I0606608

Should Have Called Dibs

The Friends Group Series Book One
Ana Blessing

Contents

Copyright © 2025 by Ana Blessing

Published by Ana Blessing

All rights reserved.

No part of this publication may be reproduced, distributed, or transmitted in any form or by any means, including photocopying, recording, or other electronic or mechanical methods, without the prior written permission of the publisher, except as permitted by U.S. copyright law or for use of brief quotations in a book review. For permission requests, contact: contact@anablessing.com.

This story is a work of fiction, names, characters, places and incidents are either products of authors imagination or used fictitiously and any resemblance to actual persons, living or dead, or actual events is purely coincidental.

Ana Blessing asserts the moral right to be identified as the author of this work.

Without limiting the author's and publisher's exclusive rights, any authorized use of this publication to train generative artificial intelligence (AI) technologies is expressly prohibited.

Book Cover Design by 100 Covers

Proofreading completed by Shelby Perlis (Fiverr @shelbyperlis)

Ebook ISBN: 979-8-9997462-0-7
Paperback ISBN: 979-8-9997462-1-4

Second Edition 2026

To my husband, thank you for supporting this journey.

To my boys, thank you for helping me find my creativity again!

To my parents, thank you for letting me stay up way to late reading one more chapter!

Chapter 1: The Boys Next Door

-Annie - Age: 17-

Fall

The moving trucks pulled up yesterday at the old McHenry place. Most of the summer construction trucks and crews have come and gone. Still, no one in town seems to know who has purchased the house. The only firm detail anyone seems to know is that the new purchasers had bought the house via the online listing. I am only interested because I hope a girl my age will move in next door. The McHenrys had been a nice older couple, but I'm looking forward to someone my age living next door.

However, it seems my curiosity will have to wait; the only people unpacking the moving truck look like the employees of the moving company. I have burned enough of this nice summer day—normally August calls for burning hot weather here in Oklahoma, but today offers a breeze with some clouds. With a deep sigh, I get up from the porch swing overlooking the front yard and head towards the backyard. I love being outside: I love being busy. My mom jokingly tells her friends I will outgrow my "tomboy" stage soon. She just isn't sure when "soon" is going to happen, but she says when it does, she is ready to give me all her tips and tricks. I always joke back that it wasn't like I don't wear any makeup or get dressed up here and there for church or school, I just don't overly fuss about it. I'm not bothered by the fact that all the "cutest" boys at school are my friends and not my potential next boyfriends. I've had crushes for sure, but when you aren't afraid to play tough in the school yard or talk about the stats from the football game, you become more friend material than girlfriend material. Also, there is the problem of my older brother scaring off any boy, including all his friends on the football team, my whole life.

As I make my way to the backyard, I pull my dirty blonde hair out of the way. I figure I may as well practice some goals and do some drills. The school year is fast approaching, and I need to be on my A game if I want to be starting varsity on the soccer team this season. I imagine I am running over and past other players on my way to score the game-winning goal. Normally, my brother and I have shooting contests, or he runs me through some drills. As the starting quarter-back with his senior pre-season practice already in full swing, he's spending most of his time at the high school, with the guys, or with his girlfriend Steph. Our backyard games have been minimal this summer due to all the changes, and I imagine things will continue to change as his graduation date grows closer.

I drown out the movers next door, soon losing myself in my backyard soccer game. I take a shot, in my mind scoring the game-winning goal. I throw my arms into the air, celebrating. I don't fight the smile that follows. As I celebrate, a movement catches my eye from the backyard of the old McHenry house. OMG, someone just saw me fake celebrating. I can't help as a blush stains my cheeks in embarrassment. I notice the guy walking in the backyard doesn't look like he is one of the movers. He appears to be around mine or Miles's age. He is tall, probably around 6'1 to 6'3, with blond hair. It seems like he is upset or frustrated as he paces across the backyard. I realize that I'm standing in the middle of my yard, staring at the mystery guy next door. Trying to cover my actions, I start walking over to the fence separating the yards. I figure if I can cover my mistake with being welcoming maybe he will not think too much about my staring.

My movements towards the fence must catch his attention, as he looks up at me. I can't help but be stunned by his sky-blue eyes. Well, crap, now I can feel the heat of the blush washing over my whole face, warmer than before. Instead, I wave and half-shout my "hello." He walks over, seeming to be in no rush, until he stands on the other side of the fence. He looks me up and down, then gives me a side smile before finally replying, "Hi." Before I second guess my actions I reach over the fence and offer my hand. He looks at it, this time gracing me with a full smile, before taking my offered hand. I feel goosebumps run over my skin, but I leave my hand in his as I state, "My name is Annie Campbell. Welcome to the neighborhood." He gives me a quick wink before removing his hand and replies, "Daniel Davis, and yeah, that's us: the new kids again." "Us," I start to reply, but before I can finish the comment, he states, "Yeah, me and Drew." I smile as I ask, "Is Drew your sister?" He gives a big laugh and replies, "He is going to love that you just referred to him as a girl." I'm so embarrassed, going another shade of red as I sputter out my apology of "sorry." He just laughs again. I'm staring again, but I can't seem to stop. He is nice to look at with his blond hair, blue eyes, strong jaw, and full lips. I can't help but wonder what it would be like to kiss him. If my face could go redder from thoughts of kissing him, it would, but I'm relieved for once that my face is already red from my last blush and so it can't get any redder from the thought of kissing him.

Then out of the corner of my eye, a new figure appears on the porch. Oh wow, this must be Drew. I can tell they are brothers, but where Daniel is all light shades, Drew is just a shade darker. Brown hair, dark blue eyes, and tanned skin. He is already wearing a big grin, and I can just make out the dimple on his left cheek. He is headed our way, his long legs eating up the distance quickly. He runs a hand through his brown hair before saying, "Hello, I'm Drew Davis." I reintroduce myself to Drew, thinking the whole time that these Davis brothers are going to cause a whole lot of trouble when school starts. I try not to feel weird about the fact my stomach is already having little flutters. Or maybe I'm the one in trouble, because they are both tempting me and I only just met them.

Chapter 2: I Saw Her First, I Should Have Called Dibs

- Drew - Age: 17 -

Moving sucks. My parents love to be on the move: Mom is an artist, and she loves being influenced by new people and places, so by nature, we have moved every few years as a result of her wanting to build her internal catalog. When I was younger, it felt great getting to be the new kid, the center of attention, or getting to reinvent myself as a new person at a new school. But over time, it has gotten old, not just for me but also for my older brother Daniel.

Last year, Daniel got into a little too much trouble. He got caught drinking and driving after a party, and then only a few short weeks later, he was arrested for breaking a window at a rival school. My parents started getting this idea that we needed to get out of the major metros and get into a place that gave us what they liked to call "roots." I can't say that I was all that interested in growing roots, but I did like the idea of not having to be the "new" kid again after this year. As part of my parents' new "roots" plan, they had agreed to stay in the same place to let us finish out high school. For me, that would mean being able to spend both my junior and senior years in the same school. I know Daniel was pissed; he was headed into his senior year and had all but been told he was going to be starting varsity on the football team. No small amount of fighting had taken place over the last few months, but my parents were not backing down. So, here we are in Oklahoma. My grandma had been from this town, and she'd always hoped to come back, but life had other plans. I think my grandma's memories got my parents to start their search here. Then, my mom saw the house online and was so excited, I'm not sure even Dad could have talked her out of it. According to her, this house was it: with an art studio off the garage and rooms for Daniel and me upstairs. It checked all the boxes, except it was outdated. So, they bought it via the online listing and contacted a few companies to give the place the updates it needed.

That gave us one more summer to spend with our friends, playing one more summer season of baseball with my team. I was going to miss them. Daniel had spent the summer hooking up with a new girl each week on what he called his "farewell tour" before our parents shipped us off to the middle of nowhere. Mom, in all her artist glory, had pictured the colors and light of each room, giving us options for our new spaces.

On the drive here, Daniel and Dad had been passing back-and-forth jabs. Daniel was sure that the football team sucked, and Dad kept telling him that in Oklahoma, football was the main focus. Dad had let Daniel know that the school had even made the playoffs last year. Daniel didn't want to hear it and just kept picking one hot topic after another, baiting Dad to continue their argument. I stayed out of it. I'd looked into the baseball program, and the team looked solid. I was worried about trying to make the starting lineup, but I am a good player; I'll find my place. I'd been on the competitive baseball circuits in every place we've lived since I was eight. It was something that I enjoyed, and I loved being at a ballpark.

***

When we finally got to the house, I made my way to what would be my new room. In the last house, we had to share the converted attic space. It was going to be nice not to have to share a room with Daniel. We get along fine with eleven months separating us, Grandma always called us her Irish twins and the opposite sides of the same coin. But we still butted heads here and there and I was looking forward to my own space.

As I walk around my new room, I imagine getting to make it my own. A movement catches my eye outside the window. As I move closer to the window, I realize the movement is a girl running around the backyard next door. Even from this distance, I can tell that she is hot: from her blonde hair pulled back out of her face to the lines of her body as she is zigging this way and that way, with the soccer ball at her feet. As she races across the yard, she takes a running kick, sending the ball flying into a makeshift goal. She throws her hands in the air, celebrating like she just scored the game-winning goal. She is beautiful; from the window, I can just see her profile, but she is smiling. I don't think I could look away if I wanted to. As I watch, I see her fully turn towards our house. For a moment, I think I have been caught staring but realize that she is looking in the direction of the backyard and not at me in the window. She waves at someone before making her way to the low fence separating hers from ours. From my room, I can just make out the flush of her cheeks and the full effect of her smile. Then something else catches my eye, and I get a glimpse of the person that she is waving to. *Well, fuck*, I think as my brother comes into view. I don't want him to run her off before I can even meet her. With his recent attitude, it's anyone's guess if he will be a jerk, or worse, if he will try to flirt with her to start his new school list. With that thought still ringing in my head, I hurry down to the backyard to meet our hot new neighbor.

***

I find myself rushing to move from the window through the boxes to my destination of the backyard. As I make my way off the back porch, I can tell when she spots me because she looks away from Daniel. I can't help but notice that she gives me a once-over. I don't think she realizes that she does it, or maybe she does because she gets a little blush staining her cheeks. I make my legs move just a touch faster, eating up the distance between us. I run a hand through my hair before saying, "Hello, I'm Drew Davis." She smiles and responds, "Hello, Drew. I'm Annie Campbell, so nice to meet you." I can't help but think, *yes, it is nice to meet you.*

Chapter 3: It is a Normal Day Until That Wink

-Annie-

School starts today, and my mom is running around the kitchen making breakfast for Miles and me. She keeps looking over at Miles; it's his senior year, his last first day. We all know she is trying not to cry or make too big of a deal about it, but we also know that we are going to take all the photos she wants. Even the one with the stupid back-to-school signs. It's weird to think that next year, Miles won't be here with me to experience my last first day. With us being so close in age, people have confused us for twins most of our lives. Miles has the same blue-gray eyes, but his hair is a shade or two lighter than mine most of the year. I focus my attention back on Miles talking to Dad about football; it's a constant for them at the breakfast table this time of year. Football is the sport we live for in Oklahoma. It's bred into us from an early age. I love fall weather and the Friday night lights, the Norman games on Saturdays, with a nice touch of the pros on Sundays. While fall is dominated by football, spring is when soccer will kick in, and so does baseball season. Baseball feels special to me, and I've always found it to be a sport worth following. From our town, we could easily take road trips to Kansas City to see the Griffons or to Dallas to see the Sheriffs. Dad, Miles, and I would spend the whole trip talking stats from the chances of home runs and playoff berths. Then Dad would take that experience and wrap it into a nice little piece for The Reporter, as their local Sports Journalist.

***

Coming back to the present, I look over at my brother, Miles. He is in his element this time of year, with this being his senior season of football. He has been laser-focused all summer. He is hoping to get an offer to play college ball and has been talking to a few Division II schools. As I focus on following the conversation, I realize they are talking about Daniel from next door. "He's going to be a good addition to the team," Miles is telling Dad. "We are already clicking. I think Max is a little pissed he could lose his starting position to the new kid, but I think he also knows he can't keep up with him." "I think I'm going to like having a target that can get the breakaway: it's going to be fun getting to make the long shots this season." Dad is nodding his head to Miles's points, and I find that I am as well. It will be good for him to be able to show off his long ball, and hopefully, this will help the Rams to the playoffs this year.

As predicted, Mom pulls out her phone plus the back-to-school signs, and we take pictures by the front door. About halfway through, I notice Daniel and Drew leaving their house, watching us in all our photo glory. I ask Mom if I'm done, and she agrees. I give her my sign and grab my backpack. I make my way down the driveway, trying not to rush. I smile and wave to the brothers as they make their way to one of the cars in their driveway. I walk over to chat with them while I wait. I know that Mom isn't going to be done until she gets just the right last first-day photo of my brother. "You all ready to start school today?" I ask. Drew replies in what feels like a joking manner, "Yeah, it's a new school, new kids, the center of attention kinda day." I have already gotten the vibe that he is the one who likes to lighten the mood, to try to make it easier for himself and everyone around him. The girls are going to love that mixed with his good looks; *he is going to be popular with our classmates*, I think, looking at him. Daniel is different. He looks annoyed by his brother, not seeming to enjoy the reference to a new school or new school year. But he does smile at me before saying, "Sure, if you can be my tour guide around school today." He follows this up with a wink, and I can feel a blush cross my cheeks.

He is a flirt, and I think I like it. Most of the football guys avoid me because of Miles. Miles has said to my face that he has "made me off limits" while he is at the school. So, it surprises me a little when Daniel winks at me—doesn't he know I'm "off limits," or maybe he hasn't gotten the lecture from my brother? Then, a thought gives me goosebumps: *maybe he doesn't care about my older brother's rule.* Why does that thought send goosebumps over my body? I have no idea, but I don't get a chance to think too much about it as Miles joins us at the end of the driveway. He looks relieved to be done with pictures. "I swear, she took two hundred photos of me with that sign." I laugh at this comment, because of course she did. Daniel and Drew also laugh. Before he can say another word, Mom yells from the porch, "You kids turn around, I want to get one of all of you!" OMG, my mom is going to kill me from embarrassment. Miles gives me a look, and we look at the Davis brothers. Miles is the first to move into action: "Better just suck it up, guys. Give her the picture, and she'll go inside to cry it out after we leave." The brothers share a look, and then we all turn to look at my mom. In the shuffle to turn around for the picture, I end up squeezed right between Daniel and Drew. Miles takes his place at the end, and we all smile up at Mom. I can feel the heat coming off their bodies, and it makes those goosebumps appear again on my skin. She waves us on as she heads inside the house.

Miles breaks the silence with, "Well, it looks like you two almost lucked out," as he laughs. Daniel smiles, "Yeah, almost," and he gives me a little nudge with his elbow. Drew nods in agreement at his brother, but the smile doesn't quite reach his eyes. He actually looks a little pissed. I wonder what that is about. Drew didn't strike me as the "no photos" type. Miles nods at me and says goodbye to our neighbors before heading in the direction of his car. "Let's go, Annie, I still have to get Steph on the way to school, and I don't want to be late." I say my goodbyes to the Davis brothers and make my way to Miles's car. I catch myself giving a backward glance and notice Daniel checking me out again. Before our eyes can make contact, I turn towards my brother's car. Here's hoping that this is as flustered as I will get all day.

Chapter 4: Is He Flirting with Her

My parents aren't into capturing the moment. I know Mom is an artist, but taking photos and being all mushy about the first day of school just isn't her thing. At breakfast, Mom and Dad talk with us both, asking what our class schedules look like and other back-to-school-related topics. Dad and Daniel have been talking about the upcoming football season. Daniel seems to like our neighbor, Miles, as I've learned he is the starting QB for the Rams. My brother is enjoying the fact that he may have secured the start for Friday's game over the previous starter. My brother has always liked being the best, and if I'm being honest, taking down his competition is a challenge Daniel enjoys. It doesn't surprise me at all that he is enjoying relaying this to us in great detail. I almost feel sorry for this Max guy, because I know that if my brother has anything to say about it, Max will not be seeing much game time this season. The rest of our morning is pretty normal, and Mom and Dad go their separate ways to start their days. When it's time to leave, Daniel and I head out to the car. Due to all the moves, we only have the two cars. One for our parents and one for us to "carpool" to school. Mom has promised that they are going to start to look for a third car, but I'm not holding my breath.

As we head out the front door, I can see the Campbells next door. Mrs. Campbell is holding her phone up and saying, "Smile for the camera," while in the background I can see Annie and her brother holding those first day of school boards wearing matching smiles. She looks over and sees us, and I can see her say something to her mom. Annie hands over the sign while picking up her backpack from the stairs. She starts to make her way down the driveway; while doing so, she gives us a smile and a wave. This smile is different than the one she had on for her mom's photos—this one lights up her whole face. Annie is dressed up today, which makes sense, as it's the first day. In my experience, girls normally pull out their most impressive styles for the occasion. Every time I've seen her since we arrived, she's been in soccer gear or casual summer styles. Today her hair is down in waves, and replacing the leisurewear is a maroon dress. It's hugging her body in all the right places, and it shows off her toned legs to perfection. Fuck, she is hot. I need to make a move, but I need to make sure she doesn't have a boyfriend first. I plan to get some details today. I can bring Annie into my conversations as she is my neighbor and the only person outside of her brother that I know here.

As I was plotting, I must have zoned out because Annie has walked over to me and Daniel. "You all ready to start school today?" she asks. I default to my standard smart-ass reply: "Yeah, it's a new school, new kids, the center of attention kinda day." My reply earns me a smile, and I bask in it, but all too quickly Daniel says, "Sure, if you can be my tour guide around school today." He smiles at her and then winks. What the actual fuck was that! Is he flirting with her? I look over at Annie and notice the blush across her cheeks. Damn it, Daniel needs to stop this shit—it's annoying me. We normally don't go after the same girls. His type has been the ones that throw themselves at his feet; they leave nothing to the imagination and then he moves on after the easy hookup. My type is Annie, hot without even trying, with just enough skin to tease, making me want to reveal the rest in private.

Annie's brother makes his way over, giving us both a nod as he does. "I swear that she took two hundred photos of me with that sign." I laugh, and so does

Daniel. We don't have to worry about that problem... the opposite, in fact. Before he can say another word, their mom yells from the porch, and before I know it we are lining up to take a picture. In the shuffle, I end up between Annie and her brother. I can smell her perfume, something sweet like apples, and my fingers itch to run along her arm right next to me. I look up at her mom and smile. Mrs. Campbell waves to us after she takes the picture and heads inside the house. Miles breaks the silence with, "Well, it looks like you two almost lucked out," and he laughs. Daniel smiles, "Yeah, almost," and he gives Annie a little nudge with his elbow. I nod in agreement, but also I'm annoyed; why the hell is he touching her and flirting AGAIN? With another nod to us, her brother walks off towards his car. "Let's go, Annie, I still have to get Steph on the way to school, and I don't want to be late." Then Annie gives us both a smile and turns to follow his lead. I can't help but watch her go. Her backpack is covering most of her back but I can still enjoy the curve of her ass. She makes a backwards glance, and I think I've been caught, but she doesn't catch me. She catches Daniel, jerks her head forward, and doesn't look back. I look at my brother and think *what the fuck* before getting myself in the car.

Chapter 5: Junior Year is Off with a Bang

-Annie-

I wish I had my own car. I hate being my brother's and Steph's third wheel each morning. They make eyes at each other the whole way to school. I almost jump out of the car as Miles parks. He reminds me that I'm going to have to wait for him after practice, and I remind him that I'll be ok and that I have sixth hour practice just like he does. I let him know that I'll be waiting in the bleachers if I get out earlier than he does, and then I hightail it into the building.

I head to my locker, dropping off the things I don't need before making my way to the newspaper office. This is my happy place; maybe I'm selling myself short wanting to be just like my dad, but I don't care. I love getting to do the sports section of the high school paper, and this year, I think I'm going to audition for the Visual News section of the team. I'm not shy by nature, but I am not exactly a social butterfly. I normally let QB1 have the limelight. But over the summer, I started watching sideline reporter videos on YouTube, both the football and the baseball ones. These women know their sports, and they get access to the coaches and athletes which is special. They can ask the hard questions right after a loss or get the best reactions to the big wins. All summer I have thought about this, and it's my junior year: if not now when? Also, I can figure it out now before it matters. If I suck at it or don't even get in, then I'll go back to the paper side of the team. No harm, no foul.

***

Meg is already here when I open the door to the newspaper office. She gives me a big hug; as my best friend, she knew where my first stop would be. She's my opposite in almost every way from her jet-black hair to her tanned skin, her natural Native American heritage on display in all the best possible ways. Her interests are art and fashion. Her purple dress showing off her curves to perfection. She also lives for the gossip: both the high school variety and the mainstream. "I told you that dress was going to look good on you," she beams in my direction. "Ok, ok—you are right, I am wrong, what's new about that?" I comment. I told her about wanting to audition for the Visual News part of the paper this year. She'd told me in no uncertain terms that I needed a "rebrand" or a "brand up" to get more attention from our peers. I was nervous about it, but I was willing to try a little harder with my outward appearance if it could help me get to my goal. Being the best friend that she is, Meg made sure as part of my "rebrand" to reinforce that my sports knowledge was top-notch and second to none. I just needed to show off my "camera-ready" outward appearance. She suggested maybe cutting down on the athletic wear and not wearing a ponytail 100% of the time, mixing in a few fashion pieces, wearing a little makeup, and styling my blonde locks.

So here I am, day one of Junior year, ready to make it or break it. Before losing my nerve, I sign my name on the sheet for the Visual News team. When I turn around, Meg is bouncing on her toes and gives me a little cheer. We make our way to first period, both talking and sharing information. "Any more run-ins with the hotties next door?" Meg asks me as we made our way down the long hallway. I fill her in on this morning's run-in with the Davis brothers. Most notably, my surprise that Daniel seemed to be flirting. She laughs, "Why are you always so surprised when guys flirt with you? You are hot, my friend. Also, don't

17

let Miles get to him before you can get your claws into him. Your brother is a buzzkill, making you off limits to the whole football team." I shake my head in agreement; maybe I'll go after what I want in all areas of my life this year. New Year, new Annie Campbell. I find myself liking the sounds of that and smiling. I am looking over at Meg, not paying attention in front of me, and I run straight into a hard body. Large arms wrap around me, catching me before I fall. Thank goodness he catches me, or I would have made a scene in the first few minutes of the morning, and classes haven't even started. He helps me find my feet but doesn't remove his hands. I look up into sky-blue eyes. *I ran straight into Daniel Davis*, I realize, my brain making the connection between the eyes and arms surrounding me! I feel the blush of deep red run across my skin. *I need to look up ways to control my reactions, or my skin is always going to give me away*, I mentally note to myself.

Meg clears her throat, and it's just the thing I need to break eye contact with him. "Thank you for catching me—so sorry for trying to run you over," I say as I take one step back from Daniel. He drops his hands from my arms and smiles. "Already testing my reflexes, Campbell: trying to see if I'll be able to handle the hard hits on and off the field?" "Well, I guess now I can report that you in fact can take a hard hit *and* have great reflexes," I reply. Meg next to me snorts and tries to cover it up with her laugh that follows. I had completely forgotten she was standing right next to me... To be honest, I had forgotten we had an audience at all and are still standing in the hallway. I go to introduce Meg to Daniel and just get out, "This is my best friend Meg Pat—" but the bell rings before I can complete Meg's name, indicating that first period is about to begin. Daniel turns to leave, but before he does, he says, "See you around, Annie," following it up with what is becoming his signature wink.

As soon as he is around the corner, I hear Meg next to me say, "That last name was Patterson, and oh yeah, it was nice to meet you too, Daniel Davis." I turn to look at her, and she is wearing a grin. "Annie Campbell, I think you have him right where you want him. That boy only has eyes for you, and I was standing right here." She makes a dramatic motion towards her body. Then we scramble into class before the second bell rings, just making it before being counted late. Maybe she's right, but it's too soon to tell if he's interested yet. I can't wait to find out.

Chapter 6: Friday Night Lights

The first few weeks of the school year fly by before I know it. I have more little moments with Daniel around the hallways and outside our houses, but our paths don't cross all that often. I have a few classes with Drew as we are both juniors. I've learned that Drew is a baseball player and is passionate about all things baseball. He has made friends with a few of my best guy friends, Craig Mitchell and Luke Harrison, who are also fellow baseball players. Craig has been starting varsity for the last two years as the first baseman. He's like an additional brother to me, and I'm fairly sure that he has told the baseball team to leave me alone, just like my actual brother has done with the football team. We'd become friends after we'd both been a little aggressive during a game of dodgeball in elementary school. We both got benched, I'd looked into his hazel eyes, and he'd looked into mine, and we'd agreed to always be on the same team from then on. Over the years, Craig has dubbed himself my bodyguard. It helps that he also looks like a bodyguard with his large muscles from hours at the gym, though he isn't even seventeen yet. The only thing not matching his tough guy persona is his reddish-blond curls. They go in different directions, and at least once a year, he buzzes them off in his frustration in trying to tame them. Luke, on the other hand, was a middle school boyfriend. I'd found his jet-black hair, tan skin, and brown eyes interesting. If you asked him why he'd been interested in me, his go-to answer all these years later is always my sassy attitude and my ass-sets. It quickly fizzled out as most middle school relationships do after we realized that kissing each other felt gross. Luke was the joker of our little group and said he thought up his best material in the outfield, waiting for someone to hit the ball in his direction.

Drew has already found his footing at school. True to my prediction after meeting him, he is popular with the girls. I've already had a few of them trying to hit me up for any details I have on him since we are neighbors. He has publicly sought me out to chat on several occasions, which only makes my female classmates think I know him better than I do. I have never been a gossip, and it feels weird to talk about him behind his back, not to mention I just met him, too. How am I going to know if he has a girlfriend or if he is interested in anyone? Meg loves it all; she keeps reminding me that I'm "rebranding" and that being friends with the hottest boy in our grade isn't a bad thing, not a bad thing at all.

I think Meg is also a little too interested in Drew, as she regularly checks in with me to see if I've learned anything new about him. I keep telling her that relationship statuses aren't a topic we've discussed in any detail. When he does stop me in the halls, it's to chat about an upcoming assignment or to quiz me on my baseball facts. He learned from Craig that I'm a major baseball fan, and he has started to test my knowledge. I have enjoyed our rounds of 'who is better at each position on the field.' Yesterday at lunch, we got into a great debate on who we think is taking the pennant home in October. He was all about the Arches, but I'm in for the Griffons. They have that underdog thing going for them. Eventually, I think Meg has had enough, and she just asked him outright, "Drew, anyone you left behind at that old school?" Drew flashed her a smile and said, "Nope, I'm very, very single." It's been the ongoing gossip for the last few weeks amongst the female population.

***

I had my audition for the Visual News last week, with the "screen test" being the first game of the season. It was exciting being on the sidelines in the thick of the action. Nothing is like a Friday in Oklahoma under those lights. The whole town shows up to support the Rams. I can feel the excitement the whole game. The season opener is against an easy opponent, and the Rams run the score up easily, going into the fourth with a score of 31-3. My brother and Daniel are on the cover of the Saturday Reporter, getting a lot of hype for what they could do this season and the possibilities of taking it to the state championships. Daniel had three of the four touchdowns, and Miles had run the last one into the end zone at the end of the third quarter. Coach had pulled them both for the fourth quarter, there being no need to keep the starters in with a lead that big. I got to interview my brother and Daniel on the sidelines before the end of the game. Daniel threw his arm over my shoulder during the interview, and it took all my focus not to react to this touch. I focused on my questions and got them both to answer before they headed to the locker room with the victory. My newspaper teacher told me I did a great job and that I had secured the job alongside one of the seniors to cover the athletic teams.

***

Junior year is going to be my year to shine: I just feel it in my bones. When my interview played on the morning news during first period this week, I felt the rush of being on screen and sharing my love for football. I wasn't just Miles's baby sister in the halls anymore—I was Annie Campbell, sideline reporter. I was getting a little more attention around the school. Meg was taking full advantage of my new "fame," and she told me she had inquiries about my "status" from at least a few of our classmates. The attention was new, and it felt a little weird, but it was also nice to be noticed for myself and not my brother. It's nice to have guys not get scared off by my senior QB brother or my baseball-playing best friends.

***

Tonight is the Rams' first test against one of our biggest rivals, the Trojans. They are one of the top contenders in the state, and they know it. So far, the other home games have been easy wins. After my soccer practices, I have been studying film with Miles, Daniel, Max, and any of the other receivers who show up at our house. They have been spending more time together getting "synced" so they are ready for game day. It's interesting the different things that they notice about the defensive patterns. I am focused during these sessions until Wednesday night, when Daniel brushes his hand against mine. *It was an accident*, I tell myself, until it happens a second time. I give a side glance to him, and he winks at me, confirming that it was in no way an accident. I give him a return smile, and he brushes his fingers along my arm, sending goosebumps along my skin. He turns his attention back to the film for the rest of the review like nothing happened.

***

It's my game to cover, and I'm in my jeans and Rams 00 jersey. I want to show my support for the team, but I'm not a girlfriend. Numbered jerseys are the ongoing trend for girlfriends and parents only. Steph is a prime example, wearing her Campbell 10 jersey in the stands. I see my parents in their usual section sporting their number 10 jersey, too. They wave, and Mom makes her way to the railing. "Honey, after the warmup, can you grab your brother so I can get a picture of you two on the sideline together?" "Sure, Mom, I'll try to grab Miles, but you better be ready. I bet he gives you just a few seconds to get it." She gives me the thumbs up and moves back up the few rows to sit next to my dad. My camera guy, Steven, comes over to let me know he is ready with my opening shot. I make my way to my mark and give the pre-game build-up. Who the players to watch are, and why I think the Rams have it in the bag.

After I am done, I move back to the sideline areas as the team makes their way onto the field. I spot Miles running in and start throwing warm-up passes. I keep scanning until I find the number 88, Davis. He is with all the wide receivers running up the field. I'm not sure what it is about a guy in football pads, but he looks good racing across the field. I eventually get Miles's attention to come over, and we turn and smile up at Mom. Then it's game on under the bright lights. The game is back and forth; for each touchdown the Rams get, the Trojans answer. My brother is on fire—he keeps making pass after pass, even making a few breakaways when the opportunities are open. Daniel is making the break on the defense all night. They can't keep up with him, and they know it. He even gets a few flags against them because of holding.

***

There is one minute and thirteen seconds left in the game. It's all tied up, our defense has done their job and helped the team to a three-and-out possession, and now it all comes down to this: will our offense bring home the win? Steven lets me know I need to give the buildup, so I stand with the game behind me and face the camera. I deliver my lines about what the Rams are doing and what they need to finish off this game. I recommend that they use the connections between Campbell and Davis to get into the end zone. Steven gives me the thumbs up that he got the shot, and I turn to watch the game. I can feel the electricity from the fans and the team next to me. My brother takes his place behind the center and claps his hands. The ball is hiked, and he is scrambling as he looks downfield.

I can't see the receivers from this angle, but I can tell he can as he jerks his arm back and drills the ball downfield. I look to the screen above the scoreboard and see the pass connect 15 yards downfield to number 88: Davis. The ball hits him over the left shoulder, and he can speed down the sidelines without a defender insight. "TOUCHDOWN RAMS!" is shouted by the announcers, and the fans go crazy.

I take my mark and smile into the camera, "That's another touchdown for the Rams scored by number 88, Daniel Davis. He was wide open in that last drive." I'm about to ask Steven why he hasn't turned off the camera when I finish my statement. I turn around to find Daniel behind me. "Campbell, you ready for my sideline interview?" He has a huge smile on his face, and I can't help but give him one in return. "Sure am, please step into my office." He closes the distance and wraps his arm around my waist. He answers my questions about the game, all while his hand makes little circles against my hip. I somehow get to my final question, "How far do you think you'll get this season?" He looks directly into my eyes and gives me a wink before answering, "I think it's a sure thing that we'll be headed to that state championship game in November." Then he releases me from his grip and joins his teammates in their celebration. All I can think is: *what the hell just happened?*

***

After the game, I drive home with my parents like normal and head up to my room to change into jean shorts. I know there's a party tonight, and normally I don't go, but tonight I want to. Maybe this "rebranding" is making me open up and try new things outside of school, too. Meg is excited by my confession; she's told me she'd even drive over if my brother wouldn't give me a ride. Since I've never wanted to go, I've never worried about asking, but I'm not sure what my parents' answer will be. I head downstairs and hear Miles and Dad in the living room going over plays from tonight's game. They are both animated, and it's nice to hear them firing off the play-by-play. When I enter, they don't miss a beat—they just keep catching up on the game. Before long, Miles's phone buzzes, and I can see Steph's name across the screen before Miles answers. He gives my dad a nod and starts to make his way out of the room.

I am about to miss my opportunity, so I raise my voice and ask, "Miles, can you give me a ride to the party tonight?" He pauses in his tracks and gives me a curious look, then looks over to Dad to see if it's ok. Dad gives him a nod and looks at me. "Your curfew is the same as your brother's. You two stay out of trouble." I thank Dad and quickly follow Miles out of the door. I hear him end the call, and then I'm the full focus of his attention. "Why do you want to go now, Annie?" I hear the annoyance in his tone. "Miles, give me a break, I'm a junior: can't I finally go to the same parties as you? I'm not some twelve-year-old girl trying to follow you and your buddies around, I just want to go hang out with my friends. Meg is going to join us at the party, you won't even know I'm there." "Fine," he responds. "I told some of the guys I'd give them a ride, so you'll have to squeeze in the back, ok?" That annoyed tone is still in his voice. I almost trip over my feet because standing at the end of the driveway are Daniel and Drew. I guess the other guys are the Davis brothers. I go to the front seat and my brother informs me that I can have the seat until we get Steph. Meaning that in a few short minutes, I'll be the one thrown in the back with the Davis brothers.

Chapter 7: After Party Delights

-Annie-

The ride to Steph's isn't so bad, but then it's time for me to get in the back. Daniel opens his door, and at first I think he is going to just scoot over. Then he pulls himself out of the back seat of the car, giving me an indication that I should just get in. I look into the car and see Drew looking back at me. He gives me a reassuring smile as I slide into the middle seat, with Daniel sliding in next to me and closing the door. Daniel and Drew aren't small guys; I can feel both of them against my hips and legs. I try to sit as still as I can, but Daniel is bouncing his leg against mine. Before I can look at him or react, Drew asks me about my sideline reporting job and if I liked it. I forget that I'm trying to be impressive and launch into how great it is getting to be on the sidelines. Drew asks me a few more questions about it and if I'll get to do the same thing during the baseball season. I let him know that I will, but it will be a little more limited during the season, as I'll also be in season for soccer. As if he doesn't want me to forget about him, Daniel starts to rub his hands on his leg, which also causes his fingers to run along the edge of my legs. The goosebumps run over my skin with every pass of his fingers. I turn to him, and he doesn't say a word—he just gives me a sly smile and what I've started to think of as his signature wink.

***

The party is at the old Sampsons' farm, just far enough out of town not to get noise complaints. As soon as my brother parks, he looks in the rear-view mirror and makes eye contact with me, "Annie, stay out of trouble and be back at this car by 11:45." "Ok, Dad," I comment back. Steph laughs in the front seat and gives Miles's hand a squeeze on the center console. "Let's go, Miles. Let Annie have a little fun." Then she lets go and gets out of the front seat. My brother gives me one last look and then gets out to follow her. I realize neither of the brothers has made a move to open the doors, and I clear my throat. "Y'all ready to party, or are we going to stay in the car all night?" Daniel smiles and says, "A lot of fun things can happen in a backseat," before he moves, swinging the door open. He grabs my hand, pulling me along the seat and out into the party. Drew exits the car from the other side, joining us as we head in the direction of the fire.

Daniel still has my hand in his, and I'm not sure what to think about it other than that I like it. We all follow in the direction that Miles and Steph have gone through the cars until we get to the fire pit surrounded by our classmates. Meg runs over and gives me a side eye, going from my joined hand with Daniel and back to my face. Then she slides over to Drew and wraps her arm around his elbow. She becomes the ringleader of our little group, weaving her way through the crowd to the backside of the fire and a few empty foldout chairs. By a few, I mean two chairs. She must have forgotten to tell me that we should bring something. I start to wonder if Miles brought any, but I have no idea where he and Steph have disappeared to.

I know that I'm not going to try and find him; I have no interest in interrupting whatever they are doing. A few of the other junior football players are giving out beers. The guy looks reluctant to hand it over when he knows I'm Miles's little sister. Eventually, he gives me one along with the rest of our group. Daniel releases my hand, and I feel the loss of it, but only momentarily, because he sits down in the chair and then pulls me into his lap, and I'm completely unprepared for this move. I know my face is on fire as he is so publicly displaying whatever is going on between us. Drew looks at Daniel and glares at his brother before taking a long drag of his beer and sitting down in the other open chair. He looks up at Meg and then pats his leg. Meg being Meg does the whole look around finger point thing into her chest before smiling and taking the seat offered in his lap.

As we settle in, the beer I'm sipping is starting to give me a little buzz. We start joking and laughing, Luke and Craig adding to the dynamic as always. I know that I'm also distracted from the crowd by Daniel. He is tracing little circles on my back as people come and go from our little group. It looks like other people got the memo about bringing chairs as a little circle forms on this side of the fire. At some point, Miles and Steph join our group. I'm curious where the chair he is sitting on has come from, but I'm not getting up to find out. Miles doesn't look all that impressed with me on Daniel's lap, but he doesn't call me out on it. I'm not going to call myself out on it either. This has been a great night, from the game to getting to sit here on Daniel's lap: there is no point in trying to ruin it by opening my big mouth.

Then Drew asks, "Does anyone want to play Truth or Dare?" Meg giggles in his lap and says, "I'm in." She looks over from Drew. "Annie, you never turn down a challenge, you're in right?" "Yeah, I'm game," I respond. Then, before anyone else can respond if they want to play, I hear Daniel say, "Truth or Dare, Annie?" I know I should say truth but I am a new Annie, so I say, "dare." Daniel spins me to straddle his waist, looking directly into my eyes, and says, "I dare you to kiss me." I hear my brother starting to speak, and I tune him out. I lean down with my lips meeting Daniel's in a kiss. I can feel his hands on my hip tighten as he kisses me back, upping the tempo with a slide of his tongue against my bottom lip. I am jerked out of the moment when I hear a very loud and far too close, "Annie Marie Campbell, what the fuck do you think you are doing?"

Miles sounds absolutely, positively pissed. I pull back from Daniel, making eye contact with Meg. She is smiling while giving me a thumbs-up motion, but I know my brother is furious and standing in the other direction. I turn in his direction—he isn't sitting with Steph on his lap anymore, he is standing. His hands are balled into fists like he is going to punch Daniel. I scurry off Daniel's lap before making my way to my brother. Steph is trying to get my brother to relax. "Miles, it was a dare, calm down already," I hear her saying. But I know that look. Miles isn't going to calm down... He is going to get into a fight. "Annie: to the car NOW," Miles says in a tone so much like our father's that I'd laugh if it were under different circumstances. If I don't follow his directions, this is going to get ugly. I look back at Daniel, but he just looks amused by Miles's reaction. He makes like he is going to follow me, but I shake my head no. We don't need to add fuel to this fire. Instead, I tell him, "Be right back, save my spot." "Don't take too long to get back Annie—I can't wait forever," is Daniel's reply. I follow my brother and his girlfriend back to our car. Miles isn't the only Campbell that is pissed.

***

As soon as we have cleared the first row of cars, my brother starts in. "What the actual fuck Annie?" I don't stop walking until we reach the car. I am not a child, and he doesn't get to embarrass me in front of a large group of our classmates. When I get to the car, I turn on him, and now he gets to see my anger. How dare he think he can embarrass me like that? He isn't my father, and he doesn't get to decide what I do or who I do it with. "Who the hell do you think you are Miles?" I shout, stepping towards him. I don't give him time to answer. "You aren't my father: you are my brother. I deal with you and Steph all the time making out in front of me, and you don't hear me calling you out. I already know about your stupid off-limits policy with the football team, so I was just as surprised as you that Daniel was making a move, but I wanted him to make a move." I take a breath and look at my brother.

He is still mad but not as puffed up as he was before. Steph beside him looks proud of me for saying my piece and gives me a little nod. "He isn't the right guy, Annie," my brother says, sounding more like himself. "How do you know that, Miles?" I ask. He doesn't reply. I look at my brother until he looks up at me. "You don't know him well enough to know if he is the right guy or not, and, to be honest, I don't either. But I want a chance to try, so give me that chance." Steph lays her hand on my brother's arm, and a moment is shared between them without any words being spoken. Then he responds, "Ok, Annie, I'll try, but I swear if he hurts you, I'll end him." I can't help but smile as that is my brother, my Miles. He is going to let this go for now, let me get my way, but if this goes sideways, he is going to get the last word with Daniel. I walk over to my brother and hug him. "I'm going back to the party. Why don't you and Steph take a minute to cool down before you go back?" He gives me a side hug. I head back to the party, back to see if that kiss was just a dare or if maybe it could turn into something more.

Chapter 8: Truth or Dare Gone Wrong

It's been a good first few weeks of school. This may have been the best place to end up. I am enjoying getting to know the guys on the baseball team. I even have a few classes with Annie, which have given me a few opportunities to ask her about assignments as an excuse to get to know her better. My new buddy Craig saw us talking after class on the first day. He let it be known that Annie is a baseball super fan and also his best friend who just happens to be a girl. I took it as "don't fuck with Annie" or "find out what happens" statement. Last week, between classes, I randomly threw out a bad stat about a key player with her favorite team, the Griffons, and it landed hook, line, and sinker. She looked at me with a side eye before she'd launched into how I was wrong.

During one of these sessions, we'd headed in the direction of the cafeteria, and that is how I ended up part of the lunch group. I stay talking with her as the conversation evolves and expands, around all thing's baseball. It's fun getting to talk about the sport that I love with her. It's impressive that she knows so much, and I get why she is the Visual News sports reporter. Earlier in the day, the first news ran during first period, and she gave the highlights of the football game and did a short interview with her brother and mine. I can't help but feel annoyed that Daniel had his arm over her shoulder. Her reporting also captures her interviewing a few of the volleyball players and cheerleaders. I've ended up having lunch with her and her friend's group, which includes Luke, Craig, and her friend Meg. Meg is the opposite of Annie, but it still makes sense that they are friends. Meg has black hair, tan skin, and curves for days. She knows how to draw attention with what she wears, and she says whatever she wants. I can appreciate the effort that she takes, even if she isn't normally my type. Meg has started to step up her flirting the last few weeks since I said I was single. She even invited me to the bonfire after the game tonight.

***

The football team has an epic win against one of the school's biggest rivals, the Trojans. Daniel has a great game, scoring the game-winning touchdown in the last minute. The crowd is going wild, the band is playing the fight song; it's a fun experience. I've been watching the game with what is becoming my new friend's group, minus Annie. Luke and Craig are going wild like they are football superfans. It makes me laugh, because they *do* take their football seriously in Oklahoma. Meg is standing next to me, and she leans over. "The party is going to be epic now—you really should come." "I'll have to check with Daniel. We only have one car to share," I tell her, because a party does sound fun. "I am Annie's best friend: I know where the Campbells live, so if you need a ride, just let me know," Meg says. It's only after I text Daniel that I realize that I don't have her number. I'll just have to hope that I can get Daniel to agree to this party. It should be an easy task. Daniel hasn't turned down a party that I know of since he turned fifteen. I pull out my phone and text him to figure out what the plan is for the evening.

33

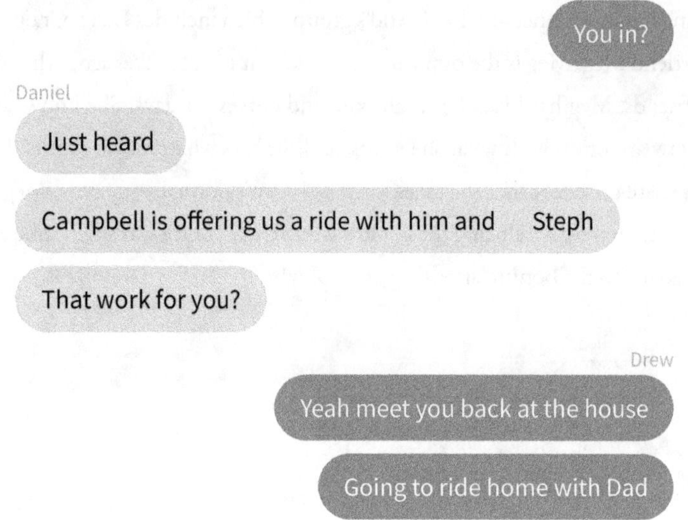

I meet Dad at the car and ride back to the house. At the house, Mom comes out of her studio in a daze. She must have gotten lost in another art piece. Dad offers to take her out of the house for a break. They tell me to have a good time, leaving before Daniel gets home with the second car about thirty minutes later. Daniel tells me that Miles texted that they will be ready in five minutes. We locked up the house and headed towards the Campbells' driveway. We chat about the game, about what we think a party in Oklahoma is going to be like. I say that I just hope it doesn't include a cow pasture, which makes my brother laugh so hard he is holding his side when Miles makes his way out the front door. It's not just Miles but Annie who comes down the driveway. Either Daniel didn't know Annie was coming, or he left that very important detail out of his texts. She looks a little surprised to see us, but she calls shotgun, climbing into the front seat.

We take the back seat. Before Miles reverses the car, he looks at his sister and informs her she is going to be moving to the back seat when we get Steph. She looks back at the small space between us, shaking her head. Miles drives the few blocks to get his girlfriend. Steph makes a move like she'll just join us in the back. Annie opens the door, telling her she is going to be moving. I go to open the door, but Daniel is on the same side of the car and beats me to it. He jumps out of the car, waving Annie towards the seat between us. She looks in with scrunched brows, and I give her my best reassuring smile. She smiles across the seat. She is going to have to straddle the console with one leg next to mine and one next to Daniel.

Daniel moves back into the car. It's a tight fit, and he pushes her against my side. I feel bad for Annie; we are both over six feet tall, full of muscle from our athletic activities, and we are not small guys, so we take up the backseat of this Subaru even without her thrown between us. I do like that Annie is wedged against me… which means that she is also wedged against Daniel, I reluctantly realize. I need to break this silence to stop thinking about her next to me. Her skin is soft against my leg, and I need a real distraction. So, I start asking about the sideline reporting. She looks over at me, giving me the highlight reel; if I had not already been at the game, this would be the recap I'd need to be prepared to talk about the game the next day. She is animated. I can tell she absolutely loves reporting. I wonder if she is going to be doing this for baseball, so I ask her. She lets me know she will, but be limited reporting due to her soccer schedule. Out of the corner of my eye, I see Daniel run his hand along his leg, but he isn't just rubbing his leg, he is also running his fingers along her leg. I want to grab her and pull her into my lap, but I fight the urge. His move makes Annie turn towards him, and I know I have lost another round to my brother.

***

We arrive at the farm, where there are already lots of upperclassmen camped out around the large bonfire. Miles gives Annie a lecture, and I can see her roll her eyes. Steph, being the only other girl in the car, backs Annie up, and maybe it's just me but it feels like Annie doesn't come to many of these victory parties by the way her brother is lecturing her. Miles and Steph get out of the car, and I realize the three of us are still wedged in the backseat. Annie breaks the silence, and before I can move Daniel grabs her hand and they leave the car. I open my door, following like a third wheel, and I lose another round.

I am trying not to stare at Annie and Daniel's hands still entwined. This is a nightmare, being interested in a girl and watching her fall for my brother right in front of me. I need to cut my losses. The problem is that I haven't been paying much attention to other girls; Annie had gotten my attention both with her body but also with all our conversations over the last few weeks. *Cut your ties, man*, I mentally think. We made our way to the bonfire, where Meg appears. Her gaze runs over Annie and Daniel's hands before her eyes run over me. She steps to my side, wrapping her hand around my elbow, and tells us to follow her to the back of the fire. She stops in front of two chairs. *I guess no one in our car got the memo about bringing our chairs,* I think. "Sorry, I only brought the two," Meg says to the three of us. "I messaged the guys, but they didn't answer, and neither did you, Annie Marie," Meg says, giving her friend some sass. A few of the guys are making the rounds and handing us four beers. The guy handing one to Annie looks hesitant but finally hands it over.

Daniel releases Annie and takes one of the two seats, then pulls Annie down on his lap. I am glaring, I can feel it; my eyes connect with Annie and she looks puzzled by my expression, so I take a long drink of my beer to reset my face. I turn away from them and take the other chair. I look up at Meg and pat my leg. She does a whole act, making a show of walking over and sitting in my lap. She does feel nice against my side. I wrap my arm around her back and settle it on the curve of her hip. Before long, others surround us, from my teammates to other guys from the football team. I can see Miles and Steph at the edge of the group making out. At some point, we all are handed another round of beer. Craig and Luke show up and are like Frick and Frack when they arrive. They are both sarcastic and love to be the life of the party, and it's entertaining watching them try to one-up each other. Craig notices Annie on my brother's lap and gives a little scowl. I still don't fully believe his whole 'friend' protectiveness of her. *Is it a friend thing or a don't want to admit I have feelings for her thing?* I wonder for the hundredth time. I need a change of subject, so in my brain, I make a rash decision to change up the dynamics of the night.

I ask, "Does anyone want to play Truth or Dare?" Meg giggles on my lap before saying that she's in. Meg quickly challenges Annie. Annie straightens her back before replying, "Yeah, I'm game." Before I can ask anyone else if they want to join, I hear Daniel ask, "Truth or Dare, Annie?" She hesitates for a moment before replying, "Dare." I watch as my brother picks Annie up, moving her to straddle him, and then he says, "I dare you to kiss me." I should look away, but I am curious if she'll do it, and she does. I close my eyes and try not to react. I still have Meg on my lap, or I'd remove myself from this moment. Then all hell breaks out, and her brother is shouting and causing a scene. Annie leaves with her brother, and Daniel just sits in his chair, giving the impression he doesn't have a care in the world. Knowing my brother, he probably doesn't care that he just pissed off the QB. My brother does what is good for Daniel: end of the story.

Meg wiggles in my lap and says to the group, "So, anyone else want to join in on a game of Truth or Dare?" It seems to break the ice, and we get a game going. We have a mixed group of girls and guys, and the game has the normal amount of truth and dare activities, from more kissing to a few shirts being removed. One girl asks for a truth, and she is required to tell the group whom she would kiss, marry, or fuck. This gets the group laughing again. I lose track of time as we work our way through the group. My dare is to remove my shirt, and it's warm enough by the fire that I don't have any problem with it. Meg gives me a look of approval before returning her gaze to the other players. At some point, Annie returns and takes her seat on Daniel's lap, but I am doing my best not to look over and to just enjoy the game. Before I know it, Miles is getting Annie's attention and pointing to his watch. Annie stands and starts to tell everyone goodbye. Daniel stands with her. I look at my phone, and it's only 11:45. Is he really headed back with them? We are never home before midnight. When I don't make a move, he asks me if I have a way home. I tap on Meg's hip, "Can you give me a ride home?" She gives me a grin, "Sure." I look over at Daniel and Annie, "All good here." They walk off towards the car. I take another beer and try to drown all thoughts of Annie Campbell out of my brain.

Chapter 9: What Are We Now

After the blow-up with Miles, I walk back to the party. I am trying not to focus on the eyes of my classmates following me or the girls leaning together, whispering, and looking in my direction. I wanted to kiss Daniel: I enjoyed kissing him, and I'm not ashamed about it. Would he try to kiss me again? Now that was the real question. If my brother ruined this for me, I am going to find a way to embarrass him in front of the whole school, or maybe the whole town... why stop there, the whole state! I look at Daniel as I approach. He is in the same place, laughing with some of the football players, but as I get closer, I catch his eye and he directs all his focus on me. A smile breaks out across his face, and I earn that wink. I can feel the smile on my face, and I walk over, feeling more confident with each step closer to him. "Is this seat taken?" I ask him. He looks me over in a slow review, then pulls me down into his lap.

This time, sitting in his lap feels different. I'm closer with no space between the side of my body and the front of his. Daniel has wrapped his arm around me and is running his fingers along the space between where my jersey ends and my jean shorts start. His fingers are warm over that small piece of skin, and I can't help but want a little more. I look over to Meg and Drew, who are a little more snuggled up than when I left. Drew's arm is around her waist, and he is without his shirt. I can't lie, I do notice that he is toned in all the right places, the shadows from the fire catching the lines of his abs as I look. Then I try to look away, because why was I even checking him out? Why was I checking him out? My brain is in hyperdrive, so I focus back on the fact that Meg looks happy next to him. I'm going to have to ask her about this tomorrow. She has been asking me a little more about baseball over the last week. I should have been suspicious, but we'd had lunch with baseball players for years, and I thought she was just trying to be included in the conversation a little more. Now, looking at her on Drew's lap, all the pieces connect; this girl was playing the long game. *Way to go, Meg*, I think.

I'm brought back to the present with Daniel whispering in my ear, "So, about that kiss." I turn to look at him, and he is smiling, but his eyes are drifting down to my lips and back to my eyes. I lick my lips, remembering his lips on mine, and my eyes go wide. I know I should be speaking, but I'm enjoying just looking at him, looking at me. His free hand reaches and lays against my neck, and he gently pulls me forward. This time, he is the one kissing me. It sends shivers down my spine and heat over my body. I sigh, opening my mouth a little, and he takes this as an invitation to run his tongue along my bottom lip. It feels good, so I repeat the move with my tongue on his lip. I'm not sure how long we kiss, but when he pulls back to look at me, I am breathing a little hard and my heart is racing. He winks, and I know I smile. This is starting to become a pattern I can get used to. He releases my neck, and I turn back to my friends still playing the game of Truth or Dare and rest my head against his shoulder. Who knew parties could be so fun? I make myself a promise: I'm going to make an effort to come to more parties this year. After all, I am "rebranding."

Time feels like it has passed too quickly. Before I realize it, Miles is standing and making the *look at the clock* motion to me. I check my phone and it's 11:45; with curfew at midnight, it's time to go if we want to get home in time. I move to stand, and Daniel helps me with a little push of his hands. He moves while giving his friends a nod before his hand takes mine again. Daniel asks his brother if he's coming, and Drew asks Meg for a ride. She is trying to play it cool, I know, but I can see the grin on her face when she says, "Sure."

Daniel leads me to my brother's car, with our hands intertwined the whole time. My hand feels small in his, and I like the feeling. Up to this point, I haven't been involved with football players. I've dated a few guys, but they had been fans versus players, and it's easy to feel the big differences already. I can't help wondering what else will be different.

***

At the car, Daniel opens the door for the backseat, and I scoot in with him following me in before shutting the door. I make to scoot to the empty seat that Drew had been in on the drive here, but Daniel wraps his arm over my shoulders and pulls me against his side. I'm not going to fight it because I like the fact that he doesn't want to let me go. Looking forward, I can see my brother's reflection in the mirror and his pinched eyebrows. I just give him a big smile in return. He is not going to make me want this any less. Miles drops off Steph first; it isn't lost on me that he walks her to her front door, and it takes at least a few minutes longer for him to return. While he is away, I lean my head on Daniel's chest, wrapping my arm around his waist. It's not the most comfortable position, but I'm not pushing my luck with Miles. This is nice, and I'll take what I can get. I do watch the clock slowly counting down to midnight. Our house is only five minutes away, but I'm starting to get concerned that we will break curfew if my brother doesn't make his way off that porch. But then Miles appears, jumping in the car, and we head towards home.

I break the silence. "We are going to miss curfew after my first party, Miles." He makes eye contact with me in the mirror. "Dad only cares that the car is in the driveway at midnight, we're fine." And true to his word, we pull into the driveway at midnight. Dad opens the front door, giving Miles the thumbs up, and shuts the door. Miles looks back at me, all smug. "Told you." "Ok, ok, but that was close and you know it." My brother laughs and lets me know he knows exactly how long it takes to get from Steph's house to ours. I hold out my hands to stop him. I don't want any more details about his activities with Steph. We all get out of the car, and Miles heads towards the door. When he notices that I'm not right behind him, he turns. "Dad will notice if he doesn't hear you come in with me." "Well, cover for me like I've covered for you." Letting out an annoyed sigh, Miles says, "Five minutes, Annie. Then it's on you."

***

Daniel looks amused when I look back at him. "So, I guess you are the good girl that everyone has been saying you are. I've heard references to your 'first party' all night—your brother seems to be on high alert and now watching you freak out about curfew." "Ok, yes, tonight is the first football party I've been to, but..." I trail off, thinking fast because I don't want to sound lame, but it's all true: all firsts. "But...?" he responds, fully turning to face me. I'm between the closed car door and Daniel. We haven't moved much since getting out of the car. He takes a step closer, and I feel my back against the car. "I'm rebranding," I blurt out because I don't have anything else to say, and it's true, it is the main focus of my junior year so far, even if the only person who knows it is Meg. "Rebranding, that's interesting. What does rebranding mean, Annie?" It is probably my brain making his voice sound deeper, right? I shake my head to try to lift the fog that has made me delay and lean my head back to look at his face.

Standing up now, his size is more noticeable. Looking up at him, I want him to kiss me again without anyone watching, but he is just looking at me, waiting... Oh that's right, he asked me a question. "It means that I'm not going to back down. It means I'm going after what I want." Daniel takes another step closer, and now I'm pinned between the car and his body. I can feel his hard muscles against my curves and the warmth of his skin against me. My hands have moved to his pecs. "Glad to know you want me, Annie," he chuckles before he wraps his hands into my hair and gives it a small yank to direct my face into the correct angle before his mouth descends to mine. I thought the other kisses were hot, but this one, without witnesses, is earth-shattering. He doesn't wait for me to open; he uses his tongue to open my mouth and slide inside. I respond with my tongue running along his mouth, and I know I moan, it feels so good. My hands, which had once been resting on his chest, are now gripping his shirt and pulling him against me. I am lost in this kiss, all the sliding of lips, tongues, and the feel of his hands wrapped in my hair. As it continues, he releases my lips with his own before he kisses across my jaw. He gives another little yank to turn my head as he kisses his way to my ear, then down my neck. It leaves a path of fire over my skin and goosebumps over my whole body. I've lost myself in this moment. I don't care how long we have been outside until I hear the front door and a throat clearing. My hands that had been pulling Daniel into me are now pushing him to no avail. He's too big for me to move, I realize, unless he wants to be moved. He looks at me and then looks over at the front door, giving me a little space to look around his body.

My dad is there, not looking mad exactly, but also not looking pleased about finding his daughter pinned against the car. "Annie, it's time to come inside, say goodnight to Daniel," Dad calls from the porch and shuts the door again. Daniel laughs and takes a step backward towards his house. "See you around, Annie," he gives me one more smile and that wink, then turns, walking to his front door without a backward glance. I take a deep breath and make my way inside. It isn't until I'm in my room that I realize I didn't even exchange numbers with Daniel: I have no way to communicate with him until school on Monday. This is going to be the longest weekend of my life.

Chapter 10: Hangovers Suck
-Drew-

After Daniel and Annie leave the party, I keep drinking. The game of Truth or Dare has continued. I've gone a few more times, selecting 'dare' every time. I'm now in my boxers and my sneakers. I can tell that Meg is appreciating all my body, and if I'm being honest, I've noticed a few other girls enjoying it as well. As it gets later, the groups start to dwindle down, and even I know it's time to go. Meg is almost asleep against my chest, and I realize that I need to wake her up. I have no idea how to get us home, plus I'm not in any condition to try to drive us home in her car, even if I could. She smiles up at me when she opens her eyes, then she asks me, "What time is it?" I have no idea. I stopped checking my phone, enjoying the party and the buzz of the alcohol in my system. I grab my phone from the pile of my clothes. Checking the time, I respond, "Almost 2 a.m." Meg jumps out of my arms, wide awake. "We have to go—my parents are going to kill me, I am WAY past my curfew." I stand up and hurry into my discarded pants and shirt, she looks over at me, a look of disappointment over my skin being covered. Then she turns, walking in the direction of the remaining cars. I follow her, noticing the swing of her hips as she quickly makes her way to a little blue car. I climb into the front seat.

***

Meg looks worried and keeps checking the clock as we head in the direction of town. I feel bad—I should have asked her when she needed to be home when I'd asked for the ride. Trying to lighten the mood, I break the silence, "So, is this a good time to tell you, I have no idea how to get home?" My comment does what I had intended: it gets her to laugh. She has a nice laugh, and I enjoy that I was able to give her a moment to relax. I know she is worried about the consequences of staying out late. "Well, it's lucky for you that I know where you live," she responds. We share a smile and a comfortable silence as music plays in the background for the remaining trip to my house. She pulls up in front of my house, and I open the door to get out quickly, knowing that she's already way past her curfew. I've had fun with Meg tonight.

She isn't the girl I had hoped to hang out with, but I'm glad she is the one that I did. I turn towards her. "Thanks for the ride, I had fun tonight. Any chance I can get your number?" I must have said the right thing because she smiles, holding out her hand. I unlock my phone and hand it over. She opens the texting app, typing in a number. She hits the send button, and I can hear the ding from her phone as it lights up. She does something else on my phone before closing the app and handing it back to me. "I had a great time, Drew. Now get out of my car, I'm already so late." I can't help but laugh and step out of the car. I shut the door, and she is already down the road before I make it to the front door. I head up to my room. Mom and Dad really haven't enforced curfew, so I'm not worried about the time, but I do try to be quiet as I make it down the hall. When I get to my room, I flop onto my bed. I start to scroll through some apps when I remember that I need to save Meg's number on my phone. I open the text app and see the message she sent to herself from my phone.

Drew

Hey hottie, this is Drew Davis

That is the message she sent herself from my phone. I laugh. Meg is just the right amount of confident. Then I go to edit the number and laugh out loud again. She has saved her name into my phone as "Meg with the Nice Ass." I mean, she does have a nice one, I'm not arguing that point at all. I don't normally save girls in my phone with the description of their bodies, but in this case, I wasn't the one to write it, so I figure it's ok to leave it like it is. Before I leave the app, I text back.

My phone pings back quickly.

I plug my phone in and pass out. The next thing I know, the sun is coming through my window, and I feel like death. I remember that I drank way too much last night. I spend most of the weekend hanging out around the house and maybe working on my abs.

Chapter 11: Am I Getting Good at Flirting?

-Annie-

Meg texts me to ask about what happened after I left the party with Daniel. We chat back and forth most of the weekend about it, and my frustration that I don't have his number. Meg thinks I should ask Miles, but I am not going to open that can of worms. My brother hasn't brought up the party, so I'm not bringing it up either. We are living in our silent agreement not to discuss the events of Friday night. I also learn from Meg that yes, she does in fact think Drew is hot, and she, in more detail than I need, describes what he looks like in just his boxers. She has been texting him all weekend, and I'm happy for her. Meg has always gone after the guys she wants and it looks like Drew is no exception.

***

Before I know it, it's Monday morning and I'm back at school, putting my things away in my locker before first period. I'm lost in my thoughts when a shadow falls over my locker. I turn, smiling, as my shadow just happens to be the guy that has been on my mind all weekend. "Do anything interesting this weekend?" Daniel asks as he leans on the locker next to me. I act like I'm thinking about it and respond, "You know, I can't recall anything worth noting." He laughs next to me, "Is that right? Here I was thinking about the girl I kissed against a car." I turn my body towards him to look at him after that comment. He smiles and gives me a wink. "Knew I could get your attention with that," he replies and takes a step into my space. Then he reaches out, taking a piece of hair between his fingers, and leans down and says, "Maybe we can do it again soon." Before I can reply, he turns and heads down the hallway. My heart is racing, thinking about the fact that he wants to kiss me again, and I know that I'm looking forward to it. I'm daydreaming as I turn back to my locker, grab what I need, and head off to first period.

I make it just in time as the second bell rings. Meg gives me a questioning look from her seat. I give her a smile and point to my phone. I take my seat, hiding my phone in my notebook, and text Meg.

I put my phone away before the teacher notices and makes me lock it away for the day in the office. I tune back into what we are learning, but my focus isn't on school, it's on the sky-blue eyes of a very distracting boy. As soon as the bell rings, Meg and I get together to discuss her plan. She lays out phase one of the plan, and it's not bad. She wants me to tell Miles that I have a ride with her after school. However, I'm not going to get a ride from her. She, meanwhile, is going to text Drew after she sees my brother leave, since she has his number, and ask him if they can give me a ride. We both know that the brothers are carpooling to school. Hopefully, he'll say yes. She'll ask him if they can give me a ride, as she isn't able to because she has to go to work, resulting in the objective of phase one. I'll be able to get a ride home with them. Phase two is all on me to casually ask for their numbers in case this happens again. Meg has given me a few ways to spin it, from not waiting to make her the middleman, or the fact that we are neighbors and you never know when you'll need that cup of sugar.

***

It is a good plan. Meg is truly a mastermind at this. I love that my best friend is a schemer and feel so grateful that she is on my side and not someone else's. I never could have come up with this on my own. The rest of the day goes pretty well. We gather at our normal lunch table now with Drew, Craig, and Luke. Conversation flows from sports to the paper we have to write for history. It's a fun group, and I'm glad how it has worked out. Meg and Drew are not talking directly, but they are giving each other looks across the table. I'm going to give

Meg a hard time about this; normally, she is the direct one. It isn't like her to not just act after what she's told me about their texting and flirting over the weekend. After we work out this plan, I'm going to have to ask her what her phase approach to dating Drew is going to be. I text Miles right before sixth period to set the plan in motion.

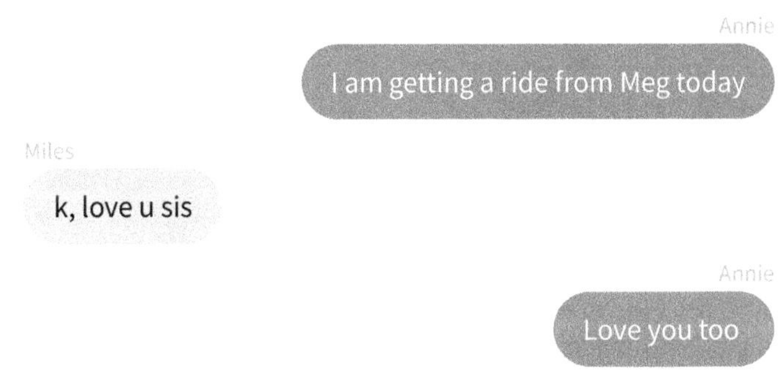

My brother is a man of many words. I mentally check off step one of the plan. I head to soccer practice, losing myself in drills until the coach blows the whistle, ending practice. I take my time dressing today. Normally, I rush to get changed to give myself time to walk around the school to wait in the bleachers for football practice to end. I know that Monday is a normal practice for them, but it still goes a few minutes longer than our offseason soccer practices. I check the time before texting Meg to start on the next part of the plan.

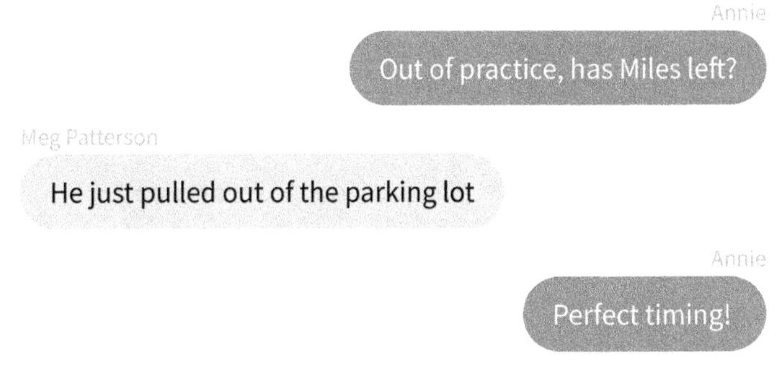

I have to wait for a full five minutes, which feels like forever. Then I see the ... indicating that Meg is working on a reply and the message isn't far behind.

OMG, I'm doing this. I look into the mirror one more time. My hair is up in a ponytail, and the makeup is mostly gone from practice. I have changed back into my t-shirt from earlier, but I stayed in my shorts at Meg's suggestion that my legs are my best asset. She said I should use my best asset to my advantage at every opportunity. I shake my head at myself. I am so not good at this. I look at myself again in the mirror and make sure to think "rebrand," then turn to leave the locker room. I make my way to the parking lot, spotting Drew and Daniel leaning against the trunk of their car. I up my tempo to a small jog. As soon as I'm in front of them, I give a small grin. "Thanks for the ride, I appreciate it." Drew is the first to answer: "No problem, Annie, it's not like we are going out of our way to get you home." Then he gives me a little shoulder bump to make sure I get that he is giving me a hard time. Daniel looks me up and down from head to toe and winks before commenting, "I don't mind waiting when you look like that." I try not to blush, I feel like he is always trying to push that line with me. Before I can respond, Daniel pushes off the car and climbs in. Drew climbs in the front, and I slide in the back.

***

The drive isn't bad as our houses are only about five minutes from the school. Daniel and Drew are talking, but I can see Daniel checking me out in the mirror. I try not to pay attention, and I'm also trying to think about how to start the conversation to get the phone numbers. Meg had made it sound so simple. For Meg, this would have been simple, but for me it is pushing past the nerves in my stomach.

Daniel parks the car, and I realize it's now or never. I have to ask to complete the third and final stage of the plan. I clear my throat, "Thank you guys again for the ride and for waiting for me. I feel so bad about it. Thank goodness Meg had your number, Drew. Since we are neighbors and just in case my ride cancels again, do you all mind if I get your numbers?" I know that I say all of this in one long run-on sentence, but it's out of my mouth and I feel so much better about it. Drew is the first to answer, as I predicted he would be; of the two of them, he does seem like the one that is the most helpful. "Sure." He gives me his number, and I add it to my phone and send him a message to give him my number.

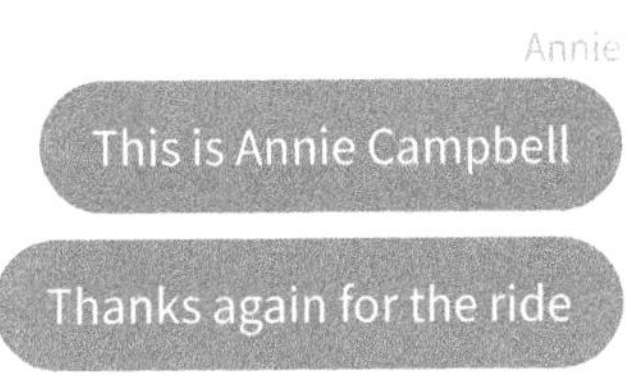

I look up at Daniel. He has turned in his seat to half face me. A sly smile crosses his face before he says, "Well played, Annie." He gives me his number, which I type into my phone, trying not to let his comment make my hands tremble. I send him a message.

I look up and smile at them both. Then I mumble my "Thanks again" and scoot out of the car and walk towards my house. It takes all my internal self-talk to walk all the way inside and close the door without turning around.

Chapter 12: Focus on Being Her Friend

The Monday after the party, everything returns to normal. The school is gearing up for the next football game versus the Tigers, which is already being hyped by Annie on the Visual News clip during first period. She still draws my attention, I can't help it, but after the party, I am definitely not going to make a move. I do have some sense of pride, and I don't want to hear her tell me that she is picking my brother over me or that she thinks of me as her "friend." I've decided that I'll push my crush to the back burner, refocusing my attention elsewhere. I can be friends with Annie. I do enjoy the fact that she knows her stuff when it comes to most sports. I learned the other day that basketball isn't her thing, which makes me want to learn some random facts over the winter to throw out at lunch just to see if she'll take the bait. Until then, I'll enjoy the fact that we can spar over football and the postseason baseball still being played.

I'm sure I'm not the only one who thinks that lunch is the best hour of the day. Since the day I followed Annie to the lunchroom, we have formed our little group. I love that they took me into what is their very small but fun group. Today, when I get to the table, Craig is giving Annie crap about her loyalty to the Griffons. "There is no way in Hell the Griffons are going to win their division, much less the Series." "Well, I think you're wrong, Craig—at least they made the postseason, unlike the Sheriffs," Annie jabs. I've learned he is a big Sheriffs fan.

"Oh, Annie, you've done it now," pipes in Luke in his dramatic fashion, and Craig starts on this next statement against the Griffons. I look at Meg and she tells me, "They have been doing this for years, you'll get used to it." I focus on her, replying, "Well, that makes me feel better. I thought I was going to have to get involved, but if this is normal, I'll just sit back and enjoy the show." It earns me a little smile from Meg.

***

Today, the conversation is flowing around the usual topics, but unlike last week, I do find I'm glancing more and more in Meg's direction. She is sitting across from me, and I take a moment to really look at her, not comparing her to anyone else. Meg's beautiful with her long black hair and tan skin. I can also appreciate all the curves that she takes care to show off. Meg may not talk sports, but she will give out random gossip facts that make me wonder who her inside sources are. I have enjoyed texting with her, and I think I'm going to double down on my efforts with her as my new target. The thought gives me a new focus, and I look into Meg's brown eyes and think, *let's go*.

The rest of the day is pretty uneventful; class is class after all, and it can only get so interesting. That is until I check my phone after sixth period and see that I have a few unread messages from "Meg with the Nice Ass."

Meg with the Nice Ass

So you owe me a favor, right?

I was supposed to give Annie a ride home and I totally

forgot I have first shift at work tonight

I check the time, realizing Meg sent this message in the last few minutes. So, I open the keyboard and reply.

I look up from the text to see Daniel coming out of the football facility. I speed up and join him in walking towards the car. "We are going to have to wait a minute. I offered a friend a ride home—she'll be here in just a minute," I let Daniel know. "Ok, cool, no problem," he replies. Look at me go, I decided today we would be friends, and I'm already putting it into action. I give myself a mental pat on the back. True to my word, I see Annie come around the end of the building by the football parking lot. She looks more like the first day I met her, hair up, minimal makeup, and her legs on full display in her shorts. Ok, so I may have to take back that pat on the back I just earned because, I can't help it, my body responds to her. I take a deep breath and get Daniel's attention. "My friend's here." He looks up and gives me a surprised look, which quickly turns into his sly smile as he looks Annie up and down.

Annie stops next to me and offers us a thank you for the ride. I don't wait for Daniel to speak, and I respond, "No problem, Annie, it's not like we are going out of our way to get you home," giving her a little shoulder bump. She smiles at me but turns to Daniel after he says, "I don't mind waiting when you look like that." I roll my eyes, I know I do, and then I push off the car and climb into the front. The ride home is short. Annie really could have run home with no problem, but it wasn't hard to wait for her either. Daniel and I get started on our normal, how was practice routine, trying to one-up each other with the weights and reps we do. Daniel is a tank, where I'm a little more lean muscle, so he loves that he can always get a higher weight number than me. As the younger brother, I have accepted my lot in life, at least for now.

***

When we get to the house, I turn to open the door, but before I can, Annie is talking. I can tell that she is nervous as she is talking in one long, sentence. She eventually gets to the part that is probably what made her nervous in the first place as she asks for our numbers. I'm kinda surprised that we haven't exchanged numbers already at lunch, so I don't have any problems telling her my number. I look at my brother; she doesn't have his number. Then I register his smile, and I know that he is playing a game with Annie. Should I warn her, or would she think I'm overstepping? We just met. I decide to leave it alone: I'm trying to be Annie's friend. I'm not going to be the guy friend who tells her who she should or shouldn't date. "Sure," I respond and give her my number. My phone pings with a message.

Annie

This is Annie Campbell

Thanks again for the ride

I save her number in my phone as Annie Campbell. As I am editing my phone, Daniel turns and replies, "Well played, Annie" confirming my earlier thoughts about this being a game to him. He does give her his number, and before Daniel or I can exit the car, Annie has jumped from the backseat, making it to her door in a half-run half-jog, never looking back. I have to agree with Daniel... Annie played that pretty well.

Chapter 13: It All Started with a Text

-Annie-

My phone vibrates in my hand as I walk to my room. Before checking, I try to calm my nerves. *It's probably just Meg anyway*, I tell myself, taking a deep breath. I open the home screen and navigate to my unread text messages. I have three of them. As I predicted, I have one from Meg and one each from the two Davis brothers.

Then a message from Drew.

My heart is racing when I open the third message from Daniel.

Ok, it worked, but now I have to flirt over text. I normally do well in person when I can read the other person's body language. I've never been a flirty texter; my last few boyfriends had texted like my brother, in a few short-word responses. I learned it was better to call to talk or video chat. I make my way to my room, and I hit the call button next to Meg's name. She answers after only one ring—she doesn't even say hello, she just launches into her question. "So, I repeat, did it work?" "Yes, it worked Meg, but now I don't know what to say." I fill her in on the original text and Daniel's response. "Oh, he is good," she laughs over the phone. Then she asks, "When does he normally come over to watch games with your brother?" "Normally on Tuesday and Thursday, why?" I reply. "Tell him the game is on, then don't text him again. Make sure tomorrow, when he comes over, you are wearing those shorts." I thank her and end the call.

Then I set my phone down in my room and head back downstairs. I chat with my brother about when we are going to watch game film tomorrow. He lets me know it will probably only be Daniel and Max. After dinner, I head back to my room to work on homework. I am trying to avoid my phone, but it vibrates on the nightstand. I have looked at the same math problem three times and still have no idea what it is asking me for. I need a break, and the vibrating phone is a really good excuse to take one now. I tell myself I know a lot of people, I'll have some text from one of my friends. There is no way that the messages are from a haunting set of blue eyes that are taking up so much space in my brain. Pulling up the messaging app, I smile when I see that all my missed messages belong to one individual and his name is Daniel.

My fingers want to reply, but I'm trying to follow the plan that Meg set for me. I put the phone down and move away from it like it could explode at any moment. I turn back to my homework, trying to focus on the math problems in front of me again. The numbers start to blur even worse than before. I can't focus, so I give up trying to finish this tonight. I check the time, thinking that I may as well get ready for bed. After I finish, I pick up my phone to set my alarm, and it opens back to the text with Daniel. My willpower is awful, and today has already pushed my normal breaking point. So, it's no surprise that I cave.

I know that is the end of the conversation for tonight. I set my alarm like I'd planned before our little exchange. I lay in bed, wondering if I have a better pair of shorts I can wear tomorrow. *Game on indeed*, I think before drifting off to sleep with a plan I thought of all on my own.

***

I wake up to the sounds of my alarm and stretch. If I'm being honest, I'm not much of a morning person. I set my alarm to a time where I know I can lie here for a while, and eventually I'll actually get up. I remember the conversation with Daniel. Wide awake now, I remember what the day ahead holds for me. I go to my closet. Meg has been trying to get me to dress up more for school. Last year, I even let her convince me to buy a few dresses. Not the going-to-church style dresses, either. The ones that are within the dress code, but at the very limit. Meg loves to make sure all her effort doesn't go to waste. Who wants to make the effort if it just gets you sent home or it gets covered up by a spare hoodie offered by the school? Meg has perfected the *just getting by* vibes with most of her school looks. She has been trying to get me on board for at least the last two years. She says if she had legs like mine, she'd be pushing the length limit every day, including the winter months. I never really thought about it. Until this year, I'd worn a lot of leggings, athletic-themed clothing, or jeans, except on dress-up days or picture days. The first day of school, I wore a new dress, and I liked the way I felt in it.

It was also a confidence boost when I caught Daniel checking me out. Craig had also commented in class to the effect that I was Annie all grown up. Craig being my best guy friend, I knew he was giving me the only form of encouragement I was going to get from him. We had an understanding: I helped him secure dates, and he tried not to overstep as my friend with guys interested in me, outside of the baseball team, of course. Craig had been the number one reason most of the girls in school kept me on their good side. Until the Davis brothers' arrival, Craig's red-blond curls and smile had made him a top interest. Craig hadn't been quiet about the fact that if a girl bad-mouthed me, it didn't matter if they gave him the best sex of his life, it was a deal breaker. As weird as it sounds, it was nice to know that I was more important than his latest hookup. I check the time on the dresser, and in my sleepy haze, I realize I have been daydreaming for way too long about this outfit choice.

I grab the dark blue dress that Meg swears matches my eyes. With that decision made, the rest of my morning goes pretty smoothly. When I am downstairs, Mom compliments the outfit choice and asks me if it's picture day. I have thrown off Mom. I give her a "Nope, that isn't until mid-October" reply, and she just shrugs at me with a smile. Then she follows up with, "So, what's the occasion?" I'm saved from answering when Miles lets me know that he wants to get to school a little early. I'm sure it's not school-related and more related to getting some extra time in with Steph. I don't want my mom to start asking me questions about boys. None of us needs that this morning. I don't want to talk about boys in front of my dad and brother. It's already embarrassing enough that they both caught me kissing Daniel on the same night. I quickly tell him that I'm all ready to go.

Miles and I say goodbye to our parents before making our way out of the house. To my delight, it just happens to be when the Davis brothers are exiting their house, too. An idea pops into my head, and I go with it. Addressing Drew, I say, "Hey, mind letting me bum a ride to school this morning? Miles wants to get Steph and have some alone time." I made the little air quotations when saying "alone time." Drew doesn't miss a beat. "Yeah, don't want to mess with that all valuable 'alone time.'" He uses his hands to make the quotation marks back at me. We both laugh. I appreciate that Drew is so easygoing. I can see us being good friends.

Miles looks over at Daniel and gives him a 'sure' head nod. Miles takes off for the car without a backward glance. I jokingly shout after him, "Yeah, love you too, don't have too much fun without your third wheel." I can hear him laugh as he shuts the car door and drives away, leaving me with the guys. I turn to them, without so much as looking at Daniel, I walk around the back of the car and climb into the backseat. Drew doesn't take the front seat this time; he opens the other side door, climbing in next to me. Daniel, at some point, gets into the driver's seat, looking a little annoyed. Drew starts the conversation, "Hey, did you see the game last night?" I realize in all my stress over Daniel, I didn't see the game, so I reply, "No, I missed it, can you catch me up?" That is all the introduction Drew needs before giving me the play-by-play of the playoff game between the Fighters and Meteors. I do direct my eyes away from Drew, finding Daniel's in the rear-view mirror. It causes me to shiver, and I quickly turn back to Drew.

We get to school pretty quickly: the drive is short, and the athletic parking lot is easier this time of the morning. I do get absorbed into the recap with Drew. It's obvious that he loves baseball—he has been talking with his hands, making the motions of swinging a mini bat when he gets to a home run in the recap. When Daniel parks, I grab my backpack and slide across the backseat, following Drew out of the car. He keeps talking, never stopping in his recap coverage. Before I can close the door behind me, it slams shut, startling me from the baseball stats and having me look at Daniel. "Oh, sorry that got away from me," he says and then loops his arm around my waist. Drew turns to face away from us, but he continues the recap at a faster clip. As we hit the sidewalk, he finishes. "Sounds like I missed a good one, text me a reminder next time so I can share my highlights." "Yeah, that sounds great, Annie. I forgot I have your number; I'll do that next time." Then Drew says goodbye and walks through the main do ors.

Daniel's arm is still around my waist, so I turn towards him and say, "Hi." "Oh, now you are talking to me," is his clipped reply. But he doesn't sound mad, he sounds impressed. "Again, Annie... For such a good girl, you sure are trying to tease me. From what I gathered from the guys, this isn't your normal play." Had he been asking other people about my dating history? Who were these "guys?" So many questions pop into my head. But before any of them could leave my lips, he says, "The dress looks good on you, Annie, but..." He bends down, brushing his lips against my ear, and whispers, "I think it would look better on my bedroom floor." Then he kisses the spot right behind my ear, unwraps his arm from around my waist, and walks away. I think he just broke my brain, giving me that image to think about. If my dress ended up on his bedroom floor, which stands for my brain to reason, I'd have to be undressed. My mind is now imagining what it would feel like to have Daniel undressing me. I think my plan backfired.

Chapter 14: Fitting Into My New Role

The next morning, I can't help but be impressed with the game that Annie is playing. I also learn I'm 100% in the friend zone with Annie. Since I had already read the signs, it doesn't bother me as much as I thought it would when she pulls me into her latest play.

Mornings aren't planned in our house so it's a little random that we end up leaving the house at the same time as the Campbell siblings. Annie waves, walking over to me, almost completely ignoring Daniel. She asks me, "Hey, mind letting me bum a ride to school this morning? Miles wants to get Steph and have some 'alone time.'" I take a side glance over at Daniel, taking in his amused expression. I play up that I understand the feeling and it makes Annie laugh, and I know I am playing my role to perfection.

She waves goodbye to her brother without even looking at Daniel, walks over to the passenger side, and scoots into the backseat. If she wants to ignore Daniel, I'm game to help, so I don't go to the front seat like I normally do. I open the back door on the driver's side of the car, joining her in the backseat. It's a tight fit with my legs hitting the driver's seat, but I can tell it's having a fun effect on my brother. He has never enjoyed having to play second fiddle to anyone, especially me. He gets in the car and pushes the seat back just enough to let me know that, yes, he noticed. I'm not where I belong in the front seat and yes he is going to make this uncomfortable for me as a result.

I don't give in to his action but instead turn to Annie, "Hey, did you see the game last night?" I ask her, because I assume this will get a conversation going. She surprises me a little when she replies, "No, I missed it can you catch me up?" That is all the introduction I need before diving into the play-by-play of the playoff game between the Fighters and Meteors. For the five-minute drive to school, I catch her up. She gives me her almost undivided attention. She doesn't make fun of me when I make my mini-home run batting motion. I continue the recap until we are almost at the front doors of the school. When I catch Daniel giving me a look, I determine it to mean 'get it over with.' I make quick work of wrapping it up and say goodbye to Annie before walking away. I give myself a mental pat on the back for playing my friend role so well.

As I enter the school, making my way to my locker, I notice Meg talking with a group of girls. I make my way over to the group and wrap my arm across the top of Meg's shoulders. "Good morning, ladies," I say and smile at the group. I'm not sure of the other girls' names, but both give Meg a nod and quickly find a way to head off, leaving me and Meg alone as people come and go heading towards first period. "You sure know how to break up a crowd," she laughs. "It's my secret power, shhh, don't tell anyone," I reply and remove my arm from around her shoulders. I earn a smile from her. "It will be our little secret." She lowers her volume to just above a whisper. The bell interrupts us before the conversation can progress. "See you at lunch. We'll have to see if my powers can scare off anyone else," I say. I can just make out her laugh over the crowd as I walk away.

***

Nothing of note takes place the rest of the day, and lunch has all the same players.

68

As I'm sitting in fifth period, I can feel my phone vibrate in my pocket. I adjust my position in my desk to make it look like I'm stretching to cover up the fact that I'm pulling my phone out of my pocket. I open the text app and see "Meg with the Nice Ass" has sent a text.

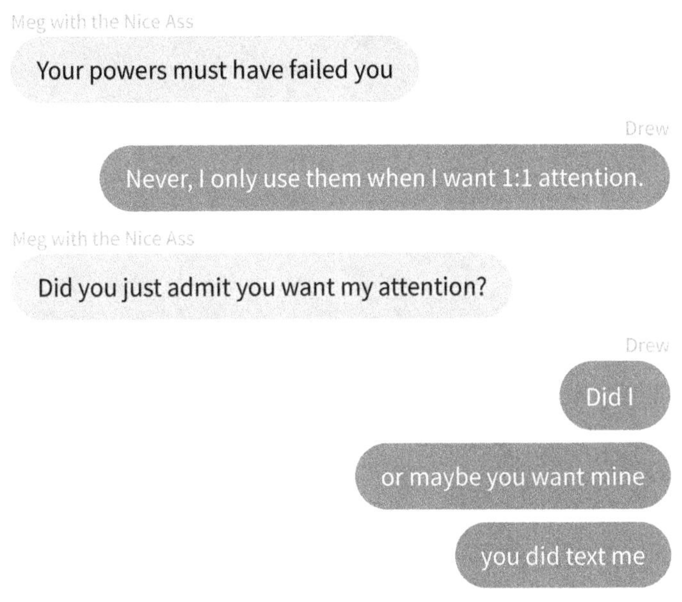

A voice clears next to me, and I look up into Mrs. Smith's face. "Anything you want to share with the class, Mr. Davis?" I shut the phone. "No, can't say I have anything interesting to share." Mrs. Smith lets me know she better not see my phone out again or I'll be handing it over. I apologize, and she goes back to the lecture. I glance over to Annie; she's covering her smirk. I have a feeling that she will be having a laugh about this with Meg later. I can feel my phone vibrate a few more times in my pocket, but I wait until I'm walking to baseball before looking at it again.

I have your attention, aren't you in class   replying to me?

No reply, oh no did you just get your phone taken?

I'll take the silence as a "yes"

Later Mr. Abs

A little smug aren't you?

My good looks are the only reason

you're getting a reply right now

Oh, did the shirt have to come off as   collateral?

Who knew I'd regret not signing up for AP   English

Didn't you see my abs as I walk to baseball?

I guess it's your loss

Later Meg

I think I need a pic as proof

Later Mr. Abs

I almost send her a picture of me showing off my abs. She asked, after all, but then I played it up, sending her a random photo from the internet of a guy with a beer belly. I shut off my phone as I entered the locker room. I haven't made the team officially, but the coach said that being in the sixth-period workout practice time would help me get to know the team and get me up to speed on the expectations. The guys aren't making it easy on me, and I'm ok with that. I don't want any handouts as the new guy, and they haven't offered them. The locker room talk is in full effect as we dress out for practice. I take my spot alongside Luke and ask him what's the latest and greatest. He looks over his shoulder, then clears his voice. "Craig isn't going to like it, but the guys can't get over the new and improved Annie Campbell." "What is new about Annie?" I question. I mean I haven't known her long, but she has been pretty consistent over the last few months. Luke looks around again, seeing no sign of Craig, so he replies, "Annie hasn't always come to school looking like a freakin' model. Annie's always been hot, don't get me wrong, but this year, well, she is dressed to impress, and everyone here is appreciating it." As he finishes, Craig comes through the locker room door. Before I can learn anything else, Luke is asking me about the game last night, and I give him the out before Craig can catch on to our previous conversation. As I follow him out of the locker room, I can't help but feel a little disappointed about not knowing her before.

Chapter 15: Who Knew Game Film was Going to Lead to so Much Drama?

-Annie-

I don't see Daniel for the rest of the day. Craig tells me after third period that my dress is too short. Knowing Craig so well, I know he isn't impressed with the fact that I'm getting more attention today. He is the best bodyguard a girl could have. I smart off to his comment with, "You know I have one in my closet that just covers my butt, but I didn't want to be sent home." He nudges me, "Stop trying to get me into fights, please!" I give him a nudge back, "No promises." I get a few compliments throughout the rest of the day, boosting my confidence that this "rebranding" is doing the job.

Before fifth period, I get to walk with Meg to class. We've been trying to connect on all things boys between classes. We would have normally chatted in detail over lunch, but with the guys joining us, it seems a little awkward, especially since the guy I want to talk about is the brother of one of the guys in our little group and is also the guy Meg wants to talk about. "So, what's the plan for tonight?" Meg asks. "I don't have one, other than wearing those red shorts I love," I tell her. "Those shorts do great things for your butt: great idea, approved." She acts like she is checking off a box on one of her books. "What about you, any plans for Drew?" Meg looks so excited. "I'm playing the long game at the moment. I think I'll text him when I get into class. Can you let me know his reaction?" she asks me, knowing that Drew and I both have English together this period. "You want me to be your spy," I mockingly gasp and look around. "Yes, you are my best insider source." Meg is all smiles as I reply, "Ok, ok but if I'm caught, tell my parents that I love them." The bell rings and we separate quickly, slipping into our respective classrooms.

We are covering the Great American Authors, and Mrs. Smith is laying out how the rest of the school year and Christmas break will play out with our current reading assignments, required papers, and due dates. In the next aisle, I can see Drew moving in his seat. His phone is now wedged between his book and notes. Meg must have sent the message that she said she would. I'm trying to pay attention to Mrs. Smith, but I'm a little distracted trying to catch Drew's facial expressions as he is focused on his phone. Mrs. Smith is cutting down the aisle, and I know he has been caught. He plays the apologetic card and slides the phone back into his pocket. He gives me a side glance, and I can't help the smirk crossing my face. The rest of the class moves by quickly, and Meg is waiting for me outside class.

***

"So, what happened?" she asks, bouncing on her toes. I give her my perspective on his reactions, including him getting caught. She laughs and pulls out her phone, opening it with a smile across her face. I glance at her phone; "Drew with the abs" is typing out a message. "Did you give him that name in your phone?" I ask as we both wait to see what Drew has to say. "Yes, if you must know I saved myself in his phone as 'Meg with the Nice Ass.'" OMG. "Of course you did," I reply. "How can I be you in my next life?" I ask her. "Rebranding, my girl. Look at you," she replies, waving at me in my blue dress. "My work has just started, and you already seem to have learned the skill of using what God gave you." She says this with so much passion. "Well, thank you, my rebranding mastermind," I say and wave goodbye as I head to the girls' locker room to get ready for practice.

***

I'm in my room working on homework when I get a three-knock tap on my bedroom door. "The guys are headed over," Miles tells me through the door. "Ok, be right down," I shout back. Then I scramble around to change out of my soccer gear into a form-fitted t-shirt and my little red shorts. I make my way down to the game room. A few years ago, my dad convinced my mom that it would be a work investment to get a projector screen installed so he could watch in great detail the games he was covering for The Reporter. Mom likes to give Dad a hard time about it because it was also the same year the Kansas City Football team had won their conference and were headed to the championship. Miles and I loved it, and so did all our friends. Who doesn't want to have almost a whole wall to watch the game across? Since Miles has been the starting QB since last year, it has been a twice-a-week event to have guys over from the team to talk about the defenses they will be facing. They run a play and stop it at different points if one of them sees something useful. I love getting the insider experience into the prep work that goes into executing the upcoming Friday night game. All the antidotes I learned here have helped me write articles last year and are helping me feel comfortable on screen delivering the Visual News each week.

***

Miles is connecting his school laptop to the projector when there is a knock on the back door. Everyone knows to come around to the back on film night. I walk over and open the door: Max and Daniel have shown up at the same time. I yell over my shoulder to Miles, "Max and Daniel are here." I do my best game show host move, directing them towards the couches. Max laughs at me and gives me a side hug. "Always good to get a warm welcome from one of the Campbells." "I live to serve at the pleasure of QB1," I joke back, sending a dig at my older brother. Max takes a seat on the end of the couch, his normal spot over the last two seasons. I turn and smile at Daniel. "Nice to see you, Davis—come on in, why don't you," I say because he hasn't moved from the back porch into the ho use yet.

He walks up to me and, in front of both my brother and Max, wraps his hand around my waist. He pulls my body against his, and his lips land on mine in a kiss. It surprises me... I didn't expect him to do that. I figured we would do the whole flirting-teasing thing that we had established over the last few weeks. Just as I'm settling into the kiss, I hear a "Cut that shit out, Davis, or I'm going to take back my invitation," Miles says in his grumpy tone. "Annie, don't make me kick you out," he warns when we don't immediately end the kiss. I step back from Daniel, and he winks at me before shutting the door, taking my hand and leading me towards the couch. He sits down in the middle, leaving the opposite end of the couch from Max open. "You're in Annie's seat, man," Max says to Daniel. Daniel doesn't even respond. "It's ok, Max, I am good on the end today," I hear myself say. I mean, Max is right; I normally sit in the middle of the couch. It's my unofficial spot during these review sessions. Before I can think too much about it, I sit down and we get to the game film.

***

The Tigers have a good defense: they like to throw a lot of one-on-one coverage. At least that is what they have done so far this year. The guys focus on the plays and coverages, starting and stopping plays over the next hour. About five minutes in, Daniel places his hand on my exposed thigh. He acts like it's the most natural thing in the world that his hand should be on my leg. When he is lost in the review, he starts to tap his fingers against my skin. I feel the goosebumps as they appear across my legs. I try to keep focused but soon realize I've missed all the comments about the last few plays, as my mind has been hyper-focused on his hand and his fingers on my leg. "Earth to Annie," Max laughs from the other side of Daniel.

I jump: oh gosh, what have I missed? Max gives me the out I need and repeats his question, "I was asking you what you thought about the defensive tackle." I think back on the film. "I think the o-line is going to have to step up their game—if this film is any indicator, he is thirsty to get the sack. He has been able to get a lot of them so far this season. Miles needs to make sure he is ready to scramble if the line breaks." I say with confidence to Max. "Annie, glad you could join us again, I'd agree with you," my brother says. He has turned toward me, his eyes going to my leg before turning around. I know he saw Daniel's hand on my leg, and I know, as my older brother, it is killing him to try not to overreact at this moment. I double my efforts to focus on a few more plays. Miles closes his computer in no time, all the plays covered for tonight.

We all stand, and without thinking about it, I stretch, making a small, satisfied groan. I hadn't realized I'd been holding my body so tight. I open my eyes. Max and Daniel are both looking at me with a look of interest. My brother's jaw is pinched. I wonder if I should be worried about him breaking a tooth. I hadn't done it on purpose; it was a natural reaction to my stretch. Boys are weird. Daniel wraps his large hand in mine. "Walk me home, Annie." I'm about to tell him ok, when Max opens his big mouth, "Dude, you live right next door! But you know, Annie, I think I'm scared of the dark. I need you to walk to my car—come on Annie, please, baby?" I know Max well enough to know he is putting on a show and playing up the tension in the room. Also, I know that Max isn't a huge fan of Daniel; he lost the starting position to him back in August. Daniel releases my hand quickly, and before I know it, he has Max pinned against the wall.

I watch the situation from outside of my body. *What the hell just happened?* Miles jumps between them, pushing Daniel off of Max. Daniel looks like he is about to throw a punch but before he does, I grab his arm and say, "I'll walk you home." I tug on his arm, and he lets me pull him out through the back door onto the porch. I don't stop, leading him through my backyard, and head for his front door. Before I can take more than a few steps in that direction, he turns and tugs me in the direction of his backyard. I follow him through the gate in the direction of his porch.

But we never make it to the porch, because in a flash, he has me pinned against the side of his house: his hands are in my ponytail, yanking my face up to meet his. After the events of the last few minutes, I wasn't expecting another kiss—I was going to be happy that no one was walking away with bruises. Now I'm here, pressed against him and the house. He is a little rough in this kiss, all the gentleness from earlier gone. He pulls my face back with his hands in my hair, looking me straight in the eyes. "Stay away from Max, Annie. Or the next time he smarts off, I'll shut him up." He removes his hands from my hair and makes his way up the stairs and into his house, not once looking back at me. For the second time in minutes, I think: *what the hell just happened?*

Chapter 16: Rebranding Lessons

-Annie-

By the time I get home after the events between Max and Daniel, the room is empty. Max has left, and Miles is already back in his room. I'm glad that I don't have to face him because if I know my brother, and I think I do, I'm going to get an earful about not dating his teammate.

The next morning, it becomes clear that my earful is going to take place whether I want it to or not. Miles is pretty normal in front of Mom and Dad, but when we head out to the car, it's clear my brother isn't going to avoid the conversation any longer. I make a move to head to the Davises' front door, but before I get two steps in that direction, Miles says, "Annie, I'll drive you today, I don't even have to get Steph. She's riding with friends so that we can chat." I could keep walking and ignore him, but I love my brother, and sometimes I even enjoy his company. So, I know that I should get this over with so we can both move on. I reply, "Sure, let me send a quick text."

I'm not sure why I lie, but I don't want to make it seem like my brother controls my actions either. I want Daniel to think of me without being tied to Miles. I get a reply back in short order, and it's a one-word reply.

Daniel's one-word response bothers me. Before I can dive too deeply into it, I put my phone away and follow Miles to the car. He starts the car, turning the radio so low that it's a hum in the background. Before he even puts the car into drive, he clears his throat. "Annie, Davis isn't a great guy, and before you interrupt me or get angry, remember that I've spent the last month having to be in a locker room with him. Even before whatever it is that you two started." He is wearing a serious look on his face. "Why should I care if he is a good guy?" I say, knowing that I do care, but I'm not about to give in to Miles. "Annie, give me a break. You've only ever dated guys that are generally well below your level and that are not bad dudes," Miles throws back at me.

"Davis has spent the last month giving us the details about all the girls he's been with. I don't think you want to add to his number. If he adds you to his number and brags about it, Annie, I'll kick his ass, and I have no problem admitting it." Miles sounds like he really would commit an act of violence; his hands on the steering wheel are so tight, his knuckles are turning white. "I'm not going to stop talking to him, Miles," I say, continuing when he glares at me. "But I'm in no rush to be anyone's next number—we aren't even dating," I reply to him, giving him more information than he probably cares to have. We pull into the parking lot, not directly next to another car. He parks the car and turns to look at me. "Annie, you're my sister. I realize you are going to date guys, I'm not an idiot. I just want the guy you are interested in to be interested in you the way you deserve." "Thanks for the information, Miles. I really will keep it in mind,"

I reply. I truly appreciate that my older brother wants to protect me. After we get out of the car, I add, "Love you too, Miles." This earns me a smile from my older brother before we both head into school in opposite directions.

***

When I get to my locker, Meg is already there. She looks behind me, and I'm sure she is looking for Drew because, for the last few days, we have been arriving in a very close window. Trying to draw her attention, I tell her I rode with Miles today. "You'll have to make eyes with Drew later," I tell her, and she replies, "Well, why did you do that and ruin all my flirting plans?" I fill her in about the events at the end of watching the game film and my conversation with Miles. By the time I relay all this, Meg is giving me a little worried expression. "It sounds like Daniel is a player, Annie. I'm going to have to agree that you don't have any experience with guys like that. Isn't Daniel the first boy you've kissed outside of already calling the guy your boyfriend?" Meg asks. "I kissed Jake during Spin the Bottle in middle school, and he wasn't my boyfriend." Meg lets out a sigh of desperation. "Annie, you are making my point even easier because you're right, he wasn't your boyfriend when you kissed, but he was by the time we started school the following Monday." I think back on it; she's right, Jake had been my boyfriend very shortly after the very public peck on the lips during Spin the Bottle. Meg and I start walking to first period before she says, "Just be careful, ok? And unless he calls you his girlfriend, please for the love of God, Annie, don't think you're the only girl he's talking to." I tell her ok as we walk into first period, and the subject is dropped.

***

I haven't seen or gotten a text from Daniel all day. A part of me felt like maybe my brother was right, and I should stop whatever this little flirting thing is with him. It is killing me not to text him. It's been a little daring and adventurous, the flirting like we have been doing. Maybe I should do a little 'rebranding' on my relationship image if both my brother and my best friend are in agreement that I've been playing it safe all these years. But I also know that I don't want to be an easy score or be a quick add to some guy's number. I'm pulled from my warring emotions and thoughts by the ping of my phone. To my delight, it is the person that my mind has been debating all day.

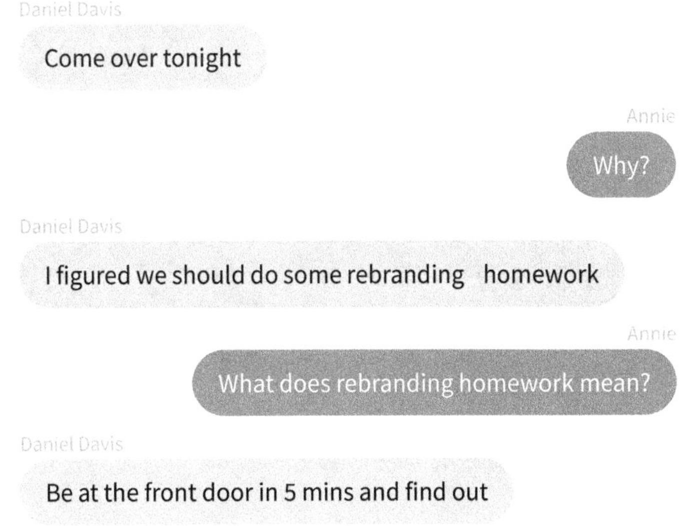

I set the phone down, taking a deep breath. Should I go over, or shouldn't I? Between Miles and Meg's conversations today, I've gotten in my head. I'm enjoying the kisses and stolen moments, but do I want him to ask me to be his girlfriend? I'd be lying to myself if I said that I don't. On the other hand, I've also never had the rush of lust that runs through my body when we are kissing or touching. It's something that I do want to explore; it's a new part of me I'm just finding. This year is about finding a different Annie, rebranding me from the version Miles and Meg talked about today. My mind made up, I grab a pair of sneakers, making my way downstairs. I tell my parents I'm going for a run, and I'll be back in about thirty to forty-five minutes. They both give me mumbled agreements from somewhere in the house. I leave the house, quickly crossing the yard to the Davis house, and knock on the door.

It's only a matter of seconds before Daniel is there opening the door for me. "What a surprise to see you, Annie, why don't you come in?" he says to no one but me. I enter the house, and it's the same house footprint as it was when the McHenrys had lived here, but it now feels more fresh and open. There are art pieces scattered along the living room walls and bookcases. Daniel breaks my review of the house by asking, "Do you want anything to drink before we go upstairs?" "Yeah, that would be great," I can hear my voice reply, but my brain is focused on the phrase 'go upstairs.' When I'd come over, I hadn't thought about what or where we could be hanging out. I guess my brain has assumed someplace like the living room, but it seems like Daniel has other plans. I follow him and we go into the kitchen. His parents are talking at the table. Daniel introduces me quickly. They let me know I could come over any time. Daniel hands me a bottle of water before taking my other hand and leading me away from the kitchen. I rush to say goodbye to his parents.

***

We are going up the stairs and down a hallway to the room at the end. As we walk down the hallway, I can't help thinking to myself that one of these rooms is probably Drew's. Is Drew home? I almost ask Daniel but think better of it. He opens the door, and I step into his room. His room is pretty straightforward: there's what looks to be a full-sized bed, a desk, and some nightstands. He has an overflowing laundry basket in the corner. There is a frame full of football team-themed posters, as well as a few of the team's very famous scantily clad cheerleaders. While I've been looking around the room, Daniel has taken a seat on the edge of his bed. He is watching me as I take in his space. "Come here," he says. I look back at the closed door. My action must give away my concern about his parents being in the house because he says, "Annie, they don't care what we do in here, they won't be checking in on us if that's worrying you." It was at least a little of what was worrying me. My parents have a no-closed-door rule, and Dad had a practice of randomly coming by to ask a question. I've seen it play out on more than one occasion with Miles. It cracks me up every time Dad came downstairs, telling me and Mom that a crisis had been diverted.

Now here I was, with a boy behind his very closed door. Daniel speaks again. "Annie, I said come here." I jerk my head at these words; his tone had been on the edge of commanding, but now, looking at him, he gives me a wink, and that seems to relax my body. I set my water bottle on the nightstand and step between his legs. With him sitting on the bed, our faces are even and it's nice being his equal. "You want your first lesson, Annie?" he says. "I'm ready, what do you got for me Daniel?" I say as confidently as I can. "Take what you want," he says, inches from my face now. I know I pinch my brows a little—*what does he mean, take what I want?* Then I look at him I know I want to kiss him, so I close the gap between our bodies and do it. I'm not in control for long before he pulls me on top of him and spins us down on his bed, effectively kissing my doubts away.

Chapter 17: I Didn't See it Coming

-*Annie*-

The next month and a half fly by, and it's early November before I realize it. Between school and covering all the sporting events for the Visual News, I've been more than busy. I still haven't gone on an official date with Daniel. I blame it on his and my schedules. We have found times to connect behind closed doors, at least once a week. Daniel and Drew's parents have a very laid-back approach. True to his word, I've cared less and less that his parents or Drew are in the house. He's started calling these visits my "rebranding in-person/in-home lessons" each time we push just a touch further. I was enjoying the ability to have him alone behind a closed door. The last time I was over, in the heat of the moment, it wasn't just my layers being removed, but some of his had been discarded too. I had enjoyed the feeling of his hands on my bare skin, but the alarm on my phone went off, telling me curfew was approaching. The night ended with Daniel pissed, and trying to convince me to break curfew. I'd gotten dressed, making an excuse about not wanting to be grounded, but in reality, I'd been relieved.

***

Outside of our "lessons," I've only seen Daniel on the rides to school or at the occasional party we'd attend. I've started riding with the Davis brothers each morning to school and riding with Miles home. Daniel and I hang back and make out in the car before the first-period bell rings. He walks me to the front doors before disappearing to his classes. Meg and I have talked about it. She loves that I am happy and getting a healthy amount of make-out sessions in a week. But she has some concerns that Daniel and I don't hang out much in public. She is afraid that maybe the lessons behind his closed bedroom door are moving a little fast. I've been making excuses about the lack of public appearances, and Meg eventually lets it go for now. We agree that once football was over, it would be better, and he'd probably ask me to be his girlfriend.

***

The Rams have made the playoffs and have already won their first few rounds. Tonight's game is the semi-finals against the Trojans. All the local news stations are hyping it as the game to watch in the state. Miles and Daniel are the poster boys of the team, and Mom has recorded each of the times they have been on the news. The scouts are in full force, seeing how the guys deal with the spotlight and the pressure of the win-or-go-home environment. For all the playoff games, I have gotten to be field side during the fourth quarter only. Coach is trying to reduce the number of distractions, and keeping the sidelines under control is important to him. I've planned to sit with Drew, Meg, Craig, and Luke and cheer on the team until I have to go field side.

***

When we get to the neutral game site, I can feel the energy and the excitement of the fans. I'm in my 00 game jersey with layers underneath to keep me warm.

I had hoped Daniel would get me a jersey, but I didn't ask, and he didn't get me one. "I still don't get why he hasn't given you a jersey," Meg says as we wait for the game to start. "For the millionth time, I didn't ask, it's not important," I reply. "Annie, you shouldn't have to ask—he should want to see you in his jersey." She leans out and addresses Drew. "What the hell is wrong with your brother anyway?" Drew makes a face, and I save him the trouble of responding, "Meg, you know that isn't fair to ask Drew." She crosses her arms, giving me a little scowl. Drew puts his hands up, "I have no idea what is wrong with him. Can we pretend that I'm not affiliated with him, please?" He gives her his best puppy dog eyes." "Ok, you are forgiven." She wraps her arms around his waist, and he returns the move and kisses the top of her hat-covered head. "I, on the other hand, will remember and hold it against you every chance I get," says Luke from Drew's other side. "I only care if he upsets Annie," pipes in Craig. "If he does that, do you have an issue with me kicking your brother's ass?" Craig adds. "Nope, feel free to kick away," laughs Drew. I appreciate how he takes all of thi s in stride.

***

Meg and Drew started dating "officially" a few weeks ago. On one of the car rides to school, Drew asked me if I thought Meg would go on a date with him. I had probably been a little too excited and enthusiastic, saying that she would love to go on a date with him. He had laughed, thanking me for the encouragement. They started dating, and the small moments of PDA quickly escalated to full on PDA at every opportunity. From them sitting next to each other at lunch, to them making out between classes, they were not afraid to show their affection. I am happy for them both, but also a little jealous. Daniel still hasn't asked me to be his girlfriend. Our moments of heat-filled bursts, play out behind closed doors or small moments at parties. "Can you two please just get a room and leave us out of it?" Craig says, bringing my thoughts back to the present. "Yuck, yuck, and yuck," Luke says, making the *I'm going to puke* motion at the two of them. "You, my friend, can F-off," Drew says to him, throwing him the bird in the process.

***

We enjoy the build-up to the game and proceed to chant, scream, and cheer on the Rams through three tight, back-and-forth quarters. I tell my friends I'll see them after the game and head down to the area where I'm meeting Steven to get on the field for the Visual News. I already miss the view I had of the whole field from the bleachers, but I'm also enjoying the action of being right here. I hear the fans cheering above us, but I can also hear the guys on the sidelines hyping each other up or getting into it about what they have to do the next time they take the field. I do my setup piece and get the thumbs up from Steven after I finish. I go back to the game, not wanting to miss a thing. He gets game shots that he will be able to clip to go with the summary I'll do.

I'm watching from my spot when the Rams' defense gets a big interception. The crowd is going crazy behind me, and the energy is raised to another level. The Rams defender is tackled short of the goal line. Steven points the camera at me, and I say my piece: "That could be just the play the Rams need to secure their ticket to State. Lopez made a great play on the ball and came up with the interception. Now it's up to the Rams offense to complete the job." Again, he turns back to the game and the line of scrimmage. The tension is high with seconds left in the game. We are currently behind by 3; if the Rams score, they can burn the clock down. I am trying to remember to breathe as my brother snaps the ball. The Rams get minimal yards on the first and second down, but then magic happens on the third down. Miles has to scramble, but he draws some of the defenders, and that leaves Daniel wide open for the touchdown. I turn to the camera, beaming, "It's another connection between Campbell and Davis to secure the Rams their ticket to the state championship in two weeks!" The clock ticks off the seconds until the team then fans storm the field, and I watch from my sideline position.

Steven asks me if I think I can get any player's attention for an interview. I know I need to at least find Daniel, Miles, or even Lopez, as they had all had big moments in the game. I see Daniel and wave him over; he is headed my way when a cheerleader—Sam, the captain—cuts him off, throwing herself into his arms. I watch him wrap his arms around her before she kisses him. I look away, shocked. I can't move. *What the hell did I just see?* In the new direction I'm looking, I spot Lopez and without a look back, I head his way with Steven hot on my tail. I get the first reactions from him and a few of the defensive players. I give Steven my mic and let him know that I think we are good. He agrees, taking the mic, and we say our goodbyes.

I am not going to cry in front of all these people. *I will not cry* I chant over and over in my head as I get my phone out of my pocket and text Meg.

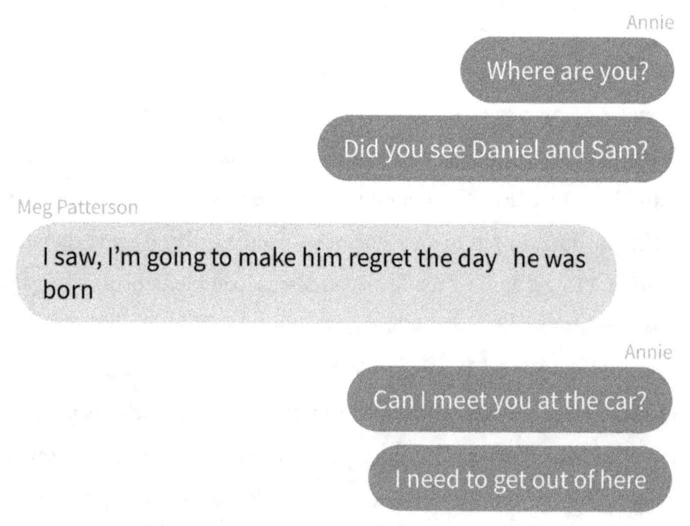

I think I blacked out on the way to the car. I don't remember saying anything to anyone. I'm so focused on the thoughts running through my head—*do not cry, do not cry, you will be so embarrassed if you cry*. I finally make it to where I can see Meg's car. I've never been so happy to see her and the guys. I take off in a run to close the distance and end up in Meg's arms. She wraps her arms around me, and then the tears I've been holding start to fall. Meg has one of the guys drive us home; I'm not even sure if it's Craig or Luke. I know it's not Drew because I'm sandwiched between him and Meg in the backseat, crying on my best friend's shoulder. If I wasn't so distraught, I'd find it weird how silent they all are.

Chapter 18: Be a Shoulder to Cry On

I'm not sure how we got to November, but here we are. I think the reason that October flew by is that I finally got up the nerve to ask Meg out. We kept going back and forth in our text messages, but I wanted to take her out. I talked to Annie about it on one of the school drives. Annie had been so positive that Meg would go out with me. I asked her out the next time I saw her in the halls. She had been bouncing on her toes when she'd said she'd love to go out with me. Bouncing on her toes is like her happy dance, I've learned.

***

Our first date was to the movie theater, followed by milkshakes at the local ice cream shop. Meg was easy to talk to, and her confidence was always present. Walking back to the car after ice cream, I grabbed her hand, only releasing it to get into the car. We held hands all the way back to her house. I walked her to her door. I asked, "So, how much time before your parents come out to check on you?" She replied, "You have about ten minutes, make them count." Then I wrapped my hand around her waist, kissing her, and I did make those ten minutes count until a woman clearing her voice startled me. "Ok, Mom, I get it, I'm coming in." Meg gave me one more kiss and went inside.

***

Over the next few weeks, we tried to play it down in front of our friends, slowly introducing the fact that we were dating. Somewhere along the last two weeks, we had both fully given in to the lust of wanting to be touching or kissing all the time. Meg was a good kisser, and I was perfectly fine kissing her whenever and wherever she wanted me to. We had even ended up in the office because neither of us had heard the bell. We'd gotten off with a warning but got a lecture about PDA in the halls and practicing safe sex... which had me now thinking about having sex with Meg.

I wanted to invite Meg over, and I knew my parents wouldn't care. I wanted to see if we could skip the party after the football game on Friday. I knew both my parents would go to the playoff game and wouldn't rush home. Daniel would probably take Annie to the after-party; it's the one place he showed her off on his arm. I could see where things went, maybe sex, maybe one or both of us removing clothing. I'd be ok touching her curves or letting her enjoy touching me. I hadn't been given a lot of good opportunities to get my hands on her curves without clothing getting in my way. My fingers itched to feel more of her tanned skin without meeting any interruption.

***

We arrive at the game with our friend's group, carpooling to the game in Meg's mom's SUV. Meg has been giving Annie a lecture about Daniel that I can't help but overhear. I've been starting to worry that Daniel is using Annie, personally.

I keep wondering if we were good enough friends now that I should tell her. *Would she trust me?* I don't know if I want to risk her friendship over Daniel. He is never with her at school, unless it is in front of everyone at one of the parties. I overhear Meg telling Annie he should have taken her out if he wanted access to all her treats. Annie makes some excuses but I'm not buying it. I know Daniel, which makes me a little concerned for Annie. I try to break the tension between my girlfriend and friend, and I think I pull it off. I pull Meg into my arms before getting Craig and Luke to make puking faces as I put my arms around my girl. I let them know that they can F-off and continue to enjoy holding Meg.

***

We chant and cheer as the Rams go back and forth. They win for a while, then lose when the Trojans get a touchdown. Annie leaves to go do her Visual News reporting in the fourth quarter. The Trojans hit a field goal to take the lead with six minutes to go. The offense does nothing on the next drive. It's starting to get into the last two minutes of the game, and it's not looking like it's going to happen for the Rams. There is almost no time left on the clock, and we don't have the ball. Then one of the Rams defenders gets an interception and makes it almost thirty yards toward the Rams' end zone. The offense takes the field, and it's not looking good. Daniel is double-teamed, and the running back keeps getting stopped. Then on the third down, Miles scrambles out of the pocket, drawing defenders, making them think he is going to run. I see Daniel wide open in the end zone, and so does Miles, because the pass connects— it's a touchdown. The student section goes crazy. When the clock hits zero, the team storms the field. I am happy for my brother. It hasn't been easy, but he seems to be doing the work here to be different than he was back at our last school. We are about to head out when I hear Meg say, "Who the fuck is your brother kissing ?"

I have no idea: I wasn't focused on the field. I look around, trying to locate him, and find him not with Annie in his arms but with the cheerleader captain. I saw him talking to her after practice a few times but hadn't thought anything about it. Maybe my thought about him changing was premature. Every time up until now, they had only been talking; it hadn't even looked like flirting if I'm being honest. I look for Annie, worried about her. By the time I spot her, she is interviewing Lopez. "Maybe she didn't see," I say to Meg. She gives me a serious side eye replying, "Even if she didn't, everyone else has eyes, they all saw." She has a good point—people are going to talk about this, as it was pretty common knowledge that Daniel and Annie were hanging out. Meg looks down at her phone. "Shit, she saw, we have to go."

As we all rush to leave the stadium, I look over at Annie giving her mic to the camera guy. She looks sad, but that's all I can see from this distance. Our little gang makes our way as quickly as we can to the car. "Did you know?" Meg asks me. "No, I have only ever seen Daniel with Annie at our house, I swear." I must look sincere because she drops it. I spot Annie in the crowd and tell Meg. She turns around, and Annie runs, launching herself into Meg's arms. Annie is crying; there is no missing the sobbing sound she makes against Meg's shoulder. It is one of the saddest things I've had to witness. Craig, Luke, and I look at each other, not sure what we should do. Meg hands Craig the keys before she opens the back door of the SUV and climbs in, pulling Annie in behind her. I slide in next to Annie and shut the door. Meg and I have a little moment over Annie's head. Looks like our night at my house is going to have to be postponed. I swear, my brother ruins everything.

***

The drive home isn't as full of fun as we had all expected after a win. The only sound is the radio and the small sniffles that Annie is making next to me. Craig is gripping the steering wheel with white knuckles. I know he wants to get his fists into Daniel. I don't blame him. Daniel blindsided her out there in front of the whole school. When we get to the house, Annie isn't crying, but she has fallen asleep against Meg's shoulder. "Can one of you carry her?" Meg asks the group. "I got her, I'm already back here," I say before Craig and Luke can answer. I open the door and then scoop Annie into my arms. She leans her head into my chest. Meg opens the garage with the code she has memorized, I'm sure from all the times she's been over. I carry Annie to her room, and she wakes up as Meg directs me to which is her room. She blinks a few times, and it must register that I'm carrying her. "You can set me down, Drew. Thanks for this." She waves over her body in my arms. I let her go at the threshold to her room. "No problem, Annie, let me know if you need anything." I turn to Meg, giving her a small kiss and lowering my voice. "Rain check on our plans." "Yes, rain check for sure." She steps up on her tiptoes and gives me another kiss.

***

I head back outside, rejoining Craig and Luke, who are waiting. "How is she?" Craig asks. "Well, she woke up, and Meg is going to stay here tonight," I say to them. "Don't ask anything else because I don't have any idea how she is doing." "Your brother is an asshole. I swear, the next time I see him, I'm going make sure he understands Annie was the wrong girl to mess with," Craig says to me. I agree with him; my brother is an asshole, but fighting Daniel isn't going to help Annie—knowing Annie, she'd be more upset with us. "Annie didn't deserve that," Luke says into the silence. "No, she didn't," I agree, then add, "But she also doesn't deserve her best friends fighting her battles. She would be pissed at any of us if we touch Daniel." "She'll get over it, eventually," Craig says, but he also looks a little less on edge. "Ok, so we don't kick your brother's ass tonight, but if he does something else to our girl, I'm only going to pretend to hold

Craig back," Luke says, making us all laugh a little. The guys leave shortly after agreeing that we will follow Annie's lead.

Chapter 19: Rumor Mill

My friends are the best. Meg stays with me all night after the football game. I feel drained, and we change and go to sleep after Drew leaves. At around 1 a.m., I hear a soft knock at my door. I quietly move off the bed, trying not to wake up Meg, and crack the door open. Miles is standing at the door, which is already surprising enough, but then I notice his swollen eye, and I know I have missed something. "Are you ok?" he asks me quietly. I step into the hallway because I don't want to wake Meg. "What happened to your face, Miles?" I respond, not answering his question. I can imagine, but I want him to tell me. "I told you: if he hurt you, I'd end him. I wasn't joking, Annie."

I look at his throwing hand, and it's swollen; the skin on his knuckles has scrapes and scabs forming. "Miles, what did you do?" I say as I return my gaze to his swollen eye. "I made sure in a straightforward way that he knows that messing with you was the wrong move." I know Miles thought he was doing the right thing, but now I'll be dealing with a fight on top of the fact that Daniel publicly kissed Sam. I cover my face with my hands, taking a deep breath. *It is going to be ok,* I chant in my head as I move my hands away from my face. "Follow me, tough guy," I say to my brother. I head in the direction of the kitchen to get him some ice. State is only two weeks away, and he can't have that hand out of commission for that game. I refuse to be the reason the team doesn't have my brother on that field.

***

The next day, after a few more hours of sleep, I think I'm ready to talk about it. Meg gives me the room to process and work through my feelings. I've gone from blaming myself and the fact that I hadn't pushed him to take me out, to blaming myself that I hadn't gone further with him behind closed doors, to finally blaming him for stringing me along and very publicly embarrassing me. It can't be called cheating, but it feels like it to me. When I've finished my rant, Meg takes the silence to mean it is her turn. She tells me, in no uncertain terms, that my blame game is bullshit and that his *cheating* on me is an asshole move. She gets a look on her face of pure scheming and it's a little scary to see. She lets me know we aren't "rebranding" anymore; we are going for "revenge."

She goes to my closet, moving clothes around. She pulls back to study her handiwork. I see a week's worth of my tightest jeans, shirts, and my shortest dresses. "You are going to show him what he is missing out on" Meg says with her hand on her heart. I hug her then I let her lead me through her plan for "revenge." I'd much rather get lost in this than wallow in the sadness I am feeling.

***

By Monday morning, Meg has set all the players in motion. I make a mental note to never get on my best friend's bad side. She made this all look too easy to put together. She texted me yesterday, letting me know that I'm going to still get a ride from Daniel and Drew this morning. I think she is crazy, but I'm going to follow her orders to a T. Then, starting on Tuesday, she is going to start picking us up. I guess Drew wants to distance himself from his brother, too.

So, here I am, looking at my reflection in the mirror: promising myself out loud that I can do this, I will not let him see that he hurt me. I check my reflection one more time. This red dress hugs all my curves, and it is just long enough that I won't get sent home. Meg informed me that for my walk to the car today, it would be completely ok if I wanted to pull it up a few inches to expose a little more of my legs. I adjust it in the mirror and agree with her assessment that this dress makes me look like my legs are miles long. I still want to pull it down immediately after I do it, but I'm on my "revenge mission". I grab my bag, skipping the coat—because I didn't wear the dress to cover it up—and head down the stairs. I avoid my parents and brother this morning, instead shouting my goodbye down the hall before I head out the front door.

Drew is waiting on the porch eating what looks to be a folded waffle. When he sees me, he takes a quick swallow, followed by a choking sound. I rush over to him and give him a few pats on the back before he rights himself. "Meg said you were on some "revenge plan", but damn, Annie, are you going to kill my brother." I smile; it's so like Drew to take my mind off my nerves and get me to smile. "I'll take that as a compliment," I say. "As you should," Drew replies before adding, "Daniel should be out any minute. I'm warning you, your brother did a number on his face." That should bother me, but it doesn't.

True to Drew's words, Daniel comes out of the front door a few minutes later. His face is swollen and bruised. When he spots me, he looks pissed. His eyes take a scan from my head to my toes. "I told Annie we would take her today," Drew says, playing the role that Meg assigned him perfectly. We both head towards the Davises' car. Drew and I take seats in the back. I don't look once in Daniel's direction. At school, I get out and start to head off with Drew. Daniel grabs my arm, stopping me before I can get out of his reach. His voice is low but not low enough that Drew can't hear. "What the fuck are you wearing?"

"It's called a dress, Daniel," I respond, proud of myself. I didn't sound anything but confident. His hand tightens around my arm, starting to hurt. "Take your hand off me, Daniel, you're causing a scene," I say. I look around: he is causing a scene, I wasn't lying. People have stopped or are walking slower, watching this play out. Daniel takes a step into my space like he used to right before kissing me *How dare he think he can still do that?* I don't think—I react by kneeing him straight in the balls. He releases my arm immediately with a grunt. I step back and find Drew next to me, and he gives me a little nudge before saying loudly for the onlookers' benefit, "Annie Campbell, you just made my whole year." Then we head into the school building, not giving Daniel another glance.

***

When I reach my locker, Meg is waiting, and she has the biggest smile. Before she says anything, she hands me her phone. There on the screen is an action shot of the moment my knee connected with Daniel's balls. It's very clear from the angle that Daniel is in some pain. "Annie Campbell, I'm not sure what happened to the plan, but I 100% approve of the new direction." A few girls pass us saying, "Good for you, Annie," then continue down the hall. Craig shows up and gives me a look while handing me his jacket before saying, "I knew our little Annie had some fight in her." "Annie, please promise me my balls are safe, that looked painful," laughs Luke. Luke wraps his arm over my shoulder and walks me to class. By the end of the day, I haven't heard a thing about me being 'pathetic' for what happened at the game. All I've heard today in the hall is that you shouldn't mess with either one of the Campbells, and I'm perfectly ok with that rumor.

Chapter 20: Is it Baseball Season Already?

-Drew-

Spring

I am so ready to kick off baseball season. I have worked my ass off over the last few months. Coach ran drills in the indoor facility most of the winter. He also believes in running us. I loved every second of it, and I'm ready to prove why I should be the starting shortstop. Last week, he pulled me into his office and let me know that I was going to get the start over Michels. I should have told Meg first, but I'd texted Annie first, letting her know I was getting the start. She had been so excited for me that she invited all our friends over for a movie night at her place with pizza. Meg had given me a hard time about telling Annie first, but said she understood that baseball was one of the things Annie and I freaked out over.

***

Outside of baseball, I couldn't be more content. Meg and I have made good on the rain check and more. She enjoys driving me crazy each time she comes over to the house. Meg believes in sexy lingerie, and I wasn't complaining. She also isn't shy about sex or foreplay. She has been honest about her history and that she was on the pill. She made me work for each new base, but she also stole a few of them herself. So, it was fair to say that Meg and I were enjoying our time locked in my bedroom. To be honest with myself, I like Meg, and we are having fun, but my feelings haven't changed since we started dating. It's comfortable, which I guess isn't a bad thing.

***

I've been trying to convince my parents that I need a car. Since November, Meg has picked me and Annie up for school. But I still had to find my way home by riding with one of the guys or, in the very worst case, Daniel. In more than one worst-case scenario, I've been subjected to Daniel's new rotation of girls. There have been so many that I've stopped trying to learn their names. I am over having to play backseat to his hookups or having to bum a ride from my friends. In this, Daniel and I have found agreement, and he's backed me up every time the subject comes up. Dad told me this morning that we can go look at the used car lot next weekend. Freedom is only a few weeks away.

***

Life is looking up, I think as I head out the door when I hear the honking car horn. This is no doubt Meg letting me and Annie know that she is here. When I get to the car, Annie is already in the back, chatting with Meg. I jump in the front seat, kissing Meg and interrupting whatever she was about to say to Annie. "OK. OK. Enough already," Annie groans from the back, and then for good measure adds, "I need a car: how do I tell my parents I am being mentally scarred from having to witness my friends make out?" I pull back and smile at Meg.

101

"Well, Annie, I think a better idea than a car is a new boy toy," pipes in Meg. Annie laughs from the back seat. "Please, Meg—describe in detail the definition of a boy toy. I think Drew and I need to get the details here." "Annie, how many times do I need to give you the definition? You need a rebound from that," Meg points dramatically in the direction of my brother walking out the door. I'm still sitting sideways in my seat, and I can see Annie roll her eyes. "That—" (making the same motion Meg just made) "—is the reason I don't want a boy anything," Annie replies. I interject with my hands up, "For all boykind, we aren't all like—" (making the same mention as both of the girls towards my brother) "—that." For good measure, I wrap my hands together in a prayer position, "Please, Annie, don't forsake us all." My actions have the desired effect, causing them to start laughing.

***

At lunch, Craig, Luke, and I are all geared up and talking about the first home game tomorrow. If all the talk in the state is right, we have a pretty good chance of making the playoffs this year. The team's seniors just missed out last year, and it's the goal they have painted on the wall for this year's team. Meg hasn't let the boy toy conversation from earlier go. She has been peppering Annie with a new game: Yes, No, or Maybe. Meg announces after grabbing lunch that *yes* means Annie's interested, *no* means, well, no, and *maybe* means that Annie could be convinced if, say, a shirtless picture could be produced. All three of us guys mostly tuned out after that because Annie is pretty much saying no to every name that Meg has thrown out. The highest rating a guy got all lunch from what I couldn't help but overhear was a *maybe*. The rest of the day zooms by as I focus on the first game.

I want a low-key night in before tomorrow. I have a few tests, unfortunately, and I need to keep my grades up to play, so I make it a priority to stay in and study. It helps that Meg's parents have a standing Thursday night family night, no friends or boyfriends allowed, so I can't distract myself with my naked girlfriend either. So, I'm trying to focus on my homework when my phone vibrates on the desk.

Five minutes later, I join Annie in her backyard. We kick the ball around, and we play a game of HORSE, trying to match each other's goal distance and angle. Annie kicks my butt, being the soccer player after all. "I feel wronged: unfair advantage to the actual soccer player on the field," I say in my best commentator voice. Annie smiles, "Next time we need a study break, you pick the drill, bet I can beat you on one of those baseball speed drills." "Oh, do you think so? Game on, Annie," I reply. I have never wished I owned a ball machine more. I want to see if Annie could face down a fastball. We call it a night so we can both get to studying. "In case I don't say it tomorrow", she says, "Good luck, Drew, I can't wait to see you on the field." Annie gives me her full-on smile and I know I give her mine. "Thanks, Annie, I'll see you on the sidelines for my post-game int erview."

Chapter 21: Game Day

-Drew-

The day passes quickly leading up to the game. I know I go to school, take my test, and have lunch with my friends, but it's like I'm on autopilot. My body and brain are all counting down to the opening pitch and my time on the field. Meg wishes me good luck, giving me a kiss at the front door of the locker room. She realized today at lunch that she will have to find a group to watch the game with because Annie will be in the dugout with the team. "You going to be ok in the stands?" I ask her. I want her to be here, but I don't want her to be lonely. "I'll be fine, promise," she replies. That settled, I head into the locker room and focus on the game.

Coach gives us a review of the game and the batting lineup. I'll be the leadoff batter this game, so I'll kick things off when it's our turn to bat. Then we get dressed out in our red home jerseys. As the new guy, I was the last one to pick my number. I have historically worn 11 in all my youth baseball, but when it wasn't available, my backup was my birthday: 17. Craig was already number 11, so I was hoping for 17 when I got to pick my number. It turned out to be one of the open numbers, and I grabbed it. We make our way onto the field, for the first inning, we get three easy outs and head into the dugout to get our gear for our turn at bat.

***

The first and second pitches are low, giving me some breathing room to take a risk with the upcoming pitch. I am focused when I swing on the next pitch; my bat makes contact, and I feel the vibration of the bat in my hand. I know it's a solid hit. As soon as I complete the swing, I drop the bat and take off for first base. I check the coach, and he gives me the go signal, so I round to second base. I make a slide as I see the second baseman reaching to catch the ball. My hand hits the bag, and I hear the call of "safe." This is the rush I had been waiting for. This is where I am the most relaxed, the most myself.

***

The game zooms by before I realize it, and it's the top of the seventh. The Rams are up 3-1, and all we have to do is secure two more outs to win the game. We only have to keep them from scoring, and we will win the home opener. High school ball only goes to seven innings, and I always wish we could play until the ninth like the pros. As the shortstop, I'm laser-focused, ready to adjust to where I'm needed. The batter is a left-hander, and I know that puts me in play to cover second if Matthews gets pulled on the hit. And almost like by thinking it, I put it into existence—the guy hits a line drive between second and first. Matthews has to take off to cut off the ball. He scoops it up and sends it flying to first, getting the first out that we need. I am ready at second to tag out his teammate on the run, completing the double play to secure the win.

After we shake hands, I see Annie waiting next to the dugout. She is already talking to Matthews, but I walk up and stand beside him, listening to the interview. "How does it feel to secure the first win of the season?" Annie asks.

"It feels great to get to come out here and win for the Rams. Expect more of this for the rest of the season," Matthews says and gives his best smile to the camera. Annie looks at me and asks, "Drew, it's your first game in a Rams jersey, how's it feel?" "I think red is my color," I joke before turning a little more serious, "It was a great game and I look forward to what we can do as a team for the rest of the season." Annie turns back to the camera, and Steven gives her a thumbs-up. She gives him the mic and turns back to us. "Way to go: you not only scored a run in the first inning, but you got the double play to finish it off." Annie is beaming at me and pulls me into a hug. I enjoy the fact that she is excited for me. "Thanks, it was a fun game, lots of opportunities for defense today," I respond. She smiles as she makes her way to the fence to join Meg. I give her a wave as I head into the locker room, counting the days until I can get back on the field.

Chapter 22: Things Aren't the Same

March charges on with home and away games, and it's April before I know it. We have completed twenty of the thirty games that we will play before the state tournament. We have won fifteen of those games, making it seem like the state tournament is going to be in our future. Coach has been impressed with the stats I'm putting up. My bat has been on fire, and I'm sitting pretty good in the .280 to .300 range for the season. I've even gotten a good number of home runs in the books, hitting some of my favorites in the bottom of the seventh to bring home some Ws for the Rams. When I'm not out on the diamond with the guys, we have all been trying to support Annie and the girls' soccer team. They only have five games left before the end of the season. It doesn't look like they will make the state tournament this year, but that isn't for Annie's lack of trying. She is a force to be reckoned with out on the field. She is a forward on the team, and when she gets the ball, she drives towards the goal with singular focus. It's impressive to watch. I can't say that I cared about soccer much before meeting Annie. It's been fun trying to understand and figure it out. All of us guys try to make Annie crack up before each game with our stupid signs and cheers. She always breaks, shakes her head at us, and then as soon as that whistle sounds, she is off.

✳✳✳

Today's game isn't much different, with Annie racing down the field. I'm always impressed that she can run that fast with a ball between her feet and not fall on her face. The athlete in me can acknowledge that it looks difficult. I'll confess to anyone who asks that there is no way in hell I could do that. Ask me to sprint to a base, make the double play, or slide home, I've got you covered, but don't ask my feet to do anything besides run. I'm all hand-eye coordination. Annie does some fancy footwork with the ball, gets by the girl, and kicks the ball towards the opposite side of the goal. "Goal Rams" is announced over the speakers. Craig, Luke, Meg, and I jump up to cheer and chant to celebrate the goal. It is Luke's turn to pick the chant, and we shout, "Annie, Annie, if she can't score, no one can." Annie gets a hug from her teammates and then gives our group a wave in acknowledgment. We all sound ridiculous, but it's nice to know that Annie is enjoying it. The Rams get a win tonight, and we all agree while waiting for Annie after the game that we should go to the cafe Meg works at to grab dinner.

Meg and I are standing next to each other, but we aren't touching. It's been weird over the last month. We haven't had a lot of opportunities to hang out alone. Most of the time, we see each other at school or one of these group events. We still text all the time and talk on the phone at night, but it's not feeling the same for me. We have been talking about prom and making deposits on the tux and the limo, but I never really asked her to go with me; we both just assumed we would be going together. Meg had started planning it with Annie before she planned it with me. I've seen a few guys do the epic prom-proposal, but when I pointed one out the other day at lunch, Meg had rolled her eyes and told us all about how she thought they were lame. I did ask her what color I needed to match, and she'd been impressed that I asked before she could organize it. Now, I bring my thoughts back to the present and wrap my arm over Meg's shoulder. She returns the gesture and wraps an arm around my waist. Why does she still feel so far away?

Annie appears, her damp hair pulled back and no makeup on. When we suggest the cafe, she says she's game. Craig asks her to ride with him, and as they walk away, I hear him asking Annie about what he needs to order for prom. I hear her say, "Just don't buzz off the curls, and I'll take care of the rest." That dude is so far behind... At least he has Annie to help him. "Do you want to drive together or meet at the cafe?" I ask Meg. We both have cars now, so this is a standard conversation for us these days. "Let's drive separately. I have to go home after dinner to study for that test," she replies. I don't think I should read more into this, but just a few months ago, I feel like we would have driven together to give us both a few minutes alone to sit in the parking lot and make out before going ho me.

Chapter 23: Yes, No, or Maybe

-Annie-

Meg was not letting up about my next guy. She had started two weeks ago asking Yes, No, or Maybe about guys around school. The first few days, I had pretty much said no to each new name that she listed. "Aaron?" "No." "Aaron K?" "No." "What about James?" "No." This has been our pattern. Each lunch, she had a list of guys. It isn't that I'm not attracted to any of them or that I didn't think of some of them as nice guys. Rather, I didn't trust myself to make a good choice. I had gotten pulled in by a guy because I had lusted after him, and look where that got me. Meg was determined to get a *maybe* out of me and would love to hear a *yes*. I worried about saying either, because I know my best friend. I know that she will start her next plan or scheme. Today, she went as far as telling me I needed to figure out at least two maybes, as prom was right around the corner. "Are you telling me that I can't go in the same limo with you all—" (I wave at our little friends group) "—if I don't have a date?" I ask her. "Nope, you aren't allowed to join us," she says in her most serious voice. "Annie, you want to go to prom with me?" Craig asks next to me. "UGGGHHH, Craig, that doesn't count," Meg says in annoyance. "Well, I need a date, too; I don't want to be cut out of the limo," he responds. "You aren't helping her, Craig, you know that, right?" Meg says, staring him down. "Wait, Craig, I thought we agreed neither of us could ask Annie?" Luke snaps. "Well, I made that deal to get you to ask

Kim." Craig shrugs as if it isn't a big deal. "I say they can't go together—I agree with Meg." Luke gives Meg a nod from his side of the table. "Everyone just calm down: no one is being cut from the limo, date or no date," Drew cuts in and takes Meg's hand on top of the table. She gives him the same look she just gave Craig but doesn't contradict his statement. Luke starts a conversation about whether anyone has the answers to the math homework, and the subject change is just what I need.

***

Soccer practice goes long today, and Miles left without me—I just know it. We have a game at the end of the week, and Coach wanted us to run a full scrimmage today. When we go back to the locker room, I don't even change back into my school outfit. I know that I am going to have to walk home because there is no way that Miles is still here. Just in case, I walk to the parking lot, finding it mostly empty, and Miles's car is not one of the cars left. I start to make my way across the lot to the sidewalk, heading towards our neighborhood, when I hear a "Hey, Campbell, wait up." I turn and find Max walking out of the football locker room. He jogs over to me. "What are you still doing here?" I ask him, because from the look of the parking lot, the team was dismissed well before I made it to the lot. "I was talking to Coach about some colleges I could try out for as a walk-on next year. He thinks after winning state, he can use that to help me get into the summer practices at State," Max replies. "Well, that's pretty nice of Coach to help you with that, and good for you for not stopping if you want to play college ball," I reply. "Thanks, Campbell. Why are you still here?" he counters. "We scrimmaged today, so practice ran long. I'm just about to walk home," I reply. "Don't be crazy, Campbell. I'll drive you home." He smiles and looks over to his SUV. "Are you sure, Max? I really can walk home." Max shrugs his shoulder, "Yes, Annie, I'm sure. I don't mind." "Sure, then I'll take the ride:

to be honest, my legs are not into any more miles today." My comment earns me a smile. As we walk to the car, Max says, "How have you been anyway? Since the end of football, you haven't been to any of the parties." I go to make an excuse, but then I change my mind, "I just didn't feel like adding any flame to the fire, to be honest with you." "Well, I've missed seeing you. If I text you next time we are meeting up, do you think you'll come?" he asks me. I smile as we get into the car. I open the door and get in. "Yeah, I think I'd like that."

After Max drops me off at the house, I feel a little lighter, and when I get to my room, I pull out my phone and text Meg. She is going to freak out with my revelation.

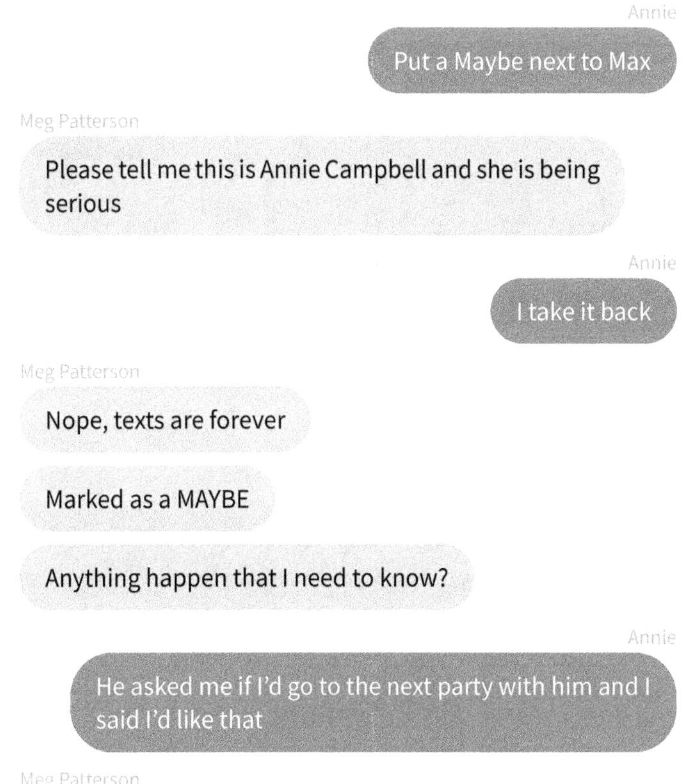

That isn't a maybe Annie that is a YES

Annie

Whatever you say, he hasn't asked yet

Meg Patterson

I bet you get that text by Friday

Annie

Well what you betting?

Meg Patterson

I win I get to pick your outfit for the party   from my closet

Annie

If I win?

Meg Patterson

Then I'll let you dress me

There is no chance I'm losing

***

The Thursday night after my soccer game I get a text from Max, as if he scheduled it with Meg to come right before the end of our bet.

Max Nell

Nice win today Campbell

Annie

***

Meg is so excited on Saturday morning at her house. She asked me to come over to try on some outfit options before tonight. Three different outfits are laid out on the bed, ranging by levels of exposed skin. She keeps looking at the clothing and looking at me. "What is the plan: do we want him to lose his mind or make him want to jump your bones?" I go to answer, and she keeps talking out loud. I realize she is thinking and not asking me for my opinion. I did agree to let her dress me if she won the bet, and she won fair and square. She finally hands me a black mini dress. "Try this one on—I want to make sure it isn't too long on you." I don't argue with her. I change into the dress, and I look at myself in her floor-length mirror. It's a scoop neck top that gives a taste of my cleavage, and the skirt is nowhere near long enough, coming to barely mid-thigh standing up. Meg joins me at the mirror, thinking about the outfit and then looking at what she has laid out on the bed. "I should have you try on something else, but this is the first one I picked out before you came over. and I still like it best. "That's my final decision," she says as she picks up the other outfits and puts them back into the closet. I change back into my normal clothing, and we hang out until I need to go home to get ready for my date.

***

I am about to come downstairs when I hear the knock at the front door. Before I get there, I can hear the door open and my brother asking Max, "Why are you here?" Miles lets Max know the plan was to meet at the party. I come down the hallway right before Max can answer. When he sees me, he gives me a look that starts at my legs, hovering over the curves that the dress is accentuating. When his eyes finally make it to my face, he is wearing a little smile. "I'll see you at the party, man," he says to my brother before he makes his way over to me, "Annie Campbell, you look good all dressed up. Has anyone ever told you that?" I blush; my skin is the worst. "Thank you," I say. Then he takes my hand, and we walk out of the house past my brother and onto the driveway. Max is nice, but I don't get goosebumps when his hand is in mine, at least not yet. He opens the door for me, and we head off to dinner. We have a fun dinner, talking mostly about football, and then we head over to the party.

Max opens my door for me, and I wrap my arm around him as we walk to the bonfire. He asks me if I want anything to drink, and I let him know that I do. He lets me know he'll be right back, and I head over to my group of friends. "How's it going?" Meg asks, bouncing on her toes in excitement. "It's been nice," I reply, because it has, but it hasn't been anything more than that. I think I have deflated Meg because she stops bouncing. "Just nice?" she questions. "It's early, it could get better," I try. "Yeah, maybe you need him to kiss you first." "Yeah," I agree. "You're probably right."

Max finds me holding a can of beer and a bottle of water. He hands me the beer and cracks the lid on the water. After he takes a drink, he wraps an arm around my waist. Again, it just feels like an arm around my waist: there are no goosebumps or warmth to my body.

We have fun at the party. Near midnight, I let him know it is time to head home. We both say our goodbyes and head out. At my house, he walks me to my door. We say our good nights, and he leans in, placing his hands on my hips. He kisses me and I kiss him back. It's a nice kiss, but I can't find the spark to let it continue. I pull back, thank him again, and slip inside the house. I let him down easy the next week at school, letting him know that I had a great time, but I think we are not meant to be more than friends. Craig and I move forward with our plans to attend prom together, and Meg keeps us on the list for the limo.

Chapter 24: Didn't Think Prom Night Would End Like This

-Drew-

It's the Saturday of prom, and Luke, Craig, and I are hanging out in my living room, talking baseball and watching the Griffons on the TV. The plan for today had all of us guys at my house, while all the girls are meeting at Annie's. That way, the limo could pick us up and drop us off at the same spot. Luke asked Kim last month to be his date. Annie and Meg have both made a huge effort to bring her into the folds of our little group. The three of them have been huddled up, talking all things prom and schedules all school week. The three of us guys had known that we didn't want anything to do with the details. We had told them to just tell us when and where to be and we would make sure we arrived on time. We had, in reality, put in a little more effort. We'd organized ourselves to make sure that we each had our tux and the corsage for each of the girls. They sit safely in my fridge, waiting for the designated time for us to get them and head over to the Campbell house. My phone vibrates in my pocket, and I open the message from Meg.

Meg with the Nice Ass

This is your 30 minute warning

Drew

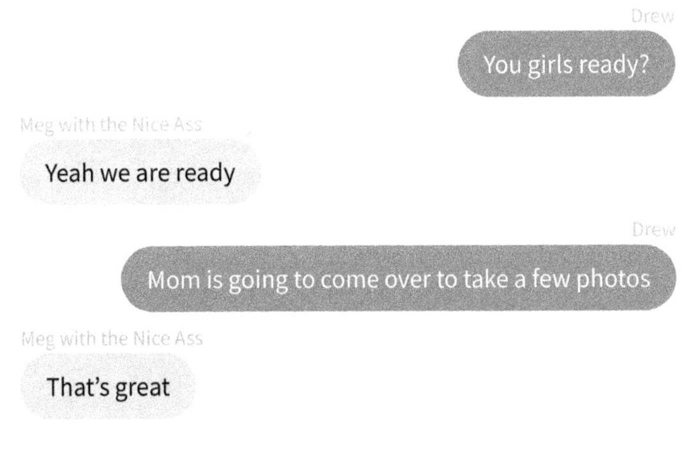

I let the guys know that we should probably head up and get dressed in our tuxes. It takes us no more than ten minutes to get ready. We run into Daniel in the living room. He is going with a group of his football friends and is about to leave the house when Mom comes out the door of her studio. She is holding her digital camera. "Can I get a few of the two of you all dressed up?" she asks. We give Mom the photos she is asking for, and then my brother heads out the door. I join the guys in the kitchen followed by my mom. "Smile, you three." She snaps a quick photo of us with the corsage boxes. "You coming over to the Campbells to get a few more pictures?" I ask. She smiles at me. She looks almost surprised that I asked her, maybe because Daniel hadn't. I'm glad I asked. I pull out my phone and text Meg.

***

We make our way to the front door, and as we near the Campbells' porch, the door swings open, and I get my first look at Annie. She may be my friend, but I can't help noticing the way that the blue prom dress is beautiful on her. The slit up the leg is a tempting thing to see. I have to make sure that my gaze doesn't linger too long. From behind her, I can see Meg, and I take in my girlfriend.

She has her black hair curled, and it falls down her bare shoulder. She is wearing a bright pink dress that matches my tux vest, and it shows all her curves. "You look beautiful," I say as I walk up to her and kiss her. "Thanks, you aren't looking too bad yourself," she replies. The moms take over, and we spend forty-five minutes doing every prom pose known to mankind. Mom and Mrs. Campbell are clicking away, happily shouting directions. The only thing that saves us from another thirty minutes is the limo arrival. Before following Meg into the limo, I hug my mom. "Thanks, hunny, for letting me come over," she says as she heads towards our front door. We all climb into the limo, and then the fun starts.

***

We have the limo driver play our favorite songs on the speakers, and we laugh and sing along to the lyrics. We make it to the event center, and it's decorated with balloons and streamers, all centered around our prom theme: Heroes and Damsels. We stand in line and take the required photos with the backdrops. Then we join the others on the dance floor, and we dance the night away. Annie's brother wins prom king, and Annie is yelling and cheering with excitement that we mirror, getting a few laughs around the room. Miles just laughs on the stage at us all. As the night winds down, they start to play a few slow songs, and I wrap my arms around Meg. It's nice to have a moment with just me and her. "You having fun?" I ask. "Yeah, it's been a great night with friends," she replies. Then it's time for the after-party.

***

The limo drops us off back at the house, and we all agree to be back in ten minutes. The girls take off towards the Campbell house, and the guys make our way to mine. We meet back outside. It takes the girls fifteen minutes, and we give them a hard time as we jump into two cars and head out to the bonfire. When we get to the party, Luke and Craig grab the chairs from the back, and we set up near the other guys on the baseball team. It's a normal party, people chatting or couples making out, snuggled by the fire. I see my brother across the fire with a new girl he started dating on his arm. I look around, realizing I haven't seen Meg in a while. I ask Craig if he's seen the girls, because I notice that Annie is also missing. He gives me a shrug. "Last time I saw them, they were headed towards the car." "Thanks," I say and make my way towards the car. I overhear, "You have to tell him soon, Meg." I know that it's Annie's voice and that the 'him' being referenced is me.

I'm not trying to overhear the conversation, but I feel weird about the fact that I have even heard this much. *What does she have to tell me?"* I clear my throat, trying to make my presence known. "What are you girls doing out here?" I ask, as lighthearted as ever. "Oh, just talking," says Annie. She looks over at Meg. "It's ok, Annie, I'll talk to you later," Meg says. Annie gives me a look as she walks away, and I don't get the feeling that this conversation with Meg is going to be fun. "Everything ok?" I ask after I know Annie is out of earshot. Meg isn't smiling, and her expression is more serious than I'm used to seeing on her. "I don't think this is working," she says, direct as always.

I should be shocked or hurt that she is doing this tonight, but also, I've been thinking that things haven't felt all that great lately either. "I don't know what happened, but I don't feel like we are connecting anymore," she continues in my silence. "We feel more like friends that have sex occasionally and less like boyfriend and girlfriend," Meg looks at me. "Does that make any sense to you?" she asks me. I've been trying to let her talk and get out what she needs to say. She is looking at me, and I know she is waiting for me to say something. I run my hands through my hair, and then I look at her. "I understand. I had noticed some distance, but I thought it was just us being busy." "Yeah, I think that is a part of this. I'm sorry, Drew," Meg says, looking so sad. I move to sit by her on the trunk bed of the SUV. I give her a side hug and say, "It's ok, Meg, we are still friends." We sit like this for a while in silence, then Meg moves to stand, and I remove my arm from her shoulder. "I think I should head back to the party." She looks me over. "You going to be ok?" "Yeah, I'll be ok, I'll head back in a few," I reply. After she leaves, I think about the last month, and I know I should have read the signs; we'd been more friends than in a relationship. I can't remember the last night she'd been over to my house. At the beginning of this relationship, we wanted every ounce of alone time we could get.

"You ok?" I hear from behind me. "I thought I'd check in on you. Meg said she told you," Annie says, looking at me with concern on her face. "I'm ok. I mean, this isn't the way I thought prom night would go, but I'll be fine," I reply. She nods her head in agreement. "You going back to the party?" "I think I'll stay here a little while longer," I let her know. Annie sits next to me on the SUV trunk. She doesn't say anything else, and we sit in comfortable silence. It's nice to have someone here, and we stay there in our bubble until the others appear at the end of the party.

Chapter 25: Closing of One Door

Everyone knows by Monday that Meg and I have broken up. "Do we need to find a new place to eat lunch? Are we now a group divided?" Luke asks me. "Stop being so dramatic," I tell him, "I'm not going to divide up the group." I jab him in his side. "Fine, I'm not asking again: if it's awkward, then it's on you because I asked," he says as we make our way to the lunchroom. We are the first ones at the table, and it doesn't take long to have the others join us. Meg sits across from Luke with Annie in front of me, joined by Craig. It is weird to see Meg on the other side of the table, if I'm being honest; she's been sitting next to me for the last few months. But also, I don't mind that she is sitting next to Annie. Maybe with some time, this will not feel so weird. Maybe we can still stay friends after all. Annie interrupts my thoughts with a statement. "I'll be in the dugout for today's game." "Did you ask Coach for the jersey we talked about?" Luke asks her. "UGGGH, I forgot with all the prom stuff last week," she says. "Any chance that you guys could help me out? I feel bad that I keep wearing my football jersey. At least it's the right team across the front." She gives a little smile with her comment. "We got you covered—we can't have our girl wearing the football team's gear at our games, right guys?" Craig says, all animated. "I totally agree, it's blasphemy," I interject. And just like that, we all fall back into our rhythm.

***

Annie does indeed get the baseball jersey from Coach, and she gets to report that the Rams make the playoffs after we get the W against the Eagles. We have been on a roll, and it feels like a great way to go into the state tournament. I haven't let the breakup with Meg affect my game. If anything, I'm not feeling the guilt of being distracted. I can fully focus on what I need to do. I was able to get on base with each at-bat in the last two games. I make some great defensive plays to get some key outs before the other team can get a run on the board. Our spirits are high as we head into the state tournament. The team has a playoff tradition of getting their numbers cut into their sideburns, and it looks a little crazy, but it's tradition, so I have 17 cut into my left sideburn like all of the others. Craig left his red curls on top like a fohawk with his number in his now short sideburns. He tells me he is starting a new style, but I'm not convinced.

***

We win the first playoff game easily, 4-1, but we don't get as lucky in the next game, and we lose 2-3. The letdown is hard, and Coach gives us a talk about holding our heads up high and thanks the seniors for all they offered during their time with the team. He tells us underclassmen that we can expand on this next year if we are all willing to do the work during the offseason. Coach asks me to meet him in his office before heading out.

***

"Coach, you wanted to see me?" I say at the door of his office. "Yeah, Davis, come on in," he says, pointing to the chair. I sit down, then he launches into the conversation. "You had a great season. I already had some of the scouts asking about you during the season. We haven't talked about it, but what are your goals when it comes to baseball? Do you want to go pro when you graduate next year?"

Did I want to go pro? Yeah, I'd thought about it, but it was the dream of every little boy who puts on a baseball jersey and walks onto the diamond. "I would love to go pro," I tell him. "It's not a sure deal, Davis: you made some great stats this season, if you put in the extra work, you could easily get signed into the minors next year," he finishes. I ask, "Anything I can do over the summer to help get my name out there?" "Actually, that is why I wanted to talk to you in here. My buddy is the coach of a traveling team out of Missouri, and he is looking for a strong shortstop. I've given him your information. It could be a good opportunity for you to be seen by scouts in those markets. Talk to my buddy and your parents, and think about it as an investment in the dream." I thank him for the information and the reference. The season may not have ended the way I had hoped, but this opportunity is a door opening I had only dreamed about.

***

When I make it to the parking lot, my car is the last one other than Coach's. Standing next to my car, looking at her phone, is a beautiful blonde. I know it's Annie, but I can't stop my brain from noticing that she's beautiful. "What are you doing out here?" I must have startled her because, she jumps and almost drops her phone, placing her hand over her heart in surprise. "God, Drew, you scared me." She continues, "I told everyone I would ride home with you. I could see the disappointment earlier when you left the field. I figured you could use the company."

I feel a little pressure in my chest. Annie has always been special like this, always knowing when to show up for people, for me. "I think we should go get ice cream," she says as she makes her way to the passenger door. "Yeah, I think I could go for some ice cream," I smile back at her and hop into the driver's seat. Over ice cream, I fill her in on what Coach said about the scouts and the travel team. "You think you'll do it?" she asks me after I finish. "It's too early to tell. I'll have to talk to my parents—the team is currently out of Missouri, so I'm not sure of all the logistics of it yet, but I am curious," I tell her.

"Drew, you could make it, I can see it now—" she holds her spoon like a mic. "Making his first start for the Griffons is number 17, Drew Davis: he shows off his ability to be dynamic in the infield at the shortstop position, and his on-base performance is second to none." She stops her pretend announcing and smiles at me. I let myself imagine it, the dream of getting to take the field, getting to call what I love my job. "Promise me that you'll get me box seats when you're famous," Annie says, smiling. "Promise, if I'm ever famous, I'll always have a seat for my Annie," I answer. Later, as I drive us home from the ice cream shop, I realize I'm happier than I thought I'd be after the biggest loss of my life, and it has a lot to do with the girl sitting next to me and the fact that she believes in me.

Chapter 26: Juniors No More
-Annie-

I'm sitting in the crowded arena in Tulsa with my parents, waiting for graduation to finish. "Miles James Campbell," is announced over the sound system, and my brother walks across the stage and takes his diploma. We make so much noise in our section that he looks up at us all and waves. I notice Daniel Jace Davis getting announced and see the Davises' cheering a few sections over. They keep announcing names, and I start daydreaming. It's weird to think next year will be the last year of high school; it has gone by so fast, and yet I feel like I was just a freshman.

I have to start applying for colleges. I've been researching the idea of going into journalism, with a focus on broadcasting. Drew inspired me when we talked about the possibility of him making it to the minors and even making it to the pro level. As much as I could imagine him taking the field, I was starting to imagine what it would be like to be the one to do the on-field reporting. I have already talked to my newsroom teacher, and she told me that I'll be secure in my position on the Visual News for my senior year. She'd given me some things that I could improve when it came to being aware of the camera and the angles for interviewing, but she'd said it was clear that I'd loved being ready to capture the moment for each sport I'd been able to cover. She'd even offered to put together a highlight reel that I could submit as part of my applications.

***

After the graduation ceremony finished, we headed home to a house decorated with Miles's face from kindergarten until his senior year. Mom had gone all out and had invited family and friends. Dad started the grill out back, manning his station of the party. I'd helped for as long as I could until I needed to escape. I'd made the rounds already, talking to all my aunts, uncles, and cousins, and I wanted quiet. I'd gone to my mom's bench in the back corner, hidden away by the hedge of the hydrangea bushes.

Quiet at last, I thought. "Boo," comes from the other side of the fence, and I jump. Hands raised, Drew stands up. "Sorry, I couldn't help it." He smiles, showing off his dimple, "Are you hiding from all the family members, too?" "Yes, it's Miles's graduation, and I'm the one stuck all day helping all our extended family and my parents," I say, letting out a sigh of exhaustion. "Can I join you?" he asks, adding playfully, "Please say yes before they find me." "Yes, hurry or you'll give away our position." I watch Drew jump the fence, making it look far easier than I know that it is.

We hang out on Mom's bench for a long time. It's easy talking with Drew: there doesn't seem to be anything we can't talk about. I'm so comfortable with him, and before I realize I'm doing it, I say, "Can I tell you a secret?" "Yeah, Annie, I'd love to hear your secrets," he responds, looking both a little mischievous but also looking serious, too. "I want to be a sports broadcaster." He smiles, "Annie, I don't think that's a secret—you do an amazing job on the Visual News, you'd be great at it." "You think so? I know, I love doing it! I have a lot to learn, but I think I'm going to look into schools that have a focus on developing my skills. Maybe I'll be interviewing you on the sidelines after a game one day." He gets all animated and in his best imitation of a TV sportscaster says, "Now down to the field with Annie Campbell: she's joined by Drew Davis after his game-winning home run, back to you Annie." I laugh at his awful imitation, but it would be pretty great to hear my introduction before getting the exclusive. "You should probably focus on your on-field performance... I don't think you are destined for the booth," I say, nudging him with my elbow. "Yeah, you're probably right about that.

I was meaning to tell you and then got busy—Mom and Dad agreed to the travel team. I'll be staying in a spare room with one of the other guys' families until August." "Drew! This is great news, I'm so happy for you," I respond, because it is great news. "Keep me updated on how the season goes," I tell him. "You know I will, you're my favorite person to talk baseball with, but don't tell Craig I said that—it may reduce the guy to tears." Drew is almost laughing by the end of his reply. "What will you be up to this summer, Annie?" "I'll be in Texas most of the summer visiting my grandparents, and then we have our last Campbell family adventure cruise before Miles heads to university," I respond. Drew's phone starts ringing, and he flashes me the screen with his mom's name. "It appears I've been noted as missing in action." We both stand, and before I can second-guess it, I lean in and hug him. He wraps his arms around me in return. "See you at the end of summer, Drew," I say, pulling back. "I'll miss you, too," he replies before jumping back over the fence. I make my way towards my own house to see if Mom or Dad needs any more help.

Chapter 27: I Sent it by Mistake

-Annie-

Summer

It's been a fun summer. It was nice to visit my grandparents in Texas. I got to go on some college visits to a few colleges, but mostly I've been enjoying the fact that my grandparents have a pool. I've spent a large portion of my visit lying by the pool, getting a great tan, and checking off my summer reading for my upcoming senior year. Mom and Miles join me at my grandparents' house for a few days before we head to Galveston to hit the cruise ship for our last family vacation before Miles starts football camp at his university. Miles and I have one request on the ship, and that is that we get Wi-Fi so we can still text our friends. Mom and Dad agree on the condition that all dinners are phone-free... for everyone but Mom. She gets her phone to capture all the moments and adventures during the cruise. We all have different activities throughout the day

.

***

Today, I take myself poolside again, trying to soak in every last drop of summer. I've been texting Meg about a few of the cute boys here at the pool. She's been asking me if I'm in the new bikini we picked out together before I left. She follows the message with a selfie of her looking all sad. Before I can reply, the waiter shows up to give me my smoothie. I fumble my phone for a second, trying to hold it and the smoothie. Thank goodness I don't drop either, and the waiter moves on to the next customer.

I'd settled for this smoothie because even though I turned eighteen in June, and I was able to drink at the port stops in Mexico, the boat upheld American laws. The smoothie tastes good, and before I set it down, I decide that I should send Meg back a selfie of my own. I open my phone, taking a photo of myself with my smoothie and its little umbrella by the pool. I type out a comment I know will make Meg laugh, then put my phone down to enjoy the sound of summer and pick up the book I still need to finish before school starts in a few weeks.

***

I've been reading the book for a while when my phone vibrates a few times on the table. I mark my place in the book and open my phone. I almost drop the phone when I see who has replied to my photo and my comment. OMG, I must have hit a wrong button or two and selected Drew's name. I think it must have happened when I'd almost dropped it earlier. It wouldn't have taken that many actions; he was the only other person I'd texted in the last few days. Our conversations had been about baseball and jokes about the summer reading list dragging on. It had not been half-naked selfies and definitely wasn't like my last text message.

Annie

Suns out, girls out! What do you think?

Drew Davis

Did you mean to send me this?

I don't mind if you want to send me more

Annie

OMG, sorry about that

Before I can text anything else, I get a photo back. It takes a little time to load, and before it finishes, I get another message.

Drew Davis

Figured I'd send you mine to keep it even

Suns out guns out, what do you think?

And before you ask I did mean to send the picture

The photo loads, and it's a selfie of Drew outside at the baseball field with his shirt off, flexing his bicep. He is all tan skin and abs, muscles for days until they run to the edge of his pants. I think I stop breathing, looking at his body like this. *What has travel baseball done to Drew? Did he have all these muscles before he left?* Before thinking better of it, I hit the button to save his photo.

Annie

In full honesty, I saved the photo

Drew Davis

And I make his photo my lock screen like I said I would. It's not like I can't change it later. But here alone at the pool, I can enjoy the picture of my next-door neighbor. I'll worry about changing it back later: right now I'm on vacation after all, and Drew handed me the best eye candy of my summer.

Chapter 28: I am Flirting with Her

Getting to be on this travel team has been an amazing experience, and I'm glad that my parents heard Coach out about the opportunity. I was offered a room with one of the other players who lived more centrally to get to all the tournaments, so I've had to catch up with my friends via text messages all summer. Craig checks in the most, letting me know he has a girlfriend now from the next town over, and she happens to be friends with Meg's new boyfriend. He'd asked me if that was weird, and I'd told him the truth, that it wasn't. Meg and I can be friends; we'd had our fun, and it had fizzled out. *High school relationships aren't meant to last anyway, right?*

I've also been texting Annie. We both signed up for AP English senior year and have been working our way through the reading list. We'd gone back and forth, complaining about the books. We'd started on different books at the beginning, but then decided we should read the same book so we could complain to someone who could understand our pain. To be honest with myself, I would have put off the reading until I got home from this travel season, but when Annie had texted asking me if I'd started, I made quick work of ordering the list to my temporary home for the summer. I wanted a reason to keep catching up with her. Her messages slowed down this week. She said her family was going on a cruise as a last family vacation before Miles headed to university. So, I wasn't expecting to hear from her much over the next week. I was going to miss her messages.

***

At practice, it was hot, like stupid hot, and a lot of us had already taken off our jerseys when practice ended, trying to cool down. My temporary roommate, John, was asking some of the guys if they wanted to meet at his house because he has a pool. Most of the team agreed to head over. When I grab my phone, I can see I have two missed texts, so I swipe and open the app. I am not prepared for the photo from Annie. She looks so fucking good, sitting in a little red bikini holding up a tropical drink with the pool behind her. If I wasn't already shocked at the sight of Annie almost naked on my phone, I would have been faster to read her message that follows the picture.

What do I think? *Hot as hell* is what I'm thinking, but I don't think Annie meant to send me this picture. I'm actually pissed when I think about who she could have meant to send it to. I take a deep breath in and out, thinking about how I want to respond. I send her a quick reply trying to play it off. She doesn't answer right away, and I check the time of when she sent the photo. The timestamp says it was over thirty minutes ago. I make to lock my phone again, about to join the guys, when it vibrates in my hand. I see the notification with her name, and I can't fight the smile at her return message. I can almost see her face when she realized that she sent that picture to me. I want to ease her mind, because if I know Annie, she is trying to figure out how she is going to cover up this mistake. I realize that I'll just return a picture. I hit the button to take a picture, and I flex my bicep as I take it.

I look up from my phone, and a few of the guys are watching me. "I'm texting a girl back home." They laugh. A few ask if I should take their picture to see who

135

she likes more. I give them the bird and look back at my phone when it finally vibrates again with a new message. I know I smile at her reply of saving my photo and I confess in return that I've already set hers as my lockscreen. We exchange a few more messages and this feels like we are flirting. True to my word, I've made the picture my lock screen. I will enjoy getting to see a bikini-clad Annie every time I go to open my phone. The guy next to me notices the picture. "Is that your girl? Well, damn, she is fucking hot, man. If she stops being interested in you, give her my number." I don't correct him about the fact that he called Annie 'mine.' I don't want to give him any ideas, and I like the idea of thinking of her as mine. "No way in Hell, dude." I throw back, causing him to laugh. But he's right; she is fucking hot, and I need to keep her focused on me and not on whoever this photo had originally been meant for.

***

I wait a few days and then text her a photo of me and a few of the guys in the dugout. We are all dressed in our jerseys, smiling to capture the moment after a big win at a tournament. I play up the reason for the text being about the tournament win and not the fact that I want to talk with her. Or the fact that I'd love to get another photo of her.

Drew

Just won the second to last tournament of the summer

Annie Campbell

That is amazing

PS: Nice Photo

A photo of Annie appears in the thread. She is in a red formal mini dress. God, she looks good in red with her summer-tanned skin still sporting her freckles across her cheeks. She's got her hair done in curls and she has on a touch of makeup. She must be going to some formal dinner on the cruise. She is beautiful in this photo, there is no denying it. But I have seen Annie in person, and I know I prefer her with hair pulled back and not a stitch of makeup to be seen.

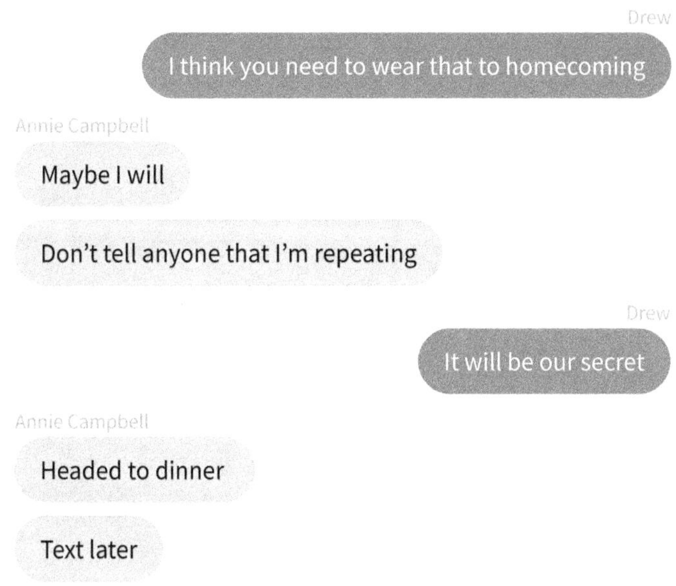

We do text again later and over the next few days. In fact, we've texted more than we've texted all summer, and none of it has been related to the summer reading. She has far surpassed my messages with Craig now. We don't send any more photos, but we flirt through our messages. I find myself counting down the days to get home. I want to see her in person. *Will our flirting lead to what I have been daydreaming about?* I want to touch her tanned skin, and I want her to let me kiss her. I'll ask her on a date this time before anyone else can get in my way. I'm so ready to be done playing baseball, which isn't something I've ever thought before in my life.

Chapter 29: My Best Friend is Better Than Yours

-Annie-

We have been back from the cruise for almost two weeks. My parents are leaving with Miles tomorrow to take him and all his stuff to the university in Texas. They insisted they needed to get him settled before football camp starts. I get the house to myself for three whole days, and it's the first time in my life I'll be home alone. Mom and Dad agreed that Meg can come over. We are going to make a girls' weekend out of it. She has been dating a new guy she works with at the cafe. We have so much to catch up on, and I think I have a confession to make to my best friend.

***

Waving goodbye to my family the next afternoon is sad. It's weird to think that when Mom and Dad return, it won't be with Miles. I text Meg to head over when she wants, and I lounge around the house until I hear the doorbell. I race across the house, yanking the door open to reveal my best friend. We both reach out and we hug and bounce, because well, Meg always bounces a little when she's happy. We break the hug and grab her stuff from her car. We take seats on the couch and start our in-person recap of what we have missed being apart over the summer. She tells me all about Tom, the guy she has worked with for a while but never gave more than a passing glance. Her eyes look all dreamy as she talks about him. Has she ever looked like this? I try to think through all the years, and I come up empty.

I do feel a pang of worry when I think of her time with Drew and about the fact that Drew is her ex. I have to tell her about the flirting, but I'm not about to interrupt her telling me about Tom. "Annie, he is just the best guy I've ever met. I can't wait for you to meet him tonight," she beams. I may be having a few friends over tonight to celebrate the upcoming school year and the fact that this is the first time I've ever had the house to myself. I've invited the friend's group and let Meg know she could invite a few other people but that we aren't having a full-on party while my parents are away. "I can't wait to meet him," I tell her, because if he can make her this happy, I want to make the effort to get to know him, too.

***

Our conversation is interrupted by the vibration of my phone on the coffee table. Meg grabs it for me and freezes, looking at the screen. At first, I was concerned I had a text that my parents were coming home. Then my brain clicks, and I realize I haven't changed my lock screen since the cruise. She is looking at a shirtless Drew on my phone. She looks over, and her smile surprises me. "Annie Marie, have you been holding out on me?" She flashes me the photo on my phone. It makes little butterflies spring to life. I'm not sure when it happened, but I'm crushing hard on Drew Davis. I cave, word-vomiting all the details of us texting all summer. The mistake at the pool leading to the photo of me and the return photo he sent and how it became my lock screen. I tell her the part I've been the most worried to confess, that if we played the game from last spring of Yes, No, or Maybe with Drew. Without a doubt, he would get a YES from me.

She sets my phone down on the table and grabs me into a hug. "Annie, this is perfect—you two would be so cute together." "You're not mad at me? I mean you all dated for months," I say into her hair as we are still hugging. Meg pulls back, holding my shoulders. "Let's talk facts: yes, we dated, but it was never more than hooking up. I broke up with him, so as long as it doesn't bother you that we dated, it doesn't bother me." *Did it bother me that they had been together?* Honestly, over the last week, I've been more worried about her reaction to my crush. Because that is what I had on Drew.

After the first photo, he had sent me another of him with his jersey on in the dugout. I'd sent him one of me in my formal dress before the state dinner. I got butterflies talking with him that I hadn't gotten before the photos. I was curious to see him in person to see if this spell would continue, or if it would feel weird in person and the butterflies would flutter away completely. "It doesn't bother me," I tell her truthfully. I give her all the details about how I'm feeling and the concerns I have. "What if this is just one-sided? We both know Drew never wants anyone to feel awkward." "Oh, Annie my girl, I've got just the plan." Meg doesn't give me details. I should be worried, but I know Meg. I know that maybe this time it is better not knowing what she is planning for me. We continue to catch up on other hot topics while we make our way up the stairs to my room to get ready.

Chapter 30: A Baseball Jersey Never Looked so Good

Annie has invited us over while her parents are out of town. I gave her a hard time when she invited me, referencing, "Where did my sweet Annie go?" She sent me back an angel emoji. I followed with 'I'll be there' and told her to 'look for the guy from my photos.' I feel like I'm that guy from last summer, crushing on the girl next door again, but this time she has been flirting back. I'm concerned about Meg... When she ended things, we stayed friendly. I heard from Craig that she has started dating someone new, and I am happy for her, but is trying to date her best friend crossing a line? It feels like it could be, and I have been worrying about it, knowing that I want to flirt with Annie in person. Meg is going to be at this little party too—*will that be weird*? I can hear people outside my window, and I pull the curtain to the side. I can see Craig and a girl walking up to the gate, with Luke and a few of the guys from the baseball team shortly behind them. Taking one more deep breath, *hear goes nothing!*

I wave at the guys. "Long time no see, Davis," Luke says as I round the corner into Annie's backyard. "Glad you didn't forget about us in all our summer GLORY," he laughs and gives me a fist bump. I joke, "What can I say, I'm a big deal." This makes the other guys laugh, and we start to give each other a recap of the summer. For a few guys, it is more of a recap of the girls of summer. The girl of my summer comes out of the downstairs back door, and I can't seem to focus on what the guys are telling me. Craig playfully punches me in the gut. "Cat got your tongue, man? You zoned out, I was asking you about travel ball." "Sorry, I did zone out," I reply and give him the short and sweet version of the season.

As I do, Annie makes her way to the others in the group. She is giving hugs and welcoming people as she makes her way around the group. When she gets to us, she pauses, listening to me finish my review. Before Craig can ask me any follow-up questions. I scoop up Annie into what is supposed to be a friendly hug, but I know I pull her a little closer, pressing her body against mine. I pull back and give her a big smile. "Missed you, Annie." When I release her, Craig wraps her in a big hug and spins her around, making her laugh, "Missed you, too," Craig says, giving me a hard time mimicking my words. Luke pipes in, "Where is my Annie hug? My arms are right here." Annie steps out of Craig's hug and into Luke's arms.

If I didn't already know that they both were her friends, this would feel awkward, watching her being touched by them both. As I think it can't get any weirder, Meg and her new guy appear. It's not awkward to see Meg with another guy. I feel awkward because I can't seem to stop looking at Annie in front of her. Annie isn't in some skimpy outfit; she's dressed in jean shorts that show her legs to perfection and a tank with an open Griffons jersey over the top. She is the most dressed down I've seen her for a party, and it's the best I think she's ever looked.

Meg breaks into my thoughts by asking, "Anyone game to play any Truth or Dare?" Everyone seems to nod their heads in agreement, and we head onto the porch set up with chairs. "I'll start," Meg offers. "Annie, Truth or Dare?" I get a weird feeling of déjà vu. "Dare," Annie answers, looking a little confused at Meg. I start to panic. I will not let what happened at the party last year happen again. *She isn't going to kiss anyone but me,* I think as I hear Meg say, "I dare you to kiss Drew." Annie's eyes open in shock, then narrow at her best friend. Annie walks over to stand next to me.

Annie whispers when she is standing in front of me, close but not touching me, "Drew, either sit down or lean down so I can complete my dare." I lean down and whisper back, "All yours, Annie." She wraps her hands in my hair, then she uses her hands to pull me to her. Our lips meet in a crash. I wrap my arms around her back and pull her into my chest, enjoying the fact that there isn't a place our bodies don't touch. I let her drive the kiss, and she runs her tongue along my bottom lip before she sucks it into her mouth. I hear a whistle, and that seems to bring Annie back from taking the kiss further. She runs her tongue along my lips one more time before breaking the kiss. Her hands moved during the kiss to wrap around my neck. She pulls back, and I have to force myself to release her. She takes a small step away but stays next to me on the porch. She turns and faces Meg. "Truth or Dare?

***

Much like the last time we played this game, most of the players chose to dare each other, and it resulted in the removal of many clothing items. By the time it gets to me, I'm finally a little more settled from the kiss. My heart doesn't feel like it's going to hammer out of my chest, at least. "Truth or Dare, Drew?" Craig asks me. "Dare." He looks at Meg. *Why is he looking at Meg?* He gives her a wink, then looks at me. "I dare you to spend seven minutes in heaven with—" (he drags a long pause, looking around the group before saying... "—Annie." I think our friends are scheming, and if it continues, I'll have to send them each a present, because they are giving me alone time with Annie. I've never been more excited to make out in a closet.

I offer Annie my hand, and she wraps her fingers in mine, and then she leads us into her house. But we don't stop downstairs; she rushes up the stairs, almost pulling me along. I haven't been in Annie's house a lot, but I think we are headed towards where I remember her bedroom being. She opens the door and pulls me in behind her, shutting the door. I don't hesitate. I pin her against her bedroom door: this time, I'm the one kissing her. I pull her little trick from earlier and suck her bottom lip into my mouth, and I give it a little nip with my teeth. Annie gives a little moan. I am getting hard just kissing her. I can feel my dick pinned between us. I've never been this turned on after a few minutes of kissing. Maybe it is the fact that I've wanted to kiss Annie for the last year. Or the fact that I've been staring daily at the photos she's sent me. If she were anyone else, I'd push her, maybe figure out a way to get my hands under her shirt. My mind is conflicted because I want that, but I also know taking my time with Annie will be better. I start to bring the kiss down from the inferno it started as. I break the kiss and pull back to look at her. Her lips are swollen from our kisses tonight, and her pupils are so big, I almost can't see the blue-gray of her eyes. I am enjoying seeing Annie undone by me. "Why did you stop?" Her words break the silence.

Why had I stopped? I am trying to get blood to return to my brain. "I wanted to look at you, Annie. You're so fucking hot in this jersey." My answer makes her smile, and I know that I'm wearing the biggest smile on my face, too. "Do you want a picture? It will last longer," she smarts off. Her brain is responding better than my own. I pull my body back from pinning her against her door. Her eyes seem to follow my movements, and as I reach into my pocket, her eyes go wide for a second before registering that I am pulling out my phone. I pull her back against me and turn towards the camera. I whisper into her hair, "Say cheese, Annie." I snap a few photos of us in this moment and then lock my phone. I want to stay in this room alone with her for the rest of the night, but I know someone is going to come looking. So, I take her hand back in mine and guide us back to the party. When we get back, the group gives us all whoops and whistles, causing Annie to blush. They aren't playing Truth or Dare anymore; everyone is hanging out and catching up. I pull Annie into the porch swing, and she snuggles into my side. I wrap my arm around her shoulder, and I don't leave this spot for the rest of the night.

Chapter 31: My Friends are Masterminds

-*Annie*-

Meg's scheming hadn't taken any time at all, and it shouldn't have shocked me. I should have known that her suggesting "Truth or Dare" was a play, but it was also something she was known to do at parties, suggesting a fun game to play as a group. She'd been the one to suggest Spin the Bottle at one of our first middle school parties, so she had played into her strengths well. We had circled up around the porch and the chairs we had set up earlier with Tom. Tom had come over early to help, and he seemed really into Meg. I'd been surprised because he isn't Meg's normal type. He is still cute with his brown hair and green eyes, but he's just shorter and a little less athletic than her history of boys. Maybe she needed something different because I overheard her say *love you too* when he'd gone to move his car into the driveway as people showed up. It was nice to see my friend so happy. Some of the group sat, and some of them stayed standing against the railing. I'd wanted to stand by Drew, but I am still a little unsure of where this flirting is going. Even though Meg has told me she was ok with the idea of the possibility of Drew and me, I wasn't 100% sure she had told me the truth.

Meg, ever the ringleader, announced, "I'll start." She smiled and didn't even look around our group before she said, "Truth or Dare, Annie?" "Dare," I say. It has become my default in this little game. "I dare you to kiss Drew," Meg replies. I know I look shocked, and I try to cover it with a smirk at her. I guess this was her very public way of giving her approval. No one was going to be able to say I was a bad friend when she had been the one to push us together. I look over at Drew standing at the railing. He is also looking a little shocked at the dare I have been given. When his eyes connect with mine, he gives me that dimpled smile, and I'm moving in his direction before I can think better of it.

Since he's standing, I can't just kiss him. He's going to have to help me, and I say so when I reach him. I think he is going to sit down—it would be easier after all, and a chair is on the other side of his body, but he surprises me. Instead, leaning down, he whispers back, "All yours, Annie." I look into his dark blue eyes, then wrap my hands in his hair, using them to pull his mouth against mine. Our lips meet in a crash, and I feel Drew's arms wrap around my waist, pulling my body against his. I started this kiss, and I want to control it. So, I run my tongue over his full bottom lip before sucking it into my mouth. Before I can do anything else, a whistle breaks through the fog in my brain. I remember that I am in front of a group of people, and I start to pull back but give Drew one more swipe of my tongue as I pull my lips from his. As I do, I notice that my arms are locked around his neck, and I have to unwind myself from his body. I take a small step away but stay next to Drew at the railing. I turn my eyes to Meg's; she is smiling ear to ear. I return the smile and ask her, "Truth or Dare?"

Meg breaks character and tells me, "Truth." My brain has to remember to work, and I finally settle on a question: "Where is the riskiest place you've hooked up?" "The back room at the cafe," she says and smiles at her boyfriend. The game moves to others in the group, and Luke is now shirtless. A few of the girls have removed clothing, but some have received dares to kiss. Danielle dares Craig to remove everything but his boxers, which he does without a care in the world. It's his turn to pick a target. "Truth or Dare, Drew?" "Dare," I hear Drew respond beside me. I am curious what Craig is going to do... *Will Drew get a dare to undress a little?* I can see the image in my head, and I'm hoping I get a look at those muscles in person. Craig, starting his dare, pulls me back to the present. "I dare you to spend seven minutes in heaven with…" (he drags a long pause, looking around the group). I swear I am going to kill Craig if he sends Drew into one of my closets with another girl. When his eyes pass over me, I know I'm glaring at him, which causes Craig to laugh. He finishes his review and says my name, and the relief I feel must be all over my face because he laughs again. Drew offers me his hand, and I gladly wrap my fingers around his. Before he has a chance to lead us into my house, I know I don't want to slip into the closet downstairs.

I want a moment with him alone, and I decide to go to my room. I take the lead into the house and up the stairs. If he is surprised by our path, he doesn't show it, and he follows without missing a step. I open my bedroom door, step through, then pull him willingly into my room before shutting the door. As soon as the door is closed, I'm no longer in control of this as Drew pins me to the back of the door and kisses me. It is clear that he is in charge of this kiss, and I can't help but moan in response when he gives my bottom lip a little bite. I want more, but as I'm thinking about moving my hands to touch him, he slows the kiss and then steps away. *Why are we stopping* is the only thing my brain is thinking, and then I give voice to my thoughts. He says, "I wanted to look at you, Annie. You're so fucking hot in this jersey." I can't help but smile. I think the kissing has fogged over his brain, too, because it's just a jersey. I look at him and see his dimple appear, and I've never felt so good wearing a jersey in my life. Then, because I have to say something, I ask, "Do you want a picture? It will last longer." Drew reaches down towards his jeans. At first, I think maybe he is going to take them off, and I'm a little disappointed when he pulls out his phone. Then he wraps his arm around my waist and pulls me against him, whispering into my hair, "Say cheese, Annie." I smile at the camera, then I smile up at him; after all, I had been the one to tell him to take a picture, so how can I be mad that he did it? It's so like Drew to take me at my word.

He leads me back downstairs, and we get whoops and more whistles, which causes heat to cross my cheeks. Drew directs me to the empty porch swing. I snuggle into his side and he wraps his arm around me. The rest of the party is pretty much us talking and laughing. A large group of people head out before midnight to make it home by curfew, leaving just Drew and me on the porch swing and Meg snuggled on Tom's lap. He whispers something in her ear, and she stands up, "I'm going to walk Tom to his car and be right back." They disappear around the edge of the house, and Drew pulls me into his lap. "I better get home too, I know you girls have a lot to talk about." He is trying not to smile, and it makes his lip twitch a little. I wrap my arms around his neck. I don't want him to go, but I know that he is right. I whisper in his ear, "Until next time," and pull back and give him a quick kiss before removing myself from his lap and standing up. He stands and leans down, giving me one more kiss. "Maybe next time we won't have so many witnesses." And then leaves me on the back porch. I'm smiling as I see him leap over the fence. He waves and goes inside. My phone v ibrates.

Drew Davis

Goodnight Annie

I'll be saving this one as my new lock screen

The photo of us smiling at the camera in my bedroom appears in the chat. We both have slightly swollen lips, but we also look really happy. Before I can respond, another one comes through. This photo, Drew is still looking at the camera smiling, but I've directed my attention to him, still wearing a huge smile on my face.

Drew Davis

I look up from my phone, and Meg has quietly rejoined me on the porch. I put my phone away, giving her a round of applause because I know she was the mastermind behind tonight's fun. I've never been so happy that my friend is the schemer she is. She makes a little bow, and then we head inside: as Drew had said, we girls have a lot to talk about.

Chapter 32: Asking for What I Want

How has it been three days since the party and I haven't seen you?

I'm right next door, all you had to do is ask   me to come over

I'm great at jumping fences

Consider this my invitation

Accepted

I should have thought about the fact that I'm dressed down. My hair is thrown up in a messy bun, and I'm wearing a pair of comfy shorts and a Rams Soccer shirt. But it's too late now to change; Drew is headed over, and I don't want to miss him. Based on the fence comment, I'm guessing he is waiting in the backyard. When I open the back door and see him lounging on the porch swing, little butterflies flutter to life. I make my way toward him on the porch swing attempting to sit down next to him. Drew must have other plans because he gently grabs my hips and redirects my body. I let out a little "oh" as I go willingly and end up straddling him. His arms wrap around my back and I'm surrounded by Drew, in the best way. Our faces are even in this position, and he leans in and closes the space.

This is the first kiss we've shared that wasn't fueled by a dare, and it's nice to know that we both want it. Maybe for that same reason, this kiss is softer, and we take our time letting our lips glide over each other. It builds, and at some point, I've wrapped my arms around his neck, pulling myself flush against his chest. His arms, which had originally been wrapped around me, are now framing my face, helping guide the direction of my mouth against his. I'm not sure how long the kiss goes on, but at some point, one of us pulls back. I don't even have the brain power to recognize which one of us it is.

I put a little space between our bodies and notice we are both breathing heavily. I wish I'd thought to turn on the porch light, but I'd not wanted to alert my parents to the fact that I was out here. I also hate the June bugs they attract at this time of year. So, I could only see his face through the shadows of light that came through the window and back door. I could stare at his face... Why hadn't I noticed how full his lips were before, or that I liked the angle of his jawline? I now want to kiss my way across it. "I like staring at you too, Annie." Drew's voice breaks the silence. His face breaks into a smile, and even though I can't see it clearly, I know his dimple is showing and I'm feeling confident in myself. I unwrap my hand from his neck, and I trace his jaw, then run a finger across the space where I know his dimple is located. "This dimple is my undoing," I quietly confess into the night. "Mmmm, I will have to make sure that I use it to my advantage, then," he murmurs in response. "Everything about you is my undoing, Annie," he continues, giving me his confession.

We sit like this, looking at each other in the half-light and shadows. It should be weird to be content just looking at each other, but it's like I'm seeing him for the first time. He isn't just the boy next door who loves baseball, the boy who is my friend. He's the boy I want to kiss, the boy who I want to discover and who I want to discover me. I don't want to ruin this moment, but I know that I want to be clear with him about what I want. "Ask me on a date, Drew." My words come out quiet, on the edge of a whisper. "I... I want this to be more than just some hookup, I want..." But before I can say anything else, Drew places one of his fingers over my lips, silencing me. "Annie." He takes in a deep breath, looking right into my eyes. "Be my girlfriend? I don't want anyone else, and I don't need one or two or five dates to know that I want you to be exclusively mine." Drew's words send the butterflies racing around my stomach again. "Ok, I'll be your girlfriend." I punctuate my words by sealing my lips against his.

Chapter 33: Go Straight to Girlfriend

I've been trying to play it cool since the party and the Truth or Dare kisses. I want Annie to want me, to want there to be an us. Her relationships for as long as I'd known her have been, to my knowledge, the small fling with my brother and the single date with Max. I want to give this a label. I want other guys—better yet, everyone—to know that Annie is mine. She wasn't an option for anyone but me. But I didn't want to come off as a controlling jerk by making her pick me so quickly. I knew from being present in her conversations last year with Meg that it caused her a lot of self-doubt when my brother wouldn't take her out, when he didn't make it known around school that they were in a relationship. I wasn't going to repeat his stupid mistakes.

So, I waited for her to text me. I check my phone an obnoxious number of times, each time greeted with our smiling faces on my lock screen and Annie's bikini-covered body on my wallpaper. For three days, I have been trying with no luck to distract myself. I've even tried to finish my last book for summer reading, since school starts next week. I realize it is a stupid idea when I read the same sentence four times in a row. I can't focus. I'm trying to come up with a reason to text her. Should I text her that I read the same sentence four times because thinking about her was distracting me? It isn't the worst opening. I'm still trying to convince myself that I should when her name comes across my screen as a new text arrives. I smile as I read her message about missing me. I reply quickly letting her know I'm here when she wants to see me. She doesn't make me wait replying with an invitation to come over and I'm moving.

***

I don't waste a second; I leave my room and shout to my parents that I'm going to a friends', and I'll be back later. I hear Dad's mumbled "Ok." I leave out the back door, totally forgetting I just said I was going to a friend's house. I'd told her I am great at jumping fences, and my mind has taken me to her fence. I don't actually jump it—it's easier to enter via the gate. I make my way to Annie's back porch and take a seat in the porch swing. I only beat Annie by about a minute. She is breathing a little hard. She must have jogged down the stairs. She's covered in shadows by the limited light from the house, but I can see that she's in shorts and a t-shirt. Her hair is on top of her head, exposing the lines of her neck. In the shadows, I can't tell if she's wearing makeup, but I'd bet that when I get to see her up close, I'll see the freckles across her nose.

She makes her way to the swing, and as she sits down next to me, the thought passes that I want to have her closer. My arms wrap around her back, and I pull her to straddle me on the swing. I want Annie as close to me as possible, at all times. Especially since I know how she tastes and responds when I kiss her. The thought of our earlier kisses drives me to lean in and capture her mouth with my own. I've started this kiss slow and easy, with space between her chest and mine. However, Annie must not want that space, because she wraps her arms around my neck and pulls all her curves against my chest.

There isn't any part of my chest that is not touching hers. When I'd picked her up and moved her to straddle me, I'd not been thinking about how it would feel to be between her legs. But now with no space between our bodies, I can't help but notice that my dick is pressed into her in the most amazing way. I want to move my hips against hers or take my hands and help guide her hips to move against me, helping to relieve the pressure building inside, but a very small part of my brain begrudgingly remembers this is only our third kiss. This is the first kiss that we have started without others daring us to. My brain forms a better plan for this moment, and my hands travel across Annie's arms until they are on either side of her face. I direct her with my hands to change the angle, changing the pace of our kiss.

Eventually, I break the kiss, and Annie moves just enough that we aren't fused together like we'd been. We are both breathing heavily. Annie is beautiful even in the shadows. I can see the line of her neck, to the curve of her lips. I realize I've been staring, but I can also appreciate that she's been staring, too. I'm the first to break the silence. "I like starring at you too, Annie." My voice seems too loud against the sounds of the night surrounding us. She smiles, and it brings one to my face as well. She brings her hand to my left cheek, running her pointer finger against the place in my cheek where my dimple is. "This dimple is my undoing." She says it so softly, I almost don't hear her. I vow to smile so much my jaw hurts; I want her undone around me all the time. I know I say something along these lines to her before confessing, "Everything about you is my undoing, Annie."

I'm not sure how long we sit like this, smiling at each other. Her hand that traced my dimple has skated across my jaw and down my neck, leaving a warm path across my skin. It's a comfortable silence, at least for me. I am enjoying getting to be here with her. Annie is the one who finally breaks our little quiet bubble. In an almost whisper, she's looking into my eyes and says, "Ask me on a date, Drew. I... I want this to be more than just some hookup, I want..." I can see a million emotions cross her face. I guess this is the benefit of having been her friend for the last year. Her eyes have pinched, and her smile has been replaced by a worried expression. I rest a finger on her mouth before she gives voice to the rest of her thoughts.

It isn't that I don't want to hear them, it's just that I realize I need to make my thoughts on this subject clear to her. I'm not my brother, and I don't want her to link us together because we share the same last name. I'm not whispering when I reply, but I'm still honoring our surroundings, and my voice is lower than normal. "Annie, be my girlfriend? I don't want anyone else, and I don't need one or two or five dates to know that I want you to be exclusively mine." The look that plays out on her face now goes from a worried expression to shock and finally to that beautiful smile. I move my finger from her lips to get the full picture. She doesn't draw out her reply and simply says, "Ok, I'll be your girlfriend." Then our lips meet again in a kiss that doesn't end until what feels like hours later. I'm not even sure what time it is when we finally break apart. I know that it's time to go home, but it already feels too far away from her.

Chapter 34: First Day of Senior Year

Fall

There hasn't been a day since Drew asked me to be his girlfriend that we haven't seen each other. I think my parents have noticed the difference, even before they found us snuggled together on the downstairs couch watching the Griffons baseball game. Mom made it a point to bring up Drew at breakfast the next morning, asking me if there was anything new going on in my life. I love my mom, but I also wasn't about to tell her all the ways I had been enjoying Drew's kisses or the way that I dreamed about him touching me. I give her the PG version of my feelings. She seemed happy for me, but she did let me know that if he came over more, we'd have to stay downstairs, or if we did make it to my room, the door would have to stay cracked. She said she'd talk to Dad to make sure he gave me the same distance when Drew was over that he'd given Miles when he'd had Steph over. I thanked her, because I didn't want to discuss this with Dad; it was already more than awkward talking about it with her. I didn't even want to imagine how weird it would be with Dad. I'd leave our conversations to be around sports and journalism school, not subjects that have to do with my boyfriend's lips or hands on my body.

***

School starts tomorrow, and Meg and I have already planned to hang out and go through each other's new clothes to decide what our first day of school outfits will be. In reality, Meg will be picking them both out. I'll follow along, because as I've learned, it is easier not to argue with her about fashion choices, but also because I know Meg always picked things that made me look good and feel good about myself. I'm in my room when the door swings open. "Ever heard of knocking?" I say as she enters my room. "Nope, hadn't crossed my mind," she laughs.

We spend far too much time chatting about all things boys. She tells me her worries about not seeing as much of Tom, since he goes to a different school, and I fill her in on my non-PG-rated thoughts about Drew. "Annie Marie, you are already thinking about third base? Way to go, you little vixen," she comments after I finish telling her the direction of my dreams lately. Meg is the only person who knows that this is a big deal. I haven't done a lot with guys; I've been to third base, but as they say, I've never made it all the way home. I'm not in a big rush to get there, or at least I haven't been before Drew. Now, though, it seems like something I'd like to get to. I'm probably rushing these thoughts because with him, it doesn't send a rush of fear or worry through my body, thinking about being naked in front of him. When I think of the idea of being naked with Drew or having sex with Drew, it feels exciting: it feels like something that would just be a continuation of the lust-inducing kisses we have shared.

Meg breaks my train of thought, and I'm grateful. "Annie, you do deserve him, you know. I'm glad to see you so happy." I hug my best friend. "Thank you for listening—this must be so awkward since, you know, you have dated him already," I say into her hair. She pulls back from me and gives me a stern expression. "This is the last time I'm going to say it, and I hope you are listening.

You and Drew don't bother me at all. We had a moment, and it wasn't right: he never looked at me like I saw him looking at you at the end of the party, and before you ask—" (she waves her hand to make the stop motion) "—that doesn't bother me either." She takes a dramatic sigh. "Ok." I give her another hug. "Ok," I say again into her hair. "You know you're the best friend a girl could have, right?" "Well, duh, I mean that should be obvious by the number of hours I've spent trying to improve your wardrobe," Meg laughs. Her comment makes me laugh, too, and then we turn our attention to the wardrobe in question. Meg makes quick work of sliding hangers in my closet, speaking out loud as she does, "No, definitely not, Annie, why do you even still have these?" She holds out a few ugly dresses and then discards them to the side. "Now this," she says, holding up the new navy dress that I bought on my own during the cruise, "I need to see on, because I think it's the one." I take the dress and try it on, and Meg loves it, doing her little happy toe bounce.

***

I wake to a vibration from my phone the next morning before my alarm can sound. I give myself another moment to stretch and remember why I can't go back to sleep before the phone vibrates again. I lift my phone and see an alert that I have two missed texts from Drew Davis.

Drew Davis

Good Morning Angel

Working on a nickname, what do you think?

Annie

Good Morning hot stuff

161

I am wide awake after our little flirty exchange, and I do as I promised and get into the shower. I am up so much earlier than I had originally planned, but now I have time to do those waves Meg has been helping me to perfect. When I look in the mirror after an hour, I'm proud of what I've done. My dirty blonde hair is falling in waves down my back. I've done some makeup to make my eyes stand out, and I've applied a clear gloss to my lips. The navy blue dress was the right choice; it hugs my breasts and then falls down the rest of my body, not hugging my curves, and is just on the right side of the required length for school, still showing off my legs. When I'm ready to head down to breakfast, I text Drew.

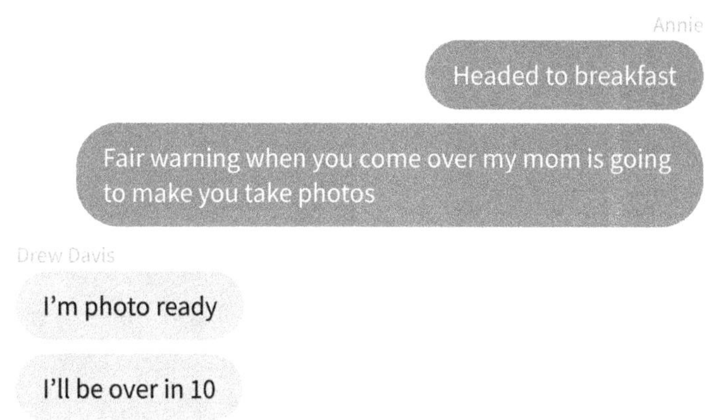

When I get downstairs, Mom jumps up and gives me a huge hug. "Oh, honey, you look so grown up," she gets choked up. "Thanks, Mom. By the way, Drew is headed over. I'll drive with him today." Mom then focuses on worrying about making sure she has enough pancakes to make Drew a plate. I should have asked him if he'd had breakfast, but I didn't think this was going to be her response. Dad pipes up from his spot at the table, "Sweetie, it's fine, he probably had breakfast already." Mom gives him a side eye, and I'm saved from her reply by the doorbell ringing. I make the dash to the door and swing it open before checking the window next to the door.

Will my body ever not have butterflies when I first see him? I think as he is revealed, standing on the porch. Instead of coming inside, he grabs my hips and pulls me into a kiss on the front porch. "Good morning, Angel," he says against my lips, and it sends a shiver over my body. He chuckles, "I think that I got the approval I needed, Angel." His dimple appears, and then he is pushing me back towards the house, taking my appearance in from head to toe. "Damn, Angel, you're beautiful." The little butterflies go crazy in my stomach. "Thanks, hot stuff," I reply, then shake my head, "Nope, I don't like it, I'll think of something better." He laughs, and I can't help running my eyes over him again. He is dressed in jeans and a red polo shirt that hugs his arms, showing off his muscles. I grab his hand and warn him on the way to the kitchen about my mom and the waiting breakfast.

***

True to my text, after getting a few pictures of me with the back-to-school sign, she insists that Drew take a few with me. It feels like we have taken hundreds when I tell Mom we really have to go. She gives me a hug, and I can see how hard she is trying not to cry. I give her another hug and tell her I love her. Then Drew takes my hand, and we head towards his car and the start of senior year hand in hand.

Chapter 35: Yes, We Are a Couple

-Drew-

I woke up early on the first day of school and couldn't go back to sleep. I was not in a rush to get ready. It is only going to take me fifteen minutes when it is time. Instead, I started to think of nicknames for Annie. I'd always called her Annie, but I'd always loved calling my girlfriend something special, and I wanted something special for Annie. I went through the usual suspects—sweetheart, baby, babe, honey—and none of them felt inspired or made me think of Annie. Maybe I'd need to let this go until later. When I'd thought to text her good morning, "Angel" had popped into my mind. I liked it, and hopefully, she would too. We exchanged a few messages, and then she said she was going to shower.

I couldn't help but imagine her naked body. I could feel my dick getting hard as more images played out in my mind of the water running over her body in places I haven't yet touched, but I wanted to. I had to jump out of bed and take an extra-long shower, thinking about her. After releasing my tension, I got out of the shower, dressed, and headed downstairs. Annie texted that I could come over, and I figured I'd better check in with Mom or Dad that I am leaving. Heading to the kitchen, I found it empty. Mom has been focused on her art due to her upcoming show in October. As I figured, they both weren't up, so I grabbed a pastry from the pantry and ate it as I grabbed my backpack from the hook and headed over to Annie's.

***

Now, I ring the doorbell and take a step back. To my luck, Annie is the one to answer the door. I reach out and take her hips in my hands, yanking her against me and kissing her. I keep it short because I know Annie's parents could appear at any point from the house. I test out the nickname by saying, "Good morning, Angel." I feel the shiver run through her body at my words, and I know that is all the approval I need. I smile and give her a little push towards the door, releasing her hips. I hadn't taken the time to appreciate her back-to-school efforts before, but now I give myself a moment to run my eyes over her. She's curled her blonde hair and done her makeup, somehow making her eyes appear bluer and bigger. If you ask me, I think she is drop-dead gorgeous without any makeup at all, but I can't deny that when she plays up her features with makeup, it's fucking hot. As I continue my scan of her body, I take in the dark blue dress that hugs her boobs. I want to feel them in my hands and taste them with my mouth, but I have vowed to myself that I am going to savor Annie. I have all the time in the world this year to do it. I give myself a mental shake, refocus on her, and lose myself thinking about her legs in that dress.

I verbalize my thoughts by saying, "Damn, Angel, you're beautiful." Annie looks me over, too, and then says, "Thanks, hot stuff." Then she makes a face of disgust before telling me she can do better. She grabs my hand and leads the way to the kitchen, giving me a heads-up that her mom is making pancakes. Mr. and Mrs. Campbell are already at the kitchen table, and the two empty chairs both have pancakes and sausages waiting. Even though I'd had the pastry, I sit down next to Annie and enjoy breakfast with them. Annie's dad asks me about my pick for the winner of this year's pennant, and the conversation finds a pretty good pace until it is time for us to leave for school. Annie's mom follows us to the front porch and, true to what I witnessed last year, she takes an endless number of photos of Annie with her back-to-school sign. She even asks me to join Annie, getting more than enough photos of us with the sign. I take Annie's hand, and we head to my car.

***

We had decided yesterday that even though Annie has a car now, too, we wanted to go to school together, and since we both have sixth-period athletics, it would be easy to wait for each other at the car if one of us is running behind. I park the car, and Annie makes to open the door, but before she can, I say, "Wait a minute, Angel. I think that's my job as a dutiful boyfriend." She smirks and says, "It is? Well, by all means, Dimples." Then I get one of her big smiles before she says, "That's it! That's your nickname, it's perfect." I show off my dimple: "You're right, it's perfect." I exit the car, making my way to her side, and open the door. She steps out, and I can't help pulling her in for a quick kiss. I like that since she's my girlfriend, I get to do that now. She blushes a little, looking around at all the other students in the parking lot. "Angel, get used to PDA, because I have absolutely no willpower when it comes to wanting to kiss you." "Mmmm, I could get used to PDA, Dimples," she says in far too sexy a voice for the school parking lot when I don't have time to push her against my car and perform said PDA due to the photos delay. Instead, I hold out my hand and she takes it again as we head into school.

***

I leave Annie at her locker, and then I head to mine, promising her I'll see her at lunch. Unfortunately, we don't have the first three periods together or even in the same wing of the building. At least we have lunch together with all our friends, and I can't wait to see her then. The morning passes pretty quickly, and it's lunch before I know it. When I see Annie, a guy is following at her side, talking to her. I can tell from this distance that whatever they are talking about is something that is interesting, as Annie looks all animated as she speaks. The guy is hanging off her every word, and I can't blame him, because I get it. But also, I don't like it. Instead of waiting for her to spot me, I make my way towards them.

When I do, I wrap my arm around her shoulder. "Hi," I whisper in her ear. I have interrupted, but I can't say that I feel sorry about it, with her focus now on me and not the guy she was talking to. "Hi," she says, then she refocuses on the other guy. "Sorry, this is Drew," she says to him. "Drew, meet Travis. He is going out for the Visual News second sports reporting spot this year, and he was asking a few questions on the workload." I give him a nod and say, "Nice to meet you, Travis. My girlfriend here—"(I wrap my arms around her a little tighter, pulling her into my side) "—did a great job making last year's reports, so you couldn't have a better guide." I'll give it to the guy: he doesn't seem to be bothered by learning that I'm her boyfriend, but he does move to put some distance between them as we continue towards the lunch room. "You are welcome to join our group for lunch, and I can give you some information about the events you could be asked to cover," Annie says to him. "I mean, if it isn't a problem, that would be great." Travis gives a little look in my direction. "Yeah, no problem man—more than welcome," I make sure to add to the conversation. When we make it to the table, Travis makes the wise decision to sit next to Meg on the other side of the table from me and Annie. I have to remove my arm from her shoulders, but I think the point was made. She's not available, because we are a couple.

Chapter 36: Asking Me On Our First Date

The first week of school has flown by, and Drew and I have settled into a pretty nice pattern. I've told Meg about Drew's little reaction to Travis the first day before lunch. She'd laughed so hard because, according to her, he was marking me as his territory. I hadn't thought of it like that, but it didn't bother me then and doesn't bother me now. Partly because he hadn't been, in the moment or since, rude to Travis. Also, it had been nice having him call me his girlfriend without prompting. I had felt a little bad about not introducing him as my boyfriend after realizing during my retelling of the event to Meg that I'd just introduced him as Drew. He didn't seem like it bothered him, so I was trying not to overthink it myself.

***

Travis had gotten the audition, and tonight was his screen test at the first home football game of the season. He had unofficially joined our little friend's group, even though he was a junior. He knew a lot about sports, so it seemed like a good fit. I had coached him on a few of the seniors he should ask for interviews after the game. Part of me was a little jealous to not be on the sidelines, but I realized that this also gave me one night to be with my friends and boyfriend in the senior section and to be part of all the chants and cheers. Meg and I had gone all out with the team stickers on our faces and the Rams colors painted into our hair. The guys had not agreed to the stickers, but they eventually gave in to having colored hair. Drew wanted us to have matching hair, so he was the only one of the guys with the half-and-half look, the others having opted for the one-color look.

The game was against the Cardinals, and it was a pretty even game most of the night, with the Rams holding them off on defense. I enjoyed getting to be a fan and not the reporter tonight. I got to sing the school's fight song and do all the cheesy chants backed up by the music from the marching band. The highlight of the game was when, during a timeout, Drew leaned over and asked me, "Angel, do you have any plans tomorrow?" "Nope, I'm just planning on homework and maybe inviting my boyfriend over to watch the game." My reply makes his dimple appear. "Well, tell him to get lost, ok? Because I'd like to take you on that date we've been talking about." Those butterflies start to flutter in my stomach again. I want to joke back, but I don't, because it's nice he is asking me on a date. "I'm all yours, Drew," I reply and kiss him. The rest of the night, I'm not as focused on football; I have a date tomorrow with my boyfriend, and it seems like a much bigger deal to focus on.

***

I have no idea what to wear, I think as I look in my closet. I think this would be easier if I knew what we were doing. When I'd asked Drew on the way home, he'd said it was a surprise. I hadn't pushed because I liked that he was planning this for me. But now, looking at my closet, not knowing was making everything feel like the wrong choice.

After our little exchange, I still have no idea what we are doing, but I do know Drew would prefer I wear a skirt. With that as my focus, I find my favorite jean skirt and I pair it with one of my Griffons tanks. Meg would have been appalled, as she would have picked one of my more fashionable tops to go with the skirt.

After changing into my outfit, I look at my appearance and like what I see. I hadn't tried too hard, and I am comfortable. The tank top is a little low-cut, and the skirt is just long enough. I am hoping the combo will drive Drew crazy. I hear the doorbell and grab my bag, making sure I have everything. I head down to my first date with Drew, butterflies along for the ride.

Chapter 37: Getting to Know You Better

Walking up to Annie's door, I start to wonder if I did the right thing not telling her where and what I have planned for tonight. I've been hoping that our little text message conversation an hour ago has at least eased her mind on the dress code. When she'd referred to clothes as optional, I had groaned into the silence of my bedroom. Here I was trying to plan this pretty PG first date: playing mini golf and then enjoying Annie's favorite pizza place, followed by ice cream, if she wanted. Then she went and started talking about "optional" clothing, and my brain started trying to figure out an "after" ice cream destination where clothing could become optional.

I need to stop thinking of Annie without her clothing... It is just making me hard. I do not want to show up at her front door with a hard-on. I take a deep breath and try to think of ways that I can improve my batting average. I start to mentally run myself through all the tips I've been given from coaches over the years. When I feel myself adjusting back to normal, I continue up the porch steps and ring the doorbell.

Thank God I've taken the time to get my shit together, because Mr. Campbell is the one who answers the door. "Davis, come on in. I think Annie is going to be down any minute." I follow his directions and enter the house. Mr.

Campbell goes back to watching the baseball game. Before the inning is over, Annie appears from the direction of the stairs. No wonder this girl has been making so many appearances in my wet dreams. Dressed in a Griffons low-cut tank and jean skirt, she is fucking with my mind. Her long blonde hair is down, and I want to tuck it behind her ear to pull it out of her face and then kiss her, but her dad is right behind me on the couch, and it feels weird to make out with her in front of him. "You ready?" I say to her. "Whenever you are," she replies. She tells her dad goodbye. As we leave, he offhandedly reminds her that curfew is midnight. Annie comments back, "Got it, Dad."

***

As soon as the door shuts behind us, I wrap my arms around her in a hug. "First the jersey and now this," I say as I run my hand along the side of her tank. She smiles and doesn't answer me with words; she wraps her arms around my neck and pulls me into a kiss. It's short and sweet, but it makes me hard again. She is going to be the death of me. I don't ever remember any time a girl has driven me this crazy without at least a majority of her clothing removed. Now here Annie is, fully clothed and making me wish I could cancel the date I've planned, haul her over my shoulder, carry her to my bedroom, and have her breathless and naked against me. "Earth to Drew," she says as I have been lost in my thoughts. I step back and offer my hand, "You ready to go on this first date?" "Yes, but are you going to tell me what we are doing?" "It's more fun if I don't," I say as we head towards my car.

***

It's a short drive to the mini golf. Even though I've been Annie's friend for over a year now, I realized while planning this date that I have some gaps to fill in as far as her interests, likes, and dislikes outside of the sports area. I've asked Craig and Luke for ideas for this date, since they have both grown up with Annie. We had thrown out the idea of the batting cages, but I've ruled that out as a first date because baseball was already so much a part of our friendship. We'd been talking about bowling or an arcade, something competitive and light for a first date, when the idea of mini golf had come to me.

I want to learn more about her, and I think about a question game I saw online when looking up first-date ideas. "Let's play a game of ten questions each while we are on the drive to our date destination," I suggest to her. "Oh, interesting—so we can ask any ten questions we want, no topic is off limits?" she asks. I give her hand in mine a little squeeze. "Yes, nothing is off limits, unless you want it to be." "Who gets to start?" is her response, looking excited next to me. "If you want, you can, but make it an easy one," I say. Annie acts like she is thinking. "What's your favorite color?" I'm able to easily say blue, I almost say blue-gray like her eyes, but it sounds a little too cheesy even inside my head, so I keep the answer to just blue. "What is your favorite color?" I return the question to her. "Crimson." I do a really bad game show announcer impression and tell her that's one down and only nine more to go. Annie thinks a little bit before asking, "What's your favorite movie?" "*Sandlot*—it's classic." Then I double down on the question, and she answers, "The newer *Romeo and Juliet*."

"You have to ask the next few first, I need time to think," Annie says. "Ok, fair point," I say, then think about what I don't know about her. I ask, "Have you ever dreamed about me?" She fidgets in her seat before answering, "Yes, you've had a few appearances." "Dare to elaborate?" "Does it count as another of your questions?" she counters. "Sure, going to answer?" I squeeze her fingers. "More or less, it's just us making out." Her answer makes me want to dive into the "more" part of her statement, but I don't get the chance. "What about you, have you ever dreamed of me, with details, Dimples?" she interjects to make sure she doesn't have to use another one like I just did, smart girl. "Yes: the first time was you reminding me I missed the English test." She laughs, and I continue, "But after that bikini picture, I had one where I got to remove it, and it was very detailed in all the best ways." I glance over at her to read her reaction and can see the blush on her cheeks. She meets my eyes for a quick moment, and if I'm not reading her wrong, she looks intrigued. "Happy to share all the details with you at some point, Angel." But I think it's my turn again. "What was your first thought after meeting me?" "Wow," she says, and then, "What about you?" "I thought you were hot." I smile when I reply. I think I've lost track of the question number total, as we continue to ask them so quickly. At this point, it's less about getting in all ten questions and it's about getting to learn more about Annie.

She interrupts my thoughts with her next question, "Where has been your favorite place to live?" This is a really good question. With the hand holding hers, I rub my thumb in a small circle against her skin as I think through the long list. As a teenager, I've probably been the happiest here in Oklahoma. That isn't just because of the girl next to me, but because I've made some good friends, and Coach has been helping me with the possibility of the next steps with baseball. But it seems like too easy an answer, and I know Annie will call me out on it. "I liked living in Colorado," I finally answer. "How long did you all live there, and why was it your favorite?" Annie asks. "We lived in a lot of different places around the state for like eight years. Mom had been inspired by all the natural wonders. We got to do a lot of hiking and outdoor adventures—we even worked our way to class four rapids by the end. Daniel and I had thought we were so cool when we came back from that trip, just to have most of our friends act like it was pretty normal to complete." I finish my thought and take a peek at Annie before refocusing on the road.

I hadn't meant to bring up Daniel; our years in Colorado had been our closest, and it had just been easy to picture him and me on those adventures together.

Well, fuck, I think, I just killed the good vibes on our first date, but before I can start to get inside my head about it, Annie asks in a serious voice, "Is it weird for you that I was with him first?" We haven't talked about the fact that Annie had dated Daniel. I knew at some point it would have to be discussed. I wish I wasn't driving the car right now. I want to watch her reactions and make sure she understands what I was about to say, but I know I can't, and it would be better to get this conversation over with now, so we don't have to have it ever again, and we can both move forward. "I'm going to be honest, so yeah, it bothers me a little. If we are going to talk about it, there has been something that I'd like to ask about your relationship, but you don't have to answer if you don't want to." She squeezes my hand, then says, "I want your honesty always, Drew. I'll do my best to answer if you want to ask." I clear my throat before asking, "Did you sleep with him?" I am not sure what I hope to gain by knowing: already I can feel jealousy take over my mind, thinking about him and her. But when she'd asked, it was the nagging question in my head. *It's better to know now at the beginning, isn't it?* I think. "No, Drew, we didn't," Annie answers me, and I can't help the relief that washes over me. I squeeze her hand again and say, "Ok, so with that covered, we can both agree that the subject of you and Daniel isn't something either of us needs to talk about in further detail." "Totally agreed. Daniel is your brother, your very annoying older brother, end of the story," she states, and I kiss her hand.

"You know, I think you have dominated the last few questions," I say, changing the subject. "I think it's my turn to ask you a few. What do you think is my best feature?" "Your ability to do that: make something easier, to lighten the mood," she says. It's not the answer I was expecting, but I appreciate it, because it's about me as a person. "What about physically, and you can't say my dimple?" I respond, because I already know that one. I can feel her eyes glaze over the parts of my body she can see. "From what I've seen, I'd say your—" (she takes a long pause) "—Fine, ok, your chest and abs are amazing, and I want to touch them." With her little confession, I see the blush on her cheeks again. "Angel, I can whip this shirt off, and you can touch them right now if you want," I say, only half joking, because if she asks me, I'll do it. "Drew, focus on the road," she laughs at me. "Ok, ok, I'll focus, but you say the word, Angel, and I'll get topless for you any time." "Deal" is her flushed response.

I know we are only a few minutes from the mini golf and our time for questions is almost over, so I ask one of the questions I remember from my internet search on this topic. "What's something you've never done in a relationship?" Maybe my previous question skewed her response, because when she answers, I can't help it: my dick twitches. "Sex," she answers with a little breath. "You?" she follows up quickly. I'm trying to get the thoughts in my brain to click, thoughts are running around from *She's a virgin, I could be her first, How is that possible?* "Drew, did you hear my question?" Her words break through the brain fog of her reply and the tailspin it sent me into. I think, *I can't say anything sexual, I've done my fair share of hooking up... The only things I haven't done aren't worth mentioning.* So, I say the first non-sexual thing that comes to mind. "I've never said I love you." Before either of us can respond further, I make the turn into the mini-golf and it's just the distraction we both need.

Chapter 38: Mini Golf Delights

-Annie-

I'd been distracted during the car ride with our game of questions. It has been a good idea so far, and I've been enjoying talking with Drew. Then he'd brought up Daniel when telling me about Colorado, and I just couldn't help but ask if it bothered him that I've been with his brother. I was worried that I'd asked the wrong question; this was our first date, maybe I should have waited for a better time, but I had already asked the question out loud before I could wonder if it should even have been asked. Drew impressed me with his honesty, then shocked me with his follow-up question, asking if I'd slept with Daniel. I answer him quickly, "No, Drew, we didn't," and as soon as I say it, he lets out a breath and his body relaxes. I hadn't noticed how tight he'd been holding himself. In a lot of ways, I am glad we got over this subject so quickly and directly. I don't want Drew thinking about me with Daniel, and I know I've never been more relieved that I'd never gotten that far with Daniel. Because this thing with Drew already feels like so much more, and the butterflies in my stomach flutter in agreement.

In normal Drew fashion, he changes the subject to something more light-hearted, asking me about his best feature. I'd answered that it was this, his ability to make things easy. He'd always been able to do that, make a conversation easier and lighter. To make me forget why I'd been nervous or make me laugh when

I'd been too serious. His follow-up of physical features made me think a little more. I looked him over in the driver's seat. He was physically distracting: could I answer 'everything?' We'd made out, and I'd felt all his hard muscles against me, but I'd yet to feel them, to trace them, to explore them. How could I pick one without having touched them? He'd already ruled out me getting to reference his dimple. Then I remember my wallpaper screen and answer with his chest as his best feature. In typical Drew fashion, he'd offered to undress for me. If we weren't in the car, I'd have gladly accepted his offer, but I remind him to focus on the road. When he says, "Ok, ok, I'll focus, but you say the word, Angel, and I'll get topless for you any time." It's easy to answer "Deal" because it is something I want, and if the butterflies in my stomach are any indication, I'll be saying the words sooner rather than later.

My mind is picturing getting to run my hands over his body when he asks me, "What's something you've never done in a relationship?" I am in a fog of lust thinking about him undressing for me, and my answer of "Sex" easily escapes my lips. I shocked myself a little; I should have said something or anything else. But the word is already out there, so I quickly try to cover it by asking, "You." He doesn't reply as quickly as I would have thought after my reply, and I tap my fingers against his and say, "Drew, did you hear my question?" He squeezes my fingers and then shocks me again, because his answer isn't easy or sexual, it's deep, and I'm impressed by his confession of never having said *I love you* to anyone. I feel like his answer is the one I should have said also, because I've never said it either, but I also don't regret my answer because it's true, and sex does seem like a thing I could be interested in getting to do with Drew. I can't help but think before I can stop my brain, maybe he can be my first, and I can be his too. Before I can focus on this thought deeper, Drew is turning the car into the parking lot of a mini-golf center.

I forget to play a version of myself that isn't competitive from the start. I make the ball into the cup at the end of the first hole in only two shots, and it takes him four. I don't hesitate to say, "Should I take it easy on you?" He gives me a smile that sends heat over my body, then replies, "Never take it easy on me, Angel. I like to earn my wins." At some point, I throw my hair into a messy bun on my head because it is getting in my way when I was trying to putt the ball. Drew just looks at me and shakes his head, then returns his focus to his next shot. At the end of the hole, he places his hand on my neck and whispers into my ear, "You trying to distract me, now all I can think about is kissing you here," and he rubs the pad of his thumb against a sensitive spot near my collarbone, sending goosebumps over my skin and a shiver up my spine. I try to focus and reply, "Who is the one distracting whom now?" He pulls me into a kiss, then pulls away, removing his hand. "I'm always game for distractions, Angel." Then he places his ball down on the next marker and takes his shot, looking back at me with his dimple on full display.

We go back and forth like this through the eighteen holes of the mini golf course, being competitive but also getting lost in little touches and moments of distraction. It's so easy with Drew—the butterflies come and go, and I realize they aren't so much about my nerves but more tied to this feeling of happiness or, in some moments, tied to a feeling of wanting. He wins by hitting a hole-in-one through the little windmill on the last hole. He holds off his celebration until I've missed the same path, and it's clear I'll be having to take more shots to get the ball to the cup. He wraps his arms around my body and picks me up, spinning us around in celebration. Still holding me up, he leans into me and kisses me, causing those little butterflies to make another appearance. A throat clears in the background, and Drew pulls back but doesn't set me down right away. He turns and looks in the direction of the sound. It's a guy with this family, and his wife gives him a little bump of her hip. "Leave them alone, the kids are still putting anyway." She looks over and winks at us. Drew slowly lets me slide down his body as he sets me down, then says, "Sorry about that." He takes my hand, and we drop off our clubs at the door. We all but run across the parking lot to his car, laughing the whole way. When we reach the car, he spins me against the passenger door and kisses me. I can't help but lose myself in his lips.

We do eventually break the kiss, and he helps me get into the car. When he reappears in the driver's seat, he starts the car, puts the car into drive, takes my hand, and asks if I'm hungry. "I could eat," I say, and he drives us to my favorite pizza place in town. When we sit down, he says, "You want the one with olives right?" "Yes, please," I reply, impressed that he remembered my order. Over pizza, we have easy conversations flowing from school to sports and talking about what colleges we are applying to. "Aren't you hoping to get a major league deal?" I ask him when he surprises me with some of the colleges he is applying to. "Yeah, I mean that would be the best outcome, but I know that it's a long shot. Coach and I have some good backup schools that I'd be able to grow and develop at if no offer comes." He is so relaxed giving me this explanation, and I'm impressed with his ability to reach for his goals while having a backup plan in place. I've been focused on getting in at Norman; it's my dream school. I tell him, "It's the college I want to attend so bad. I've got backups, but they feel like I'll be settling and not really where I'm meant to be if I don't get into Norman." "You'll get in. You work hard at school, and I bet your Visual News clips can help," he replies. "Thank you, I hope so," I say as we continue to discuss the pros and cons of each of our opportunities over the rest of dinner.

***

When we climb back into his car after pizza, I check the time, and it's only ten o'clock, giving us plenty of time before curfew, but I'm not sure if this is the end. It's already been an amazing night. "Are we headed home?" I ask, trying to gauge his plan. "I was thinking dessert if you wanted," he replies. I can't help but think of more kisses with him as dessert. I want more, but he interrupts my thoughts. "We can stay in town and go to that ice cream shop, or we have enough time to drive to that shaved ice place by the lake." This isn't the dessert I was picturing, and I can't help but feel a little disappointed. "Let's get shaved ice," I answer. It's more time alone with him, getting to hold his hand in this little first-date bubble. Over the drive, we talk and then fall into a silence that is only broken by the low volume of the radio in the background.

I really don't want shaved ice, and as we get closer, I finally break the silence. "Can we go somewhere else, would that be a problem?" "Sure, no problem, where are you thinking?" Drew asks. Where am I thinking... Where is somewhere we can stop: where is somewhere we can go and not get interrupted? "Let's go to that place by the lake, the one that is near the boat ramp but is off in the trees," I say, and my skin is on fire because I know this is the place people go to make out or hook up without being caught. *Does Drew know this?* I'm not sure if he does, but I want a moment with him alone, not on my back porch swing: somewhere I can touch him and he can touch me and I don't have to worry about being caught by my parents. "You sure?" he says, squeezing my hand. That is his way of letting me know that he does in fact know what goes on in the woods near the boat ramp. "I'm sure," I say, and he turns at the light away from the shaved ice place and towards the lake.

***

No one is in the lot when we arrive, and Drew drives his car into the farthest and darkest parking spot of the lot. I should have grown nervous the closer to this moment we got, but I'm not. I'm excited... I'm turned on. I want to be able to feel his body with my hands, and I want to feel his hands on mine. Drew clears his throat after parking and turning off the car. Our hands are still the only things touching. *How do we make the next move? What even is the next move?* There is no room in the front seats, and the seats are separated by the console between us. Drew clears his throat again before saying, "I'm not sure what the plan is from here, Angel, but nothing comfortable is going to happen in the front seat." I know I turn my head and look at the back seat. His car isn't huge, but I have to mentally agree that the backseat is bigger, and there isn't a console separating the sides of the car. "Yeah, we should move to the back," I hear my voice say, but I don't sound like me, not really; my voice sounds different even to my ears. I release Drew's fingers and open the door, stepping out into the cooling September night air. Goosebumps appear over my skin, and I'm not sure if it's just from the cool breeze running over my exposed arms and legs. Drew exits his side of the car, walks over, and opens the back seat door. Before I can think better of it, I take his hand and scoot inside, dragging him behind me.

Chapter 39: I'll Never Think of the Backseat the Same Again

This first date with Annie is so different from any first date I've ever had. I chalk it up to the fact that we don't have to get to know each other and aren't working up to a first kiss or a questioning touch. We've already worked through the nerves of first touching, making it feel easy. When we are playing mini-golf, I don't question if I can kiss her between starting the next round. I don't question running my hand along her neck after she pulls her hair up in a messy bun. It doesn't feel like Annie is holding back, either; she's been grabbing my hand or my forearm when we walk to the next starting point during mini golf. On the way to the pizza place, she'd offered her hand to me in the car. During dinner, we sat facing each other, and we'd still found a small way to touch, our legs bumping under the table. But it wasn't just the touching that was easier—it was the conversation. I'd been worried that I'd direct all our conversations to be around sports with her. I'd been focused all junior year on keeping it on sports after all, with the occasional school assignment thrown in. I should have known that other subjects would be just as easy as our sports conversations. We talked about a lot of things over pizza. It was surprising to me that she was so nervous about getting into Norman. She was so smart, and when she did the Visual News, you could tell she loved telling others about sports. She is a natural behind the camera, but I may have been a little biased, as I've always thought she was gorgeous. I seemed to surprise her too, when I told her I was applying for col lege.

***

After pizza, I get worried when Annie asks me about going home. *Have I been reading this night wrong? Is she already ready to go home?* I reply, "I was thinking dessert if you wanted." I continue when she didn't reply right away, "We can stay in town and go to the ice cream shop, or we have enough time to drive to that shaved ice place by the lake." I'm not sure which emotion is going across her face, but it's not excitement. What feels like hours later, she finally says, "Let's get shaved ice." She offers me her hand to hold, and I take it, trying to reassure myself that I'm overthinking this. On the drive, we have some conversation, but it falls off a little as we near the shaved ice. Her hand is still in mine, or this silence would feel uncomfortable. I try to focus on the radio, but I'm a little distracted by the feeling that I've done something wrong after pizza. Maybe I was trying to throw too much into tonight. Maybe I should have picked only one thing to do. Annie breaks the silence: "Can we go somewhere else, would that be a problem?" she asks. *Shit, here it is*, I think, but I reply, "Sure, no problem, where are you thinking?"

Then she makes all the worry go away with her suggestion. "Let's go to that place by the lake, the one that is near the boat ramp but is off in the trees." I have to try not to laugh. A guy on the baseball team works for the lake's main office, and he has made it common knowledge that if you need a private moment, it is one of the few gaps in the camera coverage. He has even shared with us all the paths you should drive to not trigger the ones that are near the boat ramp that the lake patrol monitors. *Has this been why she didn't want dessert?* She wanted us to have a totally different kind of dessert. I like her option better than shaved ice, too. "You sure?" I ask, squeezing her hand as I do, because I know that once we set the destination, I'll have a really hard time doing anything else the rest of the night. At her "I'm sure," I hit the blinker to turn in the direction of the parking lot.

***

We are either here early or other people have found a new spot, because we have the lot to ourselves. I do my best to remember the path and to get us to the part of the lot that is completely dark. I turn off the car, and we are in the dark, the only light source the half-moon in the sky, more than a lot away over the boat ramp. I am looking at Annie, trying to figure out the next move and realizing that the best move would be to get us into the backseat. With that decision clear, I say, "I'm not sure what the plan is from here, Angel, but nothing comfortable is going to happen in the front seat." Annie is already shaking her head in agreement when she answers, "Yeah, we should move to the back." My dick twitches, not only at her words but in the breathy way she says them. She is the first one to get out of the car. I don't leave her waiting long and quickly join her on the passenger side of the car. I open the back door, and then Annie takes my hand and pulls me behind her into the backseat. As I let her pull me, I th ink, *I'd let her drag me anywhere.*

***

Once in the backseat, we both react. I'm not sure if I pull her to straddle my lap or if she climbs on top of me. Our mouths fuse, all tongues and sliding lips. I register her fingers twining into my hair and pulling me closer. I also register that in this position, her jean skirt is pulled up, exposing most of her thighs. It wouldn't take much effort to pull it up, exposing more of her to me. But my hands are currently wrapped around her ass. No sooner are they there before

187

I'm pulling her body against me, rubbing her pussy against my dick. I groan into the kiss, all the while thinking that fuck, does it feel good to have the friction of her against me, even if it's between layers of clothing. I may have started the move, but Annie has taken the lead. She is grinding into me and swirling her hips; this must feel good for her, too, because she is letting out little moans. She starts to pull back, and my brain wants to protest. "I want it off, Drew," she says. I wish it wasn't so dark. I'm not able to make out much detail about her face, and I wish I could see her flushed cheeks, but her tone is all breathy again, and I know that she's turned on.

I don't make a lighthearted comment. I don't ask her what she means. I remove my hands from her ass, find the edge of my shirt, and rip it over my head. After all, I'd told her if she asked me to, I would. Her hands are on my chest before I can even return mine to her body, and they are soft and warm against my skin. I place my hands on her thighs, right at the edge of her skirt, running my fingers along the edge while she takes her time feeling my chest down to the edge of my jeans. I don't mean to, but feeling her trace the edge of my abs causes me to flex, and she groans. I run one of my hands up her waist and over the side of her boobs, up to her neck, and pull her mouth back to mine.

We sit like this, kissing and Annie running her hands over my chest, until I can no longer control my brain. I remove my mouth from hers, but I'm still kissing her body. I kiss and suck my way down her jaw, then further down her neck to the spot I'd touched during mini-golf that made her shiver. As I enjoy the taste of her skin, she moans "Drew" into the silence, and I can't help it; I smile into her skin and say, "You can say my name like that any time you want, Angel. Maybe I'll even get you to scream it for me one day." The thought of her screaming my name sends another twitch straight to my already hard dick. I keep moving down her exposed skin until I meet the edge of the tank top.

I want it off, so I reach to the bottom hem of the tank top, bringing it up enough for my fingers to graze the skin between her tank and the top of her skirt. I speak against her breastbone, "Can I take it off?" A breathy "Yes" escapes Annie's lips, and then I pull the fabric out of my way. She still has on a bra, and before I can even ask, she's taken the lead again, removing her right hand from my body, bending it around her back, and unclamping the material. I can feel more than see the material fall into our laps. Fuck, I wish I could see her boobs, and I mentally make a note to undress her under better lights next time, because I know that we will have many more times like this in the future. I pull her body into my chest and kiss her deeply. I can feel her boobs against my chest, and the raised nipples brush across my skin.

I repeat the same path from before but meet no interruptions as my mouth kisses along the top of her boob before kissing over her nipple. I run my tongue over the raised peak, causing her to moan my name again. Annie wraps her hands into my hair, pulling my mouth harder into her boob. She is grinding into me in slow, seductive moves. I move my hand up and wrap it around her other boob and enjoy the feel of its weight in my hand. *She's got great boobs*, I think as I suck the nipple into my mouth. She arches into my efforts and pulls me harder into her body, then moans "Drew" next to my ear. I continue sucking, licking, and touching her boobs, earning more and more moans from Annie. I need a position change to do what I want to do next, so I half spin and lay Annie's back against the backseat before I continue to kiss my way to her belly button. I run my tongue along the seam of her skirt. I'm just about to push the skirt out of my way when the silence is interrupted by a buzzing alarm, and I freeze.

Chapter 40: Interrupted

I'm not sure how to handle all the sensations running through my body. Every-thing is on fire, and I want to pull Drew closer. After he pulled off his shirt, I couldn't stop my hands from discovering all the planes of his body. Because of the dark, I can't see them with my eyes, but that almost makes it more exciting. I can feel his dick move in his pants beneath me, and it makes me hotter and bolder. He isn't just kissing my mouth; he is kissing down the skin of my neck, sucking the spot from earlier, and I burn hotter. He isn't there for long before he moves his lips lower and lower before stopping. *Why is he stopping?* I think, annoyed. I feel his breath across my skin as he says, "Can I take it off?" I quickly respond "Yes" and then mentally add that I want him to take them all off. I want nothing separating me from Drew. My brain refocuses on the feeling of Drew pulling my tank up and over my breasts before it is thrown somewhere in the car. *But it's not enough,* my brain screams. Feeling bold, I reach behind my back and undo the clasp holding my bra around my body, letting it drop. I'm not sure if it's the dark making me bold or the groans that are escaping from Drew, but I feel wonton in this moment with him. When my bra drops onto our laps, Drew lets out a deep groan and pulls my body against his and it feels amazing. My breasts feel heavy, and my nipples are peaked: when they brush against his chest, it sends a rush through my body. I can't help thinking I'm going to burn up here in the backseat of his car.

He keeps kissing me, and it's not just on my mouth. His lips are following the same line he'd just kissed, but this time there isn't a stopping point, and his mouth continues a path down the top of my breast to my raised nipple. I can't help myself as his tongue flicks against it—I feel his name leave my mouth and my hands grip his hair. What he is doing is sending pleasure to my clit, and I can't help but grind it into him through our clothing. I feel like I'm chasing this pleasure he is generating in my body. I'm not sure I knew that his kissing and touching my breast would generate this feeling of need. I've felt lust before, but my brain registers that I've never felt it this strongly, with this desire for more, I need so much more. Drew must be reading my mind as he lavishes his undivided attention on my breasts, sucking and licking and wrapping his hands around th em.

Then I'm moving, and I can feel my back against the seat. I can see the faint line in the dark of Drew above me. My brain can't understand how he did that without his lips never leaving my body but has no problem with the new direction of his kisses down my stomach. I feel myself arching into him as he continues to move down running his tongue around the very edge of my belly button. He doesn't stop there long before he is running his tongue along the edge of my skirt, and I know without a doubt that his next destination is my clit. I'm so ready to feel him there... when I hear the alarm in the dark. I freeze, thinking that we've been caught almost naked in the parking lot. I feel Drew's forehead rest against my stomach and his deep breaths across my skin. He isn't moving or rushing to cover our bodies. "It's my alarm," he says into the dark. "I set one before leaving your driveway, because I didn't want us to miss your c urfew."

Damn, what time is it, I think, and as if he's reading my thoughts, he says, "I set it for 11:30, just in case we lost track of time or had driven to the shaved ice place." He has been so thorough with planning most of the events tonight, and before I can thank him, he pulls his head off my stomach and says, "We better get dressed and head out if we want to make it home in time." I sit up and start trying to feel around for my top or bra, coming up empty on both. "Here's your bra, I think your tank top is in the front seat," Drew says from beside me. "Thanks," I respond as I pull the straps on and secure the clasp of the bra behind my back. He already has his shirt on when he leans into the front seat to grab my tank and hands it back to me. I pull it over my head and down my sensitive skin. "You ready?" he says next to me in the back seat. "Ready when you are," I respond. Drew opens the door, and the overhead light is harsh, making my eyes adjust to the scene in front of me.

Drew's hair is sticking up in random places from where my fingers have been, and his lips are slightly red and swollen from our kisses. I can see that he is making the same review of my appearance. A smile breaks over his gorgeous face, showing off that dimple I can't resist. He pulls himself out of the car and puts his hand out to help me. When we are both standing outside, he leans down and gives me a soft kiss, and I shiver. "You cold?" he asks, standing back up. "Yeah, a little," I say, because the night breeze over my too-hot skin is chilly. "Hold on, I think I have a hoodie in the trunk," he says as he heads towards the back of the car. He comes back holding out a baseball hoodie. I take it and slip it on; it smells like him, and I savor the smell.

We both slip back into the front seat. We both reach for the other, and our hands interlock on the console. Drew drives us home. We both seem a little lost in thought, and the only sound is the radio. It doesn't bother me at all: it's exactly what I need. I need it to cool down from our activities by the lake. When Drew pulls into the driveway of his house, it is 11:58, and we have two whole minutes to spare. I'm the first to break the silence. "Great idea with the alarm, we would have totally missed curfew without it." "Yeah, I would have spent all night with you, if we hadn't been interrupted," he says.

"Walk me to my door?" I ask. "Lead the way, Angel," he says. As we are walking up, Dad does his move of opening the door, making quick eye contact, and shutting it again. Drew laughs, and I forget he hasn't been present for one of Dad's curfew check-in and run acts. "You'll get used to it," I say, joining in on the laugh. "If you say so, Angel," Drew says, still laughing. We make it to the door, and I don't want to go in, but I know I have to, so I turn and look at Drew in the porch light. "Thank you for the best first date. I think if you ask me out again, I'll say yes." Drew smiles and takes a step closer. "Well, Angel, I'm going to book you every Saturday, so add me as a recurring event in your calendar." "I like the sound of that, consider it done," I say back. "Can I kiss you goodnight, or is your dad going to pop up again at any moment?" Drew whispers, like he thinks my dad is on the other side of the door listening. I wrap my arms around his neck, pull his face down to mine, and kiss him, but I pull back after just a quick brush of our lips. "Looks like we made it ok tonight, Dimples." Drew steps back, and I open my door. We both say goodnight one more time before I slip into my house. When I get to my room, I pull my phone out of my bag and set the event in my calendar. Then I text Drew the invitation.

As I get ready for bed, I mentally play out the night again in my head. Drew really made me feel special tonight. Not only physically but emotionally. I can't help as I settle into bed feeling so happy, thinking, *It wouldn't be so hard to fall in love with someone when that someone is Drew.*

Chapter 41: Homecoming
-*Drew*-

I've lost track of time, and I blame it on Annie. *How is a guy supposed to focus when he's got a girlfriend like her?* We've gone back to the lake each Saturday in September. So far, we've only gotten to the top half of our clothes, and each time we are on the edge of one of us making the next move lower, my damn alarm kills the moment. We have agreed it is a requirement to have it set, because we both get lost in the kisses and touching. The worst time, in my personal opinion, had taken place last weekend when Annie asked me to lie down on the backseat, then she'd kissed her way down my chest while her hands had skimmed over my dick through my pants. She'd been unbuttoning my jeans when it had gone off. It was physically killing me each time we got this far and had to stop.

***

Also, it was getting old not being able to see her skin in the dark. I needed to get her over her worries that her parents would see my car at the house, and they'd know what we were up to in my bedroom. I asked Dad if I could start parking my car in the garage. He'd told me he didn't have a problem, but since most of the random stuff was Mom's, I should ask her. Over dinner, I'd asked her, and she'd played twenty questions with me on why I'd wanted to park the car in the garage. I'd tried to say it was easier, etc., etc., but she kept asking. I finally confessed, "So that when Annie and I want to come home from a date, her parents don't know we are here, right next door." Mom smiled at me with the confession and gave me her permission to start the cleanup. I've worked on it a little every night over the last two weeks, and I am almost done.

***

Tonight, Mom joins me in the garage, inspecting my work. "You've done a great job out here, hunny," she says, walking around all the bins against the wall. "Thanks, it will be easier to find your extra supplies for sure," I say to her, pointing at the many bins of similar painting materials. "You've never worked so hard to have a girl over before, hunny. I'm impressed," she smiles. I want to tell my mom that Annie is different, but then I know she'll ask me why. I have a lot of reasons, but I'm not sure I can give a name to all of them. "Thanks, Mom. Yeah, she's pretty special," is the version I give her. Mom eventually heads back inside, and I pull my car into the open side of the garage, feeling pretty happy with my accomplishment.

***

It's the week of homecoming, and while I've gone before, we seniors all seem to be taking it to an extreme. It's like since it's the last one, we have collectively decided to give a shit about all the little details. It's been fun getting to do little couples outfits with Annie, and my favorite so far is the dress-up day theme 'dress up like your future career.' Annie is dressed in this little light blue pantsuit, and she even has one of the karaoke microphones. I'm dressed in my travel baseball uniform, complete with a ball cap and sunglasses on top of my head. We are different but we complement each other, and it feels good to think that we want to be in careers that aren't complete opposites, like what we want to be now would still work into the unknown future.

Again, Annie makes me think differently, because I'm pretty sure that before her, I'd thought of the future in weeks or months, but with her, I've started thinking about how we could make it work into college and maybe, just maybe, after that, too. Tomorrow is the homecoming football game, and the dance is Saturday. The girls of the group have again made all the plans. Annie told me today that they all agreed we'd save a limo for prom and that we should meet at the restaurant, meaning each couple would drive separately. I'd almost asked why we couldn't double up into one car and then thought better of it, because if we were in our car, then each couple could go wherever we wanted to after. I was personally going to try to talk Annie into finally making it to my bedroom. I needed to see her in the light, and I was over trying to make the backseat of my car work. I was ready to spread out on my bed with her next to me.

***

On Saturday morning, the idea got even better when, over brunch, Mom informed me that she and Dad would be going on a short trip to a gallery in Texas that wanted to house some of her new works. She'd asked me to make sure to get some pictures of us all dressed up, and I reassured her that there would be no lack of photos if Mrs. Campbell had anything to say about it. Mom laughed and agreed. I grabbed my phone to text Annie and update her on our new opportunity.

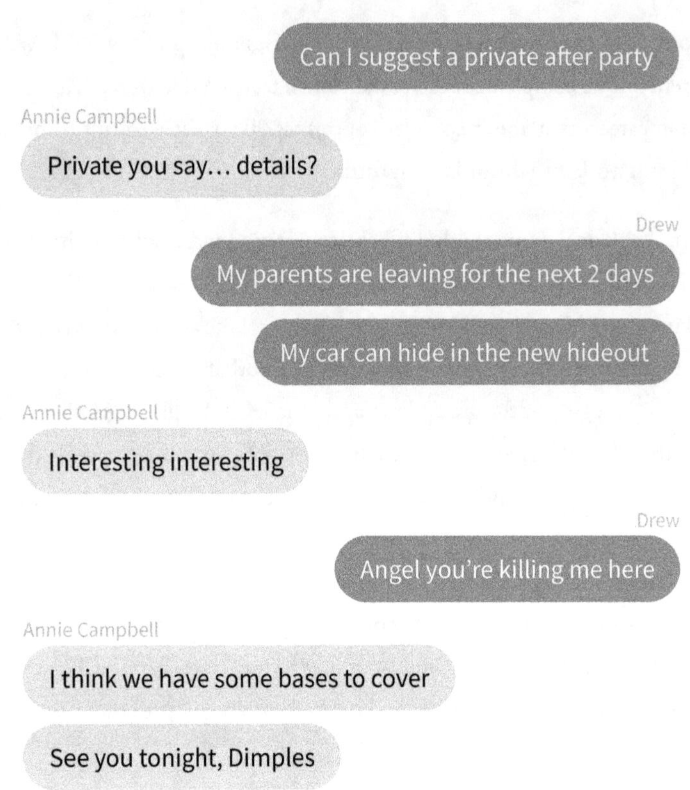

For the first time in a long time, I really hope she isn't talking about baseball with me, and that when she says *bases*, she means we can finally make it all the way to third.

***

I'm dressed in my black shirt with a red tie as requested by Annie. She is wearing that dress from the summer, like she said she would. Since we are driving separately, the rest of us aren't meeting until the restaurant. I head over a little early before the appointed time. Mr. Campbell lets me in again. He's got the playoff game on. I sit down on the couch and we both get lost in the game. It still seems so crazy that Coach thinks that I could make this my career, that I could be good enough to be the guy fans like us are screaming and cheering for in the crowds, attending the games, or in front of their TVs. We are so focused on the game that I jump when Annie's lips kiss the back of my neck by the base of my hair. "Shit, you startled me," then quickly amend, "Sorry, Mr. Campbell" because I hadn't meant to say *shit* in front of her dad. "No, problem, Davis, she's a silent assassin," her dad says, and we both laugh.

I get up from the couch and can't help but appreciate the long tan legs on full display in that red mini dress. I think the picture over the summer had been taken from the wrong angle because this view of her long legs and the dress barely covering her ass is the stuff of my dreams. "I think Mom wants to get some photos if you are ready," Annie asks, smiling at me. "You look amazing, and yes, I'm ready for pictures," I finally form words. Annie's dad waves goodbye to us, and we go out front. Mrs. Campbell, as predicted, takes so many photos. I ask her if my mom can get a few, and she says she will edit some and print me the best ones.

***

At the restaurant, we meet the lunch crew and their dates. Craig is now dating a girl named Kayla, who seems nice, and Luke is with Katie, who is a junior on the soccer team with Annie. Meg is still dating Tom, and they are on round two of homecoming. We sit at a circle table and joke and laugh for far too long. Annie and I are touching in some form or another the whole time. Holding hands, my arm along the back of her chair. My hand resting on her exposed thigh. We eventually decide we are fashionably late and should head to the gym to make an appearance since we are all dressed up.

When we get there, the dance is going full blast, with people dancing and hanging on the edge of the dance floor in groups. We all group into the photo booth and take a ton of crazy and fun photos. Then it's time to dance. It's a lot of pressing bodies together in rhythm to the songs that play over the sound system. They throw in a few slow songs, and we break into our couples. Annie wraps her arms around my neck, and I wrap mine around her back. At some point during the last slow songs, she places her head against my heart, and I rest my chin on her head. It's easy to hold her like this and get lost in the moment. When the music changes back to the latest pop star chart-topper, I lean down next to Annie's ear and say, "You ready to get out of here, Angel?" She wraps her hands in mine and leads me toward the doors of the gym. We cross the dance floor, leaving our friends, and I let my girlfriend lead the way to our next destination.

Chapter 42: Under the Lights

-Annie-

It's been dream of a night at homecoming. Dinner is a blast with our friends;
we've been laughing and sharing little memories to embarrass each other. Even
Kayla and Katie get into some of the jokes. Tom is the only one a little outside
of the conversation, but I think he is so into Meg that he isn't talking; he looks
happy all the same. We don't talk about sports unless it comes in the form of
Drew sharing the story about the time he wore his very white baseball pants
in middle school without underwear, and it rained, and they'd become very
transparent. Or when Luke retells the time he missed a grounder with his glove,
causing the ball to crash into his face, and the next week he'd told everyone the
bruise was from a ninja fight. Drew and I are involved in the conversation, but
I'm also focused on his fingers brushing my thigh or noticing when his arm is
over the back of my chair. I'm always aware of him and his touches.

***

We eventually make it to the dance, and we goof around and have fun. I'm sure
at least one of our group photos is going to make it into the yearbook. We dance
and have a good time. There's the normal grinding of hips and line dances that

everyone can do, but it's the slow dances that get my heart racing. During them, my body is swaying against Drew's, and I can't help that my mind drifts to the fact that we are skipping the after-party and going back to his house, his very empty house. All the messing around we've done in his backseat has been in the dark. The little butterflies that I thought had been resolved have returned, thinking about being alone with him in his house. I've been listening to his steady heart during the last slow song, and it's been calming, so when he says next to my ear, "You ready to get out of here, Angel?" I'm ready to see what happens when we get under his bedroom lights. I grab his hand in mine, leading us towards the exit, waving to our friends but not stopping to say goodbye.

***

Drew drives his car straight into the empty side of his garage, then hops out and opens the door for me. "The vehicle has successfully reached the hideout," he says in his best sidekick impression. I take his offered hand, and he pulls me into a kiss and shuts the door of the car. We enter the house, and he leads me up the stairs. We stop at the first door on the left, and he opens it for me, but he doesn't enter. He stops at the threshold, letting me be the first to enter his room. "After you, Angel," he says and it's so like Drew to give me one more choice, one more stopping point before we start the next moment together.

"Well, thank you, Dimples. I think I will," I say as I step through the open door into his room. I'm sure he's cleaned up in preparation for tonight, because his room is spotless, and the bed is made. "Did you clean for me, Dimples?" I tease him. "Next time you'll get to see it like normal, but today I wanted to impress you, Angel," he says, leaning against the door frame. I take in the pictures of his life that decorate his walls. A lot of Little League team photos are featured. He also has a board decorated with some more recent pictures of our friend group taken last year at the semi-final football game. I try not to get hung up on the fact that his arm is wrapped around Meg's shoulder rather than my own, and I make my eyes move on. Then I land on our back-to-school photo my mom took and the one from the party, where I'm looking at him, smiling, and my heart and mind settle. I move around the space and make it to the window, realizing he looks out on our backyards. I pull the blinds shut, blocking the view of my house. I turn and finally look at his bed, but I don't sit down. Instead, I walk back to Drew, wrapping my hands on either side of his handsome face, and pull him into his room and into a searing kiss.

Drew's hands wrap around my ass, and before I know it, he is lifting me, and I'm wrapping my legs around his hips. We are moving, kissing, and then we are falling and kissing. We land on his bed, and he moves his hands from my ass to break the fall and to stop all of his weight from landing on me. But my hands aren't worried about catching me; they have made their way to his hair. I'm using them to fuse his lips to mine. I realize he is still holding up half of his weight with his arms because they aren't on my body, and I pull his face away from mine by tugging his hair just enough to say against his lips, "Touch me." I quickly return my lips to his, and finally his hands are on me, his weight pushing me further into the mattress.

I move my hands from his hair to his red tie, and I start trying to figure out how to take it off, but I'm having no luck. I think I make an annoyed sound, because Drew is laughing against my lips. He pulls back and his hands join mine, making a quick jerking motion. Creating a big enough loop to slip his head through, he pulls his head down, and I pull the tie off and throw it onto the floor. The first clothing has been discarded, but I'm hoping it's not the last of the night to decorate his bedroom floor. He makes like he is going to start to unbutton his shirt, and I say, "Stop, I want to do it," and brush his hands away from the buttons. He wraps his arm around my waist and flips our position. Now, I'm the one on top. It will be easier to undo the buttons, and I start to make my way down his chest. I kiss my way along the skin I'm exposing, one button at a time, until I reach the top of his pants. His chest is fully on display. I sit up a little and look over all the tight muscles I've been touching in the dark. He is so hot, his shirt open, looking at me like I'm the sexiest girl he's ever seen.

My hands find his belt and release it, then slide the button of his slacks through the loop. Finally, I slide down the zipper. I look up, and Drew is watching every move I make, like it's the most interesting thing he has ever seen. I feel bold with his eyes on me. I move to the end of the bed and say, while moving my hand in a back-and-forth motion towards his body, "Off, Drew. I want them all off." He blinks a few times, as if he isn't sure what I want off.

I can see the moment it clicks and that dimple appears. He rolls himself to standing and makes quick work of the shirt, then slides his pants and boxers down to the floor and steps out of them. His dick springs out, and I can't help but make a small noise in the back of my throat, because he is hard and big. At least the biggest I've seen. I may not have had sex, but I've given a few hand jobs and a few blow jobs, and I know he is bigger than anyone I've been with. I know I'm staring as he kicks off his slacks. I'm not sure how long I've been staring before I hear him chuckle and say, "Annie, my eyes are up here." I run my eyes back up his abs and chest to his eyes. "You," I point at the open spot on the bed. "There." He does as I've asked, and before he is even settled back on the bed, fully naked, I've climbed between his knees and wrapped my hands and lips around his dick.

Chapter 43: Making it to Third

-*Drew*-

I'm not sure how I end up as the one fully naked when all I wanted since I knew we'd have the house to ourselves was to see her skin exposed in the actual light. She'd been trying so hard to get my tie off that I'd decided I should help her. She pushes my hands away when I try to help with my shirt next and she starts fumbling with the buttons, I flip us so she can have better access. She is so fucking hot in that red dress, straddling me, and I register that after she finishes with my shirt, I'm going to focus on removing it from her body. She is kissing down my chest, as she releases each button. Her lips move over my abs until her lips are at the top of my slacks. Before I can reach for her, she is pulling on my belt, releasing the clasp, then the zipper.

***

In a flash she's at the end of my bed, out of my reach. At first, I'm concerned that something happened, because she moves too quickly from touching to removing herself from on top of me. I'm about to ask her if she is ok when she says in a firm voice, "Off, Drew. I want them all off." Her command is followed with this little up-and-down motion, and it finally clicks; she's telling me to lose my clothes—ALL of my clothes. I can't help the smile that covers my face, because I like that she is the one leading us to the next step. With my brain understanding what she wants, I roll off my bed and slip out of my shirt and already undone slacks, also pulling my boxers and socks off in the process. They join the other discarded items on my bedroom floor. I do register as I pull my pants down, and my dick is revealed, that Annie makes a small little gasping noise. My hard dick reacts to the sound, and I can't help the small twitch that happens in response. I look up at her, and she is staring: not at all of me. She is focusing solely on my hard dick: jutting out from my body.

I can't help but say in the silence, "Annie, my eyes are up here." A blush appears across her cheeks, but her eyes and head make their way to my face eventually. She does take her time, looking at my body. When our eyes meet, she says again in a firm voice, "You." She points at the open spot on the bed where I'd been before I'd undressed, then finishes with "There." I don't say anything; I follow her command again, because when your girlfriend is looking at you like she wants to devour you, you follow her directions. I'm barely back on my bed before Annie is back where she'd been after unzipping my pants, and I think she'll just touch my dick with her hands, but I'm shocked when, after her hands touch me, I watch her face descend and my dick disappear into her mouth.

***

Her mouth feels perfect as she sucks the head of my dick in and out. She pulls back and runs her tongue along the tip before dipping her head back down. Her hands are wrapped around the base of me and sliding up and down at a steady rhythm. I'm not sure when they do, but my hands find their way into her hair, and I hold her dirty blonde locks out of the way so I can watch my dick disappear into her mouth. I let out a loud groan as my dick hits the back of her throat, and I can feel her moan vibrating through my dick. A glimmer of a thought passes through my mind, that I'm not sure I've gotten a blowjob where the girl moaned like she was enjoying the process just as much as I am. It's hot, and I can feel myself grow harder. I'm not sure how that is even possible.

Annie knows how to give a blow job. She keeps up this rhythm before she surprises me by taking my balls into her hand and giving them a little squeeze before she starts to use her hands again to pump up and down my dick. I am gripping her hair tighter, and I try to remember to stop, but I can't focus, and I start to direct her in the rhythm that feels the best. She lets me have control, and she works her mouth up and down me. At some point, I've also started to flex my hips and help drive my dick in and out of her mouth. She gags but doesn't stop or pull back from my dick, and I can hear my voice say, "So good, Angel, it's so good." I can only register that my balls are tightening, and I know I'm going to cum any second. I ask her if she wants to swallow, and she gives me a groan around my dick, and I take it as a yes. Then I cum inside her pretty mouth, and she swallows, and it's the fucking hottest thing I think I've ever seen. She doesn't immediately release my dick, either; she makes a few more soft passes before I see myself fall from her lips. She looks up at me, and her pupils are all big. She is wearing a satisfied grin on her face, like she's impressed with herself for giving me the best fucking blow job of my life. I lean up and put my hands on either side of her face and pull her to me. I don't care that my dick was just in her mouth: I have to kiss her.

I eventually pull her head back and say, "Angel, that's the best blow job I've ever had." She blushes again, smiling, and I pull her back into a bruising kiss. Only Annie would blush now. At some point, my brain returns enough blood to remember that I'm completely naked and Annie has only removed her shoes. She did all that to me, and she's still fully dressed. With Annie straddling me, I think to myself, *I can fix this situation quickly* and remove the dress. I move my hands from her face and brush them down her neck and to her back. I move my kisses to her neck, and I'm sucking and kissing a path towards her exposed collarbone. My fingers find the zipper, and I pull back to look at her, because I know that I want her to let me. "Can I undress you, Angel?" I ask. Her eyes have been closed, and they open to look at me. "I'm not sure why I'm even still dressed," she says and gives me a smirk. "I'll take that as a yes, Angel," is my husky reply, and as I go to pull down the zipper, she says, "Please do."

The zipper slides down her back easily, and I don't meet any resistance. The dress slides down to pool around her hips. For a moment, I'm focused on how I'm going to get the dress from around her hips. But then I look up, and all I see are Annie's exposed boobs, and I forget about the stupid dress. Annie wasn't wearing a bra, and her boobs are now fully on display for me. Annie's boobs aren't new to me; I've felt and tasted them, but only from the backseat of my car in the dark. There is something about getting to see them all peaked in front of me that just breaks my brain. I wrap my arms around her bare back, and I pull her across my lap, leaving no space between us, and at the same time I dip my head to suck her left nipple into my mouth. Annie arches against my arms and drives her boob more towards my mouth. I release the left nipple and blow a little on it, and she moans, "Drew." I can't help the smile that appears on my face or the thought that runs through my head, that my name has never sounded so good. I turn my face and give her right nipple the same attention. I'm not sure how much time I kiss and suck on her nipples, but she is grinding more and more into my hips on my lap. She's worked my dick back to a hard-on, and the only thing between us is the wet-feeling panties that she is grinding between my dick and her pussy. I look down, and I'm annoyed that the dress is blocking my view. I make the mental decision that it's time for Annie's clothing to join mine across my bedroom floor.

Chapter 44: Lost in Time

It's turned me on far more than I expected it to, having Drew's dick in my mouth. Maybe it's due to the fact that this is the first time I've seen it or touched it, but with each stroke of it in and out of my mouth, I can feel my body reaching. When Drew wraps his hands in my hair and flexes his dick to hit the back of my throat, I moan. My brain is trying to remember a tip or trick that I'd read about in some online article, or was it in the last book I'd read? My brain can't focus, I know it has something to do with a guy's balls and touching them. So, I move my hand away from his shaft and run it over his balls, causing a deep groan to leave Drew's mouth and his hands to tighten harder into my hair. I mentally note that the move is a solid suggestion before I move my hand back to grip him. The tempo increases, and Drew is driving his hard dick in and out of my mouth faster and deeper.

Drew is long and thick, and it doesn't take long for him to start hitting the back of my throat every time he drives himself forward. It causes me to gag, but I don't stop because his words of "so good" have me wanting to push him to the edge. In no short time, he says, "I'm going to cum, Angel, do you want to swallow?" I don't want to remove him from my mouth to answer, so I groan and keep moving my mouth over his dick. Drew thrust a few more times, and I can taste his cum on my tongue—salty and just a touch sweet—before swallowing it down. His fingers have loosened in my hair, but I don't immediately remove my mouth, until he's gone soft.

When I finally release him from my mouth, I look up at him. He is watching me, and he looks so satisfied and sexy. It makes me feel powerful, knowing that I've made him look like this. But I don't get to sit with my feelings long before the hands wrapped in my hair are wrapped around my cheeks and gently pulling me up over his chest, leading me to kiss him. He uses his hands on my face to pull us apart and says in a deep voice, "Angel, that's the best blow job I've ever had." I can't help the blush that spreads over my skin at his confession, and before I can think of some witty reply, he is pulling me into his kiss.

***

I'm lying over Drew's naked body when he moves us to seating, his back against his headboard. I'm now straddling his hips, and my dress is pulled up around my ass and waist. His hands start moving over my neck and then down my back. I think he's going to be moving them to my exposed ass that my thong isn't covering, but he stops at the top, his fingers brushing the edge of the zipper. And my mind shouts *yes*. But he doesn't start moving, and I can feel him as he pulls his head back from my neck, which makes me open my eyes to see what is going on. Our eyes connect, and he says, "Can I undress you, Angel?" Then I smart off some question about why I'm not already undressed, which causes him to laugh and reply, "I'll take that as a yes, Angel." I can feel his fingers moving the zipper down my back, and I think, *"Please do."*

It feels good to have my dress opened and removed from my sensitive skin. I can feel my nipples harden further as they are exposed to the air and released from the cups of the dress sliding down my body. I've opened my eyes again, and I watch the material sliding down and puddling around my waist. I look up at

Drew and watch his expression change as he notices that I'm topless in front of him. He doesn't say anything, just wraps his large arms around my waist and dips his head.

His mouth sucks my nipple, and I can't help arching my back. The only thing holding me here is Drew's arms, supporting my weight. With each suck or flick of his tongue, I feel the pulse at my clit. He removes his mouth from my nipple with a pop, and then gently blows air across the wet skin, and I can't help the moan that escapes me. He moves his mouth to my other nipple and repeats the same moves, sending my body to an inferno. With each pass of his tongue, I can't ignore the pulsing at my clit and my core, and more and more, my need is focused on the desire for friction at my clit. His dick is wedged between our legs, and as he's sucked on my nipples, he's gotten hard again. I use this to my advantage, and I'm grinding my clit against him through the material of my thong. It feels so fucking good, I can't help but double my efforts of grinding my hips up and down to give my clit the best sensations.

***

Before I know what is happening, Drew is rolling us, and he is pulling his body away from mine. I open my eyes and wrap my hands around his forearms at my side. I want his body back: I want the feel of him underneath me. He must sense my frustration or confusion because he says, "I need the dress off, Annie—lift your hips for me, Angel." I try to focus and realize that his hands are holding the dress and trying to work it down my hips. I release his forearms and lift my hips. He pulls the dress down my legs and discards it to the floor. Now the only clothing on my body is my little red thong, which just covers me. I'm watching Drew look over my body, and his hands are running over the edge of my closed thighs. "Angel, you're so beautiful, and while I could look at you all night like this, I think it's my turn to taste, so I need you to open your legs for me." That is all the direction that I need, and I spread my legs open. Then, I hear the worst sound in the fucking world: his phone alarm.

Chapter 45: Curfew Be Damned

After I've pulled the dress off Annie, I take a moment to look at her sprawled across my bed. She is the hottest thing I have ever seen. Sure, I've fantasized about her like this, with the support of the bikini photo and the touches I've gotten of her body in the dark, but nothing compares to the girl in front of me. Her hair is in tangles and draped over my pillows, her eyes are unfocused and lust-filled, and her lips are swollen from more than just us kissing. Mentally, I capture all the details of her body to recall for the rest of my life. As I continue my review, I see I've left a mark on her neck, and she'll give me heck about it tomorrow.

When I look at her boobs, they are all covered in similar marks from my sucking and kissing. Then I reach her little red thong, the only material on her beautiful body. I groan, "Angel, you're so beautiful, and while I could look at you all night like this, I think it's my turn to taste, so I need you to open your legs for me." She doesn't say anything, but she moves her legs, opening them for me, and it's all the welcome I need. But before I can even move my hands from the side of her thighs, I hear the sounds of my alarm.

***

That thing has the worst and most fucking annoying timing. I want it to stop, so I begrudgingly leave Annie on my bed and search the floor for my slacks. I find them, pulling the phone from my pocket and shutting the midnight alarm off. Annie got an extended curfew to 12:30 tonight. I set my phone down on the side table and look back at her. She hasn't moved, and all I want to do is join her on the bed. We do have thirty more minutes. It takes less than one to get from my bedroom to her front door. Before I can give voice to my thoughts, Annie says, "Drew, I think you left something unfinished." "Mmmm, I think I was about to give you a taste, wasn't I?" I say and join her back on the bed, moving myself between her open legs.

***

I don't rush my way to her pussy. I kiss her inner thigh, and she moans. I kiss my way to her clit; I suck it through the red little thong, and she arches off the bed. I wrap the sides of the thong in my hands, pulling it down her beautiful, toned legs and discarding them to the floor like the rest of our clothing. I look over at her pussy, and it's like it's calling my name. I need to taste her and make her feel as good or better than she'd made me feel tonight.

I finally get my first real taste when I press a kiss to her clit, and she wraps her fingers into my hair. I smile against the little nub and suck it into my mouth. Her response is so similar to mine when she'd sucked on my dick. She moans, and I can't help but feel good about the fact that I am doing this with her and to her. I focus my efforts on licking down her pussy. I don't think she realizes that she is grinding her pussy on my face, but she is, and it's turning me on. But this isn't about me, it's about her, and I keep licking, sucking, and then I rub my finger up and down her wet pussy, sliding my finger into her. She's so tight, and I can feel the muscles of her pussy wrap around my finger. I groan and tell her how tight she is and how much I like it. After I feel good about her taking one of my fingers, I add another and start to really slide them in and out of her pussy, setting a rhythm. I know this is good for her because she is moaning my name and rocking her pussy into my efforts. She moans, "Drew... please, please," and I know she must be getting near her orgasm. So, I go back to sucking on her clit and look up at her. She is gorgeous: her eyes are closed, her hands are clasped into my sheets, and her body is all lines of tension. I feel her body start to clamp down on my fingers, and her eyes fly open and look right at me. She all but screams "DDRREEEWW" as I can feel her come undone around me.

***

I remove my fingers from inside her pussy and bring them to my mouth as I sit back from her body, then lick them clean of her juices. I tell her how good she tastes. I look at her over my hand, and she is frozen, watching me. Before either of us can make another move, noise comes from the floor by my desk. We both look over, and at first, I can't connect what is making the sound, but it seems Annie does because she jerks up and attempts to cover her naked body. "That's the location app sound." I must look confused, because she continues. "It means at least one of my parents has located my phone at your house and has pinged my phone. It means my parents know I'm next door at your house, Drew ." *Oh shit, we've been caught,* is the thought that comes to my mind. I scramble to collect our clothing. Annie quickly dresses and goes to her phone. "Shit, I have four missed texts and then the ping." She types out a quick reply and shuts her phone. "I'm so going to be grounded." I check the time, and it is 1:10 a.m.; we have missed her curfew by a lot. I want to regret it, but I can't make my mind think logically. It was totally worth getting to taste her and watch her face as she o rgasmed.

✳✳✳

We are fully dressed now, and I walk over to her, giving her a hug and a kiss on the forehead. "You have any regrets?" She pulls back and looks me straight in the eyes. "None, but be prepared, I'll probably be grounded through at least two Saturdays for this little rebellion." I shake my head and say, "Let's get you home before it becomes three." This time, I take her hand and lead her down home.

Chapter 46: Worth the Consequences

My body is humming in satisfaction. I've never felt this good. After what Drew did to me, I feel boneless, and my mind is broken. Watching him lick his fingers as he pulls back from my body is the most erotic thing I've ever seen. I've started to take in his hard body, and the thought that maybe we should keep going crosses my mind, when the silence is broken by the location app ping. I remove my eyes from Drew and look in the direction of my discarded bag. The sexual tension has left my body, because I know that my parents have pinged my phone as a warning: they know I'm here. My brain tries to find a clock, and since this is my first time in Drew's room, I have no idea if he even has one. Drew looks confused at my panicked expression, and I give him a quick summary of what the sound is and what that sound means. I attempt to cover my breasts as I scramble to get out of Drew's bed. After my words, Drew is scrambling to find our discarded clothes. I am most worried about my dress—I can't go home naked. I grab the red material and pull it on. Before I can attempt to pull up the zipper, Drew has his hands at my back and is pulling it up for me. Then he goes back to getting into all his layers.

***

Instead of trying to look around for my thong, I go to my bag and pull out my phone. "Shit, I have four missed texts and then the ping," I say to Drew. Then, I text my mom back as quickly as I can.

I type out a quick reply and shut my phone. "I'm so going to be grounded," I think, and then realize I've said it into the room. Drew is now fully dressed, and he walks over and gives me a hug and a kiss on the forehead. "You have any regrets?" he asks against my still-too-warm skin. I have absolutely, positively zero regrets. It will suck being grounded, but I'd make the same choices all over again to be with him like tonight. I pull back and look him in the eyes, "None, but be prepared, I'll probably be grounded through at least two Saturdays for this little rebellion." He makes a joke and takes my hand and walks me home.

***

Mom and Dad are there right away, and Drew apologizes for breaking my curfew. He lets my parents know that he will do better and set an alarm next time. I did my best not to laugh, because he had set an alarm, and my actions had us forgetting it had even gone off. My dad gives a mumbled, "Do better to remember that, Davis," comment before stepping back, effectively telling me to get inside. I want to kiss Drew but think better of it. He lifts our clasped hands to his lips, giving my hand a quick kiss before releasing me and backing down the steps. "Good night, Angel. Thank you for the best homecoming on record." Then he takes off across our yards to his house. I turn back to my parents. Mom gives me a little smile because Drew did make a really sweet gesture in front of them, but my dad still looks pissed, so I make my way inside.

***

I head to the kitchen because that is normally where these conversations take place. Normally, it's been Miles in these moments; I've only heard them from the stairs while I eavesdrop. I know not to get into details about why I missed curfew—Miles had tried that once and gotten grounded for a whole month. So, I sit down and wait for one of my parents to say something. They share a look, and Mom gives Dad a little head nod, which I think means he is about to start—he is the king of curfew after all—so it surprises me when Mom speaks.

"Annie, we expect you to be able to honor the curfew we give you. We know you are a senior, and that is why we even extended the curfew, but that is no excuse to not be home on time or at least text us where you are." Before I can interject, she continues, "I realize that the location app is for emergencies like we discussed, but when you were more than thirty minutes past curfew, your dad and I got worried. So, I pinged your phone." I take a second to hear the message my mother is trying to give me. I feel a little relief, because unless I've heard wrong, Mom just let me know that Dad has no idea that she pinged my phone at Drew's: my location for the night is only known to her.

I know the silence is meant to allow me to say something, and I take a deep breath. "I'm sorry, I lost track of time with everything. I promise it won't happen again." My parents share a look, and then my dad says, "You're grounded for the next two weeks. You can attend football games only on Friday, because of the Visual News, but we expect you home right after. Also, you'll only have access to your phone when away from home, so hand it over." I can't say I didn't see it coming. I'd even told Drew I would be grounded for two weeks. I make one small request, "Can I text Drew that I'm grounded before I hand over my phone?" "Sure, send him one more message, then I'd like to go to bed," Mom says. Dad heads in the direction of their room and Mom stays seated at the table with me as I pull out my phone and text Drew.

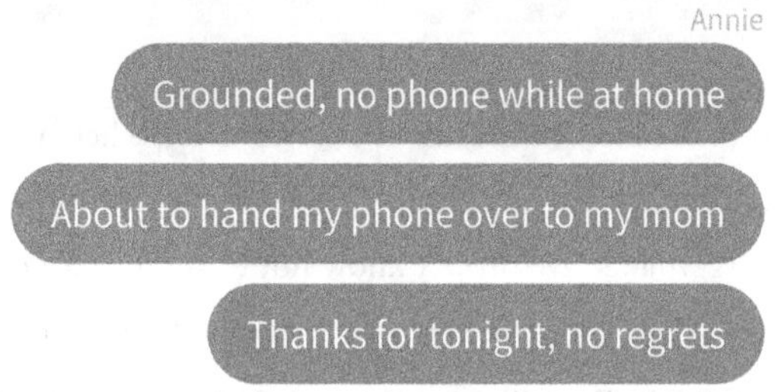

His reply is immediate, and Mom lets me read it before I hand over my phone.

I smile as I close my phone screen, getting one more look at Drew's body on my lock screen, and hand over my phone. "Thanks, Mom," I say to her as I walk to my room. "I have no idea what you mean," she says and gives me a little wink before heading towards her bedroom. It's not until I reach my room and I look in the mirror that I realize it's clear Drew and I had at least been making out, because my hair is all mussed, and when I go to comb it back from my face, I'm greeted by at least two hickeys along my neck. I make quick work of brushing out my hair and head back into my room to change. Only when undressing do I realize that I never did find that red thong before leaving Drew's bedroom.

Chapter 47: Time Flies When You're Falling

We haven't had the same opportunities since homecoming night to be completely alone in either of our houses. Annie served her time being grounded, which also meant that for two weeks, *I* felt grounded, because the only person I wanted to be going out with on Saturday night had been locked behind the walls of the house next door. I've tried to focus on myself, but I'm rather boring, I've decided. I've had to relieve myself more than a few times, using images of her from homecoming to fuel my thoughts.

The second Saturday, I asked some of the guys if they wanted to go see a movie. I needed out of my house that looked out over hers. A few of the guys from the team had thrown me a bone and gone out with me to see the latest action-adventure. It was an 'ok' movie but, when I drive home, I looked over at the Campbell house and just wanted to go see my girl. My only saving grace is that I get to see her each morning during the school week. I've gotten up early and been over at her house way too early to get extra time with her. Her parents seem ok with me being at breakfast even if she is grounded, so I start a new routine. We use the extra time in the parking lot to catch up on kisses. I can't touch her like I want, but the kisses are burning and get my heart racing.

***

When Annie is finally given her phone back and released from her two-week sentence, we agree that the alarm is a 'stop and put on clothing, no excuses' alarm. She's been so sick of having to stay home that we both agree to go to the batting cages to get out. She's been good at it, but I make a point to join her in the cage. I step behind her, helping her with the motion of her swing. I am making up a reason to touch her; I want to feel her against me. Annie knows I don't need to help her, but she does a little wiggle in my arms, pushing herself into my body more as I help her. It looks like I'm not the only one wanting to touch. When I took my turn, I didn't have the guy change the speed of the machine: it was fun to hit the ball at this lesser speed. I do love the crack of the ball against the bat, and I've connected on all the balls left in our bucket. After the last ball connects, she whistles playfully, asking me for an autograph. "I want the first official autograph when you make it to the big leagues," she says. I promise that if I make it, the first autograph will be for her. She pulls my helmet off my head, then pulls my body against hers, kissing me deeply, not caring who's watching.

***

We've taken to hanging out at one of our houses almost every day. We do try to connect with our friends, too, but it feels good to be together, no matter the event or activity. Annie is still the girl who loves sports, and she plans a few events around baseball and football. Tonight, she's invited everyone over for the Norman game. Before her, I didn't get into college football, but watching with her is entertaining. She yells at the TV, telling them, *pass, pass, pass* or *get him, get him, get him*. It is a close game; she's even gotten up from next to me, pacing the living room. Most of our friends are pretty big fans, too. It makes these game nights fun and full of conversation. Craig has joined Annie in her pacing as Norman drives the field on offense. Luke is sitting on the edge of his seat, focused on the plays—he has even stopped his wisecracks. I watch, and when the QB connects with the tight-end, the group goes crazy. Craig wraps up Annie in a hug, and Luke joins them in the celebration of the touchdown and eventually the win. Everyone goes home, and I'm the only one here now, snuggling my girl on the couch, kissing her occasionally. Her dad has established a pattern of coming to the end of the hallway but not into the room to tell us it was almost curfew. He is the "curfew king," as Annie calls him at the end of the night. Annie always walks me to the front door, and we steal one more moment before I have to head home.

***

Annie comes over to my house a lot, but she's yet to be completely comfortable messing around like we did after homecoming. Sure, we've removed clothing again, but it is only in half measures and never both of us at the same time. I understand her position; even if my parents don't care, they are in the house. I've let her know that in all the years I've been bringing girls home, I've never had them check in, but she isn't convinced. She tells me more than once it would be her luck that one time she'd give in, we would be interrupted. She'd never be able to show her face at my house again. Her other reason is that we both tended to be vocal in our climax. She gives me the example of me chanting "So good, Angel" at a pretty loud volume on homecoming night. I joke back, "At least they would know that something behind my door was SOOOO GOOOOD," and she throws a playful punch into my upper arm. She replies, "Well, in that train of thought, they would also discover that I know your name," and she jokingly moans, "DDDRRREEEWW." That sound from her turns my blood to fire, and I want to get her undressed again.

***

Thanksgiving is next week, and Annie is going to be gone all week, visiting her grandparents in Texas. I'm not looking forward to almost a week without her. We've planned a full day of activities to do today before she leaves tomorrow. I suggested to my parents yesterday that they needed to get out on Saturday night. Mom has been focused on a new project, and they both said it sounded like a good idea. After Mom headed back into her studio, Dad clapped me on the back. He'd told me to have fun, but that he wasn't old enough for grandkids. I'd told him he didn't have anything to worry about. He'd patted me on the back again before walking away. I mean, I did want to have sex with Annie, but I wasn't going to rush her to it. I wasn't going to try to squeeze our first time together in before my parents got home from a date. Her first time should be special, and I am still trying to figure out when she might let me know she is ready and how to make it something we both never forget. Tonight, I am ok with getting her completely naked in my bedroom and having her shout and moan my name again. She'd be able to be vocal to her heart's content with the empt y house.

***

Now, I am trying to be patient in my room, waiting for her to text me. I lost my patience by noon, I'm "pathetic". I picked up my phone send a message to her.

Drew

You almost ready?

Annie Campbell

225

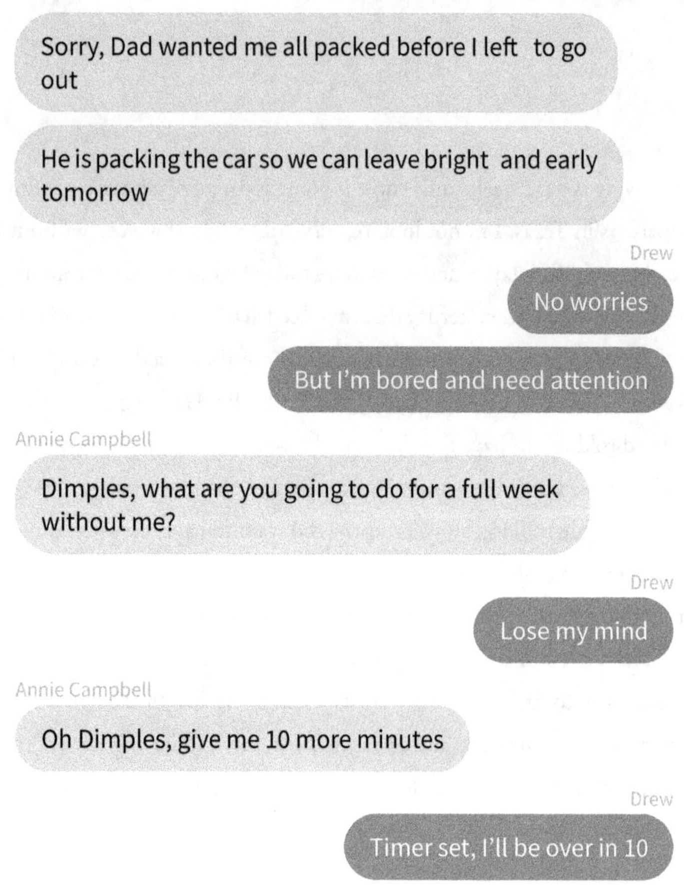

I don't know what I'm going to do for a week without Annie. I'll make sure to get in all the drills Coach has given me. I've already planned a few times at the batting cages with Craig and Luke. I'm sure I'll see Daniel at some point over the week since he will be home. Maybe I'll make the effort to see if he wants to do any gaming while he is home. That is one of the few things that Annie isn't into. She's humored me, watching me and the guys playing the latest football game, but she mostly looks at her phone, snuggling into my side while we name-call and give each other shit.

***

It's hard to think of my life over the last four months without thinking of moments with Annie. It's easier with her than any other relationship I've had before. In past relationships, I've had thoughts of the girl being clingy or that I've gotten bored in their company. In the case of girls like Meg, things had faded into friendship. With Annie, we'd started as friends, and the chemistry has only increased; there has been no hint of it decreasing as we spend more time together. I wanted to chalk it up to the fact that we haven't had sex, but I can't because I've noticed my heart racing in weird moments. Moments like when we are just snuggled together, or when she is talking to me about my future career. As I think about this feeling, I think she may be leading me to have to find a new answer to the question, "What's something you've never done in a relationship?" I check my phone. The ten minutes are up, and I'm done waiting to see my girl.

Chapter 48: Best Laid Plans
-Annie-

After Drew texted me to check in, I've been scrambling to finish all the tasks that Mom and Dad have for me. I'm finishing when I hear the doorbell. I can hear Dad and Drew talking about the upcoming Kansas City game on Sunday. I like that Dad is making an effort to get to know Drew. He still calls him Davis, which cracks me up a little. I'm not sure why he started doing it, but it's stuck. I grab my bag and head down the stairs. They've changed subjects to baseball, and I know that I need to get Drew out the door quickly. Baseball is the game they both can spend hours on, passing back opinions and facts. When I round the corner from the stairs I can see they are still standing by the door. Drew turns to look at me, and he smiles. I can't get over how good he looks—it is constantly catching me off guard. I love seeing that dimple before he returns his attention to the conversation with Dad.

Joining them in the hallway, I interrupt by reminding them that we have a booked bowling alley lane we don't want to miss out on. Dad reminds me like normal that my curfew is earlier tonight due to our drive tomorrow and I hold up my phone. An alarm is already set for 10:30 p.m. Drew chuckles at my side, because it's the standard thirty minutes before my actual curfew so we can give ourselves time to calm down and, in some cases, find clothing that has been removed. I give him a side glance to cut it out, and he just laughs harder. Dad doesn't get what is so funny and, thank God, he doesn't ask what is funny. I grab Drew's hand and say goodbye to Dad. I drag Drew towards his car, laughing along with him the whole time.

***

We do really have a lane at the bowling alley scheduled. We are meeting as a friend group to have a little time together before the holiday break. Our friends are already setting up the lanes when we arrive. Craig is single again, having broken up with his last girlfriend. He's bullied Travis to join us tonight. According to Craig, it's okay to be part of a group of couples as long as you're not the third wheel or the odd man out. Meg and Tom are still going strong, and they've even started talking about the possibility of going to the same college next year and have been applying to a few of the same schools. Meg is anxious to get to spring and see if they get into any of the same ones. Luke was still dating Katie; they are cute together, and Katie seems like she is pretty committed to Luke.

We've split our group of eight between two lanes. Since Drew and I are competitive, we've been grouped with Craig and Travis. I'm distracted, talking to everyone, when Craig yells at me to start our lane. I look up, expecting to see my name, but it reads instead: Love Bird 1, followed by Love Bird 2, Champ, and Loser. I'm going to assume that Champ is Craig, because he'd been the one on the screen when we arrived, leaving Loser to be Travis, with me as Love Bird 1 and Drew as Love Bird 2. The butterflies flutter to life looking at the word *love* on the screen. My brain makes some connection from the butterflies in my stomach to the word love in front of me. *Is that what this feeling is? Do I love Drew?* Before I can even answer myself, Craig interrupts my thoughts. "Annie, you scared." I answer, "Never," and I grab my ball and get a strike.

After I get out of my head, I enjoy bowling with our friends. We eat all the greasy foods offered by the snack bar. Craig flirts with the girl at the register, earning us extras on all our orders. We've been sitting here for a few minutes after the last game as a group, chatting. I'm wrapped up in Drew's arms and he leans in, whispering into my ear, "My house is empty." I look at him and say quietly, "How?" "My parents are having a date night out, at my suggestion. If we want to enjoy the time, I suggest we leave now," he whispers into my ear. I make our excuses almost immediately. I am sure with Drew's smirk, our friends see through my excuses to leave, but they don't call me out on it.

***

Drew parks his car in the garage, and I don't wait for him to open my door. I get out, and I don't wait for him to lead me into his house, either. I want to be bold, and it's so much easier to do it when we have the house to ourselves. "Can you carry this for me?" I ask as I hand over my bag and jacket. He gives me a little confused look and says, "Sure." I continue, "Oh, this too." I hand over my shirt. He is smiling now and continues to follow me into the house. I don't turn towards his bedroom but towards the living room. "What about this one?" I say as I take off my bra and throw it at his head. "I think I'll be able to handle whatever you're going to remove, Angel." I hear my bag and items hit the hardwood floor, and I'm being spun around to face him before his lips are on mine.

***

"I want you naked, Drew, and sitting there." I point to a spot on the couch when we break the kiss. "Angel, that doesn't seem fair —you're only half naked" he replies. I pull out of his arms and shimmy out of my jeans and shoes, throwing them on the pile of my clothes already on the floor. I'm only left in my black thong. "Fuck, Annie" is all that he says before he strips out of all his clothing except his boxers. We are out of arms reach, looking at each other. Neither of us make the first move, just enjoying looking at all the exposed skin in the shadows of the room. "I thought I said I wanted you naked," I say finally. His dimple appears, and he leans down, pulling his boxers off and throwing them on the pile of clothing. "And I think you said sit here right," he moves to the spot on the couch. His ass looks good in the shadows, and I have to give my brain a little shake to remember what I planned during the car ride from the bowling alley.

After he sits, he looks up at me. "You joining me, Angel?" I walk over and straddle him. The only thing separating us is one very small piece of fabric. I kiss him, and the world lights on fire. His hands aren't idle: they are all over my body as we kiss. I'm not sure where my lips and tongue end and his begin as our kisses continue to build. I know I'm going to have to make my next move and break this kiss, but I'm going to give myself a moment to enjoy his hands and his kisses before I do. What feels like just minutes later, I know I need to make my move—our time isn't unlimited, after all. I don't want his parents to come home to us in the living room.

So, I break the kiss and start to kiss my way down his jaw. While I do, his hands have found my breasts, and he is running his thumbs across my nipples. This next move is going to kill me, because I want his hands on my body, but they can't stay where they are. So, I pull my body back out of his hands. My mouth moves lower on his chest. I kiss across his pecs and suck on his nipple before continuing my path. "Annie," Drew groans into the near darkness. It's the thing I need to continue to be bold and set the final piece of my plan in action. My knees hit the plush throw rug, and my face is level with his dick at the perfect level like I thought it would be. I know I have a smirk on my face at my plan coming together. I suck him into my mouth and hear "AANNNNIIEE" break from Drew's mouth, and I know I've got him right where I want him.

Chapter 49: On Her Knees

-*Drew*-

Annie was quiet on the drive from the bowling alley. It didn't feel wrong, but I also wasn't sure what she was thinking. When we got into the garage and she started stripping her clothing off, I wanted to see where she was going to lead me. I'm not a stupid man, and I know that when Annie is in control, it only means good things for me. I take each piece of clothing she offers until she's topless in my living room. I'm confused why we are here and not my room, but I'm not going to interrupt the show. She leaves her back to me, and I need to see her perfect boobs, so I drop all her stuff on the floor, spinning her into my arms to kiss her.

She doesn't want me in control, and she breaks the kiss to tell me, "I want you naked, Drew." Then she points to the corner of the couch. I can't help but point out that she's not playing fair. She pulls away from me, and it feels wrong being separated from her body. But I'm rewarded with her slipping off her shoes and sliding her jeans down her body. She's left in a dark-colored thong. I remove everything but my boxers faster than I've ever undressed in my life. We stand in silence, looking over each other in the dim light that comes from the window and the porch light outside. Annie breaks the silence. "I thought I said I wanted you naked." I smile and know that I'll do everything she tells me to do. I remove my boxers, head in the direction she'd pointed me to on the couch, and sit down.

We are now on different levels, and I have to look up to take in her beautiful bod
y.

"You joining me, Angel?" I say, because she's looking over at me. I need her to
touch me, and I need to touch her. I can't see her whole face in the light, but I
see the smile appear, and then the next thing I know, she is straddling me. Her
body is pressed against me, and her thong is separating my dick and her pussy.
She kisses me, and I am lost in the moment. I'm running my hands over her bare
ass and thighs. I start to run them up her sides, right under her boobs. In too
short a time, she is breaking the kiss, but her lips don't leave my body. They are
making their way along my jaw and then my neck. I think as she sucks on my
skin that she's probably leaving a hickey. I'll wear it like a badge of honor until
she is back in my arms. With the new angle of our bodies, I can slip my hands
between us and wrap my hands over her boobs, running my thumbs over her
raised nipples. I'm about to try to move my face to taste her when she starts to
pull out of my hands. Her kisses continue down my chest, and she distracts me
further by sucking my nipple into her mouth. I groan her name into the dark
because that surprises me and sends a pulse of pleasure through my body. I feel
her body sliding down me, and I am now understanding why she picked the
living room with the low couch. I can feel her hair tickling my thighs, and then
her mouth is around me, and I let out a loud, "AANNNNIIEE."

***

I'm not sure how she gets better each time she takes me into her mouth, but she
does. She is twirling her tongue along the head of my dick and then taking it
down her throat. I grab her hair and pull it out of her way. I wish we had better
light, but I can see the outline of my dick disappear into the outline of her face,
and it's intoxicating to watch. She has learned what is my undoing. She has me
at the edge in no time at all. I should slow her down, but I can feel my release. I

233

don't want to deny myself or her for all her efforts tonight. "I'm going to cum,"
I say, closing my eyes and leaning my head back. She works me faster, and when
I cum she swallows and releases my dick from her mouth with a pop.

Before I can even open my eyes, a voice breaks the silence. "Well, at least she
started giving head." I feel Annie freeze between my knees, and I open my eyes
to see my brother leaning in the doorway of the kitchen.

I grab the throw blanket from the back of the couch, wrapping it around Annie
and pulling her into my lap. "What the fuck, man," I shout at Daniel. He laughs,
"Man, good for you, she'd barely let me get her undressed." I don't want to
talk about Annie naked with my brother, but another part of me does feel
relieved that her time was limited with him, that he never got to see her the way
I do. "Daniel, get the hell out of the room," I say, not giving his statement the
attention I know he wants. He doesn't move and continues like I haven't said
anything. "Was she a virgin when you fucked her? I bet she was: it's the whole
reason I humored her in the first place. She was a cock tease, so I found someone
willing to fuck that didn't require all the work." I feel Annie flinch against me.

I want to shut him up, but I also don't want to leave her. She's naked in the
blanket, and I'm naked underneath her. I need to get us and our clothes so we
can get dressed. I need to remove her from being anywhere near Daniel. "Daniel,
I mean it, shut the fuck up and leave." I'm trying not to shout in Annie's ear, but
I want him to understand. He laughs and finally moves into the kitchen. I stand
up with Annie wrapped in the blanket in my arms and carry her to my bedroom.
I set her on the side of my bed. I make to go back for our clothing, and she grabs
my arm. "Drew, please don't bother with Daniel, just come back quickly, ok?" I
lean in and kiss her on her forehead. "You got it, Angel. I'll be right back." I keep
my word, grabbing our stuff from the living room and completely ignoring that
my brother is in the house.

Chapter 50: How Are They Related?

I feel powerful again hearing Drew groan my name as he cums. As I remove his dick from my mouth, I look up at him. He looks so content with his head resting against the back of the couch; his eyes are still closed from his orgasm, and he is breathing heavily. I realized tonight at the bowling alley that I am falling in love with Drew. I'm already in love with him. I'm not sure why tonight my brain clicked, but it has now, and I can't help thinking *I love this boy* as I watch his reaction to our experience together. I realize that I want to be in his lap, surrounded by him, that I want to kiss those lips and feel his hands on my body. I'm about to get up from my position on the floor to climb into his lap when my lust is doused by the voice behind me. "Well, at least she started giving head."

OMG, my brain shouts, because I know that voice—it belongs to Daniel. I freeze. I know I should move because my whole backside is practically bare, the straps of my thong the only thing that would be covering my body from his view. Drew jumps into action and grabs a blanket from the back of the couch, wrapping it around me before pulling me across his lap, completely covered. His relaxed expression has been replaced with anger. I've never seen him wear this expression, and I think that is why his words feel so jarring that follow. "What the fuck, man?" I don't turn towards Daniel when he speaks again. I watch Drew's expression, because Daniel referenced the fact that he's had me naked before.

Drew's so mad, and some part of me thinks that maybe I should have been a little more transparent about where I'd gone with my "rebranding" sessions last year with Daniel. I'd wanted to keep my mistakes with Daniel in the past because that is what they were. The temporary thrill I'd had with Daniel last year is nothing compared to the feelings I have for Drew. Drew's body is so tense. I wish I could touch him, but he is focused on his brother. Drew tells him to leave again, but it's clear we are going to hear what Daniel wants to say because he continues without responding to Drew. "Was she a virgin when you fucked her? I bet she was: it's the whole reason I humored her in the first place. She was a cock tease, so I found someone willing to fuck that didn't require all the work."

I flinch, I can't help it. Daniel's words are harsh and surprise me. *Is that what had been going on last year?* My conversation with Miles comes to mind about Daniel's locker room bragging. I'd been the next notch in his belt. He'd wanted to be able to brag about taking my virginity. I've never been so happy that things didn't go further. I only register the conversation has ended when Drew wraps his arms around my back and my knees, lifting me as we move from the couch. I want to wrap my arms around his neck, but he's got this blanket wrapped so tight around me that I'm cocooned against him. He carries upstairs and sets me down on the edge of his bed. He moves like he's going to leave, and I untuck myself from the blanket and grab his arm. I don't want him to go back down there and get in a fight with his brother. I hear my quiet voice in the dark. "Drew, please don't bother with Daniel, just come back quickly ok?" The room is too dark to see his expression, but he leans down and kisses my forehead gently before saying, "You got it, Angel. I'll be right back."

***

I get up and turn on his bedroom light while he is downstairs. True to his word, he's back quickly, still naked but carrying a pile of all our clothes. I get up, still wrapped in the blanket, and help him with shutting the door and turning the lock, because who the hell knows if Daniel will try to interrupt us again? Not that we'll be doing anything to interrupt, but still, it makes me feel better to lock him on that side of the door. I can still appreciate the view of a naked Drew as he walks over to his bed. He does have a nice ass, and I appreciate seeing it in the light of his room this time and not the shadows from earlier. He drops the pile on the end of his bed, grabs his boxers from the top, and covers my view of his ass. I let out a little sigh and join him beside the bed. He hands over my jeans, and I drop the blanket to the floor. He does turn to watch me pull them up, saying, "Is it normal to feel disappointed when you get dressed? Because that is what I feel when you cover your body." "Nope, I thought the same thing when you put on your boxers." It's easy to say the truth with him. My words earn me a peek of his dimple, and we continue to get dressed. After we are fully dressed, I check the time. We still have about thirty minutes before my warning alarm. When I look up, he is sitting on the edge of the bed. He's pinching his eyebrows in worry, completely zoning out.

I put the phone back down stepping between his legs and place my hands on either side of his handsome face. "What are you thinking? "I'm sorry. You didn't deserve to hear any of that." He raises his hand in a gesture toward the direction of the living room. He continues, "He's an asshole, I'm sorry." I tip his face up to make eye contact. "You don't have anything to be sorry about, if anything I should be apologizing." He goes to interrupt me, and I rest my thumbs against his lips, stopping him from interrupting me. "No, hear me out. I'm sorry that I didn't see through him last year. I should have at least prepared you by telling you what had happened and what hadn't. You didn't deserve him trying to push your buttons talking about me like that."

Drew lets out a breath against my thumbs. He grabs my hands against his face and moves my thumbs off his mouth. "Annie," he starts and takes a deep breath, "I knew you had a history, and maybe it was stupid, but I still don't want you to tell me anything outside of the conversation we had at mini-golf. That was all the information I needed." He continues, "I don't want either of our pasts to ruin this, to ruin us." I can't help myself: I step closer to him and kiss him. It's a gentle kiss. I think "*I love you*" while my lips are on his, but I don't say the words out loud because it's not the right time after what just happened. When we break the kiss, Drew suggests watching the next episode of the new football documentary we started, and I agree. Drew lets me use his chest as my pillow, and I try to focus on the episode, but I get lost in the beating heart underneath my ear instead.

Chapter 51: He Started It

Annie shocked me with her apology after the events with Daniel. She looked so worried, like what Daniel said would change how I'd look at her. *How do I get her to realize that isn't possible?* That I'm all in with her, that she's my whole world, that I love her. I don't think I can, at least right now, not with the mix of emotions in my blood. I'm trying to fight the rage that is still under my skin. So, I suggest the documentary because we need to cool down, I need to cool down. Annie is lying on my chest as we watch the show. I can't seem to focus on what is being said or who is being interviewed. My thoughts are swirling in a million directions, and my only real focus is on my hand drawing little shapes along her back. I register that I'm not just drawing any shape, I've been drawing hearts over her back because even my unconscious mind knows this girl has my heart.

***

I walk her home a few minutes before curfew, and we don't get the normal open-door thumbs up from her dad. It's going to suck without her over the next week. When did seeing her feel like air, a requirement for my body to function? "I'm going to miss you," I tell her. She gives me a little smile, "I'm going to miss you, too." We both step closer before sharing a deep kiss. "See you soon, Dimples—don't forget me while I'm away," she says quietly into the night before stepping out of my arms. "You're too important to forget, Angel." I only move after I hear the bolt slide shut.

***

The next morning, I come downstairs, and Daniel is already with my parents having breakfast. "You have a good night, Drew?" Mom asks when I sit down. Before I can answer, Daniel interjects, "I'm pretty sure he was satisfied." I kick him under the table. Mom does her little narrowing of the eyes that she does when she is trying to figure out what she missed. I turn to Mom. "It was a good night. How about you all?" "It was nice to get out. Thanks for reminding us about that gift card." Daniel laughs next to her. "What's so funny, Danny?" Mom asks. I mentally prepare for what could come out of his mouth. "Sweet little Drew, right Mom?" he says, then adds, "It's so sad you missed seeing him and Annie enjoying personal time in the living room."

Mom makes that little narrowing eye thing again, trying to figure out what she could have missed. I can tell when she gets an idea of what could have been going on in the living room, and she half chokes on her coffee. Before either of my parents can comment, I look at my brother and feel the anger in my tone. "Daniel, I'm not sure how to get you to understand the words SHUT THE FUCK UP." Mom's eyes, which had been narrowing, go wide. We may get away with a lot, and my parents may be more than understanding about having people over, but cussing and arguing aren't tolerated. "What, Drew? It's not like I said she'd missed out on your girlfriend's little performance on her knees," Daniel says with a smile on his face. I see actual red, and I stand up so quickly from the table, I knock over the chair. *Had he just said that in front of our parents?* Dad breaks into the conversation. "Daniel, that is enough. I'm not sure what the hell is going on but it's enough."

But it's not enough for my brother, because he continues. "Dad, come on, you have to know that Drew is getting my sloppy seconds with that girl next door." I'm not sure when I round the table, but I'm there in what feels like a flash, and I punch him square in the jaw, knocking him to the floor. Mom jumps up and is near the door. Dad is standing up, trying to step between us. "Daniel, when I said *shut the fuck up*, I meant it." I hear myself shouting. Daniel makes to get up and return the punch, but Dad has finally made it between us and blocks his way. Dad says to both of us, "That is enough," then tacks on, "Drew, why don't you head to your room, and we'll discuss your actions after you cool down." *Fine by me*, I think, and I leave having burned out my anger with the blow I've landed on Daniel's no longer smug face.

***

I'm responding to a message from Annie when I get a knock on my door almost an hour later. "Come in," I say and sit up on my bed. Dad makes his way into the room and sits on the desk chair. "Care to explain what happened at breakfast?" he starts. I give him a breakdown of what happened last night, trying to skim over the details of getting a blow job on the living room couch. Dad is silent and lets me give my side of the situation. He takes a second to respond when I'm finished. "You can't punch your brother over the breakfast table, Drew. I can understand that he was pushing the limits and his comments about Annie are uncalled for, but you still can't punch your brother. I can understand why you did it, but if you tell your mother that I gave you sympathy, I'll deny it with my last breath." I can't help the laugh that escaped from Dad's comment about Mom. "Your mom has suggested taking your phone for a few days as punishment for the punch, and I've agreed." I go to protest, but he holds up his hand. "Your mom wanted you to apologize, but I let her know that I didn't agree with making you do that. I've explained to her I'd have done the same thing if your uncle had said something like that about her."

I appreciate Dad trying to lessen the fallout from my punch over breakfast. "Can I have like fifteen minutes to let my friends know? I'd been planning to meet a few of them at the cages this week." "Sure, bring it down to me when you've made your friends aware," he says as he gets up from the chair and heads for the door. "Son, if I can offer you some small advice?" I look up from my phone, giving him my attention, "Maybe don't tell Annie exactly what your brother said to your Mom and me. I'd hate for her to be uncomfortable the next time she's over." It's pretty good advice, and I thank him before he leaves the room. He makes his way down the hall, and I think for Mom's benefit he says loudly, "You have fifteen minutes and I better get that phone, Drew." I open my phone, but I don't text the guys. I text Annie.

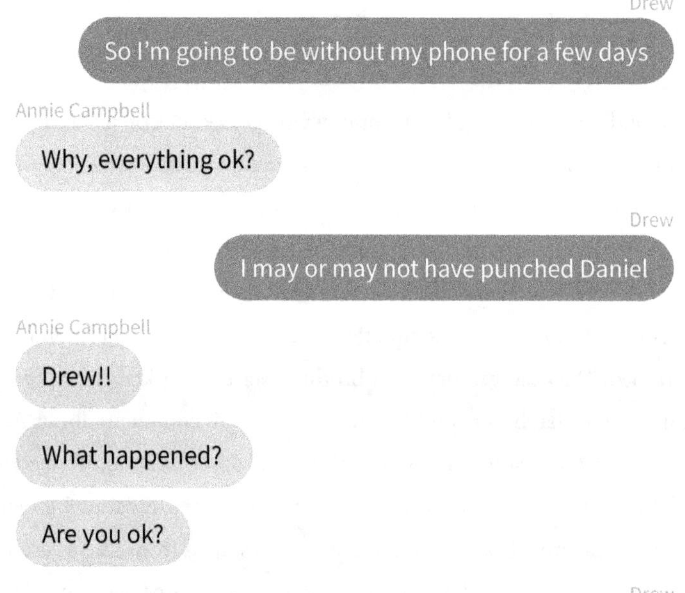

I do text a few of the guys, telling them my phone is being confiscated. I let them know when I'll be at the batting cages, and if they can make it, great, if not, don't worry about it. I hand over my phone and start to count the seconds until Thanksgiving break is over.

Chapter 52: Catching Up

-*Annie*-

Thanksgiving break has been fun with my family, and it is always great to see all my aunts, uncles, and cousins. but I've missed Drew the whole trip. I've kept texting him randomly over the week, knowing perfectly well he wouldn't see them until the end of the week. I've made sure to keep all my texts and pictures PG-rated just in case his parents check his phone. In the space left by Drew's inability to answer, I've taken to texting Meg more. I need to tell someone about my epiphany that *I love Drew*. Who better to tell than my best friend?

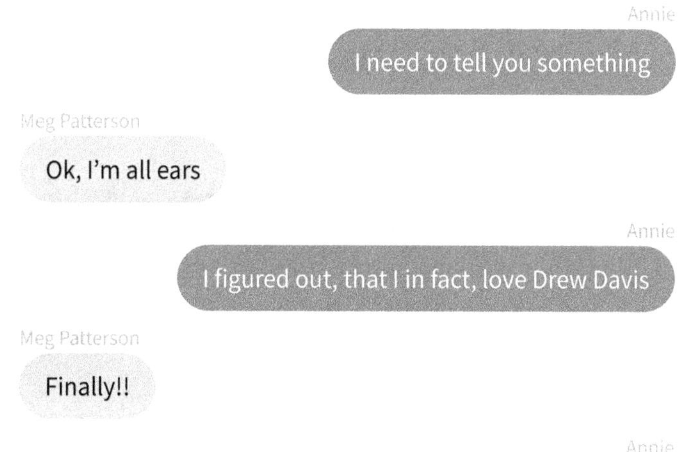

What do you mean finally?

Meg Patterson

I mean finally you two have been inseparable   since you started dating!

What did he say when you told him?

Annie

Well….

I haven't told him yet

I just figured it out during bowling last weekend

Meg Patterson

Took you long enough

Why not tell him after bowling?

Annie

Because.. ok I'm warning you I'm about to text a novel

Meg Patterson

I've got my reading glasses ready

Annie

So we went back to Drew's house…

I did a little strip clothing thing in his living room then proceeded to give him a blow job on the couch

Meg Patterson

OMG, ANNIE MARIE!!!

Proud of you for owning your sexy self

Stop interrupting

Hold comments until the end of the story

KK

So.. where was I....

Ok, so we are both naked, or mostly naked, I finish the blow job and I'm still between Drew's legs when Daniel speaks

WHAT???

Wait was he watching you blow his brother.

Sorry no more comments until you are finished

Drew covered me up in a blanket

Daniel tells him that he's seen me naked then continues to tell us that he only messed around with me last year because he wanted my v-card

Told Drew good job for getting me on my knees and getting my v-card

Meg Patterson

Gross, so glad you kept that card

I meant from Daniel

How did Drew react?

Annie

He was so mad

I've never seen him angry

Meg Patterson

Really, he'd been pretty mad the night Daniel kissed that cheerleader

Annie

I don't remember him being mad

Meg Patterson

Yeah, you had other worries

Well he was but I get it not normal Drew

Annie

After that it didn't seem like the night to say I love you

Meg Patterson

Yeah understandable

Annie

Meg Patterson

Annie

Meg Patterson

Annie

Meg Patterson

Annie

Meg Patterson

Annie

Meg Patterson

Meg Patterson

After sex, but it had been like the sex that is all feelings- so love making kind of sex

It's hard to explain

Meg Patterson

No, because its not even sex I've had before him, its different

Meg Patterson

Let's start with the words my virgin BFF

But lets go shopping when you are back

I think we should update your private   wardrobe

Meg Patterson

There's nothing like getting to catch up with your best friends. Meg has helped me get out all the worry about if he'd doesn't say it back or if I should say it first. I'm not going to rush it, but the next time I think it, I vow to myself that I'll say it out loud to him. Meg and I start a great debate on which color of lingerie I should buy. She says black, but my signature color has always been red.

Chapter 53: Saying Three Little Word

This week went by slowly without being able to communicate with her. I met the guys at the cages and took my frustration out with my bat. Craig said he was going to get me grounded during the season, so I could get some easy homers. I'd laughed, but I wasn't going to go another week without talking to Annie: even if it got me more home runs, it wasn't worth it. At home, I've avoided Daniel as much as humanly possible. We had to eat together on Thursday, but I've avoided all our living spaces most of the week. He's leaving any minute, and I am ready to see him go. Mom has been sad at breakfast. I hate to see Mom sad, but I am so ready to have the house back.

***

My phone is dead when I get it back. I put it on the charger after breakfast, and it takes forever to stop blinking the charging symbol before it finally has enough battery to turn on. I'm greeted with a picture of me and Annie, but no notifications. Maybe she didn't text me all week. I open the lock screen, and I smile because this is my favorite picture of Annie by herself. Then the phone buzzes to life, and I get so many notifications that it makes me smile. I think my girl missed me, too. I click on one of the notifications and am directed to her missed messages.

It's been 10 minutes since your last message and I'm still missing you

I still miss you

I better get details why I had to go without talking to you for a week

We ate turkey today! Oh and I still miss you

My grandma thinks you're a cutie

She also told me to have fun whatever that means

Still miss you

How many days is a few days? It feels like its been way more than a few

I should have told you to write me a paper version of text messages

I miss you, do you miss me too?

I know we said PG but I miss kissing you and the lake, I miss it a LOT

Or couches, I miss couches

I can feel the smile on my face after reading her text messages. I think my girl missed me a lot. She's right, I should have written down every time I missed her, or wanted to text her or hear her voice. She'd have a fifty-page single-spaced report waiting for her. I leave my phone on the charger and head out the door, as my girl is next door, and I don't care that it's only 9 a.m. I NEED to see her.

***

I ring the doorbell as I second-guess my decision not to text her first. They'd gotten home late last night, maybe they are still sleeping. I'm about to turn around when Mrs. Campbell opens the door. She is still in her robe, but she smiles. "Oh, Drew, Annie is going to be so happy to see you. She made it clear that you didn't have your phone all break. Come on in—I think Annie is still asleep, but why don't you go ahead and check? Let her know her dad is still asleep, so we'll have breakfast in, say, forty-five minutes." Her mom winks at me and heads towards their kitchen. I'm not sure what just happened, but I think Annie's mom gave me permission to go welcome my girl home. I make my way quietly up the stairs to Annie's room. I think about knocking, but her mom said she may still be sleeping. I could sneak in and snuggle in with her until she wakes up. I crack the door and peek inside, and sure enough, Annie is still sleeping. I open the door enough to slip in and then shut the door again. I slip out of my shoes so that when I make it to the bed, I can slip inside the covers.

I feel a little funny, tip-toeing around my girlfriend's room. I probably look ridiculous, too. I'm not a small guy, and the room is full of sunlight from her window. I get to the end of her bed and check if she is still asleep, and she is. God, she is gorgeous, and she is just sleeping. She has her hair in a half-undone bun on the top of her head, and her face is so relaxed in sleep. I notice what she is wearing. She's in my hoodie from our first date. I can't see anything else because her legs are covered by the blanket on her bed. I move to the empty side of the bed, and I lift the covers and slip in beside her.

She had been faced in the direction of the door, but my sliding into the bed caused her to turn her head in my direction. I'm about to tell myself 'Good job' for not waking her when I see her eyelids flutter open. When she first sees me, she gives a sleepy smile and closes her eyes, but then she opens them again wide. She reaches her hand out to touch my face. "Drew?" "In the flesh, Angel," I say as I smile. "Oh, how did you get here?" she asks, giving a glance at the door. "Your mom let me in. She said we have forty-five minutes until breakfast, and she let me know I could come up." Annie smiles. "I love my mom." I make to kiss her, and she holds me back. "Oh wait, morning breath, give me one minute." She jumps out of bed and heads to the bathroom. I get the quickest glimpse of her bare legs and feet as she dashes into the bathroom. There's at least one of my questions answered.

***

After a few minutes, she comes out of the bathroom and dashes back to bed. I raise the blanket so she can jump back in. She stretches out on her side next to me under the blankets. "Hi," she says before she scoots closer, wrapping her arms around my neck and kissing me. Since we are on our sides, one of my arms is pinned against my side, but I move the other one to her waist. The kiss starts gently, but as it normally does with us, it builds. I can feel Annie's leg lift over my hip, and my hand slides from her hoodie-covered hip to her very bare ass cheek. We are still kissing, and I'm not about to break my lips from hers to ask her if she is naked under my hoodie. I let my hands slide over her ass and back, never meeting any other material. She's completely naked in my hoodie, and my brain short-circuits. But my hand knows exactly what to do.

I move my hand, sliding it back down her back, and then I rotate my wrist, and I'm able to touch her front. With her leg around my hip, she is completely open for my touch. I touch her clit, and she moans into our kiss. I break from her lips, whispering, "Quiet, Angel, or someone could hear." I return my lips to her mouth and move my fingers down through her already wet pussy. She's soaked already, and it's sexy as hell to feel how turned on she is in my arms. I dip a finger in, and she bites down on my lower lip. Now, I'm the one trying to remember to be quiet, because that move sends pleasure through me. I spend time working in and out of her before adding another finger, and she bites down again. I can't help the small groan that leaves my mouth. I know I have to make this quicker than I'd like because her parents are downstairs. I push in and out of her, setting a steady pace, then I curl my fingers each time I'm pushing inside her. The walls of her pussy are starting to clamp down on my fingers, and I know that is a good sign. We aren't so much kissing anymore as she's using my lower lip to suck and bite. She latches her arm against mine and her body goes tight. Then her eyes open and her mouth makes a silent "Ohh" before letting out a quiet, breathy moan of "DRREEWW."

I slow my fingers and eventually pull them out of her body. Bringing them to my lips to lick the taste of her off them. I wish I had more time to dip under the covers and taste her, but I know that isn't possible. She looks all peaceful with her eyes closed and her head resting against her pillow. I almost think she's fallen back to sleep when she sits up. "Drew, go crack the door open, I'm going to get on clothing and be right back. I'm not going to get caught like this and get myself grounded." I laugh but follow my orders. I'm back on her bed outside the covers when she returns from the bathroom in leggings and a long-sleeved shi rt.

I prefer her in the hoodie, but she's right, we don't want to get caught like that and get her grounded after I just got my freedom back. She walks over to me and straddles me. "I've missed you, Angel." She wraps her arms around my neck and lays her head on my chest, hugging me before saying, "I missed you too, Dimples. Let's not do that again—I hated not getting to at least have some form of communication with you." I wrap my arms around her back and hug her tighter to me, placing my cheek on the top of her head. "Agreed." We sit like this in the silence of her room, snuggled together, not talking, just being in the same space. "I love you," I say into the silence. I know my heart is racing, but I needed to say it. A week without her made me realize each day that I did and do love this girl. Being here with her now, it feels right to say it. I feel her smile against my sternum and can feel the words against my heart as she says, "I love y ou, too."

Chapter 54: He's My Biggest Fan

Spring

The saying that time flies when you're in love is true. Christmas break came and went in a flash. Drew took me to the outdoor lights display at the local college, and we'd gone on a double date with Meg and Tom. We'd even gone on the horse-drawn carriage tour. It had been nice to sit next to the boy I loved in a winter wonderland. We'd even exchanged little gifts over the break. I'd given Drew a framed collage of my favorite photos of us, and he'd given me a number 17 necklace.

***

When school began again in January, we both started the lead into our spring sports. Drew practices with the team and then he drives three times a week to do speed drills with a specialized coach. Drew's coach has told him that he needs to show his speed on the field to gain the attention of the scouts. Both sides of the ball will be important if he wants to get drafted in June. Drew has also been gone a lot on college recruiting trips for his backup plan if the draft is a bust. I've had my fair share of college visits, too. We'd even had one in Norman together; it was nice to walk along the paths around campus together thinking about the possibilities. A huge part of my brain wants him to get drafted—after all, it is the dream he is chasing, the dream that he is working so hard for. A small piece of me hopes the draft won't work out, and he and I will both end up for the next four years in Norman. I always feel guilty when these thoughts happen, because I want the best for Drew, and I want him to get his dream.

***

Outside of our crazy schedules, we've filled in our free time with each other. If we aren't snuggled up in his room, we are snuggled up in mine. Our make-out sessions feel less frenzied but just as passionate: since saying *I love you*, we both feel no need to rush our moments together. That loving each other is a long-term feeling, and we aren't going anywhere. Drew even started doing his homework over at my house. We take over the kitchen table with our work spread between us. Sometimes we work on subjects for the same class and help each other complete the required assignments. It does go faster having someone to talk through complex math equations; they aren't my favorite anyway. Mom has even started to default to making him a plate at dinner because, more times than not, he is here and hungry, so it makes sense to include him in our family dinners.

***

As Drew has spent more time with my parents, I've spent more time with his in return. Mrs. Davis is a nice person, and her art is amazing. I've gotten lost listening to her tell me about the whats, whys, and feelings behind her work. It's amazing what she can do with a little paint and a blank canvas. In February, I asked her if she's ever painted something for the boys. She told me she'd painted their favorite comic book characters a few years back, but neither of them had asked for more. I asked her if she'd mind painting something for me to give to Drew as a present on the opening day of his senior season. I didn't want to inconvenience her, but an idea had popped into my head, and I thought it would be something special for Drew. She smiled so big and started peppering me with questions. I gave her a few examples of what I've been thinking could be something special for him. She told me it wouldn't be any trouble, and she loved the ideas I'd shared.

The whole month of February, I've been sneaking to his mom's studio. She's given me a little peek at the painting. At the end of February, I got a text from Mrs. Davis telling me to come over while Drew was at his private lessons. As soon as I arrived, she looped her arm in mine and led us straight to the studio. The painting is front and center. "I have a few minor touch-ups, but I'd say it is finished and ready for game day," she tells me, beaming. There in paint is the picture of Drew and me from the party, but she's replaced the background of my room with the school baseball field, and my jersey no longer sports my favorite Griffons numbers. We agreed to have her paint me in a Rams number 17 jersey instead. "He is going to love it," she piped in when I was quiet for too long. I turned, gave her a big hug, and thanked her. Waiting until the opening day is going to kill me.

***

After all these months together and all the moments we've shared, I know that I want my first time to be with Drew, and I want it to happen soon. But I'm not about to have my first time with one of our parents in the house. I don't care how easygoing Mr. and Mrs. Davis are. I know I'm not going to attempt that at my house, either. I keep expecting Drew to bring it up, but he hasn't, and that is frustrating me, too. I finally caved last week and talked to Meg about it. Meg being Meg told me that I should just bring it up. Drew is probably waiting for me to tell him I want to because, after all, I'm the only virgin in our relationship, and he is a nice guy. I am sure she's right: he's never pressured me on any other sexual stuff. If anything, he normally lets me determine the next step or action. So, with this realization in my head, I tell myself that if it hasn't happened by prom, I'll have to come up with a plan, and because my best friend is such a great planner, I make sure she's looped in to help.

***

Tonight, we kick off our first home soccer game and my last first game after all of these years of playing. I've known for years that I'm not good enough to make soccer a career. I've loved playing and enjoy being competitive on the field—I already know I'm going to miss the heck out of it when this season ends. Drew is wearing his Rams Girls Soccer shirt with my number on it all day at school. He tells me that he has to make sure it's well known that number 28 is taken, and he has the shirt to prove it. The guys are giving him a hard time when I show up at lunch, calling him whipped and in puppy love. Drew takes all our friends' jabs in stride and proudly replies, "Yes, I declare that I'm totally whipped, head over heels for number 28!" For good measure, he grabs my face and pulls me into a kiss. This draws plenty of *yuck* and *so gross* from Craig, Luke, and Travis. Meg calls out, "Give us more," playing up Drew's actions. When we finally break the kiss I say against his lips, "I love you, Dimples," and he replies, "Love you too, Angel."

Mom and Dad drive me to my game, because as much as it's my last first game, it's theirs, too. Mom is trying not to cry, I can tell, but she's keeping it together. When we go to separate at the field, Dad gives me a big hug. "Go kick some butt," he says and releases me to head in with Mom. I'm not sure why, but I have to fight the tears now, too. Our opponents are the Cardinals, and we more than outplay them most of the match. I've got two goals and I'm hoping for the hat trick. I see my opportunity and take it when my teammate gets a break on the ball. I can see both defenders getting pulled to her and the ball. I sprint forward, she waits until the last second to pass me the ball, and it's an amazing pass.

Now it's just me and the goalie. I do a fake shift of my hips to make her think I'm going to go low but then aim high, and my foot makes contact with the ball just right. I watch it sail into the right top corner over the goalie's head. "Goal Rams" is announced over the sound system, and my teammates all come together for a group hug to celebrate my hat trick. I look over in the stands and find my parents cheering and screaming in excitement, and then I find my friends. They are all decked out: Meg has a 28 painted on her face, but the guys have all come shirtless and have 28 painted across their chests. They are crazy, but they are mine, and I wouldn't change them for the world. I point at my favorite chest wearing 28 and make a little heart with my hands. Then he makes one back at me, and I turn my attention back to the game.

Chapter 55: She's My Biggest Fan

-Drew-

Annie seems shocked that I am so into her kickoff game tonight to open her soccer season. I can't help but feel a little proud of myself for making sure to celebrate her like this. I also can't help thinking the guys she dated before me are all losers, because her smile when she saw my number 28 shirt is worth the efforts I made to get it from the local sports store. Craig, Luke, and Travis give me a hard time at lunch about the shirt and being whipped when Annie arrived with Meg. She sits down, and as she does, I reply to the guys, "Yes, I declare that I'm totally whipped, head over heels for number 28." I can't help but notice the smile and blush on Annie's face at my declaration. I lean in to kiss her, not only to punctuate my statement, but also because I can't resist her. I can hear the comments from our group. I pull back, and she says against my lips, "I love you, Dimples." I say it back, because she's mine.

***

Before the game, Luke, Craig, and I meet in the parking lot and wait for Meg to arrive. "Did you tell Annie about this?" Luke asks. "Nope, it's a surprise," I say back to him. "It's going to get fucking cold shirtless. If I didn't love Annie,

I wouldn't be compromising my body like this," jokes Craig. I try not to notice that he said the word *love* and Annie in the same sentence. I know that he's her friend, but my lesser brain doesn't like any other guy saying they love her. I have to shake my head at my thoughts. Meg finally shows up, already sporting her 28 on her cheek.

"Disrobe, fellas," she smiles and shakes the body paint. "Cold, cold, cold—Meg, couldn't you have at least warmed up the paint before applying it?" Craig is whining seconds later. Luke and I laugh until it's our turn, and then we understand Craig's complaints, because damn, the paint is freezing as she brushes it across my stomach. Craig looks all smug wearing his jacket over his arms now that his paint is dry. "Meg, I swear, did you put the paint in the freezer? My nipples are like ice picks over here," Luke comments as Meg finishes the last few swipes on his chest. "Ok, ok, I think I'm done, enough whining out of you three," Meg says, looking over all of us. "She is going to love it. Now zip up those jackets so they let you into the game." We all do as we are told.

***

Inside the game, our little fan group finds seats right at the front of the stands. I do go up and say hi to Annie's parents in the stands. Mrs. Campbell's eyes are a little red and puffy. I think she's been crying, but she has a real smile when I greet them with, "Our girl's going to kill it tonight." Her dad agrees with me before I head back down to our friends. As I rejoin them, I can hear Meg reminding the guys, "Remember that you don't go shirtless until Annie gets her first goal, ok?" "Yes, Mom," we all jokingly say together. When the girls come out, we all chant, "Annie, Annie, Annie" to get her attention, and she smiles at us, then gives me a little heart with her fingers. It's the little code we said we would do for each other on the field. It takes less than five minutes for me to be shirtless with the guys. Annie doesn't notice right way because she's celebrating with her friends, but when she does, it is priceless. The look of appreciation for us all supporting her is totally worth it. She waves to us and gives us the thumbs-up motion followed by my h eart.

She doesn't let up the whole game, and by the end, she's completed a hat trick, securing the Rams the W for the game. As soon as the game is over, I put my jacket back on to warm up my upper half. On the way out, Luke comments, "Our war paint has done its job: time to put these guns away," before throwing his jacket back on and zipping it up. We leave the stands and huddle together with her parents to greet her on the way out of the locker room. She comes out pretty quickly, still dressed in her uniform minus the high socks and cleats. We all hang back and give her a minute with her parents. I can't hear what they are saying, but she makes a motion with her head in our direction. She hands over her bag to her dad and heads to us.

I scoop her up into a big hug when she reaches us. "There's my scoring queen," I say into her hair. "I'm glad you waited until I made the first goal, or your little shirtless stunt would have been distracting," she says, the whole time smiling at me. "Oh, no, he doesn't get to take all the credit," Luke pipes in. "I had hard nipples the whole game in your honor." "I also sat for the whole game half-dressed, please give me my credit too," joins Craig. I release Annie from my arms, and she makes her way to Luke and Craig, giving them both a hug, "Thank you, guys." She repeats the process with Meg before returning to my side. "Thank you all—it was cool to have you here tonight," she says, looking around our group. "It was fun to see you kick some butt out there. I wish we could come to more of the games, but I think we start crossing paths pretty much right away," says Luke. "Yeah, I know, it sucks. I'm going to hate to miss the baseball games, too," she replies. "Anyone hungry? I could do a pizza," interjects Craig. "I'm starving," Annie says, looking right at me. I almost choke on air, because my brain thinks, *she's not hungry for pizza.*

***

Last night after the game, Annie and I got pizza with our friends and came back to my house for a quick make-out session after dinner. Annie had to go home because her curfew was earlier on school nights. Now it is my turn to kick off a season, and this baseball season is the most important one of my life. I'm going to have to prove to the scouts that I'm ready. That I don't need college ball to give me time to make improvements. I'm lost in my thoughts when I head downstairs to grab breakfast. I'm a little caught off guard when I hear my mom and Annie in the kitchen. "Do you think he'll like it?" I hear Annie ask her. Mom answers, "Well, I hope so since I spent over a month working on it." "Thank you again, Mrs. Davis," I hear Annie say. Mom laughs, "Annie, darling, how many times do I have to tell you to call me Jennifer?" "Probably a few more, but I'll try, Jennifer," Annie replies. I can't help my chuckle, because her tone makes it clear that she'd prefer to call Mom Mrs. Davis versus Jennifer. Next thing I know, Annie pops out of the open doorway from the kitchen.

"Drew Davis, were you eavesdropping?" I'm delayed in my response, because Annie is in her jean skirt and my jersey. I mean, it's not my exact jersey that is in my locker at school, but she's in a Rams baseball jersey with a number 17 on full display. I eventually look around before shaking my head no to her question, "I would never, Angel." She steps into my space and pulls me into a kiss. "So, what has you over so early?" I ask when we break our kiss. "A surprise. Cover your eyes," she says, all excited. I don't want to cover my eyes. I want to look at my girl in my jersey. A quick vision of her only in my jersey crosses my mind, and I shut it down because she wants me to follow her into the kitchen. I know that my mom is in there, and I don't need to walk in sporting a hard-on. When she turns, I do take a peek, seeing the Davis across the back of the jersey. I like her sporting my last name.

I cover my eyes, feeling her pull me through the door frame safely. We stop, and then she turns me in the direction of the table. "Ok, open." I remove my hands, and at first, I can see my mom next to Annie in my peripheral, but my eyes are completely taken over by the canvas on the table. It's clear that it's a work of Mom's; it's got her signature style, but it's the subject of the art that has me shocked. It's Mom's take on the photo I took of me and Annie from the summer, where she'd been looking at me, and I'm looking up at the camera. Mom has played down the swollen lips, but she's captured the joy that we both are feeling.

I look at this photo now and wonder if this is the moment she started falling for me, because it's the same simple smile she gives me right before she tells me she loves me. After taking in our faces, I notice that Mom has painted Annie in my jersey in the photo too, and we aren't in her bedroom anymore. Mom has captured us like we are on the field. I turn my attention away from the canvas to look at Annie and Mom. They both look so nervous about my reaction. I reach out, wrapping them both in a group hug. "It's amazing." I pull back. "Mom, you did an amazing job." "Oh, thank you hunny, it was all Annie's idea. I just put it to canvas," Mom says, patting my arm. "Well, Angel, thank you for giving me my favorite Jennifer Davis painting." Annie blushes and smiles from me to Mom. "I still think it was all your mom, but you're welcome. Happy opening da y."

Chapter 56: Acceptance

Opening day has been a great game by all accounts. I've been able to get on base with each at-bat during the game. I've even been able to steal a base, showing off my speed on the bags. I've been working so hard all off-season to be able to show what I can do on the field. In the top of the seventh, I help secure the win by relaying a ball from our outfielder to the catcher, achieving the last out of the game. After celebrating with the team, I get my sideline interview from the hottest girl at the game. It takes everything in me to not kiss her right there on the field in front of all the coaches, fans, and my teammates, but I stay focused on giving her the clip she needs. I meet quickly with Coach and he says to keep up this effort, and the scouts would start calling. I leave his office and exit the ballpark into the parking lot. I have the hottest girl waiting for me with open arms, wearing my number.

***

Annie has been checking her online portals at each of the schools she's applied to. She's already gotten the "Congratulations, you've been accepted" message from three schools. Norman is the holdout; every time she checks it, the status still says pending. I applied to the same schools without telling her. I've only been accepted at one of the three she has so far. College is my backup, but if the draft fails, I am going to be heavily influenced by her college destinations on where I should be, too. Today during practice, Coach asks me for a minute. I join him in his office to learn that he'd heard from the head coach at Norman. I'm getting an offer to play for their program—it should be updated in the portal any day. Now, I'm sitting with Annie in her kitchen, doing homework. I want to tell her my news, but I also don't want her to panic that she still hasn't heard anything. She wants into Norman so bad, I don't want her to stress even further about it with my news. So, I figure that until she's heard from them, I'll keep my news to myself.

***

Five days later, I'm lying in her bed, playing on my phone, and she's at her desk looking at her computer. She screams! I sit up with a flash. "Are you ok?" She doesn't even respond to me at first. Then: "I GOT IN, I GOT IN," she chants, spinning herself around in the chair to face me. She is up from the chair and in my lap in one jump move. "Drew, I got into Norman, I did it!" The expression on her face is total awe. Her dad bangs into the room. "What's wrong?" He looks at us, then turns towards the hallway as he says, "Annie, can you please remove yourself from Drew's lap? Please let me know everything is ok."

Annie smiles at me before jumping up, going to her dad and tapping him on the shoulder, "I got in, Dad. I did it, Norman here I come." He scoops her up and spins her around. "Congratulations, Annie, I'm so proud of you." He yells down the hall to get Mrs. Campbell's attention. When she arrives, Annie relays the same message, and her mom starts to cry. Annie and her dad pull her into their celebratory hug. For a moment, I feel a little weird just sitting and watching this family moment. If they weren't blocking the only door to the room, I'd try to leave to give them this moment. Instead, I look on at them all celebrating before I hear Mrs. Campbell say, "Drew, get yourself over here," and I join in on their celebration.

***

Annie's parents decide that we need celebratory pizza, so they go back downstairs to order the pizza, leaving us alone in Annie's room again. I lay back down on her bed like I'd been before her scream, but Annie doesn't take up the same spot on the chair. She follows me and lies down on her side, wrapping her arm around my waist and sliding her leg between mine. "Congratulations, Annie," I say because yes, I'd said it in front of her parents, but I want to say it now when it is just us. "Thank you. Now we have to see if you get in too, like as a backup option." She fumbles over her words. I get why; it's been weird trying to balance wanting to be drafted to wanting to stay near her for me, too. I know she'll support me if I get drafted—she's given me so much support already. She's always checking in with my stats and tracking them against the targets Coach has given me to strive for this season. The idea of going to the same place and not being separated sounds like a great plan to me, too. I get why she wants me to go with her to Norman.

"I got into Norman too," I tell her. She sits up, asking, "When?" I stay lying down before answering, "You can't get mad, Annie. I was thinking about it and waiting to hear if you got in." "Drew, I'm not going to be mad, just tell me," is her reply, but she is already getting that little line in her forehead that only appears when she's about to get angry. "Fine, last week, I got accepted and got the offer from the baseball coach, happy?" I am prepared for an annoyed or angry Annie, but what I get is covered with Annie's body as she positions herself on top of me. Her lips are on mine in a kiss that I return quickly. When she pulls back, she looks dazed from the kiss, and she says, "Get drafted, but if you don't, let's go to college together, deal?" "It's a deal, Angel. Where you go, I'll follow." She's becoming the center of my whole world. Then we proceed to make out until her dad calls up that the pizza is here.

Chapter 57: Almost All the Way Home

Senior prom is here, and all of us guys are following the same patterns as last year. We have our tuxes in my room, and right now we are watching the baseball game in the living room. "Man, you could be up there on that TV in a few years," Craig comments from beside me. "Don't forget me when you make it. I expect all the perks of being one of the best friends to the starting SS," pipes in Luke. "We will see, man. It would be fucking cool to be on that field, and Luke, man, I'll make sure I get you some good seats and maybe get us into the VIP section at the club," I reply to my friends. "I expect bottle service, just saying," says Luke. "Do you even know what bottle service is?" asks Craig. "It seems important in all the movies, so I declare now that we need it," responds Luke. "Has Coach said anything about the scouts at the last game?" Craig asks. "Yeah, he told me he's had inquiries about my work ethic off the field and some overall readiness-type questions," I tell the guys. "I signed an agent to represent me last week. It's weird to think I need an agent," I say. It makes it all feel real. "It's going to happen, man, I just know it. I'll be able to say I knew Drew Davis before he was famous, and I can tell them about all your wild ways in high school," Luke says, laughing. "Yeah, what wild stories are you thinking about?" I laugh, joking back with him now. "Oh, I mean he had us half naked at a *girls'* soccer game," he adds. "Oh man, I'll have to get my agent to bury that story for sure." I'm laughing, because I've been the opposite of a wild guy this last year. Between trying to do all these extra workouts to be ready for the draft and the distraction of Annie, I've been mostly a homebody, and I'm not complaining.

***

Luke looks down at his phone. "Guys, as much as I want to stay here, we better get ready—it's 4:45, and the girls said to meet at Annie's at 5." We rush upstairs and throw on our tuxes, and when we come down, my parents meet us at the bottom of the stairs, holding all the corsages. "You all look dapper," Mom says, hugging me and then handing me the red rose corsage. "I could say the same thing looking at both of you," I say in return. Two weeks ago, Annie had asked if they would be interested in being chaperones for the prom; she'd said the prom committee had some openings in the later time slots and were having trouble getting parents to cover them. Mom had told Annie it would be fun as long as it didn't bother me. I didn't care if Mom and Dad came to prom, and I'd said something along those lines to them both. Now, my parents were all dressed to go out to dinner before their appearance would be required at the prom a s official chaperones. My phone buzzes in my pocket and I pull it out to read the message.

273

Looking up from my phone, I say, "We better go and save the girls, but prepare yourselves, men: stretch your facial muscles, because we ride into the throes of battle with a camera-wielding mother." Everyone laughs, and we head out the door to Annie's. The girls are on the porch stairs, smiling down at Annie's mom, who is wielding her dangerous camera. I have to catch my breath when I get to focus on Annie because damn, she is still the hottest girl I've ever seen. In that red dress, she is drop-dead gorgeous. She looks like that character in that weird '80s rabbit detective movie, but with blonde hair.

"You guys join the girls on the steps," Annie's mom says from her position behind the camera. I walk up the stairs to Annie, and I swear, I can feel my heart beating out of my chest. She is going to kill me, and I'm just looking at her. I open the box with the corsage in it and take it out, placing it on her offered arm. I step closer and give her red lips a peck. "You're gorgeous, but I have to ask, will that rub off?" I tap my finger gently against her red bottom lip. "Well, you're pretty handsome yourself, Dimples. The package said it was kiss-proof." She smiles at me and winks. "I think we should test if that's true," I whisper against her ear, so all the parents don't hear. "I think we can arrange that," she whispers back. We are interrupted with, "Everyone look over here and say cheese."

***

We do all the staples of prom night, from the limo ride to singing along to all our favorite party songs. We eat at the fancy restaurant like we belong, dressed in all our best outfits. When we arrive at the prom, we do the typical poses before heading to the digital photo booth. Annie picks the props, giving me the fake baseball hat, and she does a little princess crown. We hit the dance floor, and we don't leave for what feels like hours. I have a blast with our friends laughing and dancing. I've also enjoyed looking at Annie. I still can't get over how hot she looks in this red dress, and I want to run my hand up that slit. Every slow song, I wrap my arms around her, pulling her into me.

This feels like homecoming but better; maybe it's because I love her now. I think I was falling in love with her then and hadn't called it that at the time, but this right here, with her head on my chest... I realize I can't see a future without her, and I vow to myself that I never will. The music changes back to a pop song, and we dance until we agree it's time to leave early, and we climb back into the limo. We are calmer on the drive home, all of us couples snuggled up and sharing touches. Between kisses, easy conversations flow, and jokes are made. The difference from last year is that the girls have arranged for us to be dropped off at our stops. Each couple will get themselves to and from the after-party. It's just Meg, Tom, Annie, and I when we stop in front of my house. "See you tomorrow," Meg says to us as we start to get out of the limo. "You're not going to the party?" I ask. "Oh, we are going to the party. It's you, lover boy not making it to the party," Meg says to me and winks.

***

I shut the door to the limo, saying to Annie, "That was weird. Why would Meg think we aren't going to the party?" I turn towards Annie, seeing a pretty pink flush on her cheeks. My mind makes a snap realization. All the pieces fall into place: why we'd come home early from prom, why Annie had asked my parents to chaperone at prom during the last time slot.

My Annie, my seemingly innocent girlfriend, had given us a very large window of time with an empty house to use to do whatever we wanted. *Sex* pops into my head. I haven't been trying to rush her to have sex—I've sworn to myself that I wouldn't pressure her, so I haven't brought it up, waiting for her to want to and bring up that she was ready. So, I've waited, and waited, and waited, and all this time I was thinking she wasn't ready when really, she'd been plotting to seduce me. I walk over to my blushing girlfriend and murmur, "Are you planning to seduce me, Angel?" She bites her red lower lip and replies, "Yes, actually I am, Dimples." Then, she grabs my hand, and we head towards my house. I use the code and let us in. She pulls me through the door and into the house. She is focused on getting us to our final destination; she isn't stripping this time. I know we both don't need any repeat interruptions, and I know that Daniel is in Nebraska, hours and hours away from ruining this night.

***

She isn't running, but she is moving quickly in her heels up the stairs, still pulling me along behind her. She doesn't wait for me to open my bedroom door: she swings the door open and enters my room. I'm ushered to the bed where she slips out of my hands. "Just a second," she says and walks back to my door, clicking the lock. "Before we do what I planned to do tonight, can you confirm you have condoms in this room?" she asks, her cheeks going another shade darker. "I do indeed have condoms in this room, Angel, but before I get them, I need to make sure you want this," I tell her. I need her to say it out loud, because I think it will kill me if we start this time and we don't make it all the way home. She starts walking towards me and says, "Drew Davis, make love to me already." She is standing between my legs in that sexy-as-sin dress as her last word finishes. My dick has never been so excited. I don't say anything, I run my fingers up that sexy slit. I look up and see that she is watching the path of my fingers. "I've wanted to do this all night," I say as I dip my face to the skin at the top of the slit and kiss it. She shivers.

I grab her hips, changing our position. She is now the one sitting on the edge of my bed, and I'm standing between her legs. I remove the tux jacket, vest, and tie, throwing them at my chair, and then I get on my knees in front of her. "What are you doing?" she breathes. "I'm going to be a gentleman and make you orgasm, Angel," I say against her exposed thigh. I kiss my way up her thigh, pulling up the red material of her dress as I go. I finally get to my final destination, and I'm greeted by a red scrap of lace covering her pussy from me. "These look new," I murmur before I suck them and her clit into my mouth. Her hands go directly into my hair, and an "Oh" leaves her red lips. I release both her clit and the fabric and then dip my fingers into the straps of the thong, pulling them down her legs. She lifts her high-heeled feet to help me remove them.

I return my attention to her pussy: it is perfect, and I don't want to waste any time before I can taste it. I dip my head down again, sliding my tongue from her clit to her core. I realize I want a better angle, so I lift her legs and place them on my shoulders, mumbling against her pussy. "Don't drop your legs from my shoulders, Angel." Then I resume my efforts of licking and sucking her into my mouth. The only sounds in the room are the sounds of my efforts and her little moans of my name. After I feel like she is ready, I slip one finger into her body, then quickly a second. She is so fucking tight—I don't want to hurt her when we have sex. I know that I need to get her body to at least one orgasm to help make the next part easier. Annie rewards me a few minutes later with her first orgasm. Her body goes taunt and her pussy pulses around my fingers as she lets out a loud "DDDRRREEWWW," and then she lets go of my hair, falling back onto my bed with a look of complete satisfaction across her face.

I lick my lips and clean up my fingers as I stand up. It's time to remove the rest of my clothing, so I start untucking my shirt and undoing my buttons. She watches me undo the buttons until I remove my shirt and throw it in the same direction as my other discarded clothes. She toes off her heels and stands up next to me with her back facing me. "I am going to need your help with my zipper," she says over her shoulder. I kiss her bare shoulder and zip the dress down, but I'm not greeted with bare skin like the homecoming dress. Instead, I'm met with a red lace corset covering her back. I groan, because I know when she turns around, Annie is going to be standing in one hell of a sexy red piece of lingerie. I can bet that it is probably a matching set to her already discarded thong. I get the dress fully unzipped, and she lets it fall to the floor in a puddle at her feet before she turns around.

The lingerie is even better than I could imagine. The lace of the corset is completely see-through, and I can see her nipples peeking out between the mostly transparent pattern. "You are going to kill me," I groan, grabbing her neck and pulling her against me into a bruising kiss. I say, "Bed, Angel," and point at my bed. She takes my directions and climbs into my bed facing me. "Undress, Drew" she says, looking at me. I follow her orders: removing the tux pants, my boxers, shoes, and socks. I look over at her watching me. She looks so turned on, and I can't help feeling some pride at the fact that I'm the one undoing her.

I reach into my nightstand, pulling out the condom. I place it on the edge closest to my bed, so I know where it is when we are ready. I join her in my bed, pinning her under me, and she wraps her legs around my hips. My dick is resting against her clit, and it would take just a move of either of our hips to slip inside of her. I try to remember that I need to get her worked up again to make this easier for her. So instead of moving to enter her, I move my lips to hers in a deep kiss and my hand over the raised nipple covered in the thin red fabric. She moans into our kiss when I rub and pinch her nipple. I repeat the move on the other nipple in the same pattern. She is moving her hips in little circles, rubbing the head of my dick against her clit, and I think this is my sign that she is ready and that she wants more. I'm reaching for the condom when I hear the front door slam shut.

I freeze, and so does Annie.

***

My mom's voice sounds loud in the silence, "I can't get a hold of Drew. I've texted him and called at least five times, and he isn't responding," I can hear a lot of panic in her voice. "Hun, it's prom night, he is probably out with his friends." I can hear my dad respond. "Don't *hun* me, Dan; his brother's been in a car accident. We need to leave soon to try to get to the hospital," Mom says, panic lacing her words. *What the hell did she just say?* My brain isn't keeping track. "I'm going to look at the location app, then we'll have to show up at the party and try to find him without making a scene," Mom says. I'm still frozen on top of Annie, but she is pushing my chest. "Drew, get up," she whispers, and I do as I'm told. Annie scrambles to grab her dress and underwear, and she is already mostly dressed when I register my parents' voices again.

"Dan, it shows his phone is here, why would it show it is here? I know that he had it at prom, he'd sent me that photo when they left," my mom says before letting out a loud "OOOOHHH." There is silence downstairs. I know my parents have figured out that Annie and I are upstairs and probably have an idea of what we could have been doing in the empty house on prom night. What else could we be doing that would prevent me from caring if my phone existed? "Drew, get dressed," Annie says, before throwing my clothing into my lap. I look down at the pile and realize I'd been sitting on the bed naked, listening to my parents downstairs.

I'm sliding into my pants when a knock sounds at the door. "Drew, are you in there?" Dad's voice asks at the door. "Yeah, I'm here," I respond through the door. Dad clears his voice, "Son, I'm sorry if I'm interrupting something, but there's a situation," he says a little too loud. "Can I meet you downstairs in like

279

two minutes, Dad?" I reply back. "Sure, two minutes is fine," he says, and I can hear his footsteps retreat down the stairs. I slip my shirt back on and slide the buttons on the shirt closed, then look at Annie. "I'm sorry we got interrupted." I stop and run my hand through my hair. "This isn't how I saw this going." She leans into my chest and wraps her arms around me. There isn't anything sexual in this hug; she is offering me comfort, and I take it by wrapping my arms around her, too. She pulls back and gently takes my hand, leading me like earlier in the direction we need to go.

***

When we join my parents in the living room, I can see Mom crying. Her face is all red and swollen, and Dad's eyes are bloodshot. "I heard something about an accident before Dad came up," I say, offering them a way to start the conversation. I grip my fingers around Annie's as Dad says, "Daniel got into an accident at school. Looks like he may have been drinking and driving. He ran his car off the road into a ditch. The hospital says he's in pretty bad shape, and he's currently in an induced coma, but he's stable. They'd like us to be there in the morning when they run their next round of tests."

My mind is spiraling. I'm glad my brother is alive, but he is so fucking stupid for getting behind the wheel drunk again. Mom breaks the silence of my lack of words with, "Drew, hunny, we have to leave right now if we are going to make it to Nebraska by the morning." As I'm trying to process, I hear Annie. "Well, thank goodness no one else was hurt and that Daniel is at the hospital where they can monitor him." I squeeze her fingers, giving her the only reaction that my body can seem to make.

Finally, my brain starts to form words. "So what do we need to do?" Mom answers quickly, "We need to pack and leave soon. Maybe change into something more comfortable since it's a long drive." "Let me grab a few things, change, and walk Annie home. I can be ready in like ten minutes, will that work?" I ask. Mom looks relieved that I'm making this so easy, and she walks over and gives me a hug. Before I can return the hug, she's pulling Annie in, too, and I wrap my arms around both of them. "We are so sorry we had to interrupt prom night," Mom says, releasing us both. Annie gives my mom another hug, "It's ok, Mrs. Davis, we'll have other nights—you all need to focus on getting to Daniel right now." Then she releases my mom. Mom gives me a little nod, and Annie and I head back into my room.

***

"Why don't you change, and I'll grab some of your stuff for you?" I scramble to get dressed, and Annie makes her way around my room, grabbing what she thinks I'll need, including my backpack with my homework and my phone charger from the wall. When I'm done, I look at Annie. She is sitting on my bed with her knees tucked under her chin, lost in thought. "Angel, what are you thinking about?" My question startles her. She moves to stand and then makes her way beside me near the door. She steps into my arms and lays her cheek against my chest. I wrap my arms around her, and then she whispers, "That our time can be cut short before we've ever gotten to be anyone."

I place my fingers under her chin and gently tilt it up so our eyes can meet. "You are somebody to me, Angel, and we'll have a lot of time to become somebody out there in the world, too. I am truly sorry about tonight, Annie. I wanted this to play out so differently." "Stop apologizing that we didn't have sex, Drew." As she says *sex,* her face blushes red. "I'm sure we will find another time and place," she adds. I can't help it: I give her a light kiss and say against her lips, "I can't wait until then, Angel." Then I grab my bags and take them to the car Dad is packing. I walk Annie to her house, kiss her one last time, and promise to text her in the morning before jumping in the car with my parents to go on an unexpected road trip.

Chapter 58: I Don't Care Who's Watching

-Drew-

I spend a few days with my parents in Nebraska at the hospital with Daniel. The swelling in his brain has gone down, and the doctors have reassured my parents that Daniel should be able to recover from his accident. The doctor does express to my parents that they should consider possible treatment programs. Daniel's blood alcohol level had been over .30% when he'd been admitted to the hospital after the accident. Mom has insisted that I get home, because we kicked off district play, and scouts will be highly suspicious if I go MIA from the starting lineup.

Dad agreed to drive me home while Mom gets a hotel and car to stay in Nebraska with Daniel. Mom is trying to figure out if she can get Daniel any extensions at his college so he can complete his classes. He'd only been a few weeks away from the end of his semester. It feels weird returning home without even having my brother wake up, but the doctors said it would be any time now and that Daniel only needed time for his body to finish healing. On the drive back, I tell Dad that he should fly back and join Mom. I tell him I'm completely capable of taking care of myself and that I'd be so busy with baseball that I would barely be home myself. He'd said he would talk to Mom, but that it didn't seem fair to me not to have either of my parents present for what promised to be a strong playoff run. Annie texts or calls me multiple times a day while I'm gone. It's reassuring each time I see her name pop up on my phone.

***

True to my promise, I have been busy and all-consumed with baseball. We'd won our district games, then repeated our efforts and won all our regional games to make it into the top eight schools in Oklahoma. Most importantly, the state tournament. Dad has stayed with me and has shown up for every game, even though I'd told him he didn't have to. It was nice having him there to support me. Mom is finishing up in Nebraska, having helped Daniel finish his classes and enroll in a program to get help for his drinking. I've overheard a little of Dad's call with Mom last week and her telling him how Daniel had been responding to all the actions and steps they'd laid out for him.

Mom told Dad that Daniel apologized and agreed he needed help, and that he'd gotten out of control before the accident. I'm missing Mom's arrival home from Nebraska with our bus departure to drive to the state tournament. Once we leave today, we either come home champions or we don't. All of us guys are ready to get on the road; we even refreshed the numbers in our sideburns. Since shaving it into my hair, Annie traces it when we get moments alone, snuggled up at her house or mine. She runs her fingers over the almost bare patches, tracking the one and then the seven. I may or may not have fallen asleep on her parents' couch a few nights ago when she'd been doing it.

***

Annie is the best girlfriend through all the craziness that my life is right now. She finished her soccer season during districts. Since then, she has been present at every single game: home or away, it didn't matter, sideline, dugout, or the stands next to Dad. It didn't matter where she was, just that she was there at each game. The state tournament would be the one exception, because she couldn't get her parents to agree to head out with us to the tournament yet.

She went back and forth negotiating with her parents since we qualified for State. If I hadn't already been head over heels in love with her, this would have been the thing to push me to confess my love for her. She'd started her pitch by telling them how important it would be for her to support me, then for the school to have a reporter to capture all the moments with the team, and finally for her dad to get an accurate story for the Reporter. She'd finally gotten them to book a room for Saturday night, one for her parents and one for her and Meg, so they could be present at the state championship game. Now the guys and I have to get ourselves there.

***

Dad drove me and Annie to school today, so we don't have to leave my car in the lot for the next few days. From the front, Dad says, "Once your mom is home, we will head out. We may miss the first game, but we'll make it well before the scheduled second game." "Sounds good, I'll check my phone between games," I let him know. Dad parks the car, getting out and heading towards the trunk to grab my bags. "I'll meet you at the bus," Annie says, giving me a quick kiss and moving out of the backseat and off through the parking lot before I can protest her absence. I join Dad at the trunk and take one of the bags from him before he says, "Drew, no matter the outcome, you've made me proud. This isn't the end of your baseball career. Go have fun before this is your job: enjoy how good you are out there and how it feels to be with your friends."

This isn't the first time he has told me he is proud of me for all the efforts I have put into baseball, but it is the first time he has said outright that he believes it will be my career. It's always been an "if," "backup plan," or "just in case" type of scenario with Dad. I never thought he didn't believe I could do it, but he's the planner of my parents. He wanted to make sure that I've always understood my odds and the other things I have to offer outside of baseball, so to hear him say it will be my career means a lot to me, and I tell him, "Thanks, Dad. It means a lot to have your support." "Always, Drew." He gives me a quick hug before handing me my other bag. "Now go have fun, and maybe win a championship, too."

***

I drop my bags off with the coaches and they run me through the checklist one more time. I reassure them that I do have all my gear and my toothbrush. After doing all the required check-ins, I go to find Annie in the crowd of other players and students ready to give us a pep rally send-off. I spot her next to Craig, Luke, and Travis in the crowd. I make my way over and slide my arms around her waist, standing behind her. She leans back into me and twines her fingers into mine on her stomach. "You snuggle into any guy throwing his arms around you, Angel?" I ask. She laughs and looks over her shoulder. "Nope, I could tell your touch from anyone's, Dimples." I lean down and capture her lips in a kiss. "Ok, OK, I mean it, OK," Craig mocks us. "Lover boy, get your last feels, because it's just me and you in a hotel room until Sunday, and I don't put out," Craig laughs at himself. He continues, "but if you trade places with Liz over there, I could change my mind."

"Ok, gross, I don't want to hear who you would and won't put out for, Craig Mitchell," Annie says from my arms. We all turn towards the buses and Coach at the sound of the whistle. He gives a little speech about the team's hard work and how we've earned this opportunity. He ends with a dramatic "Let's take State!" "I think that is my battle cry to head towards the bus," I say against Annie's ear.

She spins in my arms and wraps her arms around my neck, pulling me into a kiss, then too quickly pulling away. "I'll see you at the Championship game, but I'll be watching all the streaming coverage I can," followed by "You are going to do so great, and I love you." I steal one more kiss from my girl and join the team on the bus, ready to have some fun playing ball with my friends.

***

We've done it: we've gotten ourselves through our games on Thursday and Friday to make it to the end, to this moment, the state championship game. The buzz in the locker room is crazy—some guys can't be still, and they walk around talking with everyone. Others are quiet and focused, zoning out to the music in their headphones. I'm somewhere in the middle. I've chatted with the guys, but I'm here at my locker now, thinking about what I have to do to help us win this game. I've been on fire the whole state tournament, and my bat and glove haven't failed me yet. Here's to hoping they don't fail me now. I've recorded great stats, but my home runs have been the most surprising. I've hit a minimum of one a game in all the state tournament games, and last game I had even gotten two. When I'd video-called Annie in the hotel after the game, she'd been so excited replaying the moments for me, she'd dropped her phone.

Coach breaks into my thoughts. "Let's take the field for warm-ups." We get a big cheer from the stands behind our dugout when we enter the field. There isn't an empty seat in the place; it is packed, and the energy is off the charts. As I walk to my position for warm-ups, I glance over the crowd, trying to find her. It doesn't take long before I spot the section of people clad in number 17 gear. There are all the people I would expect: Mom, Dad, Annie, and Meg, plus the unexpected with Annie's parents sporting Rams number 17. I wave at the crowd and see Annie lean over to my parents and point in my direction. They look over and wave back. I don't care that the stands are packed, I lift my hands in front of my chest, making the heart shape, and then point at her up in the stands. She doesn't make me wait before she does one back at me. I smile and go back to warm-ups, feeling like tonight is going to be a better night than the other games.

Chapter 59: We Are All Champions

-Annie-

The buzz of the crowd is amazing around us as the players take the field for warm-ups. I know the moment he leaves the dugout as his number, 17, races out to the field. I'm so lucky to call him mine. I hadn't been joking with him at the send-off a few days ago: I'm always aware of him. I could be in a crowded room, and as soon as he entered, I'd know he was there. I can see him looking over the crowd, and even though he is across the field, I can make out the smile before he waves in our direction. I tap Mrs. Davis's arm. "I think Drew is waving to us." "Oh, Dan, he's waving." She pokes Mr. Davis in the stomach, and they both wave. "Thank you, Annie," she says over her shoulder. He stops waving and holds out his hands in a heart, then points in our direction. I know it's for me—it's our secret game code, so I do one back at him.

Shortly after, he returns his focus on warm-ups. Meg elbows me. "Can we get snacks now that you've seen Lover Boy?" I laugh, agreeing we should get our snacks before the game starts, and I ask the parents if they want anything. With all the orders straight, Meg and I head to the concession stand. "So, is tonight a go?" Meg says next to me in line. I can feel the blush. "I think so—Craig said he'd figure out how to escape to the stairs to exchange keys." "I love that my sweet little BFF has, for the second time, planned out a whole 'get sex' plan." Meg smiles next to me. "I don't care if the fire alarm goes off, you don't let anything get in your way this time, ok?" she says. "Ok, ok, no interruptions. You make sure that my parents don't realize Craig and I have switched rooms."

She laughs and replies, "You know I will. I mean, I already brought you condoms, I'm committed to this plan." I know I blush at the word *condoms* surrounded by a crowd of people. "Ok, can you be quiet before you give the whole thing away?" I give her a little elbow to the ribs. "Ouch, ok fine, my lips are sealed from here on out. Let's get the food and go watch the Rams kick some butt." Meg gives me a side hug, and we get the snacks, returning to the stands as they start the national anthem. Moments later, the umpire says, "Let's play ball," and the players take their positions on the field.

***

Drew is amazing out on that field; if he doesn't get drafted, the scouts are stupid. He's making it look so effortless when the Rams are on the field. Earlier in the game, he completed the double play to get the last two outs of the inning. Then, to complete the last inning, he'd made an amazing diving catch and throw to get the batter out at first. The game is all tied up at 3-3, and it's the bottom of the seventh. The Rams need one run to win State. Drew has been getting on base and even scored one of the points reflected on the scoreboard.

I'm nervous, because the Eagles pitcher had a perfect inning in the sixth. Drew hadn't been an at-bat against him, but he's the second one up this inning. Matthew is the first batter, and he gets nothing: each time he swings his bat it's met with empty air. Mrs. Davis grabs my arm. "He's got this," I say out loud, and she nods her head in agreement. He's so focused in the box sets his feet and his bat in position, and the pitch flies from the Eagles player. Drew jumps back, the ball just missing his front leg. "Ball" is announced.

He steps back and adjusts his helmet, then resumes his position in the box. The pitch comes, and in the silence of the crowd, I hear the crack of the impact on his bat. It's like slow motion as I see the next actions take place. The ball is flying in the air, Drew is taking off towards first base, and the ball continues over the heads of the outfielder and the fence. Drew slows to a jog as he runs his bases with a huge smile on his face.

"HOME RUN, HOME RUN FOR DAVIS NUMBER SEVENTEEN, THE RAMS ARE STATE CHAMPIONS" is yelled over the speakers in the ballpark, and the crowd on our side of the field erupts into pure chaos. I've somehow jumped out of my seat with the crowd, but I'm not sharing the moment with those around me—my eyes are glued to Drew rounding third and meeting his teammates at home base. He is tackled almost immediately by a dog pile. When he resurfaces, he is missing his helmet, but that smile is still on his face. He looks into the crowd, and I'm sure we can't make eye contact from this distance, but it feels like we do, and he puts up his hands in a heart shape before he's wrapped into another celebration with his teammates.

***

They do the trophies and metal presentation. All the guys look so excited and happy. I can see Craig, Luke, and Drew joking around on the metal stand. They all look beyond excited. "Ready to head back to the hotel?" Dad asks us after the ceremony is over. "Well, if it's ok with you, we can take the girls back with us. I bet Drew would love to see Annie," Mrs. Davis offers to my parents. My parents share a look, then Mom says, "Oh, that would be great, thank you, Jen." She turns to me and says, "Text us when you are back at the hotel." My parents leave, and we make our way to the field. Other families are huddled up with their players, giving hugs and smiles in celebration.

291

When I see Drew, I don't wait for the others; I take off across the field. He turns to see me, and a dimple appears on his left cheek. I launch myself into his arms and throw myself around him, and he wraps his arms around me. "You are amazing, congratu—" I get cut off by his lips on mine. We break the kiss, and he is smiling again. His smile is so infectious I can feel my face beaming in return. I drop my feet back down to the dirt and step out of his arms as his family arrives. His mom takes the space I left, and his dad joins them. I grab my phone and take a picture. Then I think I become my mother, because I take a ton of pictures of Drew with his parents, and with Craig and Luke, before I hand it over to get some of us with our friends.

***

Eventually, the guys have to return to their locker room. "I'll see you later," I say to Drew. "Yeah, I'll video call when we get back to the hotel." Craig gives me a wink over Drew's shoulder. I guess Craig has kept my secret. I owe my friend. Meg and I follow Mr. and Mrs. Davis to their car in the mostly empty lot. Meg is on her phone, and then I get a ping on my phone. I look at it, expecting it to be my parents, but it's a message from Meg. Maybe she wants to tell me something but can't because the Davises would hear, so I swipe it open, and a gasp escapes m y lips.

Because I'm not greeted with a smart-ass comment about phase two of my seduction plan. I'm met with a picture. Meg may have been influenced by my mom, too, because she'd captured the moment right after we broke the kiss. Drew and I are in profile, smiling at each other: his dimple is just visible, my arms wrapped around his neck and my legs around his waist, with his hands around my waist, holding me. I save the photo and then make it my lock screen. It's now my favorite picture of the two of us. "Thank you," I tell her in the backseat as we head back to the hotel. "It was too good a moment not to capture. I think your mom's gotten into my head," Meg replies, then starts laughing. I laugh along with her, so beyond happy, and I didn't even do anything but love the boy who hit the home run.

***

"Are you ready?" Meg says from the edge of the bathroom. I look at myself in the mirror. *Am I ready?* Yes on all accounts. I'm still in my jersey, but I've changed into the little red corset underneath. I have a few condoms in my back pocket. I'm leaving my phone with Meg in case my parents text, so she can answer them. "Ok, because Craig is in the stairwell—he just texted me," Meg tells me. "I'll text Drew tomorrow if your parents are getting suspicious." She gives me a little hug before continuing, "Have a lot of fun, but remember this is a hotel, so maybe moan into a pillow or something?" I laugh so hard. "Ok, noted."

***

Craig is in the stairwell when I arrive. He hands over the key card and reminds me to get to room 326 without being seen. "Thanks, Craig." He shakes his head of half-red curls. "Let's pretend for the next thirty years that I didn't help you have sex after State, and we will call it even." "Deal," I tell him, and he heads downstairs in the direction of the room with Meg. I open the door to the third floor. I peek my head out and don't see anyone. I know from looking at the hotel map that I need to go down this little hall and make a left turn, and the room should be right there. I don't run, but I walk at a fast clip, do a little peek around the corner, then slide up to the door labeled 326 and tap the card against the reader.

It seems like it is never going to flash green. I hear the click of the lock, and I turn the handle and swing the door, rushing inside. I have my back resting against the door, breathing heavily. *Who knew that sneaking around a hotel would make you out of breath?* "Man, that was the longest ice run in history." Drew's voice comes from the part of the room with the beds. "Fair warning, I couldn't get a hold of Annie while you were gone, so she could call back at any minute, and before you say it again, no, we aren't playing a game of I'll show you mine if you show me yours." I have to cover my mouth so I don't laugh while Drew thinks he is talking to Craig. I make my way to the wall blocking the door and say, "And here I was thinking we could play that one."

***

I've startled Drew. He drops his phone in his lap, and his eyes are popping out of his head looking at me. "Annie, how did you get here?" He looks behind me like he expects to see Craig. "I ran into Craig, and he gave me this," I held up the room key, "and I gave him my free bed with Meg." "Annie, are you trying to seduce me again?" he says, smiling up at me from his place on the bed. I reach into my back pocket, pull out the condoms, and throw them at him. He catches them in one hand and looks from them to me. "Yes, Drew Davis. I'm here to finish what we started." I walk over to the edge of the bed and slowly slip the buttons of the jersey I'm wearing free.

I look at him as I do; his pupils are so large, and the dark blue of his eyes are a small ring. He isn't looking at my face, though. His eyes are on my hands that are undoing my jersey. If he wasn't breathing so heavily, I'd think he was frozen until I undo the last button. The jersey is fully open, revealing the red corset. I know he's seen me in it before, but he groans. Before I can react, his hands are on either side of my ribs, pulling me against him. Standing like this, his head is against my stomach, and I can feel his breath against the sheer fabric of the corset. I'm looking down at him as I feel him kiss my stomach through the material. He looks up at me. "Angel, you are going to kill me—you're fucking gorgeous."

I can't help the little rush of satisfaction that flows through me at his words. It feels good to know that he looks at me like this. I step back, and his hands tighten on my ribs. "Let go, Drew," I say quietly into the room. I slip off the jersey and lay it on the other bed before removing my jean shorts and shoes. I'm only covered by my little red thong and corset set now. "Fuck, Annie" escapes from Drew's lips. I step forward and slowly straddle his lap on the bed. Drew hasn't moved: he's looking up and down my body. "You can touch me now," I say before kissing him. He does. His hands start on my hips, traveling up my ribs to flick over each of my nipples, all while his mouth moves from my lips across my jaw and down my neck. "Drew, please don't make me wait," I say.

We've been interrupted too many times now that I feel like we need to get to the end quickly, or we may never actually make it. I refuse to get interrupted again. I grab at his shirt, and he helps me yank it up and over his head. I throw it on the other bed with my discarded clothes. I want his pants off. I want him naked. As if he's able to read my thoughts, he flips us, and now I'm under him. He pulls back long enough to slip his hand to the edge of his joggers, sliding them and his boxers off, becoming fully naked in front of me. OMG, he is so ripped and cut in all the right places. I could look at Drew naked all night, but I want more , I *need* more from him. "As absolutely sexy as that outfit is, I think I want it off," he says. I swallow as he runs his hands up my legs, looping his fingers into the straps of the thong. He pulls it down my legs and throws it on the pile of discarded clothes. "I'll have to sit up to remove this," I say, pointing at the corset. He settles back between my legs, and I wrap my legs around his waist. Wedging his dick against my clit, I experience a weird sense of déjà vu, like we have been here before.

"I'm good with the corset staying if you are: I like this position, personally," Drew says against the skin at my throat before he dips his lips against my skin.

"Mmmm" is the only sound I make as my thoughts are distracted by him moving his hands up and over my breasts, then down over my nipples before I feel his body move back. His dick isn't pinned against me anymore, but he replaces the space with his fingers. He runs his fingers from my clit down to my core and back a few times, each time I mentally send him signals to dip his fingers inside me. He has different plans and merely runs his fingers back to my clit to rub a circle before returning down.

"Drew, please," I moan after the last pass of his fingers. Drew goes back and circles my clit before answering my plea by dipping his fingers into me. It feels so good that I arch into his efforts and wrap my hands around his arm. My body is on fire; it's pulsing, and all my muscles are tense. It all feels so good and yet still not enough, then I feel his breath a moment before his mouth wraps around my nipple and sucks on it. "DREEEWW" escapes my mouth. It wasn't loud, but it wasn't exactly quiet either. I know my orgasm is coming, and I know if I don't do something with my mouth, I'm going to moan or scream. I grab the pillow next to me and bite on the edge. With the next pulse of pleasure that courses through my body, I see actual stars as I close my eyes.

***

I'm only brought back to earth when Drew moves the pillow from between us and kisses me. "I really could watch you orgasm every day," he tells me as he reaches his hand for something on the other side of us on the bed. It takes my brain longer than it should to realize he has the condom in his hand and is tearing the edge of one of the packages. He removes his body from mine, sitting on his feet, and I watch him roll the condom down his dick. He returns to cover my body with his now condom-covered dick wedged against my clit again. "Annie, this could be a little uncomfortable for y—" I place my finger against his swollen lips, because I already know what he is going to say. I know that this could hurt, I'm a virgin, but I have a best friend who isn't shy about sharing details or answering questions, so I know what to expect.

I move my hips a little, causing his dick to slide down, and it now rests right where I want him. I say, "Make love to me, Dimples." He smiles against my finger, and I feel the head of his dick enter my body. He's big, but it feels good. He pulls back, and I moan with the loss of him. He pushes back in, going deeper, and I wrap my legs tighter around his hips, urging him to continue. We go back and forth like this for who knows how long, with him pushing a little in and a little out. The pressure is building inside me, and I know that he has more to give and he is taking it slow. Yes, I am glad he is easing me into this but also, I want all of him now. So, I start arching into his forward thrust, and he begins to lose control. I feel the moment of discomfort come and go just as quickly. Drew pulls back out and, on the next thrust in, pushes completely inside me: our bodies are as close as two people can be.

"You ok?" he breathes against my face. I roll my hips, feeling him everywhere. I like it, feeling more pleasure than discomfort. "I'm ok—don't stop now, Drew," I demand. I can feel his smile against my cheek before he dips his lips to mine. He is kissing me, building a tempo of thrusting and retreating. The pleasure is building inside me again, but this time it feels bigger and hotter. I feel my whole body tense around him. I don't just see stars; I implode into ecstasy. Drew's thrusts are becoming erratic and harder. His face is all tense and hard planes as I watch him move over me and into me. I watch his face as he cums with my name on his lips before pinning me to the mattress with his full body weight.

He makes a little turn to get us both on our side, wrapping his arms around me before kissing my temple. "Angel, that was amazing." I can't help thinking *ditto*, my body all tingles. I can feel him slide from my body, and I panic, grabbing at him. I don't want him to go. "Angel, let me get the condom off, I'll be right back." Drew leaves the bed, making a quick dash to the bathroom. I can hear the sink turn on and off before he returns, holding a washcloth. He hands it to me, saying, "If you want to clean up, I thought this would help."

I thank him for the warm towel, and I clean up the evidence that we had sex from my body. I make to get up, but Drew reaches out his hand, takes the cloth, and goes back to the bathroom. He returns quickly, rejoining me on the bed and pulling my back against the front of his body. I shiver, and he turns and pulls the covers over us. "You ok?" he whispers next to my ear. "I'm perfect," I tell him, because I am. I am absolutely perfect snuggled next to the person that I love on the best night of my life. *How could life ever get any better*, I think as the warmth from his body against mine drags me into sleep.

Chapter 60: The Draft, The Dream, The Aftermath

-Drew-

Summer

If I ever make it big and someone wants me to recall the month leading up to the draft and they ask what has been the highlight of the last month, I'm sure they'd expect my answer to be winning the state championship, or graduation, or the possibility of being part of the draft. Still, those guesses would have all been wrong, because the biggest moment of my life in May was making love to my girlfriend for the first time. Yes, I've had sex before her, but sex with her wasn't like any of the girls before her. It felt like, for lack of a better word, more. We'd fallen asleep after our first time together and I'd spooned her against my body the whole night. It all felt a little like a dream until Craig came into the room and grumbled, "Do not thank me for getting you laid. Annie has already done it, and it was weird."

***

Graduation and all the events feel like a blur, from the last days to all the good-byes with our fellow classmates. I love that the school doesn't do graduation in alphabetical order and that I get to sit next to Annie and our friends through all the events of the ceremony. I am behind Annie when her name is announced, and I shout along with her family in the crowded arena. When I hear "Drew Joseph Davis," I hear my family and give them a look, holding up my diploma and waving it in their direction. Craig gives a bow to the lady giving out the diplomas, which gets a laugh from the audience. Luke can't let Craig upstage him, and he shouts near the mic, "Looks like they passed me after all, don't look suspicious, don't look suspicious..." as he heads to the lady with the diplomas, gaining another round of laughter. Meg is the last to be announced, and we all cheer from the audience again as we get back to our seats. When it comes time to move our tassels, I grab Annie's, and she grabs mine, and we flip them for each other. We share a short kiss as our classmates cheer, celebrating our graduation.

***

Two days later, I get the call from my agent about the draft. I should go downstairs and tell my parents first, but I leave the house and walk over to the Campbells'. Per normal, Mr. Campbell opens the door and ushers me inside. "Davis, how are you?" Annie and her mom come into the open living room from the kitchen, carrying a bowl of popcorn. I blurt it out: "I'm getting drafted, I've been asked to attend the draft in person." The excitement breaks out over at the Campbells'. Mr. Campbell pats me on the back, telling me, "Proud of you, Davis." Mrs. Campbell runs over and gives me a hug, saying, "Anyone watching you play knows it's what you're meant to do—congratulations, Drew." Annie drops the popcorn before jumping around her mom and kissing me, not caring that her parents are right behind her. When we break the kiss, she tells me, "I always knew you would make it." Mr. Campbell says we need to celebrate with a dinner out and that they can postpone the movie night. I ask if my parents could join us, and then I go home and share the good news with them as well as our dinner plans. The night out with both our families is a blast. Our parents laugh and share all our embarrassing stories. The whole time, I hold the hand of the most beautiful girl. I know that I want her to be part of all my big moments.

***

A few days after the family dinner celebration, I walk over to the Campbell's house when I know that Annie isn't home. Mr. Campbell opens the door, looking a little confused. "Hi, Davis, good to see you, but Annie isn't here." I tell him I've come over to talk to him about something. He seems a little worried but welcomes me into the living room. Before I can even start to ask if Annie can travel with me to the draft, he says, "Drew, I know you love my daughter, but you are just starting your career. I can't give my approval yet. Let her go to school, let her go get her dreams, too, and then ask me again. I'll be ready to approve then. You're a good guy, and I know she loves you too, but please, just wait." My mind was not prepared for his speech. What did he think I was going to ask him? Replaying his words, I realize he thought I wanted his approval to ask her to marry me. For just a split second, I see it all in my mind: us engaged, us married, us getting to set up our first place together, but then just as quickly, I see that she'd follow me if we got engaged now. She'd put her dreams on hold for me, and I don't want that. I want Annie to get her dreams, too, and not feel like she'd given them up for me. I thanked him for the advice, agreeing that I love his daughter and that getting engaged now isn't the right time. After he looks satisfied, I address the actual reason for my visit, having Annie come with me and my parents to the draft. He tells me that if Annie wants to go, it isn't a problem with him. I thank him for his time and leave with a lot more on my mind than when I showed up.

***

Now I am sitting here at the draft in my suit and red tie, with my parents and Annie. She is in a beautiful red dress that matches my tie, and my hand is resting in her lap. She has both her hands wrapped around mine. Dad leans in. "Heard anything?" "My agent said he'd text me when it's about to happen," I reply. We are six guys into the first round, and my agent estimates that I will probably go early in the second. He'd received an indication that a few clubs are interested and that I impressed in the media interviews a few days ago. I am trying not to show my emotions on my face, but my brain is going in a million directions. I eventually focus on Annie's fingers sliding over the top of my hand. I'm so lost in thought that I jump when my phone buzzes in my pocket. I feel sick with the nerves as I reach into my pocket for my phone. My agent's name appears across the screen, and I swipe open the message.

Well, fuck, is the first thing that goes through my mind. *$3 MILLION* is the next thing that flashes like neon lights in my mind. I squeeze Annie's hand to get her attention, because I know my time is coming. She looks over, noticing I have my phone; I turn it to her. As she reads the message, her eyes go big, and then a smile appears. "Drew," she whispers. "I know, be ready to be on camera, Angel," I say, smiling back at her. The announcer says that Arizona is making their selection, and I look over at my parents before I hear, "With their first-round pick, the Arizona Sands select shortstop Drew Davis." I make sure to smile at the camera crew in front of me before pulling Annie into a hug and a quick kiss. I hug both my parents before making my way to the stage. I get handed an Arizona hat, and I place it on my head before shaking the hands of the announcer. Cameras are clicking, and I don't have to remember to smile, because my dream just came true.

The reality sinks in when my agent joins me backstage. He goes over the next steps of now being a drafted player. I'll do some press, and he is sure that I'll get some calls to do some sports radio interviews. He tells me that I'll play out of the minor league group for Arizona in Scottsdale; the club has recommended apartments that work with the baseball players, but we can deal with that in the next few days. He tells me to start packing, because I'm now a pro baseball player. I get a call from the organization welcoming me to the club, and they let me know we will finalize the paperwork, signing bonus, etc., in the next few days, but for today, they tell me to enjoy the moment. Then, in two weeks, I'll be expected in Arizona, and we can get serious then.

I thank them for the opportunity before the call ends. When I finally see my family again, I feel like I've been through a whirlwind. Mom comes up to me: her eyes are all wet, and it looks like she's already cried and that she may start again now. I pull her into a big hug. "Mom, don't cry." She mumbles against my chest, "These are happy tears." She rejoins Dad. He hugs her and kisses her forehead. Annie is standing back. I think she is trying to give us family space, but I'm not having it; she's going to be my family one day, and she needs to realize that none of these moments are just mine, they are ours. I pull her into our little circle and against my side. She comes without hesitation. "So, what's next?" Dad asks. "Well, I was thinking dinner, I'm starving." This gets everyone laughing. We head to dinner, and I forget for a few hours that I'm about to move away from all of these people I love, and that I'm not going to have this summer with Annie, because the dream is now real.

The next week and a half are a blur of phone calls and planning. My agent does the real work: I just have to agree or disagree with his approaches or suggestions. The only call that I have to make is to the coach at Norman to formally withdraw from my collegiate offer. He tells me congratulations and wishes me the best. I get calls about a lot of things and have to lock in a furnished apartment quickly. The club is letting other guys know that I have an extra room available to rent. The only thing that I have left to do is pack. Looking around my room, I have no idea where to start. When did I forget how to pack? We'd moved every few years until getting here. I hear a knock at my open door. I expect it to be Mom or Dad. They keep checking in to see what they can do to help, but to my surprise, it is Daniel.

He got home from his rehab program right before the draft, but he didn't feel like it was a good time to act like we were all good. I'd appreciated him skipping the event, because it had given me the extra spot for Annie to be with me at the draft. "You need any help?" Daniel asks from the doorway. I am about to say no, but for some reason, I say, "Yeah, can you help me tape up those boxes and then fill them with the clothing from the closet?" "Yeah, no problem," he says, and we work on our tasks. The clothing is an easy item to take; it's the rest of it that I am overwhelmed by. How much to take and how much to leave here? My eyes drift over the pictures I have decorating my walls, the little league memorabilia, the trophies... I think I'll leave them. One item gets checked off in my mind. I keep scanning the walls, checking yes or no in my head on whether I should pack it or not. I end up looking at the painting of me and Annie. "Drew, you ok?" I hear Daniel say from the edge of my closet.

"Yeah, yeah, why do you ask?" I say by default, still looking at the painting. "I don't know, bro, the fact that you haven't moved for like five minutes looking at the painting? Did you all break up or something?" I flinch at Daniel's question—not because of his tone, he hadn't said it as a jab to be cruel or spiteful like when we'd had the last run-in about Annie. It's almost like he is trying to be kind. I flinch because he assumes that we broke up and that we didn't make it. "We are still together. I guess I got lost thinking about how we'll make it work, that's all." I run my hand through my hair and turn back to my task. "Drew, I never said it, but I'm an ass for the stunt last fall; she never looked at me like that," he says and points at the painting. "You are an ass, I agree." I face my brother, and we share a little look. Then the moment passes, and we go back to work. I look at the painting and make a mental note that I need Mom's help to package the painting so it can travel to Arizona with me.

***

I leave tomorrow, and all my boxes are in the garage, ready to load into my car. Dad is going to make the road trip with me, and Mom is going to fly in tomorrow to Arizona to make sure I have all the stuff I really need when we arrive. I wanted Annie to come with me, but a part of me knows it is going to be easier to have this first separation where she has support on standby. She's been excited to my face, but I know my Annie, and she is hiding her other feelings away. I've seen looks of sadness pass over her face quickly yet more often as tomorrow's date approaches. I called Meg yesterday to make my plans for Annie. Meg is going to take off from work the day after I leave and spend the day uninterrupted with Annie. I'd taken over a few bags of Annie's favorite snacks to Meg's house to supply the girls' day. "Drew, you didn't have to do this. I could have bought snacks for us," Meg had said when I'd shown up with my haul of items. I'd let her know it was the least I could do, that she was the one who was going to have to make sure our girl didn't fall apart. Meg had hugged me and promised to take care of Annie, then said, in true Meg fashion, that I better go kick some ass to make it worth it.

I'm getting off my last call with the club before I leave for Arizona when I hear Annie's voice from the stairs saying, "Have a good dinner," and the front door slamming shut. I hear her hurried footsteps up the stairs, and then she is there in my doorway. God, she is beautiful, she's just in a pair of shorts and a T-shirt. She smiles and comes in, shutting and locking the door behind her. "You expecting any calls?" she asks over her shoulder. "Nope, I'm all yours for the night," I reply. Annie turns, already removing her shirt and tossing it to the floor.

"Well, what are you waiting for then, Dimples?" She removes a new piece of clothing with each step into my room. She takes off her bra and her shoes, finishing by kicking her shorts and underwear off. I take her lead and strip out of my shorts, boxers, and t-shirt as quickly as humanly possible, and we meet next to my bed, fully naked. I reach out, pulling her gorgeous naked body against mine, and kiss her. She wraps her arms around my neck, and we kiss, standing naked against each other until one of us gets us falling onto my mattress. I eventually grab a condom, roll it on, and enter her body in a slow slide. Somewhere our quick start of undressing and hard passionate kisses has morphed into slow moves and touches. Neither of us seems in a rush to reach our climax; it feels like we both want to savor this moment, not knowing when the next one will be.

I am sliding slowly in and out of her, watching the way her face changes with each slide. Her eyes are watching mine too. It feels like both of us are trying to memorize each other in this moment of our bodies being connected, trying to savor every detail to help us when the distance will be the only thing between us. She wraps her fingers into the back of my hair and looks directly into my eyes before saying, "I love you, Drew Joseph Davis." She's told me she loved me daily since the day we both declared our feelings, but for some reason, this one feels bigger, like a moment that I'll want to remember until I die. I run my hand up her side until it is on her cheek before I say, "I love you more than you can imagine, Annie Marie Campbell." I kiss her, and she kisses me back. We don't break our kiss until we each see the same stars.

We've been lying naked in post-lovemaking bliss, wrapped around each other. My fingers are playing with Annie's long hair, and she's drawing little hearts against my chest when I hear her say, "I'm going to miss you, Drew. I knew that when you got drafted that you'd have to leave, but I wasn't prepared for this feeling: this feeling of dread and sadness mixed in with all the happiness and pride I feel." I take my time before answering. "I'm going to miss you too, Annie," I reply before I move us to our sides so we can look at each other. I think it's time to address the elephant in the room. I don't let her lead us in this part—I want to start.

"I love you, Annie. We need to come up with a plan to make this work." She replies, "I love you too. What is your plan?" Oh shit, what is the plan? *Do I have a plan?* I know that I don't want to go days without talking to her, but I also want to know what she wants and what she needs, so I reply, "Well, I want to talk about it with you." She gives me a smirk before saying, "Oh, I see, Dimples. You want me to plan." I can't help but laugh and say, "I mean you did plan my seduction twice, and both were very, very good plans." She gives me a playful little smack of her hand on my bare chest before saying, "Ok, fair point, I'm good at plans." We both go silent, and I watch her think. I see when she makes a decision. "We need to have three non-negotiables: like, we have to talk every day could be one." She has read my mind, and I smile, praising her idea and adding a suggestion. "Maybe make sure we do video chats at least three times a week." She agrees, and we both sit thinking again in silence.

Phone sex pops into my head; I can't help it with her naked body in my arms. Before I think better of it, I say, "I want to say phone sex—does that make me sound like a perv?" She laughs and smacks her hand against my chest again before saying, "Yes, major perv vibes," then tacks on, "I agree with you, though. If I can't touch you," she emphasizes by running the hand that smacked my chest down my abs before continuing, "I'll still want moments like this with you, however I can get them, but only over video and no pictures." It's easy to make the deal because I understand that we don't need to risk a leaked photo with the futures we both want to have. With that settled, I suggest that we get into another round of sex before we can't.

***

Dad, Daniel, and I make quick work of loading my car the next day before my friends come over to do a big send-off. They wanted to give me my own personal pep rally. I wanted to tell them all not to worry about it, but I didn't want to sound like an ass, not celebrating one last time with them before leaving. I am not going to see my friends for a while, with me heading out now and them going off to college in the fall. Craig is going to Norman with Annie, and Luke is headed off to Texas to play for a school there. Meg and Tom are headed to the same university as Miles. Annie and I aren't separated at all this morning as we chat one last time as a group. "Drew, we better head out if we want to make it to the first stop tonight," Dad says as he steps out of the front door. I give Craig and Luke a half hug, and they both tell me to kick some ass. I wrap my fingers in Annie's and walk to the driver's side of my car.

She has been quiet all morning. I place my hands on her cheeks and tip her head back to look into her eyes. "I love you, Annie Marie Campbell." I kiss her like no one is watching. Our friends' whistles cause us to break our kiss, and she says, "I love you too, Drew Joseph Davis. Go now before I can't let you," before she steps out of my arms. I just want to grab her back into my arms, but I take the opportunity she's given me to get into the car. I open the window and wave and shout my goodbyes. I check my rearview mirror one last time to see my friends, and I almost stop the car. In the reflection, I see Craig giving Annie a side hug, but that's not why I want to stop the car. No, it's the tears I can just make out on her cheeks and the look of devastation on her face. I've never seen my girl look so broken, and I know I'm the reason for it. Who knew your dreams could have such horrible consequences?

Chapter 61: Highs and Lows
-*Annie*-

Watching Drew get drafted is the best and worst thing I've ever been a part of. I'm so excited for him and proud of him. I'm also extremely sad, knowing he is going to be gone in days, and that our time getting to walk across the grass separating his house from mine is going to end much faster than I expected. We will have to go days, weeks, and possibly months without kisses, without hugs, without me seeing that dimple in person. I should have thought about this more. I mean, I love baseball—I know the draft happens and that the guys drafted head off to play in the minor leagues almost right away.

I mean, we have a minor league team within driving distance from our house, and the lineup changes from one season to the next. At a fundamental level, I've known this would be the result of him getting drafted. I guess I've pushed all my rational knowledge to the back of my brain when it comes to being separated from him, because this feeling of emptiness is unexpected and not what I thought I'd be feeling. I sit, watching him beaming on stage in his new Arizona hat, and I try to remember to smile through my internal struggle. While he is away backstage, I talk to his parents in between rounds and watch other guys beaming on stage. For each of them, I only feel happiness at seeing their dreams come true. About forty-five minutes later, my phone buzzes on the ta ble.

I let his parents know the plan and we find the security guy. He is nice and asks all about Drew with the Davises while he escorts us to the area to meet Drew. Drew appears, talking with his agent, and I hang back, watching my professional baseball player boyfriend shine in his excitement. It radiates from him: the dimple never leaves his face as they wrap up the conversation before Drew sees his parents and jogs over to them, all sharing a big hug. He looks at me, takes a few steps to my side, and wraps his arms around me in a huge hug. He takes my hand, leading us back to the group to rejoin the conversation with his parents and his agent. Drew's dad asks the question I don't want to know the answer to yet. "What happens next?" Drew smiles at his dad and says, "Well, I was thinking dinner, I'm starving." I can't help laughing along with the group. We go to a fancy restaurant near the hotel we are staying in. I excuse myself when we first arrive to go to the bathroom, and I look at myself in the mirror while washing my hands. I will be happy: *he is still my future no matter where he is, don't stress,* I tell myself. *Leave tomorrow's problems for another day.* As I look into the mirror, I see a smile on my face, and I push all my worries away and go celebrate with my guy.

***

As soon as we get home, Drew is busy getting ready to go to Arizona. He takes so many calls in the first five days, my head is spinning trying to keep up with all the details. When he isn't on his phone, we can't be separated. Even now that almost two weeks have passed, we haven't talked about the fact that he leaves tomorrow. It's like neither of us wants to break the bubble or acknowledge the separation that is coming whether we want it to or not. When I came over a few minutes ago, Mr. and Mrs. Campbell were headed out to dinner. It's nice that they are going out, because I selfishly want time alone with him, to be connected to him

I make it upstairs, and we make quick work of getting naked. We then take our time showing each other how much we love each other. We are both taking our time, touching, stroking, and kissing each other. A moment grows where we are watching each other's expressions. I am enjoying watching his face reflect how he feels about our bodies being connected and it reflects how he feels about me. I can't help myself, and I wrap my hands into his hair and say, "I love you, Drew Joseph Davis." Drew's dimple appears as he runs his hand up my side, following a path up my ribs and over my breast. His hand continues to travel up my neck to settle against my cheek before he says, "I love you more than you can imagine, Annie Marie Campbell." I can feel all the ways he loves me, and they aren't just in the ways our bodies are connected. He seals his words with an unending kiss. I'm not even sure when it ends, because I fall over the edge into my orgasm, and Drew joins me in the falling.

***

My body has cooled down and we are still twisted around each other, naked in Drew's bed. As my brain turns back on, I take in Drew's mostly empty room. All that is left are his childhood mementos. All his newer pictures have been packed away, and the painting of us has been removed from the wall. It makes me feel good to know he wants to take it with him—to have this reminder of us, of me with him wherever he goes. The words escape me, "I'm going to miss you, Drew," and I hear the catch of sadness in my words. "I knew when you got drafted that you'd have to leave, but I wasn't prepared for this feeling: this feeling of dread and sadness mixed in with all the happiness and pride I feel."

Now that I've said the words and they are out there between us, a little weight has been lifted from me. I've been putting on an act in front of everyone, and it's been exhausting. I've hated feeling like I was somehow lying by omission to Drew. "I'm going to miss you too, Annie," he replies before he shifts our bodies so that we are on our sides and our faces are level with each other. "I love you, Annie. We need to come up with a plan to make this work." He sounds so serious about making this plan. I reply with, "I love you too. What is your plan?" "Well, I want to talk about it with you," he says with a smirk. "Oh, I see, Dimples. You want me to plan," I say and can't help the smile. "I mean, you did plan my seduction twice, and both were very, very good plans," he laughs. "Ok, fair point, I'm good at plans," I say before giving him a quick kiss.

I think over all my worries from the last five days. What would we have to do to make this work? "We need to have three non-negotiables: like, we have to talk every day could be one." Drew smiles and says, "See, you are a better planner—that is a great idea. I like the idea of talking every day. Maybe make sure we do video chats at least three times a week?" "That is a good one," I reply. Then we both sit for a little while in silence, before Drew says, "I want to say phone sex—does that make me sound like a perv?" I laugh. "Yes, major perv vibes," I reply to him before adding, "I agree with you, though. If I can't touch you," and I emphasize my point by running my hands against his abs, "I'll still want moments like this with you, however I can get them, but only over video and no pictures." "Deal, now before my parents come home, do you think we can get in another round of in-person touching?" He kisses me, and we get in two more rounds. I don't even notice when his parents come home, or that my curfew has come and gone without the ping from the location app on my phone.

***

Drew left yesterday to go to Arizona. As he drove away, I couldn't help the tears that streamed down my face. I must have cried harder than I thought, because Craig had wrapped me up into a side hug. He didn't say anything as Drew's car made the turn and disappeared. I locked myself in my room and cried for the rest of the day. Mom came up to check on me, and I told her everything was fine. She didn't seem to be convinced, but she'd left me alone. Today, I've sat on my bed all day, having emptied my body of all the tears it can shed. I feel ridiculous—we didn't break up, we are still together, but just not right next to each other. I hear the knock at the door. "Come in." I am expecting my mom again, but it's Meg. "I come bearing gifts," she announces, as she has two bags full in her arms.

She has all my favorite snacks and candies. We turn on a rom-com and munch on all the goodies. When the movie ends, I feel a little lighter, a little more human. "Thank you for getting all of this," I tell her. "Well, I only showed up, Drew ordered all the snacks and told me he thought I should bring them by after he left," she says. "Oh, Meg, am I that pathetic?" I say covering my eyes with my hands. "No, Annie, you love him, and he knew you'd be sad. It's ok to be sad when someone we love is so far away." "Well, thank you for being here," I say and mean it. "Tomorrow, we leave the house," she declares. "Yes, tomorrow we leave the house," I agree. Later, I get my first call from Drew. He sounds tired but excited about his apartment. He lets me know he will video call me tomorrow to show me the space once he and his parents actually unpack his stuff. He lets me know that he's also met his roommate, a guy named Adam Perez from Florida. Drew says he's the catcher for the team and seems like a cool dude. Then he asks me what I've been up to. I should tell him the truth, but I also don't want to bring down his excitement, so I say hanging out with Meg. We end the call by eac h saying *I love you*. I sit in my empty room and vow, *tomorrow I really will get*

***

A week later, a small pattern is emerging for my summer. Drew and I text on and off each day, and either call or video chat. We haven't gotten to that phone sex call yet, but I'm sure it will be coming soon. I've also started the part-time job I got at the end of school to help digitize all the old copies of the Reporter. I figured it would be good to say I have been in a newsroom other than high school. It is pretty easy, but the money is already being put to good use. I am saving to see if I can get a round-trip ticket to Arizona to visit Drew before I start in Norman in August.

***

Almost two weeks after Drew leaves, I turn nineteen and get a wakeup call from Drew wishing me a Happy Birthday. He tells me next year we will make sure we are together, and I make him promise. When I make it downstairs, I'm greeted with "Happy Birthday" from Miles, Mom, and Dad. It has been nice to have my brother home, and we have a family breakfast full of our sports debates. I even invite Miles to join me and my friends for our plans today. When he asks what we are doing, I have to be honest and let him know that Meg insisted on a day full of fun. He tells me he's game, and I give him the only information I have from Meg, which is to have a swimsuit, a towel, and to bring extra sunscreen. We both head upstairs to change.

***

I hear the horn from my room and know that it is my signal that Meg is here. As I leave my room, I yell to Miles, "You ready?" I hear his muffled, "I'll join you at the car in a second." As I go downstairs, I yell to my parents that I'm leaving, and they both yell goodbye from somewhere in the house. When I get outside, Meg rolls down the window and yells, "Happy nineteenth birthday, Annie Marie." Meg has always been able to make me feel so special; I'm a lucky girl to have her as my best friend. "Thank you—Miles is going to join us, I hope that is ok." I get into the car. "Yeah, the more the merrier." She grabs her phone and types a message to someone. "So," I start, "can you tell me now where we are going?" I jokingly plead. Miles has joined us and is in the backseat, looking as curious as I am about the events for today. "Guess," is Meg's one-word reply. I make an exaggerated thinking expression from the passenger seat as she is pulling out of the neighborhood. "A pool?" I guess, and Meg says, "Lame." "What about the water park?" I guess next. Meg gives me a side eye from behind the wheel before saying, "Are we twelve, no." This gets a laugh from Miles in the back seat. "Well then the lake, it's got to be the lake," I say.

I earn a smile from Meg. "Yes, it's the lake, but it's not any lake day on the beach. Tom's parents have a pontoon boat." "Do they have a tube to pull?" Miles asks from the back. Meg looks in the rearview mirror, "Yes, they have the one that sits like three to four people." "Annie, thanks for the invite, sounds like fun," Miles says to me. "Yeah, it should be fun." When we get to the boat ramp, I try to fight the little ping of sadness that passes when I think about being here at night what feels like years ago with Drew. Meg leads us to the pontoon boat. I can see Tom, Craig, Luke, Travis, a few girls I don't know, and one guy I don't know. Meg gives Tom a quick hug and kiss as she boards the boat. As I get on, I tell him thank you for taking us out for the day. Tom lets me know it isn't a problem and then yells, "Justin, come here a second." The guy I don't know comes over, and Tom continues, "Justin, this is Annie. Annie, this is Justin, my buddy from school." Justin reaches his hand out and I shake his hand. "So, you're the girl we are celebrating today," he says, giving my hand a little squeeze.

I remove my hand quickly because it felt weird, and I'm sure he wouldn't have done that with Drew here. "Yeah, that's me, nice to meet you," I say and then excuse myself to join the guys I know. They introduce me to the girls, Amanda and Emily. Tom gets behind the captain's chair and we take off for the day on the lake. We have fun swimming and tubing most of the day. The only little hiccup is when Justin starts asking me if I'd like to go out sometime over the summer, and before I can even tell him no, Craig gets involved, not so kindly letting Justin know that I have a boyfriend. Justin smarted off something like, "Well, if he's such a good guy, why isn't he here?" "Maybe because he's a pro baseball player, asshole," Luke interjects himself into the conversation.

Meg joins the conversation and gets the guys to settle, but it killed a little of the easygoing nature of the day. We all agree to head back to the boat ramp. I tell all my friends thank you for coming and hop into the car with Meg and Miles. "Sorry about Justin" is the first comment Meg makes when we get into the car. "Tom said to tell you sorry, too: he didn't realize his buddy was going to try to hit on you the whole boat ride." "He was kind of an ass," Miles replied from the backseat. "He even asked me after the whole *she has a boyfriend thing* if I'd give Annie his number. I told him to fuck off and to leave my sister alone." "My shining hero," I joke. I haven't looked at my phone all day because we'd been on the boat, and Meg had volunteered to be the official photographer. I have ten missed messages from Drew.

Drew Davis

I hate that I am missing your birthday

Back from practice, have fun on the boat

Meg sent me a picture of you in a bikini

I mean it did have other people in it too

Correction now I have one of just you

Why have I never seen you in a bikini in person?

We need to fix that ASAP!

But I have seen you in red lingerie so maybe   that kinda counts

Now all I can think about is you in lingerie

Text me when you're headed back home I love you

Annie

Just headed back from the lake

Drew Davis

You have a good time?

Annie

It was fun

We all tubed and Miles had an epic head first wipe out

Drew Davis

Did Meg capture that on camera?

Annie

Nope, she was also on the tube unfortunately

but I'll remember it forever LOL

I tell Meg and Miles that I need to video call Drew in the driveway, because I have another birthday surprise. We all pass back and forth ideas of what could be my surprise for the rest of the drive.

***

I hit the video button and the phone rings twice before Drew's face appears on the screen. "Angel, you look all sun kissed. I'm jealous, I want to kiss your skin, too." "Annie, he knows that other people are around, right?" Miles speaks from the backseat. "Oh, gosh, is that your brother? I was about to describe what happens after we start kissing," Drew says, showing off that dimple. Meg and I laugh. "Meg, thanks for spoiling our girl," Drew says, and I point the phone in her direction. "No problem, lover boy. Is phase two ready?" Meg smiles as she asks Drew.

"Wait, what phase two? Do you already know my surprise?" I say, looking from Meg to Drew on my phone. "Yeah, phase two is waiting in the living room," Drew says back to us over the phone. "You are better at planning than you think, Drew Davis," I say into the camera. We all get out of the car and head towards the front door. "Is a crazy clown going to jump out at me in the living room, because

I'll be honest, I dislike clowns, call it off," I say to Drew on my phone. Drew laughs over the phone. "No clowns, Angel, but thanks for the advice." "I'll get the door," Miles says, and he opens the door for me and Meg. I go into my house and there are so many flowers—I count a least five different arrangements. "I know you got a rose at prom, but I wasn't sure if it was your favorite, so I ordered a few kinds. I expect a report back on your favorite," Drew smiles. "They are all so beautiful, I'm not sure if I'll be able to pick a favorite," I say as I walk around, looking at all the flowers. "Thank you for my surprise, Dimples," I say, looking directly at Drew on the screen. "Oh, Angel, that isn't the surprise, those are just flowers to celebrate my girl," Drew says.

Then Mrs. Davis comes from the kitchen. "Oh, hello Mrs... Jennifer, it's so good to see you," I say as I see her. She walks over and gives me a hug. "Happy Birthday, Annie. Now follow me." I know I have a puzzled look, and I glance from Drew on my phone to his mom. "Follow Mom, she's going to show you the real surprise." I follow Mrs. Davis, followed by Meg and Miles. We enter the kitchen, and there, on an easel, is my surprise. I should say thank you, but I'm too mesmerized by it. It's obviously a painting done by Mrs. Davis; she has taken the photo from the state championship of Drew and me and put it on canvas. She's done a few adjustments here and there, but it completely captures the excitement of the moment, of the love between us. "Oh, Angel, don't cry," is what finally pulls me from my trance.

I didn't even realize I'd started crying, but I am. "They are happy tears," I say, looking at the phone. "Drew, it's beautiful, thank you." I also thank Mrs. Davis, and she gives me another hug before excusing herself. Meg and Miles both hug me and follow Mrs. Davis. I return to Drew on my phone after they leave. "When did you plan this?" "When I got invited to the draft. I wanted you to have your own Jennifer Davis painting to look at of us," Drew says. "I will have to figure out where to put it in my room, but I can't take it to college; I don't want it damaged." The thought of anyone messing it up makes me feel sick. "Well, I'll get a printed canvas of the painting created that can go with you, and the original can stay safe in your room until it can be moved to join the first one," Drew says. I like that he is hinting that we will live together one day and we'll have a set of our memories on our walls. "I can't wait, Dimples, I love you." "I love you too, Angel," Drew says from the phone. We talk until my phone flashes a 5% battery warning and we both realize the time.

Chapter 62: Call Fail

-Annie-

Two weeks after my birthday, the pattern is more or less the same, but Drew and I have started missing calls because of our schedules. We still text each day, but I'm at the Reporter when he is open to talk, and he's at practice or games when I'm free. I've tried to get out with friends, and it never fails that I'm at a movie or something when he calls. Tonight, I'm out with Craig and Luke at the local minor league game. I watch the game and imagine the shortstop is Drew and not the guy in front of me. As if I'd manifested it, my phone starts to buzz, and a picture of Drew in his Arizona jersey pops up. I swipe and open the video chat. "Angel, can you hear me?" I can see Drew, but my box is all blank. "I can hear you, but I'm at the ballpark with Craig and Luke, and I have crap signal—I don't think my video will work." I reply.

"I can call you back later?" Drew asks. "No, I can see you, stay," I say. "Man, great game today, saw the stats," Craig pipes in next to me, and then Luke directs my hand to pull the mic closer to him, "I told you you'd kick ass: you'll be moved up next season no problem with plays like that." "Thanks, guys, I appreciate it." He is smiling with the praise from his friends. "Angel, really, you can call me back after the game, it isn't a problem. Perez and a few guys are hanging, I can ju—" He gets cut off by a girl's voice. "Davis, baby, come back to the party. I thought you were going to teach me more about baseball, and I was going to show you my appreciation for the lessons." I can't help but think *who the fuck is calling Drew baby and what does she mean by appreciation?* Drew's face on the screen freezes with a girl's hand on his chest, and the call gives me the pop-up of "call failed."

What the hell just happened? I try to call him back, but my phone's signal sucks, and I keep getting a "call failed" message. I look up from my phone, and Luke and Craig are staring at me. "Annie, I don't think that is what it sounded like," Luke says, and he sounds serious, which makes me more worried. Luke is never serious: he's always the comic relief. "Really, Annie, he'd said Perez had people over," chimes in Craig. I put up my hand for them both to stop. "He said Perez had GUYS over, but I don't want to get into this with you both," I tell them. They both return their attention to the game, but I can feel them checking on me through side eyes. My phone buzzes with a text notification.

I don't answer because the few times I've tried to type something, it is all angry replies like, "Well enjoy teaching her BASEBALL" or "Why was she in your room Drew?" because he'd been in his room, that much was clear from the call. At one point, I even type and then delete another message saying, "could have fooled me." I know this is jealousy and anger, and I shouldn't say anything over text when I feel like this, so I put my phone away and sit in the stadium until the game ends, because I'm not watching the game after what just happened.

***

The guys continue in Drew's defense on the drive home, and I feel like I'm going to throw up the hot dog and crackerjacks that I had at the ballpark the whole way to my house. "Annie, I swear if I'm wrong, I'll go to Arizona myself and kick his ass," Craig says, and Luke's "Ditto" at least makes me less mad at my friends for their defense of Drew. On the rational side of my brain, I know that Drew loves me and he isn't the kind of guy that would cheat, but what I'd heard and seen had been real: I didn't make it up.

When I get home, I do my best not to rush to my room, but I can't help taking the stairs two at a time to get to my room. The video call is already ringing when I shut the door to my bedroom, and I take a seat at my desk. Drew's face appears on the screen and a feeling of relief passes through my body, because he is alone. My mind had imagined he'd answer with that girl next to him. "Angel." He says it so tentative, like he doesn't want to set me off, which does set me off a little. He doesn't get to call me Angel right now. "Don't *Angel* me right now, Drew. Explain." "Annie, please, I promise it looked worse than it was," he says, and before he can finish, I cut in, "Drew, just so we are on the same page here, let me tell you what it LOOKED like and what it SOUNDED like before the call ended, why don't I?

I hear, and I quote, 'Davis, baby, come back to the party. I thought you were going to teach me more about baseball, and I was going to show you my appreciation for the lessons.'" "Annie," he interjects with a look of pain on his face, but I don't let him interrupt me. "Then, Drew, you want to know what I SAW? I saw her hand on your chest in your room, and then the call failed." I take a deep breath, the jealousy and anger back in full force in my bloodstream. "Can I explain?" Drew says, before I give him my one word reply. "YES." "Annie, Perez had people over after the game, and at first it was just a couple of the other guys from the team, but it evolved, and a few of the local baseball groupies tagged along with Jackson."

He takes a deep breath before continuing, "I did talk with her, and she'd asked a lot of questions about baseball. I was just being nice, but then she hinted that she wanted to see my room, and I told her no, Annie, I swear. I told her I had a girlfriend, and I made a point to get up and get something to drink. She kept trying to restart the conversation, and I'd come into my room, and I thought I locked the door when I called you because I wanted to talk to you, not her. But

I must not have locked the door. I don't know how I missed the door opening and closing—I was talking with you and the guys, and she appeared behind me. After the call failed, I removed her from my room and told Jackson he needed to take her out of my apartment." He takes a deep breath and runs his hand through his hair, looking exhausted.

I take in a deep breath and try to push the anger and jealousy from my body to digest what he's told me about the events before and after what I saw. "Drew, before you got interrupted, you told me Perez had some guys over: why say it like that?" Because after all he'd said, this point still bothered me. I needed to understand. "I don't know, I didn't do it on purpose. Maybe I felt guilty that she'd thought I was flirting when I'd just been talking about baseball, maybe I didn't want you to think I'm partying in Arizona with all these girls in my apartment, because I'm not. Annie, I will never do that to us. I know what I have, and no easy offer of sex is going to make me forget that you're it, that we are it, that I love you." When he finishes, he looks so sincere, and my last feelings of anger and jealousy disappear. "Can we not lie to save the other the heartache or worry again, please? I would rather have all the details, because what I just did tonight was spiral, Drew, I..." I pause because even the thought hurts. "I thought this 'us' wasn't enough, that the distance has already gotten to us, and it's only been a little over a month." "Angel, I'm sorry, I promise," he says. We talk for a while longer, but I can't kick the pressure in my chest, the feeling that I need to be sick.

Chapter 63: All the Things I Love

It's been amazing being in a professional baseball club. All the focus we get from the coaches to the trainers is impressive. It's easy to take advantage of each opportunity that is offered, to take the advice of these people whose job it is to focus on weeding out the winners and losers. They have to determine who is worth moving up and who can't take the pressure of so much baseball physically or mentally. I don't want to be found in the group of guys labeled as "not ready." I want to make the club's investment in me worth it, because I love each game, each crack of the bat when I connect, and each play I make on the ball. It's work, but I don't feel like I'm working; I'm just playing a game that I love for money. I know I've let a few phone calls slip with Annie since I left. I make excuses in my mind that it will all level off, the season is only so long. I'll be home in the fall, and the distance of almost eighteen hours will be cut down to only four from home to her in Norman.

***

Then that stupid party happened, and the fight with Annie followed. Since then, things haven't felt completely the same with Annie, and I can't place what is wrong exactly. She said she believed me about what happened, and I didn't lie to her about the details. I'd made a mistake in how I had tried to handle the situation, and I knew it and haven't repeated it. The next day, I asked Perez to keep the groupies out of the apartment, at least for our after-game celebrations. I didn't care who he brought home to his room. He laughed and told me I was whipped. I told him he would be too if he had an Annie. He laughed before saying he wasn't sure this Annie was worth it. Being a smart ass, I pulled out my phone and showed him that bikini pic of her from last summer, which was a mistake because now he keeps asking me when the blondie was going to visit so he could see if it was worth it to be whipped. I know he is messing with me, or I guess I hope he is messing with me. If Annie gets to visit, and he hit on her, I may have to show him what it means to get his ass kicked.

***

We've made it to halfway through the season, and it's mid-July. My birthday is tomorrow. The guys found out today, and they want to have a party after the game. It helps that the day following my birthday is our off day, so we can have a little fun without impacting our play on the field. I've told them I'm in, and one of the guys says we should go to a local club that is eighteen and up. I don't see the appeal personally, but a lot of the guys are in, so I say sure. After practice, I think about what I have to do today and try to remember Annie's schedule for the day to call and fill her in on my new birthday plans. I finally figure I'd call her on the drive to the charity event I'd been voluntold to attend. The event is for the kids in the area: I have to sign a few autographs and help run a little clinic. The coach suggested in our last one-on-one session that players who do good in their communities and give the club a good name can only rise in the league. Then he'd asked me if I was interested in the event. I'd said yes, because with that little sales pitch, how could I say no?

***

I call and text her with no reply, which isn't completely weird—we miss each other, and Annie doesn't have her phone with her at all times, so I'll have to talk to her later. I'm almost to the ballpark where the event is taking place when I get a call from my mom. "Mom, how's it going?" I answer. "Oh, hunny, it's going good here. I think we may come to visit in August, to see you play *and* for work. I loved all the desert landscape possibilities." "Sounds good," I let her know, because it will be nice to have family in the stands. Mom changes the subject. "I know you're busy, but you should be getting your birthday present today. I wanted to call to let you know to look for it later." I let her know that I'll be home a little later, but Perez will be home to get the package. She laughs at me and says that will work. She tells me to have fun with the kids and ends the call with her typical *be safe* and *love you*.

***

So here I am, feeling ridiculous, signing a bunch of autographs on photos of myself in the Arizona jersey and on the baseballs the kids offer. I think almost none of these kids know who I am, but their parents know I could be somebody, so they are here in my line to get my signature. One of the boys—he's got to be like twelve—asks me, "So, like, are you going all the way to the majors? I want to see if it will be worth it to get your signature now so I can sell it later." I laugh and sign "Worth It' and my name on his ball, which gets me a laugh at least. I've been focused on each person who appears in front of me, I haven't paid attention to the line or who is up next.

I think this is why I jump when I hear a voice I'd know anywhere. "I'd like mine made out to Angel." I look up at her, because there is no doubt that my eyes are going to see my Annie. I smile and say, "I think I can do better," and I sign 'for my love' with my signature, then slide back the signed photo. "I think that will do. Thanks, Dimples," she says, and she brushes her fingers over my hand as she takes the photo. I do check the line now; there are about ten kids left. I wave over to the lady from the team who lead me over to this table. When she joins me, I ask if I can have a quick ten-minute break before starting the clinic with the kids after I finish the signatures. She tells me that is fine. Annie has moved to the edge of the little area, and it takes all my effort to give the next kid my attention, but I do because I want them all to feel special for the few seconds that they have my time.

I sign the last kid's cap, and then I seal the marker and hand it over to the team rep. I hear her giving a little *here's what's next* to the group leaders as I walk to Annie. I should say hello or ask her how she is or tell her she is sexy as hell in my Arizona jersey, but none of those things happen. I walk up to my girl and kiss her in front of all of these people. I can't help myself. I know we are around families, so it doesn't turn into anything crazy, but I have to feel her lips on mine. When I pull back, she is smiling. I finally say, "Are you my birthday present?" Annie gives a wink and says, "I left the bow in my bag at your apartment, but yes, I'm your present. Surprise." I smile and pull her into a hug. "Best present ever," I say against her ear. She hugs me back. "I'm here for the next four days. Go play baseball with the kids so we can go home." I pull back: I like the sound of going home with her.

***

I finish the clinic, and the team rep lets me know that I'm finished and can leave. Annie has been sitting in the stands with the parents, watching, and I try not to get distracted, but kids need a lot of water breaks in the Arizona sun, so I get a lot of looks at my girl. She meets me at the gate, and I grab her hand and make a run for my car. She laughs and races with me. We talk for the whole twenty-minute drive to the apartment. I learn that Mom gave Annie the spare key to my apartment, so she hadn't met Perez yet, but she'd been able to store her stuff in my room by recalling its location from our video chat tour. When we get to the apartment, all I want to do is unwrap my present, but unfortunately, Perez and a few guys are over watching the game for the majors on TV in the living room. When I introduce Annie, a few guys don't think anything of it, but Perez looks Annie up and down, then gives me a smirk. I want to wipe it from his face. "Glad to know she matches the picture, let me know when I get that chance we talked about." I grab Annie's hand and lead her, looking confused, towards my door. I say over my shoulder, "Not a chance in hell, Perez, not a chance in hell." I hear him laugh as I shut the door.

My room isn't all that impressive, but it's mine. I have the painting of us on the wall and a few other things. Annie makes quick work of looking around the room before walking back to me. "I think it is time you got to unwrap your present, don't you?" "Yes, I think I've been really good and should get to unwrap it today and tomorrow and every day until you go home," I say, my fingers sliding the buttons of her jersey free. "Mmm, I can get behind that plan," she says as she starts sliding my jersey buttons free in return.

***

I wake up the next morning to my alarm with Annie in my arms. I'm spooned around her back, and it feels like the best way to wake up. Annie grumbles about the alarm and is now back asleep; my girl isn't much of a morning person. I like that I'm getting to learn this detail about her. We've only woken up next to each other a few times, but I know they've been my favorite mornings. What guy wouldn't want to wake up to a naked, beautiful girl, even if she is a little grumpy at first? I know I need to get up and do all my pregame routines, but I also don't want to leave this bed. The only reason I finally convince myself that I do, in fact, have to get up is that I know I'm off tomorrow and we have the whole day to spend in bed. When I come back in the room, Annie stirs under the covers, and I get a muffled "good morning" from the bed. But then she throws the covers off of her and sits up, saying in her fully awake voice, "Happy Birthday, Drew," and then launches into a little happy birthday song. I can't help thinking that this is the best version, because who doesn't want a sexy naked woman they love singing them a happy birthday?

***

It has been hard not to walk over to Annie in that bed and make love to her again, but today is a game day, and games here in Arizona are played earlier to accommodate the heat, so as much as I want to, I know I can't. Later, I'll make up for our missed morning. So, I settle for the kiss she gave me before she hopped into the shower. I can hear Perez in the living room and join him to ask if we can ride together to the ballpark, that way Annie can have my car so she doesn't have to be stuck at the club all morning. Perez tells me it's my present because he didn't get me one. I laugh and say it's a great gift all the same. He gives me shit about the fact that I do have a roommate, and even though his birthday isn't until November, he could use better noise-cancelling headphones. I tell him that he can handle it for only three more days, and I return to the bedroom to get myself ready and to get at least some kisses from my girl before we leave.

***

What the fuck is going on. I think in the dugout a few hours later. I have been on

332

a pretty good kick until today, and I'm not sure why I'm so off. I have struck out on all of my at-bats except the first one. I've been slow on defense, and I can't find the right gear. I wanted to play a great game with Annie here, but something isn't clicking today. Maybe I need that rest day after all. Maybe a day away from baseball will be what I need, because I can't let this be the direction the rest of the season goes. Perez breaks through my thoughts. "Oh, lover boy, earth to lover boy." "Oh, I see I'm the lover boy. Ha ha, funny man," I reply. "Maybe you need a little less mattress exercise with Blondie before the next game," he says, laughing. "You're just jealous my mattress got some exercise," I reply. Perez loops Smith in on the conversation. "I mean, I think anyone would be enjoying mattress time with Blondie, what do you say, Smithy?" Smith looks confused. "Who is Blondie?" he asks, and Perez stands out of the dugout on the railing and looks into the stands. "Smith. she is right behind the dugout in the 17 jersey, can't miss her." Perez jumps down from the railing, and Smith jumps up and looks around. I know the moment he sees Annie, because he smiles and jumps down. "Yeah, Perez, I wouldn't mind some time with Blondie." "Well, you can go fuck right the hell off because she's taken," I spit back at both of them. "You three going to focus on the game?" the coach cuts into the conversation, and that ends anything else they could have said about Annie. I turn my attention back to the game, not that it helps, as I continue to make stupid mistakes until it's over.

***

I shower and leave quickly after the game. I'd texted Annie to wait for me, and we ride back to the apartment together. At first, we are both quiet. We hold hands over the console but listen to the radio. I break the silence. "It's ok, we can both admit it was a shitty game." Annie takes a deep breath, "I mean, I've seen you play better, but off days happen, right?" "Right," I agree. We head back to the apartment, and I get distracted from my awful play today by, and in, her body. Eventually, we do have to put on clothing to go out with the guys. I'd wanted to cancel, but she said it sounded like fun.

She's been right, and the club has been more fun than I'd originally thought. I think that has a lot to do with Annie. She's chatting with all the guys, and half the guys are already half in love with my girl. She'd even given Perez some shit on his reaction at the plate today, and it was priceless to see his face. At some point, she tells me she wants to dance, and we do: all bodies pressed together, moving to the beat of the music. "Let's get out of here," I say next to her ear so she can hear me with the music. She smiles, takes my hand, and leads me out of the club, a feeling of déjà vu playing through me.

Chapter 64: Distractions Ruin Dreams

-Annie-

I'm not sure what happened today. Drew looked like he was struggling to find his timing: his bat a second too late and his steps just a little off in the field on defense. I can't help but feel guilty. We'd stayed up late last night, wrapped around each other, enjoying each other and making up for the month he has been gone. At least tomorrow he doesn't have a game, and we can enjoy the rest of his birthday, plus I will not have to feel guilty for keeping him up too late tonight. On the ride back from the ballpark, I don't know if I should come out and say anything or not. I'm grateful when Drew interrupts me listening to the radio with, "It's ok, we can both admit it was a shitty game." I squeeze his hand in mine and take a deep breath before replying with my truth on the topic, "I mean, I've seen you play better, but off days happen, right?" "Right," he agrees and squeezes my hand back. Back at the apartment, I use my body to distract him from baseball, and we get lost in each other.

***

Eventually, I check the clock and determine we should start to get ready to meet his teammates at the club like they planned. I make the suggestion to Drew that we save water and take a shower together. I feel like I have barely said the words before Drew sits up from the bed, throws me over his strong shoulders firefighter style, and carries me into the bathroom. He sets me down on the counter and turns around to start the shower. After he tests the water, he moves back to me at the sink, wraps my hair in his hands, and pulls my lips to his mouth in a seriously hot kiss. He picks me up, and I wrap my legs around his hips and my arms around his neck. He steps into the shower and pins me against the wall. His dick is pinned against my clit. The head of his dick rubs my clit, and I moan against his mouth. He keeps up with the motion of rubbing his dick up and down my clit. He starts to move his arms, and I know I let out a frustrated groan. I tighten my legs around his waist, trying not to lose the feel of him against me.

I feel his fingers at my entrance, and I can hear my moan vibrating around the bathroom walls. He slides two fingers into my pussy, matching the rhythm to the movement his dick is making against my clit. I know I'm not going to last long, which is probably good as we don't have the time. He breaks our kiss, telling me in his deeper voice, "Cum for me Annie." He continues to pump his finger into me, curling them, and hits a new spot. My orgasm hits. I break apart, and then my body goes limp against Drew and the shower wall. He lets me slide down his body, holding me as my legs are unsteady coming down from that orgasm. He reaches around me, grabs the shampoo, and starts to lather the lotion into my hair. "What, is that all?" I say into the steam from the shower. Drew laughs and says, "I'll fuck you in this shower before you leave, don't worry Angel, but I don't think we have time for what I want to do." "Promise," I say as his hands massage the shampoo into my scalp. "Promise. Angel," he says and pulls me into another kiss before we take turns washing each other's bodies clea n.

***

When we get to the club, we are taken to a back table and a group of guys and girls are already here. I wish I knew if one of these girls was Danielle, but a rational part of my brain knows it's better not knowing. Drew introduces me to a few of the guys near us and they all say hello. They go back to talking baseball, and I listen for a while taking in Drew and his teammates. I start to make a few comments here and there, and before I know it, I'm a part of the conversation. Then Perez starts to give Drew shit about today, and I can't help myself, I call out that Perez needs to cover the plate and that he'd been a little sloppy at home. Drew doesn't look pissed at my remarks to his teammate and roommate; he looks a little proud. I think it's time to dance, and I lean into Drew and say, "Dance with me, birthday boy." He stands up and offers me his hand. "Angel, it would be my pleasure." I take his hand, and we dance to each song for so long that I lose track. It's easy to lose track of time with his body against mine. Then his lips graze my neck before I hear, "Let's get out of here." *Great idea*, I think and take his hand, and we leave the dance floor and exit the club, ready to continue our night without an audience.

***

When we get back to the apartment, I tell Drew to wait in the living room and that I need to change into his second birthday surprise. He shows me his dimple and says I get five minutes. I take off and find the little scraps of red lingerie from my bag that I'd hidden at the very bottom of my suitcase. I go to the bathroom, shut the door, and undress to redress into this little set I'd found with Meg a few weeks ago. The bra is pretty much just underwire cups that sit under my breast, covering nothing. Then, I have to pull the fabric from either side and tie it in a bow over my nipples. The matching lace garter belt and thong are also red and have little bows. Meg had said, and I quote, "It makes you officially a present to unwrap" when she'd handed it over to me at the lingerie store.

I'd second-guessed myself a few times after buying it, but after all our talk of me being his present and the other unwrapping we've done since I got to Arizona, I feel nothing but confidence now. I give myself one more look in the mirror and approve, then shout, "Drew, you can come, in but sit on the bed." I hear the door open and the slide of the lock and then Drew says, "Ok, I'm where you wanted me." I open the door and face him from the doorway. "Fuck, Annie, you really are my present." I watch him look me up and down, then down and up, his eyes growing darker with each pass over my body. "Come over here Annie, I need to touch you," he says, as if it is causing him physical pain to not be touching me right now. "No," I say and smile. "No," he repeats, and he looks confused. "I will allow you to take one photo of me like this Drew, but only for you to remember your nineteenth birthday present," I say, and as my words settle with him, that dimple I can't resist appears.

He stands up and reaches into his pocket for his phone. He holds up his phone and clicks the button once, then sets his phone on the nightstand and sits back down. "Come here, Angel. I think I've waited long enough to open my present." Drew is all smiles again. I agree, and I walk over to him and stand between his legs. His hands waste no time in going to the ends of the ribbons and pulling them free of each other, exposing my breasts to him. He closes his eyes. "What are you doing?" I ask when he doesn't open them right away. "I'm making a wish before I blow out my candles." He opens his eyes, reaches out, and pulls me to him. As his mouth wraps around my left nipple, I wrap my hands into his hair at the base of his neck, and then he pulls back and blows on my wet skin. He does the same to my right breast and then looks up at me. "Can I always blow out my candles like this?" he asks, looking smug. "I'll have to check my schedule, but I think I'll be able to arrange it for when we are together for your next birthday."

I lean down and take his lips in mine, and then it's all touching, feeling, and my overwhelming lust. I help him remove his clothing until he is naked, and I tell him to sit against the headboard. I slide my thong down my legs and kick it toward the pile of Drew's clothing. I grab the condom from the stack on the side table and open it. I join Drew on the bed and slide the condom over his very hard dick, and then I straddle his hips, hovering over him. We've had sex more times than I can count, but normally, he's been the one on top, the one controlling the moment. Tonight, I want to give him pleasure, I want to drive him wild, and I want him to be able to touch me anywhere and everywhere while I am in control of our bodies.

I move until I feel Drew at my core and slide my hips down over the head of his dick, then back up, then a little down. I set a rhythm of sliding my body up and down him until he's fully inside me and I'm sitting on his lap completely. He's been touching and kissing me while I drive our passion. But the moment I'm sitting with him inside me, we both open our eyes and connect. I roll my hips, and his flutter shut again with a groan of "Annie" on his lips. It's powerful being in control of his body, of his lust, and I do it again, earning an "Angel" from his swollen lips. I can't help myself; I capture his lips in mine, and his hands wrap into my hair at the base of my neck. I move my body up and down him in a blinding, pounding rhythm. I catch fire and explode, moaning his name into his mouth, and he captures all that I have to give. At some point, Drew starts bucking his hips into me while I still slide myself against him, around him, and the tempo shifts and grows. At one point, I can't even understand where he starts and I begin—we feel so connected that it's all the same. There is no beginning or end, we are one. And I know the moment Drew cums because he groans "Annie" into the room and captures me in an all-consuming kiss. At some point, I get fully undressed, the last pieces of the lingerie removed, and fall asleep on Drew's bare chest, body spent and mind and soul bone-crushingly hap py.

***

I wake up the next day to the buzzing of a phone. I'm still snuggled into a warm body, and I have no interest in worrying about the phone, but the warm body that is my pillow moves, and I can see from my half-open eyes as Drew's hand reaches out and picks up the phone. "I have to take this, Angel," he says but doesn't move out of the bed. "Hello?" I can hear that it is a female voice, but I can't make out what she is saying, "Yeah, Pam, I can make it in today. Yeah, 2 p.m. works for me. Oh, Pam, would it be a problem if I come early and show my girlfriend the ballpark, like the locker room and stuff? Great, thank you." He ends the call and sets the phone down before speaking. "So, Coach wants to talk to me. I'm sorry, Angel, I know we thought we'd have the whole day, but—" I cut him off. He has to go talk to his coach: if I wasn't here, he'd feel no guilt about changing the plans for his off day. "Drew, I get it, you don't have to explain. What did I hear about a private tour?" I change the subject, and he smiles. "Yeah, Pam said that I could walk you around the facility behind the scenes. I can even take you to see my locker and stuff if you want before we go." "I've never had a private tour of a ballpark from one of my favorite players... Count me in," I say and reach up to kiss him.

***

The private tour has been special. Drew stops and talks to the office staff and coaches we run into and introduces me to all of them. I can tell that he is well-liked, and he loves it here. I get a walk-through of where he eats and takes meetings before we head out to the ballpark. He takes me out to the dugout steps and onto the field. Before I can take it all in, he takes my hand and leads me to the shortstop position, his position in the infield. I spin around and take in his view. There are the obvious things on the field: the pitcher's mound, the home plate, the netting behind to protect the fans. There are so many seats, and from this view, he can see so many people, and their reactions—good or bad, fan or rival—would all be in view. "What do you think so far, Angel?" he says, standing closer to second base than to me. "I think you have the best view in the place," I say, still looking out over the stands. "I know I do now," he says for a second, and I look over to find him looking at me and not the ballpark. I can't help my smile. "What's next?" He takes my hand and walks me to home base, then he leads me to the box. I make a show of pointing to the far fence before acting like I'm in position to take a swing at an imaginary ball. Drew laughs and slides in behind my back. "I think your elbow should be here to get the best swing." He checks my imaginary bat, then points out in the direction of the fence. "Now you're ready to hit that home run, Angel." I take my imaginary swing, but instead of taking off for first, I spin in his arms and lean up to kiss him. "Home run," I say against his lips. "Without a doubt, Angel," he says back, and we wrap our hands together as we head back in the direction of the dugout and locker room to finish our tour.

***

The locker room is what I would expect, and it's nice to know now where he is when he calls or texts me after a game. He doesn't have a lot of pictures, but the ones he has are all recent. One of our friends together after State, him and his parents at State, and one of us from the draft night, with him beaming in his new Arizona hat. As we head out into the hall, we run into another coach, but this isn't any coach—this is the head coach, and Drew makes the standard introductions. "Davis, you open now to have that conversation? We can start early, I know it's your off day." Drew looks at me, and before he speaks, I say, "I am fine—I remember the way back to Pam's office, just down the hall and to the left, right?" "You got it," the Coach says. "You sure?" Drew asks with a little pinch in between his eyebrows. "

Completely, you two have your meeting." I move from his side and start to walk down the hall. I can hear their conversation start in the hallway, carrying their voices around the space. "Son, is she the reason you played like you did yesterday? Are you distracted?" I almost flinch as I keep walking. "No, sir, it was a coincidence that she happened to be here when I sucked yesterday," Drew replies. "Davis, you can't have distractions like that, not now. You need to show up every game: the organization has high hopes for you. Before yesterday's game, I had a call with the Class A coach and he's looking forward to having you join them next year, but you can't afford more performances like that." I reach the point in the hall where their voices are lost, and I blindly make my way to the secretary's desk. She offers me a seat, and I take it and sit in a daze.

I'm a distraction. His coach thinks I'm distracting Drew, and that I could cost him the next opportunity. My mind spirals and spirals over the next thirty minutes, and then I know what I have to do, what has to happen. I already feel like throwing up, but I make my fingers move on my phone, setting my horrible plan into motion.

***

When Drew joins me in the office, he isn't as happy as he was on the field, but he isn't walking like he just heard his future was on the line. *He must be putting on a show for me* is all I can think. We get to the apartment, and Perez and a few of the guys are over. I tell Drew to stay and talk with his friends when I move towards his room. When I'm in the space of his empty room, I take a deep breath, and when I open my eyes, I make myself move around his room, finding all of my things and packing them in my suitcase. I have to stop a few times, the tears I'm holding in burning my eyes, and the pain in my chest making me feel like I can't breathe. *I have to*, I chant in my head. I'm zipping my bag when I hear the door open. Drew looks at me with my bag and yells over his shoulder that they can leave without us, and then he shuts the door. "Annie, why are you packing?" he asks with a confused expression. "You don't leave until tomorrow."

I take a deep breath, because this is it, this is the moment my horrible plan comes to life, and I have to push past the lump in my throat and the burn behind my eyes. "Drew, can you sit down? I think we need to talk." He goes to the bed and takes a seat. I walk my bag to the edge of the door. I join him on the bed, but in the opposite corner. "Annie, you are worrying me," he says before I can start. I don't know how to say it; saying it is the only part of this awful plan I couldn't make myself focus on. "Drew—" I take another breath. "Drew, this isn't going to work." "What do you mean this isn't going to work, Annie?" Drew asks before adding, "What isn't working, Annie? I'll fix it." "Drew, I'm distracting you. I can't be the reason that this doesn't work for you—" He cuts me off. "Coach doesn't know what he's talking about. You aren't distracting me, Annie, it was one game." "I don't want one game to turn into two, then three, Drew. I heard him say you are already being called about moving up. That's huge: I will not be the reason you don't get the next chance." I am pleading with him to hear me, to understand that I'm doing this for him. "No, Annie, I love you. No." He reaches out and pulls me into his lap, and I should push him away, but I know that this is the last time I'll be in his arms, and that I need his touch to help me get the next words out to finish what I have to do. "Drew, I love you, too. I love you so much, but I can't have that love turn into hate or resentment if I cause your dream to come crashing down. I'm leaving, I'm going home, because for right now, our paths are going in opposite directions. I am breaking up with you." And then the tears I've been holding back break free, and Drew holds me.

This hurts. There is no softening the blow of the words I have said, no undoing them. They had to be said, and yet I feel a bad taste in my mouth. Drew holds me, and I cry so hard I almost can't breathe anymore. He holds me, rubbing his calloused hand up and down my arm. He doesn't say anything. If it hurts this bad now, what is it going to feel like when I leave, when I go back home and I can't feel him against me? The last two and a half years, he's become the person I was closest to: he's my favorite person, my best friend. I was always able to just be Annie around him, even when I realized I had a crush on him or when I lusted after him. I'd always been myself, not some manufactured version I thought he wanted. I realize, sitting in his arms, that I'll never love anyone like I love him, but I also know that this love can't hold him back from his potential, his dream of the big leagues. *I have to get up*, I tell my brain. I have to remove my body from his and let him have his dream. I'll go and try to find my own dreams, even if right now I can't quite remember what they are. I meant it when I said that if we hold each other back this wouldn't last, we'd break each other, and I don't want this love to change to hatred or jealousy. I would rather live with the heartbreak in this moment than see his love changed into hate.

I pull my head up and look into his dark blue eyes. His eyes are red like I'm not the only one reduced to tears by my words. I can see my pain being reflected in them. I can't help myself, and I push up and kiss him. I need one more of his kisses, and we cling to each other. Then I find a strength I didn't know I had, push myself away from his lips, and climb out of his lap. I look at this beautiful boy, seeing the glimmer of the man he is growing into, knowing I'm going to miss the next big moments that shape him into the man he will become.

I know my actions tonight have hurt him and will be part of his story in the worst way. But I also know that he was never going to be able to do this for us, for himself. He's always been the one to hold me together, to try to hold us together. Drew has only ever wanted the best for me, and I think that is why he isn't fighting me; he must see the truth in my words. "Good luck on the re—" My voice breaks, and he reaches for my hand, but I step out of reach. I take a deep breath and start over. "Good luck with the rest of the season." I turn and make my way towards his bedroom door and my packed bags. I grab them, opening the door, and hear him say, "I hope all your dreams come true." I take one final look at the boy I love, trying to remember every last detail of his face. I whisper, "You, too." Then I'm pulling the door closed behind me, never once taking a look back as I walk out of the apartment and to the waiting car. I can feel tears streaming down my face harder and my heart breaking, but I have no one to blame but myself.

The End...

Or is it?

Want More of Annie's and Drew's Story? Check out Making It Home

Keep Reading for a sample of Making It Home, Annie's and Drew's Second Change Romance!

Join The Friends Group either on the website www.anablessing.com or on Instagram @authoranablessing.

Join the Newsletter for sneak peeks and more!

Making It Home-Preview

Book 2 in The Friends Group Series

The Friends Group Series
making it Home
ANA BLESSING

Chapter 1: It's Not All Golden

-Annie, Age: 25-

Six years later—November

I am sick of California, as only a Midwesterner can be. I miss waving to my neighbors without getting a glare in return, driving to a place on an open highway without 24/7 traffic, and my family being within driving distance. The beach has been a highlight of being in California. I'll miss the freedom on a bad day of going to listen to the waves rushing in and out, but the waves don't outweigh my wish to go home. Or at least as close to home as I can get, knowing that Oklahoma doesn't have a major league baseball team. I've enjoyed the experience of being here in LA and getting to help cover the baseball teams here. I am the secondary sideline reporter covering the visiting team at either ballpark. It's been an experience adjusting to the pace of being at so many games, but I've learned a lot here. I love covering baseball, and it's what I was meant to do.

The Series ended yesterday, and I mostly ran background support for the sportscaster team, as neither of the local LA teams made it to the finals. As a baseball fan, it was nice to see the KC Griffons make a run for the pennant, and they played a heck of a season, coming up just short in game seven. The sportscasters on the team think they'll take it all next season if they make a few adjustments, and I am in total agreement; getting some strong pitchers and bats would get the club in a good position to take another run into the playoffs next fall. After the long baseball season, I am planning to head home for the holidays. I get be home from Thanksgiving until just after Christmas. This will be the longest amount of time I've been home since the summer before college, and I am looking forward to time with my parents and my brother Miles, who moved back to our hometown a few years ago after his college graduation.

I've gotten approval to be in Oklahoma longer because I am interviewing in both the Texas and Kansas City markets for the new positions the network has in those districts. My producer here in LA, Mac, gave me a little inside scoop during the Series coverage that I should be on my A game. He followed it up with the intel about the network getting new reporting opportunities. Mac tells me he's learned that the key markets expanding with exclusive sideline coverage are Arizona, Missouri, and Texas. Mac is like my work dad here in LA, and I think he's noticed I am a little out of my element here. Not in the work but on the personal side of life: I don't go out and socialize much, and I'm 100% focused on every extra assignment the network offers me.

I clearly have no external plans to interrupt, so they ask me to do extra assignments like I've done for the Series this year. So, it seems fitting that he'd be the one to let me know about the possibilities of getting out of the big city and back towards my roots. I told Mac he is my hero for the information. He gave me a little pat on the back and said it was the least he could do for his favorite reporter. He made the universal sign of 'shh,' placing his finger over his mouth, before telling me I couldn't tell the other reporters. I made sure to tell him that his secret is safe before heading back to work. I will miss him if or when I move on to the next opportunity.

A few days after the initial scoop, Mac finds me at my little desk reviewing player stats. "Annie, so glad that I've caught you—I may have more information about that exclusive part of the new reporter gigs." "Thanks, Mac, what you got for me?" I reply, curious not for the first time about the details. "Looks like it's going to be with specific teams, for all home and travel games. You'll be responsible from Spring Training to the Series if your team makes it all the way," he says. "Well, that sounds like an experience, doesn't it?" I say, knowing that learning one team and the players on it feels exciting. "Yeah, as I said, one of the teams is your Griffons: you'd be great since you're already an encyclopedia of Griffons history," Mac says, giving me a kind smile. "Yeah… Between you and me, I'm interested in the Missouri or Texas jobs," I tell him. "Annie, you just tell old Mac which ones you apply for, and I'll get with my contacts in those markets, give them the word on why Annie Campbell is one of a kind," he finishes and gives me a little wave before he leaves.

Before looking at any job listing or the actual teams in each market, I know I will be true to my word with Mac. I've ruled out Arizona; Drew still plays for the team. I haven't seen him in six years, and I don't think showing up to Spring training with the requirement that he has to see me every day seems like a better job. Plus, Arizona is still too far from home, which is why I'm looking to get out of LA. I fight the urge to pull up Drew's stats, now thinking about him in Arizona. I've followed his career progress over the last six years because I can't help myself. I watch his progress to validate that all the pain I caused has been worth it.

Watching him climb his way up the minors has been the validation I've needed to dull the heartbreak. Dull is the key word because I can't help thinking about him; my brain brings him up in the most random or, in this case, logical ways. I just can't erase him from my mind. Last season, he'd gotten his call-up to the majors, just like I'd always known he would, and he'd been the key player in Arizona's lineup the rest of the season.

He'd even been nominated and won his division's Rookie of the Year award. I'd recorded his first pro game because I was covering one of my own. I cried when I watched Drew take the field, his dimple on full display along with his big smile. He looked so happy, and I'd never been more proud. I'd had this pain in my chest watching, wishing I could have been there in the stands like back in high school, but I knew that was the dull ache speaking. He'd had a hell of a first game both defensively and at bat. I remember turning off the game and thinking, *He's done it, his dream has come true.*

I'd gotten lucky, and Arizona had already played games with the LA teams I cover before he was called up. I wasn't sure how we'd interact if I were the one assigned to get interviews, but I know that I need to think about it, because if his career and mine keep on their current paths, we are bound to have them cross at some point; it'd be inevitable. I guess that would be another plus of this new position—my interactions with most of the teams in the Texas and Missouri markets would have limited games with Arizona. If I got this job, I wouldn't be covering the visitors and would only be with the home team, so we'd be in the same ballpark but not on the same sideline. It would limit any on-air awkwardness; we could wave, and life would return to normal.

The only negative of thinking about making this career adjustment was the ending of my relationship with Dax. He had potential; he is in production on one of the other network shows in LA. When I'd told him about the news I'd received from a 'source' about the jobs in Texas, Arizona, and Missouri, he'd expressed zero interest in joining me on the adventure to move to another market. He'd said that LA was his market: he let me know he liked me, and the sex was good, but not enough to change his career path. I've since chalked it up to my relationship wasteland, which, if I'm being honest, all added up to careers trumping love every time. Drew was the start, maybe the most painful example, but I've always attributed that to the price of first love.

In fact, before his loss from my life, I thought that if you loved someone, it meant forever. I'd done a little casual dating in college before meeting Peter my sophomore year. Peter was studying journalism too, and it seemed like we could be headed towards real feelings, and I'd been surprised that I was starting to feel them. I'd been on the edge of telling Peter my feelings, but before I could, he'd gotten a position in Denver to cover the pro football team. He'd dumped me so quick that I'd almost gotten whiplash. I'd only dated casually again until Dax here in LA. I'd met him working on one of my 'extra' assignments, and we'd hit it off. We'd both been understanding about limited date nights and had been more focused on the sex when we had time together.

I liked him but hadn't gotten to know him well enough to ask myself if deeper feelings were possible. So, it seemed fitting that this relationship would end because I was choosing my career. Maybe it was poetic justice that I finally decided to follow my dream. I'd told my best friend Meg over video call that if I got one of these jobs, I might just need to stay away from men. She'd laughed and said that maybe I needed to avoid relationships and get a few boy toys instead.

Chapter 2: Friendsgiving
-Annie-

November

God, it is good to be home in Oklahoma, I think. I've missed getting to see my family and friends. I've been focused these first days at home on spending time with my parents and Miles. Soon my friends will be home from their respective places around the country. Meg's been off in Dallas living her best life with her roommate James Arthur. Luke has been in law school in Texas conquering the pressure of his chosen profession. Craig is in Arizona living his best life possible.

On my first night home, Miles somehow got me to agree to talk to the high school newspaper and visual news teams about my college and professional experience. Since he graduated, my brother has been teaching English at the high school. He fits the part with his shaggy blonde hair and five o'clock shadow that never seems to grow out. Along with the news teams, Miles has been working as the QB coach for the football team. He takes his coaching and teaching seriously; those kids are like his babies, and he wants to give them the best. I think it's funny that he supports the newsgroup with Dad at The Reporter, and me making good in sportscasting on TV. Miles now has his own stamp on journalism. Dad laughed when I'd agreed, telling me, "He is using all his connections for those kids. I've already visited them earlier in the fall." I'd laughed too, because it is so like Miles to want to serve others; he is a teacher through and through.

***

It should feel weird to be back in my old high school surrounded by teenagers who make you think, *When did I get old?* I'm here now, walking the halls with my brother and wondering, 'Did we look this young?' and 'Where did the time go?' He walks me by the Wall of Fame, covered with the faces of the school's most famous graduates. I can't say I remember this from my days in these hallways, but it was probably here the whole time because I see photos with pictures of mostly men dressed in athletic jerseys from the '70s and '80's.

Then I get to the end, and there we are. They have added a photo of me with my professional headshot from the network with a little tag "Annie Campbell: Network Sports Reporter" with my class year. Next to my picture is a headshot photo of Drew in his Arizona uniform with a little tag "Drew Davis: Shortstop for Arizona" and our class year.

My brother breaks into my thoughts, "It's crazy to see you on the wall, right? I remember when you were a baby," he mocks, sounding like Mom or Dad when they reminisce. "Ha ha, you're only like a year older than me, you don't remember me as a baby. But yeah, it is crazy, I don't know if what I've done is Wall of Fame worthy," I say, being honest. I don't feel all that famous, but it's cool that someone thinks I'm famous enough to be on the wall. "Well to the kids, it's enough. Enjoy your fame," Miles says, giving me a nudge before starting to walk again. I follow Miles to the newspaper club classroom, and even though it has been six years and the computers and equipment have been upgraded, the

355

room still feels the same.

***

Miles introduces me to the students, then surprises me when he asks one of them to turn down the lights as he turns on the computer projection on the wall. "I'll let Annie speak for herself; it is her job, after all." My brother gives me a slight elbow nudge and hits the play button on the video. I watch clips of myself reporting during high school at football games and baseball games. I watch small clips of myself interviewing Daniel and Miles after a game, then my post-state interview with Drew and the guys. The video clips show me in Norman, on the field at a football game, and my viral interview when the baseball team won the college division championship. The last few clips are of me interviewing players and coaches in LA.

When it ends, the kids give a round of applause, and I blush a little—it's still hard for me to be the center of attention. I can be on the sidelines and have no problem not blushing, but now I'm focused on their recognition and can't control the blush. Miles jumps in after he turns on the light. "So, any questions?" A few students raise their hands. I pick the girl in the back. "Was it weird interviewing guys you go to school with?" "Great question. No, it wasn't: it did result in me getting to know them better. It helps that they know talking to me would get them on the school TV each week." I pick a boy in the middle of the room. "Do you think you got advantages because you're hot?" Before I can answer, Miles cuts in, "Dillion, I thought we talked about being professional with our questions—calling my little sister hot isn't what I'd call professional." There is my protective big brother, I cut in to soften the blow for the kid. "I think what he probably meant was attractive," I cover. He nods yes in agreement. "Well, I don't think it hurts that people think I'm attractive, but I don't focus on trying to be attractive; I focus on being the most prepared person in the room. I want to get the best interview or coverage for my network and the viewers."

Miles gives me a nod of well done, and I take a few more questions before the bell rings, dismissing the students. Miles has football next, so he walks me out to my car on the way to the locker room. "Thanks again, Annie. I think it's good for the kids to see what they put in now can translate into a career. That it isn't just all make-believe." "Thanks, Miles. It was fun to talk to them and answer their questions, even the awkward ones." Miles laughs at my comment and asks, "What are you doing now?" I roll my eyes before answering. "I have to go home and get the house ready for Friendsgiving, which you promised to attend this year," I tell him. He laughs, holding up his hands. "I remember, I have a reminder to get rolls from the store on my way to Mom and Dad's house after practice." I hug him, and we say goodbye. Now, off to the hard stuff: cooking a meal that people can eat. *Thank God for Mom's*, I think as I drive towards my parents' house.

***

Friendsgiving started our first year in college, after we'd all missed having our lunch group gatherings over food. We'd started having Friendsgiving a few days before our actual Thanksgiving at Meg's suggestion. The only person who had never attended from our group was Drew. I'd agreed the first year, expecting him to be here, only to learn that the Davises were taking a family vacation for the holiday. As our Friendsgiving had become tradition, so had the Davises' vacations at this time of year. I thought I'd been the reason Drew didn't attend the first year, but as time has gone on, I've taken it less personally. Now, it's a fun little event I look forward to each year without the guilt or hope that revolved around Drew's absence or appearance.

I am hosting at my parents' house, as history has established, since my parents love seeing us "kids" get together. I am in the kitchen helping my mom cook. I may be hosting, but cooking isn't my strongest skill. In LA, I have lived off pre-made meals and craft services at the baseball games. The mashed potatoes, gravy, and pumpkin pie I have volunteered to make have mainly been cooked by Mom, but I'd at least peeled and sliced what I could. The doorbell sounds, and I can hear Dad talking to someone. I ensure Mom is good, covering the last items on the stovetop before I head into the living room.

Before I can fully enter the room, I'm wrapped up in strong arms. "Annie Campbell, it's nice to see you in person," Craig says against my hair and releases me. "You, too. We didn't make anything healthy in that kitchen, forgive me," I joke because Craig is a personal trainer now, focused on keeping himself and his client at their top performance. I'm not sure why I say his *client* in my head when I know who his famous client is—Drew. I should just think Drew, but my brain always edits it to client, like that will soften the blow or make the little pinch in my heart go away faster. Craig cuts into my internal thoughts with "Annie, come on, Friendsgiving doesn't count, you know that. The more butter, the better." Craig heads into the kitchen, and I hear him say hello to my mom.

The doorbell rings again, and I tell Dad I'll get it. I open the door to Meg and Luke, our little Texas transplants. "Annie, are you ready to marry me already and activate our marriage pact?" Luke says as he hugs me. "I thought we had until thirty before the pact terms kicked in," I laugh as I release him. "I guess I'll have to look into the legal language," he laughs. "Yeah, put that law degree to good use, why don't you?" I reply before he says, "Almost law degree. Meg cuts in and I wrap her in a side hug. "Missed you, BFF". I release her before grabbing the items she has in her hands. "Miss you more, Annie Marie," she tells me, willingly handing over the dishes. She turns to head back to her car as she says, "I'll be right back with the turkey." I am in the kitchen with Mom and the guys when Meg opens the door for Miles, with his hands full of both the rolls and turkey.

"He insisted on carrying everything," Meg says as she rolls her eyes. "Well, it seemed like the nice thing to do, *Megan*," Miles addresses her with a glance before setting the food on the table. "Oh, he just called her MEGAN, she must be in TROUBLE," jokes Luke. Meg gives Luke a look and turns her attention back to Miles's comment, "Is that right, Professor?" Meg quips as she moves his long, shaggy hair out of his eyes. "Oh, is it Professor now?" Miles gives her a smirk. "I think he looks like the male teacher all the girls are getting their first older man crush for," pipes in Luke. "Gross," I say, because he is my brother. Everyone else just laughs in agreement with Luke.

I trade with Mom, finishing the items that still need to be stirred. She gets hugs from everyone before heading down the hall, "You kids have fun," she says before she tells Dad she is ready to leave. My parents are invited but want to leave us all to catch up. "I'll make sure that Miles does all the dishes," I shout, and can hear my parents laugh as they close the door.

We set the table as a group, and while putting out plates and food, Meg asked me, "So when do you start your interviews?" "What interviews?" asks Craig as he sets out forks and knives. "I am trying for a position closer to home and doing some interviews with the Texas and Missouri divisions," I reply. "I'm voting for Texas—then my Annie Marie can come be my roommate," says Meg, doing her little toe bounce thing. It's her tell that she is excited about the possibility of us being in the same city again after all these years. "Which one are you hoping for, Annie?" asks Luke as he enters the room. "If I get the Dallas coverage, it would be great to live with Meg, but I'd like Kansas City as my backup. You all know they've always been my team," I reply. Luke nods in agreement, because the Griffons have always been my team, even when they had no chance at a playoff run. "Interesting," is all Craig's gets to reply before he is interrupted by Meg's "Dinner is served."

***

We spend the meal eating too much food and catching up on how life has been since the last time we've all been in the same room. Meg is over-stressed at work and says she is following my example. She is going to start looking for her next opportunity when she returns to Dallas. Miles gives her a look of concern, but it's gone before I can ask him about it. Luke tells us that he's been busy trying to finish law school and that he is the most boring. He makes sure to point out that he hasn't even had sex in months. We all can't help the laughter that follows his confession, because he makes such a dramatic emphasis on the word *months*.

Miles is the next to speak "Nothing can be as dull as returning to your old high school. Going from starting QB to English teacher isn't the stuff of dreams". Luke pipes "You heard the part about no sex for MONTHS, right?" Miles raises him one with the word "Years." This only causes us to all laugh harder. I do make a comment that we need to stop this conversation before I hear any more about my brother's sex life.

Craig loves his life in Arizona and lets us know he isn't having the same problems as the other guys in the sex department. At that, Meg pops off about the fact that she's gotten laid plenty. Then she pulls me into the conversation by asking me about my sex life. I joke about being happy on my own and that I'm all stocked up on batteries for the future. Miles makes a gagging noise and repeats my comments from earlier about not needing to hear about my sex life with or without people. We eventually move on to safer topics. We finish the meal with pumpkin pie and a toast to another year of Friendsgiving.

Chapter 3: Negotiations Have Failed

-Drew, Age: 25-

Six years later—November

It is nice to have some time off with my family after the end of my rookie year in the big leagues. The baseball season had been long and exhausting, but it was the best year of my career. Having it capped off with the win for Rookie of the Year for the division was just icing on the cake. I owe my success last season to my team: I have a great agent in Dominic Stone, who has helped me climb the ranks from the minors to the big league. He is always looking for ways to increase my visibility and continues to tell me to do things I hadn't even thought possible, like getting me to be a spokesperson for a health drink brand. He keeps telling me he is working to get an athletic clothing brand deal, but his primary focus is on the contract extension with Arizona.

My trainer happens to be my best friend, Craig Mitchell. The timing of him finishing his baseball career at Norman and graduating with his athletic training degree with a license to do personal training couldn't have worked out better. I'd asked him if he wanted to work with me in the offseason, which turned into him following me when I got called up last season. Our hard work had paid off; it was clear with the way I played all season. We'd both agreed that he'd stay on as my trainer for the upcoming season. We also decided that I would eat whatever I wanted for this break. I am enjoying not being in season and the Thanksgiving holiday before we get back to Arizona to start training for the new season. Spring Training doesn't begin until the end of February, so I have time to rest and indulge before kicking it into high gear with my diet and exercise.

So, here I am, enjoying a drink at the beach next to my parents on another family vacation for Thanksgiving. Thanksgiving has never been a big holiday in the Davis house. Mom never enjoyed trying to get all the food to come out hot simultaneously, so we'd found a new tradition for the family. I admit that my reason for starting this little tradition six years ago was to not have to be in Oklahoma at the same time as Annie. Having her just next door and just out of reach had seemed like the worst kind of torture.

I'd known that first year she'd be home, I'd been a part of the same friends group text chain. I'd seen Meg's suggestion to start a Friendsgiving when everyone was home. I'd seen everyone's excited "I'm in" comments, including Annie's. I'd sat in my room, typed "I'm in" and had almost sent it because I'd wanted to see her, to see if I could convince her to get back together, but I'd known that would be selfish.

So, the Davis Thanksgiving Vacation was formed, and I never replied to the invitation in the chat on the topic. This year, the only Davis not in attendance is Daniel. He is currently on active duty in an undisclosed location. He'd turned his life around after his college accident and worked hard to prove he had changed. He'd entered the military two years ago and never looked back. He is still cocky, but he is the best version of my brother I've known. We do video chats, and he emails me occasionally to give me updates or to ask me to make sure to include his name on presents to our parents when he's away. He'd video-called us all from his undisclosed location to wish us the best for yesterday's holiday, just in case he wasn't available again this week.

He told us that he should be back in the states in the new year, and he would make stops in Oklahoma, where my parents still live, and in Arizona to visit me when the season started. Mom and Dad told him that he better make it home safe, and he promised them to do his best. I'd told him I'd have a bed ready in Arizona and a VIP game seat waiting for him, too. He'd laughed and said the VIP treatment sounded like a plan and well deserved for all his years dealing with the smart-ass shortstop. I couldn't help laughing at his too-true description of me, and I told him to stay safe before we disconnected the call. Since our call with Daniel, we'd all spent a lot of time just sitting in the loungers at the beach, listening to the waves rush in and out.

***

It had been nice to soak in the sun, eating and drinking what I wanted, but I'm back to reality. December in Arizona doesn't feel like December. It's probably weird, but I kinda miss being cold. Arizona is the place I've been living the most over the last few years. After getting promoted to the main lineup, it is my home again. I needed to think about getting started on baby steps to training again. I'd enjoyed my break and my body needed it, but it is time now to start making small efforts to make Spring Training in less than three months easier.

I want to come into training like I'd left the season, at the top of my game. I'm working out in the apartment complex gym when my phone rings, flashing "Dominic Stone" across the screen. I swipe and hear Dominic's voice cut off my workout music in my headphones. "Drew, got a second to chat?" His voice isn't as easygoing as it was on the last call about the prospect of a new brand deal. "Yeah, Dom, I'm just working out. What's up, man?" I reply. "Drew, I think we are going to have to force Arizona's hand, open up to the market as a free agent," he says in that same serious tone. Before I can answer, he continues, "It's not unheard of in the league, and it's a common move to get a club to sign a longer-term contract with a better guaranteed payout."

I wasn't planning on leaving Arizona; I'd grown up in their system, knew the expectations, and had a great season last year. Free agency wasn't even on my radar. I re-rack the weights and reply, "Ok, so what's the next move if I go free agent? When would I find out where I'm going to land with that approach?" "The best-case scenario is that it will make Arizona put up the money we are asking for to keep you. Worst case, I know of a few programs looking to strengthen their line-ups. If I have your approval, I'll start doing some digging." "Permission granted," I reply. He tells me a few more details, and we end the call. I guess I'm a free agent now.

Chapter 4: Quiet Free Agent

-Drew-

Mid-December

Dominic has been working on getting a new contract signed, and true to his word, he's done some digging about other teams looking for a shortstop with my skill set. I don't want to feed any rumors that I am unhappy in Arizona, so we've been keeping the fact that I am going about negotiations as a free agent behind closed doors. So far, the only ripple has been a few networks reporting that I've not signed an extension on my rookie contract as expected.

Dominic has gotten some interest behind the scenes from a few ball clubs. I am still talking with Arizona regularly, and the coach has called, asking me to stay. I appreciated him calling and trying to make it work, but I want to see what else was out there, too. I've started to have a few conversations with the interested teams, Kansas City and Atlanta. I feel like I am betraying Arizona and all the efforts they put into me, bringing me up their club ranks.

Craig has been a great sounding board during our training sessions. He reminds me they still have to give me the best offer, my body will only last for so many seasons, and I need to make the most out of the years I have left. We both joke that it is a weird conversation at twenty-five, but it's the reality for professional athletes. Bodies can only take the strain for so long; my time on the field wouldn't take me to traditional retirement at age sixty.

Atlanta's been an interesting club to talk to because I haven't kept up with them much. The general manager seems like a nice guy, and he is trying to sell me hard on his vision for the club. He seems like he is trying to build a good team, but it's just that they are rebuilding, and I'm not sure about it. In the best-case scenario, a rebuild can surprise and make a big run, or in the worst-case scenario, they don't work well together, and it's a very ugly season.

The final team is Kansas City, the Griffons, Annie's favorite pro team. When Dominic had given them as one of the interested teams, I couldn't help thinking about her. I'd been guilty of doing an internet search with her name and going down the rabbit hole of watching her top interviews. Craig had walked into the kitchen, and I'd slammed my computer shut so hard, I was surprised I didn't break the screen. He'd made some off-hand comment to save the kitchen porn for when he was out of town.

***

The GM at Kansas City is trying to lock in a few missing pieces the organization felt could have helped them win the Series last year. They want to see if they can capitalize on last year's near-championship win. He's been selling me hard on the caliber of the coaching staff, the family feeling of the team, and the fact that there are no greater fans than the ones in KC. The last statement makes me look at my living room wall at the painting of the biggest KC fan I've ever known. What would Annie think if I joined the Griffons? Are they still even her favorite team? I return my attention to my phone call, thanked him for his time, and tell him we'll talk again soon. After disconnecting, I'm interested, but will I always think of her when I hear the team name? She's already the girl I can't seem to replace. Will she be the ghost haunting me every day I step on the field there? I am trying to figure it out, reminding myself she isn't really a factor in this decision.

"So, how are the negotiations going?" Craig asks when he comes into the apartment carrying bags of groceries. "I think I'll tell Dominic to rule out Atlanta. It doesn't seem like a great fit right now," I reply as I joined him in the kitchen. "So, it's Arizona or Kansas City. You have a strong feeling about either of them?" he asks while preparing our lunch from the items in the bag. "They are both good clubs, but if I leave Arizona, it would be fun to be at an organization primed to make another deep run into the playoffs." I mean it; playing in the Series, The Championship, would be amazing and more than I thought was possible. I've dreamed of getting to play baseball professionally and winning the Series like all kids do, but to think it could be possible still feels like a kid's dream, not a real thing. "I personally think we should head to KC. I think it's time to leave the desert," Craig says with a smile before turning to place things in the pan.

***

Five days after Christmas, I verbally agree to sign with the Griffons for a ten-year average salary of $22 million a year over the contract terms. I will get a signing bonus of $5 million. It's all crazy numbers, and I don't know how my agent pulled off the deal. Dominic calls and happily announces, "Kansas City, here he comes," and tells me I had better start moving. I've been taking calls all day from the Griffons GM to their ownership team, each offering congratulations and welcoming me to the team. We've agreed to keep it quiet until I am in KC in three weeks to sign my contract formally. Then we can kick off the media storm of my moving to their club.

"I think I found an apartment downtown—someone I know is recommending it." Craig has been on his phone frequently, looking at all things KC. I've even seen him looking at apartments in KC before I'd verbally accepted the offer. I realized I wasn't the only one interested in the opportunity, and I think it helped me make the decision, not that I'd tell him that. He already has a big head and enjoys telling me to do another round of the most challenging exercises as my trainer. He doesn't need to know that he influenced my choice to leave the desert. "Seems like it has an open penthouse unit, a lot of the other athletes lease or rent space in the building, so it's got a great security presence, too," Craig says as he offers me his phone to look at the photos. "Yeah, let's get in contact with the building management and lease it," I say, having looked over the information he showed me. I hand his phone back to him.

"Well... What if I told you I've already done that?" He doesn't look guilty at all for already kicking off this process for me—well, us. Craig is my roommate in Arizona, and I don't see why he wouldn't be my roommate in KC. "Send me the information, and I'll get it to Dominic and his team to coordinate payment, contract, etcetera." My friend looks a little bashful now. "Would you be mad if I sent it to Dominic, and he's already starting all of that?" Craig gives me a little smirk when he finishes his statement. I chuckle before telling him, "Nope, please tell me you've called the movers to pack all of this," I say, pointing around the current condo. "I haven't, but I will once I get Dominic and his team to get us a move-in date," he says, looking happy with himself.

"On another subject," he holds up his hands, "don't kill me for asking, but please tell me that you ended it with Mandy." "Well, I mean not officially, I'm not sure I have anything to end," I say honestly. Mandy and I have been hooking up off and on during the season. I asked her to go with me to a few events, but it wasn't more than that. The funniest part is that Craig has hated her from her first sleepover. She'd commented on Mom's painting in the living room, something like, "Who's the average-looking girl?" Craig had looked at the painting and back at me before saying, "There is nothing average about her."

If I hadn't known he loved her like a sister, I'd have felt weird about him talking about Annie like that, but Mandy didn't know that. She'd said, "Sounds like you have a hard-on for Drew's sloppy seconds." It was the wrong thing to say. "She's the only one to make him happy and not just on her back." He'd said what he needed to say and refused to be in the apartment when she was over. I should have told her to leave, but I wasn't looking to get into it with her. At the time, I was focused on sex, and it had been good with her, even if, to Craig's point, she'd only made me happy in bed. Annie's only place in my life was on that wall, in that painting, in a moment we shared something magical.

I'd let Mandy's comments go, not wanting to interrupt the good sex for the girl I didn't have. We'd text here or there, hook up when I was around, and go weeks before our next interaction. "Give me your phone, and I'll handle that too," he holds out his hand like I'm going to hand him my phone. "She can get the realty check she deserves." "I think I'll handle this one for all our sakes," I say.

Craig shrugs before saying, "Moving to KC is going to give you a much-needed improvement in the woman department." I laugh before I give him something to think about. "If you say so, man, or maybe you'll let a woman get her hook in you". I go to my room and call Mandy to let her know I'm moving out of Arizona. True to the nature of our arrangement, she tells me 'good luck,' and we get off the call within ten minutes. Now all I have to do is figure out how to get all my stuff across the country. It will be nice to return to the Midwest, and I can't help the feeling in my chest that it feels like I'm headed home.

Chapter 5: An Offer of a Lifetime

December

I jump from Oklahoma to Texas, back to Oklahoma, then to Kansas City, then back to Oklahoma, all in three weeks. I've gone through multiple rounds of screen tests with each market's production team and feel like my chances are pretty good with them both. The screen test in Kansas City felt different; it was so much easier. The producers asked me why I wanted to be the on-field talent in KC, and I'd word vomited my love for the club, even going into details about my favorite Griffon players growing up. The producers had seemed impressed when I'd been able to name players across multiple years and positions. On my way home to Oklahoma, I see I've gotten messages from both Meg and Craig. I start with Meg and open our chat.

Meg Patterson

So how did it go?

Annie

I think it went great.

Then I go to the message from Craig to see that he is just as impatient as Meg.

Annie

I don't know yet Mr. Impatient

Craig Mitchell

Tell the Network I told them to hurry it up I have plans to make

Annie

Oh ok, I'll get right on that

I'll just tell the president of the network that my buddy Craig has plans to make

So please let me know where I'll be working next season.

Craig Mitchell

Thank you

Annie

Smart ass

Craig Mitchell

I'll take that as a compliment, but I'd rather hear nice ass for future reference

Annie

Yuck, gross. I am not going to say that

Craig Mitchell

Have you seen my ass lately, I do a lot of squats

Annie

I'll take your word for it.

***

Four days before Christmas, I get a call for an official offer to join the Kansas City network division. It takes everything in me not to shout "yes" into the phone and interrupt them. I instead find myself doing Meg's little toe bounce happy dance while the producers gave me the breakdown of my offer. I would be signing a three-year deal to be the exclusive on-field talent supporting the Griffons club on the network. I'll also be the one to do player spotlight interviews before the games to be used as part of the pregame packages. The salary is more than it was in LA, so it's a no-brainer to say yes. They are even going to give me a moving allowance to get out of my lease in LA, move all my stuff, and help me get into an apartment in KC—they go so far as to send over some recommended apartment complexes for me to look at to help me start the process as soon as possible, since I need to be in KC by mid-January.

I accept verbally on the call and quickly review the paperwork before sending it to my legal expert and long-time friend, Luke. He'd been the one to help me with my contract last time, and I want to make sure he doesn't have any concerns with the new one. I want to tell someone so bad, but my parents are already in bed, and I don't want to scare them by waking them up. So, I'd started a group call with my friends Meg, Craig, and Luke.

"Annie, everything ok?" Craig answers. "Yeah, Annie, everything ok?" Meg repeats. "Did you just send me an e-mail?" Luke says as he joins the call. "I got the KC job," I half scream into my phone. My friends whistle and whoop in celebration on the line. I get statements like, "Always believed in you" to "They'd have been fucking stupid not to hire the best woman for the job." When the celebration settles, Meg asks to hear the details, and I spend the next fifteen minutes reading over the contract with them. Luke tells me he will review the agreement after we get off the call, so I won't have to wait to sign. Meg says to let her know when I move into my apartment, and she'll take a flight to KC to help me set up my apartment and unpack boxes. Craig jokes that everything seemed covered before asking me to send over the recommended apartments. He says he could save me some time researching the different locations and send me his recommendation on which ones look the best. I thank them all, because they are a girl's best friends.

***

Everything goes so quickly after I get the offer. The next day, true to his word, Luke sends me back the contract with a few suggestions, and I forward those suggestions to the network. They accept them, and I sign a three-year deal two days before Christmas. On Christmas Eve, Craig sends me his top two suggestions for apartments for lease in KC:

Craig Mitchell

I like the Plaza or Power & Light apartments. Both seem to be in good areas in the city

Let me pull those up

Where would you live?

I think I love the Power & Light if it was me

The rate seems reasonable

Yeah, better then LA that is for sure

Thank you, I'll call them tomorrow

Let me know if I can help with anything else

But not moving, use the networks money

I thought you had big strong muscles

Muscles yes, interest in moving no

LOL, I'll update you when I hear back

***

Two days after Christmas, I complete the lease agreement for a one-bedroom apartment in downtown KC's Power & Light district. It is the best option for me being single; it has a lot of things to do and places to eat nearby, and the ballpark is only fifteen to twenty minutes away. I text Craig a picture of the Welcome packet I'd gotten, and he replies that he can't wait to visit. Then I book my flight to LA, because I have an apartment to pack up and move. Kansas City, here I come!

Also by Ana Blessing

Acknowledgements

First and foremost, I would like to thank my Heavenly Father for all the opportunities he has blessed me with. Secondly, a HUGE, MAJOR, THANK YOU, to my mom for reading this book when it wasn't even finished and for reading it for what I'm sure feels like over a hundred times more. I couldn't have done it without you! To my dad, thank you for hearing me out when I got excited about each step of this journey and for telling me to follow my dreams. To my little brother, for laughing with me and telling me to make sure to write good smut, if I was doing this. To my friends and early beta readers Kayla and Maddie, thank you for supporting me by listening to me brainstorm and daydream about the possibility of this book getting published. Also, for reading that early unproofread version, I owe you all. To my Instagram family, thank you for humoring me when I only had book reviews and random post to offer. To my family, my first support group, my Husband and two Boys. I know I took hours away to bring this book to life, and you all gave me the courage and grace to accomplish this dream! I couldn't have done it without you and love you all so much.

And finally, to all of you-the readers, thank you for taking the time to read this book. I appreciate you and hope to see you again with the next one!

About the Author

Ana Blessing has always had a passion for reading, which lead to her writing her debut novel *Should Have Called Dibs* the first book in *The Friends Group Series.* She loves to watch football, baseball and tennis, cheering loudly from her couch.

She has been married to her leading man for over fifteen years. She is a mother to two wild boys, who keep her busy when she's not writing. They happily call the Midwest home along with their family cat.

Join The Friends Group either on the website anablessing.com or on Instagram @authoranablessing.

www.ingramcontent.com/pod-product-compliance
Lightning Source LLC
Chambersburg PA
CBHW071741110726
47908CB00006B/1655